SO-BYR-310

21ST CENTURY CHINESE LITERATURE

Editorial Committee for the Series

Consultants: Cai Mingzhao Zhou Mingwei

Director: Huang Youyi

Vice-Director: Fang Zhenghui

Members: Li Jingze

Zhang Yiwu

Xie Xizhang

Huang Jiwei

Qiu Huadong

Xie Youshun

He Xiangyang

Wang Xiao

Chen Shi

Hu Baomin

Li Zhenguo

Shao Dong

Hu Kaimin

THE GREAT MASQUE

AND MORE STORIES OF LIFE IN THE CITY

FOREIGN LANGUAGES PRESS

First Edition 2009

ISBN 978-7-119-05437-7

@ Foreign Languages Press Co. Ltd, Beijing, China, 2014

Published by Foreign Languages Press Co. Ltd

24 Baiwanzhuang Road, Beijing 100037, China

http://www.flp.com.cn   E-mail:flp@cipg.org.cn

Distributed by China International Book Trading Corporation

35 Chegongzhuang Xilu, Beijing 100044, China

P.O. Box 399, Beijing, China

Printed in the People's Republic of China

Contents

Contents

21st Century Chinese Literature
— Points of Departure

By Wang Meng

The *21st Century Chinese Literature* series aims to introduce contemporary Chinese literature in English, French and other languages to readers all over the world.

Chinese literature's recent path, along the country's trajectory, may not resemble a smooth highway, yet it is still the main channel toward understanding China and the daily lives and inner-world of the Chinese people.

China has been experiencing soaring development, and its links with the rest of the world have been growing closer. Even if you might not know anyone from China, "made in China" still can now be found in most aspects of your life, or as expressed in a Chinese idiom, "Look up, and see it everywhere." News about China appears regularly in newspapers, on TV and the Internet, trying to tell you what is happening in this remote yet near country called China, and what China is thinking and planning. In this way, peoples of the world have developed their general views of China.

Many of those views are often insightful. Chinese writers, like myself, have also been keeping an eye on the world. We often discuss the US, Japan, Russia, South Africa, Italy and other countries, as well as the interesting or ingenious views about China held by peoples of such countries. But we feel much regret to find

---

Wang Meng is an illustrious writer and China's former Minister of Culture.

sometimes that others' views about China are full of illusions and misunderstandings, more often than not, preconceived, arbitrary and overgeneralized. Thus, my fellow citizens and I have become powerfully aware of how little the world really knows about China, and thus we feel that the world is so near, yet still so remote.

Literature can draw us closer to communicate views and imagination about the world and life, and share each other's joys and sorrows beyond language barriers, different cultures and backgrounds or long distances. It can make you feel that people living afar are like your next-door neighbors, as you perceive and share the secret interiors of their lives and dreams. To illustrate this point, I shall borrow a poetic line from the current Indian ambassador to China, Mrs. Nirupama Rao:

"...making sense of each other,
even as realization glimmers
that, we are little morsels
tossed by the history of these parts."

It elucidates the point of departure of this series. Readers from all over the world, who are used to learning about China through foreign newspapers, TV and the Internet, may now open up these books to see China through the heartfelt thoughts and writings of Chinese people themselves. The many authors of these new short stories, living in this rapidly developing and changing, yet ancient nation, have strived to describe all that is happening in and around themselves, to give genuine dynamic expression to the intricate recent experiences of the Chinese people. Through the power of their words you will be able to catch glimpses of the real, complex and living China, as well as other possibilities for all humanity, including yourself.

The Foreign Languages Press has long devoted itself to enhancing mutual understanding between China and the rest of the world. China followers in every country probably still remember *Panda Books*, mainly published in the late 20th century. Those books collected a wide range of contemporary Chinese literary works. The *Panda Books* series helped many Chinese writers become known to the world. *21st Century Chinese Literature* can be regarded as the continuation of *Panda Books*, though its selection and editing methods vary greatly from the old series. All the three volumes of new short stories were edited by Chinese scholars, with in-depth understanding and research in contemporary Chinese literature, whose judgment and views are highly respected among Chinese writers and readers. They accomplished this editing work independently, conducive to this new series better reflecting the highly diversified spiritual quests and artistic creativity of contemporary Chinese literature.

Thus, the other vital impact of this series is to provide international sinologists and Chinese literary researchers with the view from inside, from within the Chinese literary circles widely recognized among Chinese writers and readers. These points of view are likely to differ from the general views held by other countries toward contemporary Chinese literature. It is this very difference that engenders the great potential for new knowledge and discovery.

Modern Chinese writers have been deeply influenced by literature from all over the world. We have been deeply convinced by Goethe's concept of "World Literature." We are committed to the invaluable dream of a "Tower of Babel" promoting mutual understanding among all the peoples of the world. I believe the *21st Century Chinese Literature* series will provide our own enduring great bricks in this skyward "Tower."

Chinese Miracles and Stories of the People

Li Jingze

Li Jingze. He is an eminent Chinese literary critic, is editor-in-chief of *People's Literature*, a major literary journal in China. Li Jingze was born in 1964 and entered Beijing University at the age of 16 through the national entrance examinations.

Since graduating in 1984, Li Jingze has continually done editorial work for *Selected Stories*, *People's Literature* and other journals.

Chinese Miracles
and Stories of the People

It is a snowy day, sometime in the early 21st century in China. A man travels to a large city to meet a woman there ("Taking a Rabbit, Meeting a Woman," by Yang Li). She is a friend through the Internet, with the name of "White Black-eared Bunny." He is not certain about any of her other details. He therefore takes a live white, black-eared rabbit with him, as if to attach an element of real weight to this illusionary trip.

In the city he loses his way as well as his rabbit. The whole city appears to be a vast, bustling construction site, with ever-changing geographical sights that could never be affixed on a map. When the man finds no other way through, he suddenly begins to scurry over the rooftops along the city's skyline, like the chivalrous swordsmen of ancient Chinese legend. Eventually he arrives at their rendezvous in the city center, where a fast-food outlet used to stand with the globally recognized golden "M" sign, only to be surprised. Will the real woman show up, and what of his rabbit?

The rabbit reminds me of the one in John Updike's *Rabbit Tetralogy*. "Taking a

Rabbit, Meeting a Woman," a fictional tale written in 2002, gives an account of the adventures of the main character on his way to an appointment with a woman. In fact, in this tale he is taking a journey to discover his true self, rather than the woman, as he explores his own limits and possibilities. Ultimately he may only gain another kind of reunion. The young fictionist's writing is a mix of poetry, satire and frail bewilderment, composing a worldly portrayal of the tragicomic self-consciousness of the emerging middle class in China.

In this fiction, the city and the woman, both described as chaotic, energetic, constantly changing, unpredictable and elusive, are co-referential concepts. Both are the subjects of desire and imagination, and spell out miracles as well as illusion and disillusionment, inspiration as well as frustration. The city can virtually be any city in the vast Chinese land that has grown rapidly over the past twenty years. The miraculously emerging high-rises catch by surprise the people traveling between them, and impose often hidden yet severe tests upon their lives, including their sense of self and imagination about the world.

The fiction abstracts this matrix of spatial anxiety as being lost in a boundless space, which can be as physical as a magnificent city or as intangible as the cacophonous Internet world. It could also reflect a type of "realism," describing the ever-dynamic current social realities comprising status, class, desire, imagination, convention and history. Based on urban prosperity, this social reality promises freedom in the sense of life having infinite possibilities. In such a labyrinthine space, Chinese fiction writers are now exploring paths to "authenticity."

"Who Could Shame Me?," by Tie Ning, depicts a tragic misunderstanding between a young water deliveryman and a middle-class housewife. For the lad, the woman is his "white black-eared rabbit" and embodies the values he has revered and yearned after — an advanced, fashionable, clean and affluent life. She is his "city" (*chengshi*), which plays tricks on the imagination of a youngster living a dirty, disordered and cramped, laboring life on the urban underside. The city controls his imagination from top to bottom. The youth believes that he can approach the dreamlike city, which he had gazed at from a remote distance, as he tries to turn himself into another self that had long existed in his imagination, by physically dressing up in a suit, tie, checkered scarf and leather shoes, even a walkman.

This is a cruel and bitter anti-fairytale, or rather a fairytale version of *Lost Illusions*, by Honoré de Balzac. The clumsy and naïve youth feels cheated by what he thought to be "magic." When his illusions are dashed, frightened, he confronts the woman in a suspenseful denouement.

However, the fiction carries far more meaning than only demonstrating prevalent misapprehensions over daily life. The story ends with the woman's stern self-justification.

"And so what?" the Woman would say to herself sternly, "Should I feel ashamed over his tiring labor? No...." The Woman keeps turning this over and over again in her mind. "No!" the Woman says loudly to herself.

Of course, she needs to repeat it "over and over again" and "loudly." Thus in the end, she and the virtual "white black-eared bunny" character in "Taking a Rabbit, Meeting a Woman," are quite different. The youth has taken her as the subject of his imagination out of his own wishful thinking, while in the woman's worldview, the young man is not only completely an object who is the "other," but also a stranger with unpredictable motives intruding into her castle.

She may be not guilty. But her "forced" assertions reveal her vague perception of the hard truth that her city made impossible promises to the lad, taking over his consciousness and imagination, but excluding his too real body. His awkwardness and comic inconsonance are the symptoms of such a separation of mind and body.

We have to be clear about the unique process of the development of Chinese cities in order to understand all this. In the nearly thirty years before 1978, China had established a binary social structure with a division between urban and rural areas based on a strict household registration (*hukou*) system. The urban and rural areas were hence institutionally separated. The peasants could not work and live in cities, while people in the cities were secure in having a certain social status and relationship through *danwei* (work unit) systems and the welfare-oriented public housing distribution system. This institutional design contained a complex spatial ideology in which urban and rural areas were placed at opposite ends of each other, as "distant places," so that an urban identity could only be validly established. In actuality, however, the closed and stable urban areas replicated the rural social structure.

Then in 1978, social reform and economic development began surging forward, carrying through to the present day. China has experienced rapid urban expansion during this process. Old institutional barriers have been gradually broken through and tremendous social dynamism released. By 2007, China's urban population had exceeded 500 million, not including countless rural workers flooding into the cities. The household registration system, though not abolished, could no longer stop millions of peasantry, full of dreams and desires, from migrating.

This, probably the largest human migration ever in modern history, was accompanied by the decline of urban work-unit system and the collapse of the welfare-oriented public housing distribution system. The urban areas became open, fluid and jumbled spaces. Disordered yet splendid modern cities appeared for the first time in the lives of several generations of Chinese, within a relatively short span of time, often quite overwhelming in its force.

Chinese fiction writers have been focusing their gaze on everything. They had once been used to observing the slight waves in an orderly rural society, through certain dramatically structured historical and revolutionary narratives. Now they are looking intently at a clamorous, diversified world full of relentless streams of overlapping illusions. The difficulties facing them are attentively and accurately described in "Last Tango in the Square One Midsummer Night," by Xu Kun.

The square is located at the center of a commercial residential district. Over less than a decade, such districts have become the main residential areas for Chinese people. This marks the shift from obtaining homes through welfare-oriented public housing distribution to buying homes freely on the market. The old-type communities have become outmoded, and now people do not even know their neighbors. So they walk onto the squares and into the crowds in search of some kind of public life.

However, no one has names in this obscured moonlit night world. The author narrates the story in an almost bewildered, conjectural tone, detached from all the people, who are silent, inquiring yet identifying each other only through eye contact. Finally, all eyes are focused on a pair of impassioned Tango dancers, who seem to forget everything, as if only the two of them were on the square, speaking to no one else.

This fiction leaves the readers with the question: "Who is he, or who is she?"

The stranger, as a genuinely modern figure, has been the central image of Chinese literature since the 1990s. Countless works have devoted their attention to the stranger, a product of modern urban life. The stranger is destined to rove within an open and flowing space. The perceptions, identifications and imaginings about the stranger disclose the dark area of urban life convoluted with puzzles, difficulties, possibilities and melodramas.

In the square on an obscured moonlit night gathers a range of people of diverse status and educational background. Among them, the eyes of migrant laborers and long-time urban residents are to be easily distinguished — representatives of both rural and urban areas together watching two new strangers, who are difficult to categorize and identify. The two strangers silently endure the observation of the multitude. Their freedom and loneliness, to a large extent, come from their anonymity and silence.

"The Rain Dampens the Smoke," by Xu Yigua, introduces another stranger. Although he has a well-known reputation in his city, one day to everyone's amazement he turns out to be a person completely unknown. This man had appeared to be a miracle of modern urban life, achieving a transformation from duckling to swan. He turned from being a supposedly destitute, ugly, vulgar countrified man into a successful urban resident, entering into the upper social strata, and soon on his way to the wider world. However, one day for no apparent reason he becomes a murderer.

The author discovers with a penetrating eye the confinement and detraction of human nature hidden in the promises of affluence, cleanliness, decency and success brought about by modern cities. The narrative strategy furnishes this fiction with the power of evoking the subconscious. The author adopts the mode of detective stories, and his sentimental, depressed and romantic tone reminds us of one of the earliest detective tales, *Murders in the Rue Morgue*, by Edgar Allan Poe. Poe's story told of a sudden gruesome murder of a middle-class mother and her daughter by an unpredictably dangerous force. The case is ultimately solved and the murderer turns out to be an orangutan from the South Seas — an irrational, ugly, barbaric beast and an absolute "other" object. Perhaps Xu Yigua remains unaware, but the murderer in his story indeed has a subtle similarity with Poe's orangutan — both coming from afar, the orangutan from a geographically remote place in the colonial system and Xu's murderer from a distant impoverished rural place in a binary social system.

Poe would have been aware of the interior tensions in modern cities under the colonial system or the globalizing system, which gathered, absorbed and tolerated boundless heterogeneous factors. Yet he gave up any deeper understanding, choosing to make arbitrary classifications, ascribing the crisis disturbing the superficial peace of daily urban life to remote and nonhuman objects. His fiction gives a detailed account of witnesses' contradictory testimonies regarding the language of the suspect, a key to solving the case, offering a great deal of possibilities: French, English, German, Russian, etc. Of course, it eventually turns out to be a nonhuman language that we cannot and need not understand. Poe and his readers thus would feel relieved and justified.

Xu Yigua's murderer, however, is impenetrable because he gives up on self-defense and maintains his silence. As a result, his incomprehensibility poses a question to us, instead of at all solving the problem. Such a person, holding accumulated personality-splitting tensions in the process of his transformation from rural to urban ways of life, managed to replace his local dialect with more refined standard Chinese, yet he has failed to learn English properly in any way. Still, he is unable to resist a certain thorough reconstruction by this rapidly developing world. However, there has always remained a silent area tenaciously growing in him that concealed this nameless shame and pain.

Silence has something to do with the shame of self-exposure and the reality facing the self. The exploration and discovery of silence demonstrates Chinese fictionists' sensitivity to the impact of China's enormous social changes on the mental and spiritual health of the Chinese people. Over the past nearly thirty years, China has experienced extraordinary development and prosperity. The country's transformation from long-standing agricultural traditions to modernity has relied totally on the courage, passion and strength of the Chinese people. At the same time, however, this process has certainly caused acute mental trauma. People have been so busy and stressed, and forged forward without hesitating or reconsidering. But their spirits and inner selves were not necessarily prepared for all the changes. The truth is that, all their worries were confined to a silent, sometimes subconscious, area in the body, where often hides a stranger.

Therefore, the young man in "Who Could Shame Me?" is silent because he is unable to put together any genuine, accurate self-expression when faced with this world. Fictionists have been observing the silence in people's minds, and endeavoring to describe it in words and give it some concrete form.

"Confidences in a Hair Salon," by Wang Anyi, gives a more complicated expression to silence. She takes the readers into a hair salon on a street in a big city. In the genial bucolic atmosphere there, a pregnant woman recounts her life in homely, garrulous and warm tones, leaving the impression she has been always lucky enough to hold her life steady in her own hands, despite the many bumps and jolts of this city, and she is now able to live in peace and content-ment, becoming a happy mother. The readers may even admire her ability to settle down with her husband, who turns out to be once a crafty swindler.

There is so far no silence, and the woman is not a stranger. Yet someone in the audience in the story had not yet spoken a word. At last, a single utterance could conclusively shatter all her accounts. We suddenly become alert to the silent area that the woman is try-ing to hide behind in her enthusiastic narration. Perhaps this genial woman is in actuality a stranger.

At this point, some people may not like this story: Why be so acrid? Why not be more generous in bestowing blessings on a woman who has gone through tough struggles for survival, yet retains simplicity and innocence?

However, the author's intention is not to appreciate a way of life, but is aimed at reflecting a more subtle respect for the urban experience. The silent, insidious judge simply sits there apparently unconcerned, but conveying a harsh disbelief of the woman's narra-tion through silence. The author tries to convince us to believe what we see and hear, and she achieves her goal with skillful and accurate writing. However, she tells us in the end how unreliable superficial phenomena can be, and that we must transcend the genial, familiar images, sounds and sights, to approach the silent, strange areas.

When observing cities at the beginning of the 21st century, Chinese fictionists have discerned the tremendous difficulty in as-signing an identity to a person, to see his/her inner life and real re-lationships with others and the world, in a modern city emerging on a colossal scale, including the Internet, mass media, a maze of roads and buildings, lavish material wealth, along with enormous crowds of people. There are no strangers in villages, whereas strangers are everywhere in an open, fluid modern city. We approach others through eye contact and language, which may also be a means to deeply conceal oneself.

That is precisely where the difficulty lies. It is based upon this difficulty that contemporary literary writers have developed a complex, subtle narrative art. Modern Chinese fiction of the past one hundred years has never been as sensitive as present works, which are characterized by a labyrinthine imagination, conscious differentiation between superficial phenomena and truth, deep self-suspicion, and the dilemma between living standards and moral conditions in modern cities.

"The Great Masque," by Wei Wei, contains a duckling-to-swan fairytale, as also depicted by Tie Ning, Wang Anyi and Xu Yigua in different ways. Rapid economic development and great social mobility have created innumerous miracles, by no means transcendental, in the daily life of the Chinese masses, and opened up an imaginative space filled with desire, shock and anxiety for Chinese people. Within this space, various values that urban life has promised, paraded and achieved still haunt people's minds, and self-exploration and self-expression become adventures in miracles.

The heroine in "The Great Masque," gloriously successful, is about to meet her former lover. Back in her past, miserable poverty had deeply depreciated her love. Now a whim strikes her that she will pretend that no miracle ever happened to her, and she goes to meet her former lover clothed with her former failure and destitution. She wants to find out who she really is, and how the world will treat her after she peels off her gorgeous acquired "feathers."

Therefore, she *masquerades*. This is an action precisely hitting the vital spot of the dark secrets of the urban experience — judgment by others' eyes, on which modern urban civilization definitively depends. Everything, including his or her dress styles and brands, cars and houses, appearance and manners, and activity scope and places, is classified and measured swiftly by the eye. An urban resident has to be a politician proficient in the eye's judgment, and in how to know and cope with the world through it.

This woman attempts to resist such politics of outward judgment and ridicule superstitions regarding material wealth and superficial phenomena. With a final card ensuring victory in hand, she believes she can direct a pungent popular comedy and stamp out the snobbery and vanity under her feet. She intends to transcend the eye's judgment, and prove to the others that she has a true self indefinable by any judgment by others' eyes.

Will failure turn her designed sarcastic laughter into sad tears? The problem is that this "masque" means submission as well as resistance to judgment by the eye. To the woman's astonishment, she has to retain her mask in the masquerade; otherwise there is only a completely blank, only a strange face, remaining.

This theme is even more cruelly demonstrated in "Meeting Xiao Fang Again," by Chen Xiwo. The story deals directly with the two essential factors dominating life: material wealth and the physical body. The body is intrinsically a kind of material wealth, which is extremely subject to the eye's judgment, or the "gaze," in urban life. Appearance is so important as a symbol of status and ego that it becomes a heterogeneous matter detached from one's true self. Thus body and mind are split, with the body preparing for inspection and discipline of others' gaze at any time, while the mind remains deeply worried about both material wealth and the physical body.

"Meeting Xiao Fang Again" introduces a man with little money yet a vigorous body, and a woman with too much money and an obese body. The author pushes them head on into a secret space far away from the almost transcendental eye's judgment and allows them to talk face to face despite difficulties. The two go beyond material wealth and the physical body to open their hearts, wherein reside no souls capable of fighting against material wealth, the physical body and desires. Instead, there is only silence thirstily seeking expression through fragments of memory, illusion and metaphor.

Almost every short story in this collection is concerned with fighting against the judgmental gaze, while attempting to probe through the crevices in the patchy, improvising and superficial eye's judgment, into some real realms loaded with spiritual pain.

Honoré de Balzac's realist novels trust the eye's judgment. Fictionists observe the superficial phenomena of this world and believe in their faithful reflection of its essence. But modernism is intrinsically based on the profound skepticism of the eye's judgment or "the gaze." Modern urban experience shows that this "gaze" has won such an overwhelming victory that the values subject to the eye's judgment unduly prevail in life. In this sense, Franz Kafka had to write *The Metamorphosis* to escape from the shackles of the eye's judgment and to rediscover the real personality beyond it.

This is the fundamental purpose of the "stranger" and of "silence." Contemporary Chinese fiction writers have all experienced the colossal urbanization process and witnessed the great changes in people's lives and inner beings. They are trying to tell people's stories in such a world, wherein everything is changing and all established assumptions about people are being tested, where everyone becomes a stranger and people's stories wait in silence for concrete expression.

This includes discourses on fate. In "The Great Typhoon," by celebrated poet Wang Xiaoni, the fate of the larger masses is newly scrutinized in the jumbled city. The typhoon changes people who rarely notice the weather or look up at the sky and people who live plain and simple lives but rarely too thoughtful or sensitive, suddenly transforming them into sorts of creatures with tentacles all over the body. To some extent, the typhoon turns the city into a stage for classical drama: The sky begins to gain importance in people's lives, and those people who are used to bustling through the apartment and commercial blocks and streets are thrown back, as if into open fields. By observing them, we realize that people do not only live for the moment and the present, and that life is not merely about consuming and being consumed. When a person suddenly halts to listen to the faint, fragmentary messages of fate, fiction returns to the long-standing tradition of Chinese and Western literature, as William Faulkner described in his Nobel Prize acceptance speech:

"The poet's, the writer's, duty is to write about these things. It is his privilege to help man endure by lifting his heart, by reminding him of the courage and honor and hope and pride and compassion and pity and sacrifice which have been the glory of his past. The poet's voice need not merely be the record of man; it can be one of the props, the pillars to help him endure and prevail."

Taking a Rabbit,
Meeting a Woman

— yang Li

Yang Li. Born in 1973, a graduate of the English Department of Beijing Normal University, Yang Li began to write fiction in 2002.

The short story "Taking a Rabbit, Meeting a Woman" was her fiction debut, published in the July 2002 issue of *People's Literature* and included in the Short Stories volume of *Selected Literary Works 2002*, published by Dunhuang Literature and Art Press. Her novella *Chubby Girl Tang Ping* and *Private Map* were published, respectively, in the December 2002 and July 2003 issues of *People's Literature*. Her short story "Flaming Orange" was published in *People's Literature*, March 2005; "Funeral," in *Fiction World*, July 2005; "Coal" in July 2005 *People's Literature* and the 2005 21st Century *Short Story* volume, by Chunfeng Literature and Art Press; and "Sea in Northern China," in the April 2006 issue of *Lotus*.

Taking a Rabbit,
Meeting a Woman

Zhang Kai's slight form bobbed up and down like a scrap of chaff in the crowds milling around the exit of the railway station in N city. In his left hand he held a small wire cage that he had bought at the bird-and-flower market. It held a small rabbit also bought at the market. Even with his cage, he was inconspicuous in the crowd, just as anyone from out of town come to do business here — medium height, dark blue mid-length coat, black satchel slung across his chest from his right shoulder hanging down his lower back. This shoulder bag was the only thing that made him stand out: it looked heavy, as if it held a laptop computer.

The rabbit crouched in the small cage, motionless, either napping after the long journey, or perhaps frightened by the loud noises all around. It had black ears and its eyes were ringed with black fur, in parts resembling a panda. It was gentle, shy and a bit odd-looking.

Zhang Kai's gaze was drawn to a huge billboard with a picture of a wide street going through palatial buildings. Large black characters were printed over it: "Once and for All." Along the bottom were two lines in smaller characters: "When the East-West Boulevard is completed, the 'Palace in the Wind' will play celestial music." Bemused, he knit his brows in incomprehension, and once again was engulfed in the crowds exiting the station.

Curiosity at the novelty of a strange place distracted Zhang Kai slightly from his constant thoughts of a woman by the name of "White Black-eared Bunny." She was a friend on the web, a woman who tortured him, as did her pleasant voice. She was the reason for his coming to this city, and they had agreed to meet at two thirty in the afternoon outside the McDonald's at the crossroads by the city center.

The gray city carried a cold nip in air that felt sharp, yet invigorating. At the mouth of the underground exit was the bus stop for the No. 718, which went straight to the city center. The acacia trees lining the streets were bare and black, the people all looked like little boilers in their bulky clothes, puffing white steam rhythmically from their mouths. As he waited for the bus, white crystals began to drift in the gray sky. Though they did not resemble the "great flakes of the Yan Mountains" of his imagination, they were his first real contact with snow. He felt clean and refreshed. The crystals drifted on to his face, each a tiny prick of cold, floating into his hands and melting into drops of water.

As an air-conditioned bus slowly drew up and stopped with a jerk, he climbed on and took a seat close to the door. His rabbit attracted a lot of attention, and everyone's gaze shifted to it from the windows. A little girl with curly hair, dressed in so many thick clothes she looked like a ball, stared at the cage on his lap. The rabbit sat motionless, its tail towards her, its head tucked in the corner, quite uninterested. The little girl slid off her grandmother's knee and waddled over to him, put her hand on the cage and pressed her face up close. She lifted her head inquiringly to see if he objected. Her grandmother was asleep by the window, a thread of saliva hanging from the corner of her mouth. He smiled at the child, who smiled back, "Little whitey bunny, lift up your ears... why, they're black!" She looked at him as if for some explanation.

A string of traffic lights made the bus progress very slowly, as it stopped at nearly each crossroad. Inside, everyone became drowsy from the excessive warmth. His stop was the last one, still a long way off. He could not help yawning a couple of times — so hard that tears came to his eyes. He leaned back comfortably into his seat and closed his eyes.

To reach the northern N city from his home in C city in the southwest, Zhang Kai had sat on a train for one entire day and night. Before this trip, the furthest north he had ever been was to a small town on the southern banks of the Yangtze River. Over the time planning for this trip, he had gone to work during the day and had many dreams at night. He had played out a number of possible scenarios for their meeting, which had cost him much sleep. Even when he had been on the road, he would picture the exciting moment when they would meet. He thought of her constantly, trying to figure her out, as if there were countless rabbits in his heart, each of them hopping and jumping about, making him agitated, upset and restless. As the train headed northward and her city rushed closer and closer, he had suddenly calmed down and become more confident. What's all the fuss about, he thought to himself; it's just two Internet friends getting together, there's nothing to get nervous about.

Zhang Kai's meeting with "White Black-eared Bunny" followed pretty much the same pattern of all young people who fall in love on the Internet. They had happened to encounter each other in a busy, noisy chat room, her web name had pricked his curiosity and he had started chatting with her. They had exchanged thoughts and feelings, and then QQ addresses. Then their Internet charges had risen faster than smoke from cooking stoves, as they chatted deep into the night and poured out their hearts. Following this, came extensive email communications, and long phone calls. This had gone on for one year.

Zhang Kai was the kind of young person you can meet anywhere, in the park, in the cinema, in the town square or on any street. They are clean, plainly dressed, unexceptional, with a secure job that guarantees enough to live on without any worries. Their parents are both alive, they have life insurance, and if they have never encountered any misfortune, neither have they ever run into any great joy. Of course, some say that real happiness should taste just like boiled water, plain and light. In fact, the place you would most likely run into Zhang Kai is on the bus at the height of rush hour, or perhaps hidden behind a computer screen in some company where you have gone to see an old school friend. As he works, he is also downloading some movie from the web, has his QQ window open and is chatting with some girls somewhere. Probably everyone has had a classmate like Zhang Kai: not very diligent, but always able to get fairly good grades; not a class activist in the student union, but possibly a group captain or hygiene monitor in primary school, or maybe the contact person for a student group in some obscure science and technology department in the university. He does not seem to need male friends, but neither is he particularly interested in girls. He would never be anyone you would want to either censure or praise. As you reach adulthood, you realize that there are people like Zhang Kai all over the place, particularly in various companies big and small. Here you find lots of Zhang Kais who have studied applied science, and who work silently, steadily and unobtrusively.

Before that "spring morn of a new dawn," Zhang Kai had moved smoothly along his life's trajectory. On that day, one of his colleagues noticed he was late for work. When he finally signed in with his card, then sat down at his desk, instead of setting to work right away, he sat staring at his monitor for several minutes, where the desktop showed the lovely pure features of Audrey Hepburn. Then he went into his library of downloaded photos, searched around and changed them. At lunchtime when he went out to eat, his screen displayed a picture of Meg Ryan in *Sleepless in Seattle*; at the end of the day, the face of young, graceful Julia Binoche looked out, and the last picture was of the young French mademoiselle Audrey Tautou from *Amelie*. After work, office people liked to dine together, and sing karaoke. Such group activities often created possibilities of eventual pleasant assignations between one man and one woman. Zhang Kai, however, was already squeezing on to a crowded bus on his way home. Back in his rented room, he would eat his takeout dinner bought on the way, his eyes glued to the screen watching a DVD movie, his QQ chat-room window open, until he was sure that tonight, "White Black-eared Bunny" would not be coming online. When he got up during the night to go to the toilet, his steps were light, as if in a dream, and after relieving himself, he would feel a pleasurable sense of release. In the morning, the alarm would go off just as he was sleeping most heavily, and so become quite useless. That was why he was often late. The worst instance was when he was instructed to close down the IP addresses of a couple of coworkers who were the most inveterate and frequent online chatters, and by mistake ended up closing the boss's QQ.

Zhang Kai's smooth and uneventful life had now become dis-

turbed by many small things. He noticed that all his female coworkers had copies of *Elle* magazine on their desks; that the teddy bear
given to him for his birthday by his colleagues rather looked like him;
that there were actually several different panhandlers outside the
building, even though they looked very similar. One day after work,
he went to the Pacific Department Store nearby and discovered to
his amazement that the whole first floor was devoted to cosmetics: sparkling perfume bottles, arrays of many-colored lipsticks, and
countless delicate little trinkets and other objects just as glittering
and bright as in a jewelry shop, but far more varied and interesting
as well as sweet smelling. He was filled with wonder. On the second
floor was the women's section with lingerie and clothes. A couple of
older men were also roaming about. Zhang Kai went up to the fifth
floor to the sports section intending to buy a pair of sneakers. As he
walked past the swimsuit rack, he bought a short-sleeved shirt with
bright flowers printed on it. Goodness knows when he would ever
wear it. Then he carefully read the notice announcing all the activities for a camping club. He began to pay attention to the people and
happenings around him. As in the past, he was not that engaged, but
for all that, his life had become much richer.

He had told her about many of his recent impressions, and she
responded online with a couplet of poetry:

> *Before the sun sets in the west,*
> *Before the first snow has fallen.*

She wrote for a small entertainment magazine in N city, and
also dabbled in poetry and fiction, which had not been accepted for
publication yet. He asked her, "Did you write these lines?" "NO,"

as she shook her head, and finally admitted they came from a Polish woman poet. "White Black-eared Bunny" had not seen much of the world, neither did she go out frequently. Generally, she preferred to stay home, only going out on weekends with a good friend to window shop, eat at snack shops, or see an unexciting movie.

Back last summer, Zhang Kai had suggested they meet, though he had nothing specific in mind and certainly no particular time or place. He was not good at expressing his wishes to others, or at organizing or doing anything specific. For these very reasons, when he finally got a notion into his head, it was very hard to give it up. Online, his request was heartfelt and earnest, "Let's meet once, just once." His tone was childishly obstinate, even a bit pleading as if to arouse her compassion. She dragged her feet, and they had exchanged dozens of phone calls. Each time, it was she who had initiated the long-distance calls, because she detested hearing the phone ring. Whenever the insistent sounds shattered the quiet, she would have an emotional reaction: her mind would go suddenly blank and then her hands would start to tremble. She had been to see a psychologist, who said she suffered from a minor nervous condition. The result was that she had shut off everything, both in her home and in her bag, which could ring suddenly and upset her. He had never heard of such a condition before, and could only say, "What, really?" in a bemused way. Of course, this was nothing really important; after all, lots of people have unavoidable or irritating habits.

There was silence on both ends of the phone for a while; finally she said in a very sweet voice, "All right, we should probably meet, so come." This simple sentence set him on fire. She proposed to meet in N city, where she had lived from birth, through kindergarten, primary school, middle school, university and now work. She knew this city like she knew the mole on her heel, and could find her way around with her eyes closed. He thought, she probably feels safer this way; so I'll go, he decided. She proposed that their contact signal be a "white black-eared bunny." This was both mischievous and taunting. Zhang Kai knew absolutely nothing about small grass-eating mammals, and thought that rabbits came either in black, white or gray. He was filled with excitement at the approaching rendezvous, but also worried about this request to bring a special kind of rabbit. During lunch hour the next day, he gobbled up his meal and, filled with anxiety, went to the bird-and-flower market opposite his office, and there very quickly found a rabbit with the coloring she wanted. So rabbits, too, came in all shapes and colors, just like people.

Zhang Kai promptly filled in a leave request form and submitted it to his boss. As he watched him slowly sign the paper, he recalled the two lines of poetry she had sent him.

"What, you really bought a white rabbit with black ears? I was just teasing," she giggled, covering her mouth. She looked just as he had imagined her: long black hair, a pair of bright soft eyes, and two faint dimples.

"Yes, I really did buy it, look," he said as lifted the cage to show her. The rabbit was munching a carrot, making loud noises. As he spoke, his heart gave a shudder, and his body began to tremble too.

The bus lurched suddenly and Zhang Kai started awake from his hazy dream. Outside, the sky was even darker and gave off a cold glitter, just like the lowering clouds before a storm breaks. The street surface was covered with a thin layer of ice. Everyone, cyclists and pedestrians, moved very carefully and the bus inched forward. He looked at his watch: ten thirty.

The bus stopped, the doors opened with a "*ping*" and a gust of cold air rushed in. "Oh gosh, my rabbit!" He saw a small ball of white by the door take two jumps and go bounding out of the vehicle. The cage was still cradled in his lap, but its little door was open, for how long he had no idea. The little girl and her grandmother had got off at some other station.

Zhang Kai leapt up from his seat and rushed towards the door, but it closed relentlessly. The rabbit was crouched beside the stainless steel garbage can at the bus stop, looking shifty and sly. He stared at it and banged on the door in exasperation, "Open up! I want to get off! Hey, open up!" He rushed up to the driver, a young woman, who looked at him out of the corner of her eye, but took no notice while she smoothly shifted gears, pressed the accelerator and moved the bus away. She was wearing a pair of gray woolen half-gloves with a lozenge pattern that left her fingertips uncovered. These used to be very popular north and south of the Yangtze many years ago, and were called "thunder gloves." He stared at them without seeing her sharp expression, and kept repeating, "Open the door, will you? My rabbit has got away...." He choked and stopped. The young woman did not look at him, but stared at the road ahead with a serious expression that clearly said, "stop bothering me, I'm driving!" He opened his mouth but said nothing. What was there to say, and where to start? Should he tell the driver how important the rabbit was to him? That was a long story, and where should he begin? He could not describe in just a few words its importance, and now he had nothing to show that he had even possessed one.

"How many more stops to the center of town, please?" he asked the ticket collector sitting behind the driver. She had a short upper lip and slightly protruding teeth with two large white front incisors, and actually looked at bit like his escaped rabbit. He found this mildly encouraging.

"This bus doesn't go to the city center."

"Why not?" The words were hardly out of his mouth, when they sounded silly even to him.

However, she did not mind, probably because she could tell from his accent that he was from out of town. "Things keep changing on the roads," she said, "Barely have we got used to one route than it changes, so sometimes even we don't know where we are going."

Zhang Kai gazed out of the window. The bus was passing a place teeming with workers in yellow vests, and bristling with many tall cranes. They were building a high wall or erecting billboards. Others were driving bulldozers, demolishing small shops and decrepit old houses. Metal signs hung crookedly from the broken walls — the city was undergoing rapid construction and expansion. New streets were opening up and extending into the distance where they linked up with other streets.

Whether it was the slowness of the bus or the scorching dry heating that caused hallucinations, he had the strange impression that the heights of the buildings too were fluctuating, now tall, now low. Some of them were covered in bright glass, others gave off a cold golden glow; some were in the shape of medieval castles with rough rock facing, or friezes and complicated designs. All were gray, blending in with the sky above.

He continued to gaze out of the window and happened to witness a series of traffic accidents: a cyclist slipped and fell heavily, like a door crashing to the ground, his bright handlebars twisted at an extraordinary angle, and behind him, a string of cyclists also came tumbling down; a *Santana* coupe braked suddenly to avoid a *Chery* taxi, and skidded into a public bus. As they rode along, Zhang Kai saw more and more of such accidents, one causing another, as if an invisible hand were willfully manipulating both cars and people.

The bus crept forward and came to a halt in the middle of a crossroad jammed with vehicles on all sides. There was no moving now. At this, the young driver opened the bus doors without any hesitation, and Zhang Kai jumped out. He slipped as he landed, nearly falling on his face. There had been snow a few days before, which had melted in the daytime and frozen at night, leaving ruts and runnels from the car wheels. Today's heavy wet snow was insufficient to cover the uneven surface, and had instead laid down a layer of lubricant over the ruggedness. On the exit and entry ramps, the cars were lined up without moving, no one daring to slide down the steep gradient.

Zhang Kai stood on the pavement, stamping his feet against the cold. He was undecided about whether to go back to find his rabbit or to proceed to the meeting place. If he went back, there was no guarantee the rabbit would be docilely waiting for him, so it seemed a better idea to proceed with the main activity, which was to get to the McDonald's. He might be a man of few words, but he was not indecisive: once had made up his mind he promptly set out on foot. Many people were waiting at each bus stop he passed, and a couple of them, impatient with the delay, would peel off and follow him. They very soon formed a small cohort with him at the head. The billboards all around carried the "Once and for All" sign. On one side of a six-storey building he noticed a huge map of N city. It took him five minutes to locate his position on it, and he was delighted to find that he had not gone too much off track since leaving the station. Another five minutes were spent trying to figure out the shortest route to the city center. From the map, N city looked like a huge target board: a number of concentric expressways circling the city center, the last two drawn with dotted lines, telling you that, even as you blinked, the city continued to grow. He was presently in the southeastern part, and needed to head directly northwest, across two ring roads to reach the bull's eye.

After half an hour's brisk walk, Zhang Kai was beginning to sweat with steam rising from his head. His bag seemed to be getting heavier too, but he had still not crossed the first ring road. He began to get anxious. He clutched the metal cage in his left hand — the rabbit might be gone, but he still had the cage! Now, however, it only served to heighten his anxiety about being late for his rendezvous. This was something he had not considered before, and the misfortune with the rabbit now set him thinking that, maybe in life lots of things were unpredictable. Once the seeds of doubt were sown, all sorts of questions popped into his mind and nibbled at him — that, maybe he would only reach the McDonald's totally worn out, and late in the afternoon, but the dining area would be dark because of a power-cut, with each table lit by a white candle. Not many people were eating, there was no music, everyone looked uncomfortable and almost stealthy, in a hurry to finish and get home quickly — not at all like the usual jolly bright McDonald's scene, but more like some small eatery tucked away in a quiet corner. He would order a glass of orange juice and sit at the window facing the street, no machines working because of the power-cut, but his orange juice would be cold, while he looked outside onto the rear view of "Uncle McDonald." High in the air, the big "M" sign shone bright yellow and red, and on the other side of the street, in incongruous contrast with the freezing weather, would be a billboard with a model advertising women's underwear. The little cage sitting forlornly on the table, when only a few hours before it had held a cute white rabbit with black ears, but now vanished because its owner had fallen asleep on the bus. After a tedious day and night on the train, it had finally found freedom in a strange place, or maybe it had been just dying to get from C city to N city — dimly he had a sense of foreboding.

Perhaps he should have confidence she would wait for him there, forever if necessary, but he really could not think of any good reason why. He had to admit that being late was risky, and now that the rabbit was lost, things were even worse. As he hurried past a Western food restaurant in a steel and glass building, a strange woman inside suddenly rushed up to the French windows, pressed her face to the glass and screamed at him, "You can fly, why don't you fly!"

He could only see her lips moving, and as he wondered about her, he saw in front of him, the great flyover arching over the street, like a gateway of hope.

Once past the bridge, he entered what seemed familiar territory: a wide, straight boulevard running east to west, lined with newly built houses with gray walls and tiles, which still stood empty. The black double wooden gates were only for show, the stone drums on either side looked as if they have been there forever, awaiting his arrival. Red imperial walls replaced the gray, golden tiled sloping roof-eaves layering into the distance. Sounds of music drifted through the air.

Zhang Kai had no time to appreciate the sight, because a high, solid wall reared up before him. His road was blocked. A couple of "yellow vests" were working atop the wall, making it even higher. Clearly it was freshly built, maybe even begun just that morning. He approached it as if trying to hear its heartbeat. When a Formula One racecar swerves from the track and hits the side barriers it is very hard to back away. Likewise for a person who has been moving in a certain direction, anticipating an open path, and suddenly encounters a high wall.

It was twelve thirty and he really did not have any more time to walk around in circles. He could not bear the possibility of missing her by so little, after he had gained her promise, finally made it to the city, overcome so many visible and invisible obstacles, and now all because of this wall.

"How does one get to the city center?" he asked, raising his face. The snow was still falling and he could hardly open his eyes. The workers were perched on the wall like sparrows and looked down at him curiously, without replying. There was no one else around, so he shouted up again, "How far to the city center? Is it a long way?" An aluminum-alloy ladder was propped against the wall, and on an impulse he climbed up it. The dark gray below lightened, the sky above widened, and the snow fell even thicker.

A worker with a beard was squatting at the top of the ladder watching him climb up, muttering to himself, "We only laid this much since morning, we're too slow!" Zhang Kai stooped and thrust his face close to the worker's, in an almost threatening gesture, "How do you get to the city center?" The bearded man stood up and pointed behind him. The wall stretched back into a mass of buildings of varying heights. It was much wider than expected, so two Pavarottis could have strided along it abreast without any trouble. It pretty much went in the east-west direction of the main boulevard.

At first, Zhang Kai felt awkward walking on top of the wall, from where he could see the street scene and the slow-moving traffic below. Everything was white and silent around him, only the crackling of the snow underfoot. Through the branches of the trees and the spaces between the buildings, he could see the street like a broken gray ribbon not very far away. At one corner, the crowns of Chinese parasol trees arched above him, their twigs tickling his cheeks, black bird's nests built high in the top branches. The top of the wall began to slope gently upwards, and he cast aside his previous caution and began to stride swiftly along. Probably no one had ever walked with such eagerness along this type of path before, a path in midair that had before this seen only the footprints of birds, knowing little of human feet. At this point, Zhang Kai was not even thinking of her, his haste was all in his legs not in his heart. At each street lamp, there was a pile of slippery white bird droppings on the wall, so thick that even the snow could not cover it. By the time he had passed the thirty-eighth pile, he realized that they were there because the lamps provided some warmth at night and many birds came to perch on them. That would really be quite an impressive sight.

The wall came to an end at a very narrow twisting lane. On the other side was a three-story red brick building with a huge gaping satellite dish on its roof, by a forest of TV antennae. What should he do now? There was nowhere to go. Zhang Kai did not hesitate, but just backed up a step or two before taking a running leap across the lane, landing firmly on the opposite roof. He looked down with disbelief, and then gazed back at the wall that looked like a long, winding broken tail stretching behind him. He let out a deep breath and began to run, his legs light, his body agile. Wearing only a red T-shirt, he had become a red flying bird, a singing kite, a leaping champagne cork, and was no longer Zhang Kai! Emptiness, solitude and silence expanded with every breath and step he took. Space seemed elastic, stretching ahead, now high now low, and as long as he could leap and run, could breathe, could feel that solitude, he possessed and reveled in this unseen, unknown place. All he needed was to run as fast as he could in his scarlet flight. He leapt, light as a deer, bounding past scattered piles of strange-shaped objects: an old sofa with protruding springs and foam, a coil of electric wire, the remains of a kite, piles of dead branches, and the large metal reservoir of a solar water heater. The sky was infinite, the clouds lay low, the trees reared silently, the snowflakes danced in the wind. Zhang Kai ran, leapt and shouted, his voice carrying far, far away.

When he reached the end of the building, a neat row of single-storied houses stretched before him, with sloping roofs and slightly up-tilted eaves. There was a thin layer of ice over the black tiles. He climbed onto a low wall and stepped out on to the first roof. Grasping a TV antenna with his right hand, he started to walk across. As he reached the next antenna, the rabbit cage knocked against the metal pole with a sharp clinking sound. Then he stepped out on to the roof ridge and spread his arms — "You can fly, why don't you fly?" — he swayed a few times, hoisted his bag to find his balance and then calmly walked across with small quick steps. A couple of pigeons flapped their wings and cooed at him, their red eyes staring, their heads darting about uneasily, their neck feathers gleaming with rainbow colors. An elderly woman in a down coat came out of her house, heard noises above and looked up. Her eyes widened as she let out a low, startled cry.

If Zhang Kai's footsteps had been plotted on paper, they would have formed a rising and falling curve. Walking and jumping on rooftops was extremely exhilarating. Amazingly he figured out how to quickly balance and pace himself along roof ridges, perhaps his childhood game of weaving his way along cracks in the road having been good practice. The even rows of convex tiles pressed against the arches of his feet and seemed to hear the rapid beating of his excited heart. He skipped from one roof ridge to another, from one line of houses to another, following a zigzagging route through this serene place, like some no-man's-land, feeling intoxicated with the long forgotten pleasure of walking. His footprints covered the marks of hopping birds, and a startled cat suddenly darted out of the shadows and dashed past him with all the wildness of an animal that has long forgotten it was once tame. It stopped on the opposite roof, glaring and baring its fangs, snarling threateningly, probably trying to defend its territory. Zhang Kai continued on his way, his arms spread wide, feet light and agile. If he had a tail it would lift straight up with each leap, as he felt some instinct deep in his memory now returning. Like all creatures on the move, he had an intuitive compass in his brain. As he climbed over the last roof and on to the second-floor balcony of an office building, he had not lost his sense of direction one bit. There was a small door on the wide concrete balcony leading into the building, with two guards on either side. One of them turned his head quickly at the sound and saw him. He suppressed his excitement and walked calmly over as if nothing was untoward. The tall guard put out an arm to stop him and said coldly, "Show your pass!" Reflexively he felt in one trouser pocket, which was empty. In the other he found his time card from his company, the size of a phone card, and pulled that out. The guard examined it, nodded, and let him pass, then returned to his impassive state.

He dashed into the building and found himself in a long corridor with a red carpet, with identically furnished offices on either side, very much like in his own company. Under the harsh white lights, each person sat in a small birdcage-size cubicle, eyes glued to a computer screen. Many of the men were dressed in the same style and colors as he usually wore; maybe they even wore the same brand of shirt. As he ran past, he wondered if they, too, did the same things he did to idle the time away, and it occurred to him that if he were online now he would probably meet them in some part of cyberspace. At the end of the corridor was a sash window, which he opened and slipped through without hesitating. Next door was a long, ugly gray block of old flats, the kind that was being knocked down at the rate of at least two a day in N city. They were being replaced by high-rises, which saved space and could accommodate many more people. The window of the flat opposite was open, and the sound of a merry waltz came drifting out. He noticed that there was a heating pipe that linked the two buildings. Zhang Kai took a flying leap, landed on the windowsill of the apartment, and entered an unfamiliar room.

Every place has its own smell. Zhang Kai had burst into the space of a stranger, and was instantly surrounded by an untidy, casual atmosphere. He walked around a pile of half-read magazines in the middle of the floor, noticed the wilting flowers and a reproduction of Impressionist artist Monet's *Water Lilies* on the wall. Rich music was swelling from an open TV set, which was showing the New Year's concert in Vienna. He felt bewildered by a sudden sense of warmth and peace. Gently he shut the front door behind him and ran down the rusty fire-escape at the end of the corridor.

The snow had stopped.

Just before the steps reached the ground, Zhang Kai jumped down and landed on a very soft lawn, like a drop of water, like a pause signal. He had never expected the earth to receive his feet so kindly, sending an unfamiliar feeling of springy comfort from his toes to the top of his head. He was like a bird emerging from snow and sweat, calves trembling, still seeing in his mind's eye his running and jumping. The empty cage seemed glued to his hand, though somewhere along the way the small door had fallen off.

He stood there for a moment, still thinking he had to keep running, and then, a split second later, realized with amazement that he was standing at the very place she had described in such detail in her email: a huge road junction with large buildings reflecting the history of the city at its four corners: one a 1950s Soviet-style block of city government offices; another a trade building in the Chicago style of the 1920s and thirties; the third, a Qing dynasty-style princely mansion now home to the city's Writers' Association, and the fourth leg of this square should be the famous McDonald's, supposedly right where he was standing now — but as he gazed at the dark green lawn around him, nowhere was there any sight of the huge, eye-catching yellow and scarlet "M" of McDonald's! Absolutely nothing! Beneath his feet was this expanse of green lawn, rare in a city center, quite empty, extravagant and unusual, no doubt laid over a grid of heating pipes, for how else could it remain so lush and green in the middle of the freezing winter? The traffic lights blinked and the cars moved slowly forward, no longer jamming the streets. There were very few pedestrians about.

Had there ever been a busy, bustling McDonald's here? Zhang Kai was completely nonplussed, and his disappointment nearly crushed him to the ground. In a daze, he stepped over the low bushes and walked to the pavement, stopped a passerby and asked him hoarsely, "Was there a McDonald's here, right here?" He pointed to the lawn behind him.

"Correct! For many years! A few days back, when I passed by on my way to work, it was still here. But now it's demolished, just like that!"

"Demolished?!"

"That's right, I used to pass here every day! That was some fast work — they laid this grass, now look how green it is!" The last words came drifting back on the wind.

He stayed on the spot, speechless. An idea floated in his mind:

is it possible that she is hiding somewhere to stealthily observe him? This idea, though naïve, is not impossible. He quickly glanced over this somewhat deserted intersection, thinking that it was indeed impossible to draw her out if she is hiding herself, unless she walks out herself. He raised the bird cage over his head. Perhaps, such a funny posture would be more eye-catching.

The street lamps came on, and the wind began to cut his face like daggers. Slowly he lowered the cage that he had perched on his head. Should he find a hotel and stay the night? He could get online with his laptop.... As he considered this, the cage fell out of his stiff cold hand and dropped to the pavement with a loud "*clang,*" which seemed to reverberate in his stomach. He felt too weak to pick it up. Hunger saved him, diverting his attention, so that he could gather his spirits and think. He found a small noodle shop down a winding lane, sat down and ordered two big bowls of noodles, adding a double portion of chili sauce. Gradually the heat spread through his body and his sense of reality returned. Ever since they had decided on this rendezvous, for the last two days his body had been literally on fire and functioning on overdrive. Now he had been on the point of physical collapse.

Should he keep waiting for her? Should he find a hotel and contact her online? Ask her why she had not come, why she did not wait? As long as she was willing, he would wait and search for her without hesitation. The lost rabbit, her lateness and two thousand kilometers of travel were nothing, but now for the first time Zhang Kai began to doubt: did she really exist?

Zhang Kai was someone who melted quietly into a crowd, while she, on the other hand, hid behind the mask of "White Black-eared Bunny." All those emotions that tease the human flesh tickled her body too, but she had not yet learned how to deal with them, or how to relate to others. The solitariness of puberty sometimes lasts an amazingly long time in the heart of a young woman who does not mix easily, and sometimes its influence never really goes away. After work, she would go to the market and buy a fresh fish, then return home to cook a vegetable dish and some rice to go with it. The tapping of the keyboard at night expressed many of her joys and fears. She might call a good friend to go out together the next day, but then would worry about rejection. Others mistook her solitariness for arrogance: whenever she joined a group for a bicycle excursion in the suburbs, she always rode very fast and placed herself up in front. She had once had a live-in boyfriend, but was unable to hold him back from pursuing a career in a faraway place. Beneath the ordinary exterior she presented at daily work was a secret garden of the soul that she tended carefully. Zhang Kai was a stranger who had blundered into this garden, and because he was far away and his face indistinct, she had felt safe and could be as saucy, sexy, mischievous, lively and humorous as she liked. Zhang Kai had thought this was the real "she," and had never imagined she would disappear behind the name of "White Black-eared Bunny." Perhaps her strong sense of self-preservation was similar to her dislike of the phone ringing. He had been attracted to her, had respected her terms, but had omitted trying to understand the real person in her real world.

He had never thought that, in the blink of an eye, she would become a virtual identity, a pale and faded fantasy, vanishing into the wide expanse of cyberspace without a trace, like water on sand. He needed to try to distinguish what was real in the details she had described, what were just vague hints, and what were merely the products of his own passion, imagination and desire. Starting from that quiet late night in spring, he had carefully moved toward an idealized version of her, had carefully tended the relationship for nearly a year, all in preparation for this final effort. And yet, in the end, all it had been was a small, ineffective revolt against his mundane life, a disappointing emotional experience that was now over.

The night in N city was frigid, the sky a dark impenetrable indigo, all the smoke from the chimneys streamed out in one direction, as high and thin as the clouds. Zhang Kai stopped wondering if she were real or not, he believed that she had come to the meeting place: surely she had left home early and as she had approached, she must have been thinking of getting a table by the window in the McDonald's, so she could watch the customers come in and out and recognize him immediately by the white black-eared rabbit, ready to smile as she remembered this teasing request. She would then have walked with disbelief on to the lawn, stretching out her hands with an expression of surprise and confusion. Slowly she stood up, Zhang Kai could see her, a pathetic sadness in her eyes, the kind of sadness that is hard to describe. Without looking back, she disappeared into the crowds without a trace.

Slowly he stepped over the low bushes back onto the lawn, and could not resist taking a few random running steps. The softness underfoot gave no traction, and as he strode forward, his legs felt heavy after all his earlier exertions and the laptop in his bag pressed painfully on his right shoulder, and he felt his backside sag, probably from too much sitting in front of the computer.

Suddenly, something tripped him and he went sprawling. A couple of steps away, the rabbit crouched, like a ball of white wool on the grass, motionless, its black ears raised, its dark-ringed eyes watching him.

It hopped on to his palm and curled there quietly. He could

feel the soft fur, the warmth of the small quivering body. His fingers reached out to touch something around its neck — a dark red silken cord — at some point on the rabbit's solitary perambulations through N city, it must have been tied by some unknown hand.

(Translated by Shi Xiaojing)

Who Could Shame Me?

— Tie Ning

Tie Ning. Born in 1957 in Beijing, of Hebei origin, Tie Ning was once the chair of the Hebei Writers' Association and vice-chair of the Chinese Writers' Association, and in 2006 she was elected the chair of the Chinese Writers' Association.

Tie Ning began to publish her writings from 1975. Her representative works are four novels, including *Rose Gate*, *Bathing Beauties* and *Benhua Village*, and 15 novellas and short stories, including *Xiangxue*, *The Twelfth Night*, *A Red Shirt without Buttons*, *In the Opposite Building*, and *How Far Is Forever*. She has also written prose and informal essays totaling 4 million Chinese characters, and published over 50 anthologies of fiction and prose, including the five-volume *Collection of Tie Ning* in 1996 and the nine-volume *Tie Ning Series* by People's Literature Publishing House in 2007. Tie Ning has won the Lu Xun Literary Prize, along with five other national-level literary prizes, and over 30 prizes for her fiction and prose given by major Chinese literary periodicals. The film *Xiangxue*, adapted from her novella, won a prize at the 41st Berlin Film Festival, as well as Chinese Jinji and Baihua film awards.

Some of her works have been translated into English, Russian, German, French, Japanese, Korean, Spanish, Danish, Norwegian and Vietnamese, among other languages.

Who Could Shame Me?

After breakfast, the Woman made one call after another. She was not sitting down in front of the phone, but walking about the room holding the handset — she had a cordless phone in the sitting room. There were two reasons for her roaming about and looking around like this. First, she was able to check her bright large new home to see if anything was still missing. Was everything the way she liked it? Or maybe everything was just fine. Second, she seemed to think she was imitating those heroines in foreign movies who always carried a phone around with them when making or taking a call. They would stroll about the room, the long cord snaking behind or ahead of them, looking relaxed and self-contented. The Woman too, felt smug, but she did not want to admit this, it was too petty, and her feelings surely were loftier than that. She was not quite forty, an age when the desire to imitate and to create exist in tandem.

The Woman strolled into the kitchen and noticed that the pale blue translucent water container in the dispenser was empty. She should call the water station and order another bottle, so she quickly finished her phone conversation, which was pretty pointless anyway. She dialed the water company several times but each time got a cold, bland voice, "The number you have called does not exist or has been changed." The Woman felt annoyed. This mineral water company, Qinglin Mountain, had come to her door to sell its product, and just a few days earlier she had called to order more water. How could the number now not exist? Or maybe it had been changed? Which was even more unforgivable — how can you change a number and not tell your customers, don't we need to drink water every day? The Woman called "114" for information, but was told "the company you want is not listed." Now she was really angry. "Illegal shop," "unregistered business" and other such terms flashed through her mind. She remembered that last time the boy who had delivered the water suggested she buy a batch of ten water coupons for the price of one hundred yuan. She had done so, for the sake of convenience, because it would mean she did not need to keep the exact cash on hand, and could just pay with a coupon each time. That must be their trick, to get all their customers to give them cash and then to skip town. As these thoughts flashed through her mind, she opened a small drawer by the stove and took out the wad of narrow water coupons. Well, if the company's number still existed, these were still worth some money, otherwise they were just a stack of waste paper. Then she noticed on these "worthless" slips the address of the water company, in clear distinct characters: such and such a number on such and such a street, in such and such a district of the town. So the place actually had an address, how was it she had never noticed that before? Probably it was because, if one can telephone to get the service one needs, an address is unimportant — but now it became very important. The Woman did a quick calculation of the distance from her home and decided it was about six kilometers away, a middling distance in a medium-sized town. She decided to look up the water station, spurred perhaps by the thought of that the hundred yuan (which she had actually already written off), or perhaps by indignation over being swindled. Because that is indeed how she felt, though this was not an unfamiliar feeling.

In a booming but untrustworthy business world, a wealthy but insecure lifestyle was what she had learned to live with. All promises were to be doubted, including the promise of round-the-clock hot water, never completely fulfilled, from the service company that managed these residences. However, in contrast, it had dressed up the security personnel in smart dark blue uniforms with gold epaulettes and tassels, topped with red berets, and had them marching around the premises on regular patrols, as if they were on show. Did this not satisfy both the company's and the residents' sense of self-importance, shouldn't it be enough? For the Woman, those red berets were the most hateful of all. And most particularly, when she turned on the shower and no hot water came out. She would grab a towel to wrap around her naked body, and call the service office, only to get the usual answer, "We apologize, but we are doing emergency repairs on the hot water pipes." At such moments, she was convinced that the person on duty was sitting there with a red beret perched crookedly on his head, hopelessly trying to look professional.

Her thoughts darting around like this, the Woman got dressed in a huff, locked the apartment, took the elevator down, and drove off in search of the missing water company. She quickly found the narrow street in the designated district. It turned out to be a crowded, noisy, dirty place, packed with shops and stalls selling local wares at wholesale prices: brooms, dustpans, mops, toilet paper, doubtful-quality stainless steel basins, bowls, kitchen knives, scissors, iron pots, plastic buckets...; the goods were stacked like waves on the pavements. Amongst them were food stalls and eateries, with stoves trespassing on the road itself, selling large dumplings, steamed meat buns and bowls of noodles, each cooking in their pots, belching clouds of hot steam. The whole street and all the people in it were shrouded in this pungent air, and the ground was sticky with grease, dirty water draining everywhere. The Woman in her car slowed down, carefully inspecting the street numbers and thinking to herself that, any small shop or "company" on a street as messy and crowded as this could very easily disappear. At that moment she saw the three characters "Qinglin Mountain." Squeezed between the steamed meat bun and the noodle stalls was a small shop front with a large sign above: "Qinglin Mountain Mineral Water Company." So it really did exist. The Woman parked her car by the curb, picked her way over the trickles of dirty water, and entered the shop. In the room stacked with water containers, the kid, the one who had delivered water to her house, and two companions were sitting around a two-drawer desk eating noodles from huge china bowls decorated with blue flowers, each larger than his head. When he noticed the Woman, he took his face out of the bowl and looked at her, a strand of dark spinach stuck at the corner of his mouth.

The Woman calmed down. So the water station was not a hoax, the address on the coupon was genuine, and there was a dusty telephone on the desk being used as a dining table. She glanced at the kid with the spinach and wondered how to address him. Clearly he was not yet a full-grown man, but "boy" seemed a bit too juvenile, after all, since he was no child laborer either. What about, "young man?" That sounded a bit too encouraging and approving, which was not her intention. After all, he could not be older than seventeen, with a narrow, mousy face with dull skin, an air of half-country bumpkin half-city urchin, merely a malnourished teenager.

Did she really have to put so much thought into how to address a character like this? "Hey, you," she said, and followed this with a string of reproaches about changing the telephone number without informing the customers. The Young Guy explained that the old number had been borrowed from someone else who now wanted it back, so the boss had applied for a new number, which would soon be in use. Then he muttered a number of awkward "apologies," which showed that he was new to the city and still unaccustomed to its ways. The Woman heard him out impatiently, and said, "You've delivered water to me before, please send over another bottle at three this afternoon; you have my address on your customer list." The Young Guy said earnestly that he remembered her address: No. 801, Block 5, Lakeside Park Residence. The Woman smiled to herself, not at the Young Guy's good memory, but at the thought that this town actually did not have any lake at all, yet her residential sub-division had chosen the name "Lakeside Park Residence." Did this not satisfy the subdivision and all its residents' desires to impress, along with boosting their sense of self-importance? Of course, it did! The Woman felt pleased with her own self-derision; after all, only those who can laugh at themselves can move ahead in life. She believed she was one of those.

The Young Guy watched her get into her car and drive away. He paid special attention to the white car, though he did not know the name. However, this was not important, the main thing was that a woman driving a car had come to the water station, come to this shabby, narrow room. She had come in like a gust of fresh air, sweet smelling and warm, and she had come to see him. She had been annoyed, but had not said anything too harsh, and had asked him to send over some water. She was spiffily dressed — though the Young Guy did not have enough vocabulary to describe how so.

He looked down at himself. How shabby and tatty he looked, with his county shoe-factory sneakers already worn, with a number of small holes. The Young Guy was not happy with himself, even a bit angry. He thought back to the first time he had delivered water to the Woman, but could not remember very much. The rooms had seemed very big, the kitchen especially, even bigger than his aunt's house — he was staying at his aunt's and shared a six-meter square room with his cousin. The Woman's kitchen must be at least double the size of that room, though he could not for the life of him see why a place to cook needed to be that big, big enough to open a restaurant. What was more, there had even been a "carpet" (anti-slip mat) in front of the sink! He also remembered the Woman's child, quite small, maybe five years old. The tot was playing with her mobile phone, and when she told him to put it down, he said plaintively, "Why can't I play with it, why can't I do something *totally* fun with it? I'm going to call 110...." (In China, dialing "110" is equivalent to "911" for emergency — *Tr.*) These two words "totally" and "110" had stuck in the Young Guy's memory, even more than all the fancy things in the room. After all, the apartment and everything in it were very distant from him, but the tot's "totally" struck a chord. He "totally" wished he did not have to deliver water, and could just "totally" loaf about instead. Each water container weighed twenty-five kilos, and he only earned eighty *fen* for each one delivered. On a very good day, he could deliver nine bottles, earning only seven *kuai* (bucks) and twenty *fen*. When that had happened once, his cousin promptly teased him into buying a dinner of lamb kebabs. What was left from his one-day's wages was not even enough to buy one container of water. A single bowl of noodles cost two bucks, and he had to eat at least two bowls a day because his aunt did not provide meals. Sometimes, especially when a customer lived on the fifth or sixth floor and he had to climb all those stairs hoisting the container on his shoulder, fury would surge through him, "Why did these people have to spend money to buy mineral or distilled water? Was the water in the pipes poisoned or something? Serve them right if it was!" Sometimes his thoughts ran quite wild, but he knew that he could not poison "them" because "they" would dial "110" for the police. Six months earlier, when he had first come to the city to seek his fortune, his cousin had told him about "110," and he now knew that if he ever had an emergency he should call that number. The trouble was he never had any emergency. His biggest emergency was lack of money, without which life was no fun. "110" could not help him there, could it? But now, he must go to 801, Block 5, Lakeside Park Residence to deliver water to the Woman. If these people all stopped drinking mineral water, he would no longer be able to earn even 7.2 bucks a day. His two companions, who had been eating noodles with him, chose this moment to start cracking coarse jokes. "She was picking you up, she was, she's got an itch for you she does." Something clicked in his heart — he could not explain where the feeling came from, but he just knew that now he was different from them. He even rather regretted eating noodles with them. Why did the Woman have to see him holding that bowl of noodles with the few spinach leaves floating in it? He also felt that he must change his clothes.

At three o'clock that afternoon, the Woman heard the doorbell ringing. She opened the door and the Young Guy stood there with the water container. He looked rather odd, though she recognized his face and expression as still the same person. After a moment's inspection, she decided it was his get-up that made him look so peculiar. That morning, she had not noticed what he was wearing.

His clothes and his face all seemed to blend with the dark, gloomy room at the water station, seeming to all naturally fit together, so who would pay any special attention to what he was wearing? Now here he was, in completely different clothes: an overlarge brand-new Western suit of cheap cloth that had not been properly shaped, sticking out stiffly. It made the Young Guy's head look even smaller, so that it seemed to the Woman it was not a person but the suit carrying the water container. As she let him in, there was a loud slapping sound. She looked down at his feet and saw he was wearing a pair of outsized stiff leather-soled shoes — the other part of his new get-up. She reminded him to take off his shoes, but he seemed not to hear her, slapping his way forward into the kitchen. The cuffs of the too-long trouser legs were rolled up twice and flopped in folds on the tops of his shoes, as if he had loosened his belt and was taking off his pants. She did not insist that he remove his shoes because experience told her that his feet probably smelled bad, just like the workmen sent by the service company to fix the heating or the water pipes. She always opened the windows to air the place after they had left. So let him keep his shoes on and take them away with his smelly feet in them. The too-large suit made the Young Guy's movements clumsier, as it rustled, as did the plastic cover that he ripped off the water container. After he had finally wrestled it off, he made to lift the bottle on to the dispenser. "Wait," said the Woman.

He turned and saw she had a dazzling white wad of cotton in her hand, cotton soaked in alcohol. She said to him, "I want to disinfect the mouth of the bottle first. Don't touch that part again."

He said, "These bottles are all sealed when they leave the factory."

She said, "Who told you?"

He said, "My boss."

The Woman pursed her lips disdainfully, and without hesitation, vigorously wiped the bottle, as if to show the Young Guy that she did not have confidence in his boss or the so-called seal of their factory. Up until that very morning, she had not thought of disinfecting the container, but that afternoon she decided she must. She was not particularly put out by the water company being on such a messy, dirty wet street; after all, just because you bought things in a bright, clean comfortable large supermarket, did not mean they were produced in such conditions. The Woman was the producer of a TV program and so knew quite a lot about such things. As she bent to wipe the bottle, her gaze quite naturally fell on the hands of the Young Guy standing beside her. How filthy they were, and these were the hands that delivered drinking water to people. She stood up and thought, well, I can't return the water coupons, so as soon as I have used them up I must find another water company. Then his hands, dirty or not, will have nothing to do with me anymore, just like his peculiar clothes and big shoes. She didn't care, had no time to care, about why he looked like this; next time the person who delivered the water could be wearing an even bigger suit and have even dirtier hands.

The Woman finished disinfecting and signaled to the Young Guy to install the container, then tore off a coupon for him, but he did not move. He was reluctant to leave because he felt a bit let down. His fancy get-up was his cousin's best suit, and he had made a special trip back to his aunt's at lunchtime to surreptitiously put it on. Surely, he felt, this outfit should be appropriate for delivering water to a home like hers, for a person like her. Was there any other reason? Well, he wanted to dispel the impression she had from her surprise visit to the company that morning, and from seeing him gobbling his large bowl of noodles. He was unable to sort through all the disjointed thoughts in his head, but he just knew he felt let down. It was clear the Woman had not noticed his new clothes, and by cleaning the sealed mouth of the bottle, she had signaled that she found him repulsive. He was not a very sensitive person and his judgment was often off, so he concluded pigheadedly that his new outfit was still not good enough, and remembered his cousin had a number of other fashionable gadgets. At this moment, the Woman asked, "Is there anything else?" The Young Guy explained that he wanted to tell her that when she wanted more water she could page him because he had a pager. Surprised, the Woman said, "What?"

The Young Guy was delighted by her surprise, since he wanted her to notice him. He told her again about his pager.

"You mean your company phone will be out for a long time?" she asked.

The Young Guy said, "No."

"So why would I page you?" she said.

"I just meant that, if you need more water in the next few days you can page me," he said.

"No need," she replied, "In five days time just send another bottle over."

"So you don't want my pager number?" the Young Guy asked.

"No." Her answer was very firm.

This Young Guy was becoming annoying — who did he think he was anyway, not everyone was worth her paging. And even if she ran out of water, and was unable to contact any water company, was there not water from the tap? What did she and everyone else in this town drink ten to twenty years ago? Tap water! When she was much younger, in her childhood, she had lived in a dormitory building where all the families used a single tap at the end of the corridor. On summer nights, she never washed her feet in their room, but would always go down to the communal tap in her sandals and let the water gush over her toes. Then she would drink directly from the spout, something that the adults forbade, saying she must drink cooled boiled water. But she and her friends all did the same thing, and here they were, all well developed, healthy, no one having been poisoned. These memories warmed her heart, but she did not intend to copy them. Now that she was a mother, she would never let her precious baby drink tap water, water that was not up to international standards. Her husband, who was permanently abroad on business, had come home on the holidays and was not used to local conditions anymore, even getting a bad stomach from drinking boiled tap water. That's why the Woman needed someone to deliver water, and why she had to put up with these kind of people.

Five days later, the Young Guy came again, still wearing the suit and shoes, with an added checkered scarf around his neck, which made him look extra bulky. The Woman opened the door and everything proceeded just as it did the previous time. The only difference was the Woman asked him a few questions when she handed him the coupon. Maybe she was gratified that he had kept his word, or maybe she just wanted to fill the silence. Anyway, she asked him how much he earned for each container. He said, eighty *fen*. When she asked how many he could deliver in a day, he paused for a moment. He really wanted to show off a bit, so he raised his head and said that on a good day he could deliver sixty bottles. He wanted to show that he was not to be despised, and also that he earned a lot of money. Unfortunately, the Woman was not interested; she did not want to know what sixty containers meant to him, or how much time and energy they needed, nor did she want to calculate how much sixty times eighty was. Her questions were just to fill in the space before he left. Whether he bragged or was truthful meant absolutely nothing to her, so all she said was, "Oh, sixty bottles."

Her offhand comment and disinterested expression seemed to wound the Young Guy. His huge lie and the big numbers had no effect on her, not even to arouse her scorn. There was nothing for him here, and there never would be anything for him. So why didn't he just go? He felt thirsty, and asked the Woman for a drink.

She jerked her chin slightly in the direction of the sink. Naturally it could only be the sink. Above the double sinks with the slop grinder was a long, shiny unusually shaped stainless steel tap. He went over in a daze, twisted his small head covered in dust and dandruff, and put his mouth under the cold spout.

Another five days went by. The Young Guy had not had a smooth time. His cousin had discovered that he had "borrowed" the suit and shoes, making them all dirty, and they had had a fight. Then the cousin had locked up all the things he thought to be of value. The Young Guy was no match for his cousin, who was big and strong and had lifted him right off his feet so they dangled in the air. However, he was not afraid of being beaten by his cousin — what really scared him was when his aunt rubbed her eyes and said to him, "You are living here for free, so if...." The Young Guy knew that she meant he could very easily be kicked out on to the street and that, if he wanted to make his way in the city, he would then have to rent a place. But by this time, the Young Guy was very confused and overwrought. Barely had he finished begging for mercy from his cousin, who then left the house, when he was seized with a violent desire to break open the lock on the cousin's trunk. This impulse came suddenly out of the blue, more urgent than asking for mercy, and completely oblivious to the consequences. He broke the lock, dressed himself in the clothes, and draped everything he could on, not only the checkered scarf but also a tie that he wrapped around his neck. He found a keychain with a penknife, scissors and a fake cell-phone hanging on it, and attached that to his belt. Then he daringly picked up his cousin's walkman radio and stuffed it into his pocket, clapped the heavy black headphones on to his ears, and slipped out of the house behind his aunt's back, bulky yet agile. He hurried off to the water station.

The Young Guy got on his bicycle, loaded with a container of water to be delivered to the Woman, but everything went wrong. First, his back tire went flat and he had to push the bicycle along to find a repair shop. Back on the road, all he could hear on his headphones was the song *Too Softhearted*, but the volume was so loud it almost lifted him off his seat. Actually, this wasn't too bad, as suddenly his surroundings seemed to disappear. The cars, the people, the trees, the street, everything seemed very far away; only the song in his ears carried him along, maybe it was even pedaling the bicycle for him. His vision, hearing and reactions all became deadened, and he didn't even notice when a tricycle sideswiped him and knocked him over. At that moment, the music stopped and the world flooded back. He was sitting on the ground next to his bicycle, and the container of water had rolled quite a distance away. He crawled to his feet, his suit and leather shoes covered with dust, the radio remaining silent no matter how he jiggled it; it was broken. The other vehicle had long since fled, but fortunately the water container was undamaged. The Young Guy put it back in the frame hanging over the rear wheel, and continued on his way to the Lakeside Park Residence.

It was a quiet afternoon. The Young Guy stopped outside Block 5, brushed off the thick dust on his clothes, hoisted the container onto his shoulder and went into the front hall. He headed straight for the elevator, but unfortunately, it was out of order. This was really bad news because it meant he had to climb eight floors carrying a twenty-five kilo container on his back. Maybe he should withdraw, and let someone else do it another day. But the Young Guy felt he could not retreat: his whole get-up, put together in such excitement, with such difficulty and at such risk, his broken yet fashionable headphones, along with the obstacles and accidents of his journey here, all spurred him not to withdraw. He must climb those eight floors and see the Woman. And so he started off. The overlarge shoes, heavy and loose, really hampered him badly. By the time he got to the fifth floor, his ears were ringing, sweat pearling on his brow and drenching his back. The calories in his body were way too few to support this huge effort. He stopped to rest three times before finally arriving at the eighth floor.

The Woman heard the bell ringing, recognized him through the peephole and opened the door.

Of all the times he had come, this time he looked the strangest to her. He was just a water deliveryman, and he was on the job, so why was he dressed like that? There he was, in a Western suit with a scarf and tie, with a large pair of headphones on his ears. He looked as if he were moving house, or as if he had just robbed a department store. The water container seemed almost irrelevant, yet that was what she really wanted, and why she let him into the house.

He came in, panting a bit, and all through his exertions to install the container on the dispenser, he was doubled over and pressed one hand to his stomach. It was hard to tell what was wrong. Did he have a stomachache, or a gut ache, or maybe none of those but was just exhausted? Or maybe not that either, but was just trying to arouse the Woman's attention, or her curiosity, or maybe even her pity. Trying to stir her to pity was ridiculous, but there was perhaps a hint of the spoiled child hoping to get attention, though the Young Guy probably was not aware of this. Had the Woman noticed this she would have been filled with contempt and anger, and would have ordered him out immediately.

She noted his posture and glanced at his face. He didn't look morose or mulish or calculating, and certainly not shifty; in fact he didn't seem to have the capacity to be shifty. His face was covered in a thin film of grime, like a layer of hoar frost, and a long hard gaze was necessary to see beneath it to the youthful person behind. This time she truly found him utterly repulsive. For a moment it was if he were not a human being at all, but some kind of strange monster that had barged into her home. She was not interested in why he was bent over holding his stomach. Was he sick? What right had he to be sick in a customer's house? She handed him the water coupon and told him to go.

The Young Guy took the coupon, but made no move to leave. He eyed the Woman furtively and suddenly felt a wave of dejection. Her hair today was disheveled, as if she wanted by this messiness to show her complete disdain for his sort of person, for his whole elaborate get-up. He thought, "Why can't I stay here for a minute?" When she urged him to leave, he said he was thirsty and wanted a drink. His voice sounded hoarse even to himself, and his sweat-soaked checkered scarf was bunched about his skinny neck. He really did need a drink.

The Woman heard his hoarseness, hesitated a moment and then, like the previous time, gestured towards the sink.

The Young Guy did not walk towards it, instead he took a step in the direction of the water dispenser. "I want to drink some mineral water," he said.

The Woman was standing between the sink and the water dispenser, slightly closer to the sink. They stood facing each other, about two meters apart, but it seemed much closer to her, because she had a faint but clear sense of foreboding. At this moment, the perceptive Woman still wished to assert her will, particularly if she felt insulted, and the Young Guy's request for a drink of mineral water was distinctly insulting. She stared at his narrow, shifting eyes and said, "No, you cannot."

The Young Guy straightened up, challenging, as if he were going to make a move.

The pattering of little feet sounded on the floor and the Woman's five-year-old child came in, the same one he had seen before. The tot held out a little cup and said, "Mummy, I want some water." "Move over!" she ordered the Young Guy.

He glanced sideways at the child and recalled the first time he had seen him and how he had whined to the Woman, "Why can't I do something *totally* fun?" Aha, "totally!" Today the Young Guy was "totally" not going to move away.

Sternly the woman told the little boy to go back to his room. "Go back," she ordered.

The child left, holding the empty cup. He did not cry or fuss, clearly also sensing the unusual atmosphere in the kitchen. He went back to his room and even closed the door softly.

Even more sternly, the Woman said, "Now please get out."

Despair overwhelmed him. He knew he did not want the mineral water, but then what did he want? What did he *truly* want? He did not know, had never known. But now, at this moment, he felt furious over his confusion, and even began to loathe the coveted suit together with all its bits and pieces. He began to tear them off, and his hand touched the key chain at his waist, with the penknife, scissors and fake cell-phone. He grabbed the penknife and opened it. The blade was not long but very sharp. The Young Guy pointed it at the woman in a desperate clumsy gesture, and without thinking, took a step towards her. He felt he hated her, and as the hatred welled up, he finally realized that actually he envied her. However, at this point, hatred and envy were the same to him. From envy to hatred needed no transition. He had dressed himself in suit and leather shoes just for her, and now she was as hateful to him as these clothes. But what did he want, to kill her or just to drink her water? Probably both. At this point, the Young Guy had lost control. He could not even figure out which was the greater crime, to kill a person or to force them to give him a drink of water. Everything was unpremeditated, so there were no rules and he could only play it by ear.

The Woman looked at the approaching Young Guy and began to realize the real danger. She decided he was a thief in her house, but clearly she knew her surroundings better than him. Telling herself to remain calm, she backed steadily away until she came to lean upon the stove, reached her right hand behind and grabbed the gun. Then she whipped it out and, holding it with both hands, pointed it at him. It was actually a stove lighter in the shape of a gun that her husband had bought for four US dollars at the tax-free shop in the airport at Sharjah, when he had been making a connection on one of his business trips. She was trembling inside but did her best to control her hands; she must believe that she was holding a real gun with real bullets. At this point, the Woman with the gun and the Young Guy with the knife confronted each other, for three minutes, maybe five.

The tension became explosive. The Woman felt she must say something. With the gun, she could lower her voice. Pointing it at the Young Guy, she said softly, "Get out! Get out or I shoot."

The Young Guy was stunned by the gun. It never occurred to him that it might not be real, because the Woman was so far above him — her house, her car, her life, everything was way above. So far above that you could hate it, but you could not doubt it. In the same instant that he felt total defeat, he also was struck with amazement by the gun. So this was what a gun looked like! He stared down the black muzzle, mouth half agape, and it seemed to be the real source of all his inferiority, leaving him totally humiliated. For a second, he felt like throwing that cheap, trivial little penknife behind him, its cheapness making it even more insignificant, its insignificance making it even cheaper. What should the Young Guy do? The hand holding the knife was dripping with sweat, but he did not know what to do next.

His hesitation gave the Woman strength, daringly she pressed the "trigger" and the gun popped twice. She wanted to make some kind of noise with it to frighten him further and get him out of the house faster. The sound might betray that the gun was not real, but even as she thought about it, she could not resist "firing" it twice.

Once again the Young Guy was stunned, as if he had heard a loud mocking sound, and his mortification was complete. He wanted to cast aside the penknife and throw himself on the Woman, throw himself on to that enviable and dizzying gun, on to everything that was so distant and so far above him. He actually loosened his grip on the shameful little knife. Sometimes people who are deeply humiliated possess a special kind of grim, agitated energy. At that moment, a police car had already stopped outside the apartment block, and the policemen very quickly forced their way inside. It was the Woman's little boy who had called them with his mother's cell-phone from his room. Finally, he had had the chance to *totally* dial "110."

The Woman listened to the policemen questioning the Young Guy. How could such a youngster like him break into a home armed with a knife to rob, didn't he know he was breaking the law, they asked accusingly. The Young Guy said he did not want to rob anyone. "So what did you want?" the police asked. Each time the question came up, the Young Guy just shook his head.

"Do you know what a sense of shame is?" the police asked. He said nothing in reply. "So what is there that could shame you?" the police demanded. The Young Guy thought a moment. "The gun," he said. "You were afraid of the gun?" the police asked. "No," he said, "When she pulled it out, I... I only had a knife." "You mean you were ashamed because you didn't have a gun?" asked the police.

Again the Young Guy said nothing. Perhaps embossed in his mind was that a shiny, black, smart mysterious gun would make him feel *totally* good. How he wished he could be the person holding it! By this time he had practically forgotten about the Woman.

There are times when, with almost a fierce pride, the Woman would think back to the Young Guy, because his violence and his weakness had left a strong impression on her after all. But in the end, he had been no match for her, not even for a five-year-old child. Not every child that age is able to call for help and speak clearly in an emergency, but hers was. Whenever she thought of that, the Woman would hug her little boy closely to her breast. In the following weeks, whenever the elevator was out of order and she was forced to walk panting up the stairs, she would recall what the policemen had told her that day: that they would have arrived sooner if the elevator had been working. So that meant the Young Guy had climbed up those eight flights carrying the water container that day. Even as the Woman considered this, the image of the Young Guy bent double with his hand pressing his stomach would flash through her mind.

"And so what?" the Woman would say to herself sternly, "Should I feel ashamed over his tiring labor? No...." The Woman keeps turning this over and over again in her mind.

"No!" the Woman says loudly to herself.

(Translated by Shi Xiaojing)

The Rain Dampens
the Smoke

Xu Yigua

Xu Yigua. Born as Xu Ping in the 1960s, Xu Yigua, as she is now known, after working as a postal mechanic, lawyer and advertising designer, is now a reporter covering politics and law for the *Xiamen Evening News*. After attending the Young Writers' Conference in 1990, she stopped writing for nearly ten years.

Since 2000, Xu Yigua has again begun to publish novellas and short stories, in periodicals such as *Harvest, People's Literature, October, Writer, Shanghai Literature, Fujian Literature, Fiction World*, and *Jiangnan*. Her works have often been excerpted by *Xihua Digest, Selected Stories, Fiction Monthly*, and *Writers' Digest*. She has a fiction collection entitled *Pale Green Moon,* and a correspondence and fiction collection entitled *Xu Ping vs. Xu Yigua.*

The Rain Dampens
the Smoke

Looking out the attractive high windows of Courtroom 2, you see a corner of the long corridor of the Shide Forklift Factory office building. Farther, through the steel fence of the corridor, one can see atop someone's house a red brick chimney belching smoke. The blue smoke rises from the chimney, not too strong, not too weak. The rain falls on the smoke, not too strong and not too weak. Yet, the smoke braves everything and keeps rising up. Although it is hard to tell from afar, the rain must surely dampen the smoke.

The presiding judge declares, "Will the defendant please make your final statement."

The defendant is looking toward the attractive high windows of Courtroom 2. There is dead silence in the courtroom, and the prosecutor chews his gum secretly. Both the defense lawyer and his assistant sitting in the defense enclosure are looking at their client. No longer able to control himself, the assistant hisses to the defendant, "Over there!" Their client turns back to continue staring outside the courtroom window. The assistant stretches his neck out this time to whisper to him again, "Final statement!"

The defendant's answer is hardly discernible, "The rain has dampened the smoke."

The presiding judge prompts him, "Speak louder! This is not a conversation between your own mouth and ears alone."

The defendant nods, but then shakes his head slightly.

The presiding judge tells him, "You may say whatever you wish to say, or you may want to plead for leniency from the government. Whatever you want to say, just say it."

The defendant shakes his head again, "No more."

The defense lawyer shuts his laptop a bit loudly. The thud is what a famous lawyer of his status should make. He is truly famous. His assistant is clearing up the paperclips, cigarettes, blue and red pencils, lightly and deftly.

The judge announces that the court is adjourned.

As soon as the famous lawyer signs the court record by the court clerk, he finds the defendant's wife, Qian Hong, standing right next to him. They walk out of Courtroom 2 together and go downstairs to the first floor. Only then does the famous lawyer realize that Qian Hong is accompanied by her elder brother and elder sister. Her father is too old to make it to the court. Her mother had originally planned to come but suffered an angina attack before she left home. The famous lawyer has noticed that in court, or even while being escorted out by the bailiffs, his client had not even tried to look at his wife, let alone his in-laws. Basically, he refused to look at anyone at all. Throughout the trial, he just looked out the window now and then with clouded eyes.

"We'd like to apply for another psychological assessment!" says Qian Hong's elder brother. It sounds like he is announcing a decision, but the way he is looking at the lawyer actually shows he is just consulting him. The famous lawyer starts to light a cigarette and then blows out the smoke. Seeing his assistant driving his car to the court entrance, he walks down the grand circular steps even as he turns down Qian Hong's offer to take him at a restaurant. While he is opening the car door, he sees tears in Qian Hong's eyes. He stops and seems to deliberate over the issue. Then he tells her, "There's nothing wrong with him. He's quite normal."

Qian Hong grabs a hold of the lawyer's robe, "Shuiqing would never kill anybody!"

"Yes, that is what I hope, too. Let's just wait for the verdict of the first trial."

Forty-four days ago in the evening, it had also been raining, an extremely stormy downpour. In fact, the rain had been falling endlessly for forty-nine hours already. The city's meteorological bureau said the rain was being swept in by a passing typhoon, and just one day of precipitation had already broken the record in the area's history. When Cai Shuiqing received the phone call from a chess pal, he was in the middle of buying a silver carp head at a food market. He had not needed to brave the storm to buy big-head silver carp at all. At home in the fridge there were already fresh shrimps, spareribs, two bags of fresh day lilies Qian Hong liked and the potatoes their son loved. However, Qian Hong had mentioned the night before that it had been a long time since she had not tasted the peppered fish head he used to cook.

At that time, the rain had also been pouring down outside the window. Under the antique bed lamp with a copper-tint paper lampshade, Qian Hong was reading a family digest magazine. Cai Shuiqing had bathed earlier, checked their son's homework and gotten ready for bed. He had waited in the living-room for Qian Hong as she was bathing in the bathroom. Born to a respected intellectual family, all of Hong's family members, including her mangrove-expert father, her retired professor mother and her elder brother and sisters, disliked watching TV. So Cai Shuiqing did not turn on the TV. He hunted for mosquitoes with an electric swatter in the living-room. He noticed there were only a few of them and they liked to rest on the black antique mantelpiece.

Qian Hong had come out of the bathroom and walked directly toward the bedroom. With a mere glance, Cai Shuiqing knew that Qian Hong had forgotten again to dry her feet. Qian Hong was quite careless in her ways. Cai Shuiqing put down the mosquito swatter and rushed into the bathroom to grab a dry soft blue-and-white-striped towel. Qian Hong chortled as if feeling itchy, and then giggled, "I didn't mean to. I promise not to do it again." Cai Shuiqing squatted down by the bed and wrapped Qian Hong's feet in the soft towel, starting to wipe her toes one by one. When he finished with one foot, he checked it and turned to dry the other.

Cai Shuiqing is a very neat man. Unless you looked closely at his features, you would hardly realize he was from an impoverished village where most villagers don't even know what an apple looked like. Yet he had obtained a good education. Earlier at university, Qian Hong had been at first extremely embarrassed that a guy like him would pursue her, and despite the fact that for over two years Qian Hong's parents and siblings had seemed wary to accept him as Qian Hong's fiancé, Cai Shuiqing had changed all that, bit by bit through incredible perseverance.

Cai Shuiqing started to clean up the water splashed on the bathroom floor and walls. This was his housework every day. He knew a colleague who had failed to take good care of his bathroom at home, and the moisture had accumulated so much that not only had the wooden door gone moldy, but also stretched onto the walls and the wooden floor of his living-room, turning them black. Qian Hong used to clean their bathroom at first, but then Cai Shuiqing had told her, "You're no good at these things. Let me do it." Hence, he would get into the bathroom to clean it right after Qian Hong used it, even if he had already gotten into bed first.

The thunder still rumbled and lightning still flashed outside; the rain was still spattering down earnestly. Cai Shuiqing liked the excitement of this kind of storm; it put him into a good mood. Without the thundering storm, he could not fully appreciate how warm and comfortable their home was. Cai Shuiqing held Qian Hong in his arms for a while after getting into bed. Qian Hong was reading the family digest magazine. She rolled over, saying, "Scratch my back. It's itchy."

Certainly this was an excuse. Cai Shuiqing knows it was a bad habit acquired from her grandma in her childhood. Qian Hong's mother had told Cai Shuiqing about it at tea one day, after he had already started to scratch Qian Hong's back every night. Lasting for at least ten minutes each time, the scratching carried out was neither too heavy nor too light and spanned an area neither too large nor too small. If she did not get her back scratched, Qing Hong would pout that she could not fall asleep. However, when his mother-in-law divulged the reason to him on the balcony, Cai Shuiqing had just smiled and said nothing. Actually, it had been Qian Hong who had made a show of telling her mother about it, as if to let her see what a thoughtful man she married.

While her back was being scratched, Qian Hong turned the pages of magazine. She said suddenly, "It's been a long time since I've tasted that peppered fish head you make."

Cai Shuiqing asked, "Would you like to eat it?"

Qian Hong had answered, "Sure."

Forty-four days ago during the day, it had also been pouring with rain as Cai Shuiqing pushed his way through the drenched crowds at the Yinguan food market. Many people's umbrellas were dripping and their vegetable baskets leaking, also splashing onto Cai Shuiqing. Even as he got even wetter himself, Cai Shuiqing's own dripping umbrella was dampening others too.

The fish-stand owner had been replaced by a young girl. Cai Shuiqing always bought fish at this stand, so he stopped before it simply out of habit. The young girl seemed to know him as an old customer since she smiled at him. Splitting and cleaning the fish for the customer, the girl had asked Cai Shuiqing what he would like. Cai Shuiqing pointed at a big-head silver carp and said, "Is the former owner your...?"

The girl replied, "She's my mother. Her knees ache in wet weather like this, so she didn't make it in today."

Cai Shuiqing somehow felt his own knees aching too. He bent down and rubbed his knees. Yes, the pain was becoming more obvious. The girl's talent was no match for her mother's, for sure. Her mother always cleaned the fish very well, but the girl let the fish jump and splash wildly. The fish water splashed onto a thin woman who was selecting fish at the stand. She had cursed the girl and walked away indignantly without buying anything. At about this time, Cai Shuiqing's cell-phone rang. It was that chess pal of his inviting him over the phone, "Come have dinner at my place tonight!"

"But it's raining!" said Cai Shuiqing loudly.

"Hey, it'll stop by tonight," the chess pal answered, "Let's get together. We haven't met for a while. My wife can make some kind of chive pancakes now."

Cai Shuiqing asked, "Who else is coming?"

"Just a few of us: you, Lao Fu, Lin Yuji and Zhou Weidong. Don't you want to bring your wife over?" the chess pal asked.

While saying no to the invitation, Cai Shuiqing asked, "Is it a special occasion?"

"No shit really. Just a get-together. As we can't afford a restaurant meal, just come to my place for some home-cooking. You don't look down on our food, do you?"

Cai Shuiqing said, "I always prefer home-cooking."

"Sure! Okay then, half past six."

Cai Shuiqing put the cell-phone back into his pocket, feeling greatly annoyed. The chess pal's wife was a fellow villager of his. He had met Lao Fu and others at a training class for *weiqi* (go) players. Put into the same group, they had merely played chess with one another more than the others, far from becoming close friends at all. Cai Shuiqing, in fact, rather disliked them. Yet Qian Hong had insisted that he should have some friends lest his life become too boring. Although Cai Shuiqing was far from being an unknown in their city, Qian Hong felt he was a bit forlorn despite his fame. In other words, no one seemed to try to befriend him. For example, hardly anyone would phone him with greetings for the Chinese New Year, not to mention those boisterous text messages flying around among everyone else. At first, Cai Fenfen, the director of their fellow-villagers' association, had taken the initiative to contact him, upon hearing the news that a fellow villager of theirs, an especially talented professional receiving monthly government allowance, had come to work in their city. Speaking in their local dialect, she had warmly invited him to join their association, and even suggested he give a donation to become the vice-director of the association. Nevertheless, Cai Shuiqing had right away rejected her invitation. Cai Fenfen came again, offering him the position of vice-director even if he did not donate. However, Cai Shuiqing had turned her down once more, expressing his refusal in standard *putonghua* Chinese. After realizing that he did not even want to join their association, she had stopped calling. Certainly, he ignored all activities held by his fellow villagers. As for the address list of their villagers that Cai Fenfen had given him, he directly gave it to his son to be used as scratch paper. Basically, except when forced to deal with Cai Fenfen and her association, he always ignored any such villagers' gatherings.

Qian Hong had prodded him, "It doesn't seem right, no?"

Cai Shuiqing had answered, "The most boring thing in the world is the villager's association. Just look at who these people are! If there is any time to spare, why not spend it on doing some research?" Although Qian Hong was not clear as to what his fellow villagers were like, she disliked at least Cai Fenfen, who she thought behaved too young and naively for her age. So she gave up pursuing the issue but merely kept urging Cai Shuiqing to try to make friends. That was why, when Cai Shuiqing had gotten involved with his chess-mates, learning how to be a better player, and especially since her father and elder brother both loved to play *weiqi*, Qian Hong had pushed him to treat his chess buddies to a meal at the Moon Bridge. So Cai Shuiqing had then invited his chess pals to a restaurant. She would take their son out for fast-food whenever someone invited her husband out to dinner or if he ever announced he had a social engagement in the evening.

After getting home from doing the grocery shopping, Cai Shuiqing had removed his soggy clothes, and then started to repair his umbrella turned inside out by a strong blast of wind on the way. When Cai Shuiqing had pulled the umbrella back hard in the storm, he had done it so abruptly he may have broken one of the spokes of the umbrella, which was a brand new one of dark brown and yellow checked fabric.

The fish head had been cleaned and rubbed with fine salt. He planned to marinate it in sauce until evening, so the flavor soaked the fish head thoroughly. However, since he had to go out this evening and Qian Hong would be simply unable to cook the fish head herself, he would have to cook it during the noon break. Cai Shuiqing took the fresh day lily out of the fridge, since he needed to remove the black pistils from the day lilies, a very time-consuming chore. If he failed to prepare all the ingredients beforehand, Qian Hong could never open up each lily petal to remove its black pistil. It is said that day lilies should be eaten after drying them, since they are toxic if you eat them fresh and do not remove their black pistils before cooking. Cai Shuiqing prepared them this way each time because Qian Hong loves eating fresh day lilies — cooked with shredded meat. Cut into thin strips already, the shredded tenderloin was placed next to the prepared day lilies in a food container. A note was pasted onto the container cover: "Stir-fry the two things together. Add salt and MSG. Sprinkle on some Shaoxing wine before pulling it out of the wok."

After getting all the ingredients for dinner ready, and placing the container in the fridge, Cai Shuiqing changed into a clean suit and left the house to pick up their son, a grade-one student in primary school.

Cai Shuiqing soon found his second pair of leather shoes soaked through. With no sign of letting up, the rain kept pouring down, alternating between heavy rain and thunderstorm. The whole populace in the city was hustling and bustling past one another going in different directions, each emitting their tainted mixture of rain and sweat into each other's nostrils.

Happy to eat the peppered fish head cooked by Cai Shuiqing, Qian Hong had consumed the bigger half of the fish head, stealing a kiss with Cai Shuiqing when their son was not paying attention. Cai Shuiqing was also in a good mood. Hearing the storm going wild outside while finding his own home so comfortable, he was feeling quite content. Cai Shuiqing mentioned his chess pal Lao Xin had invited him to dinner tonight. Qian Hong was happy to hear it at first, but then sounded worried, "But what about the rain?"

Cai Shuiqing's mood had deflated too, "It may stop by the evening, right?" Qian Hong ran to a window close by and looked out, saying, "It might not stop. The weather forecast yesterday said that four rain systems are gathering above the city. Lao Xin is funny. What weather he chooses to treat friends in — why in the middle of a typhoon?"

Cai Shuiqing felt even more reluctant to go now. Qian Hong said, "Well, it's his first time treating friends to dinner. He won't change his plans even if it rains harder. He must be at least earnest in his invitation. You had better go. Making more friends means having more opportunities. You should try to be less of a loner."

At 2:05 pm, Cai Shuiqing had gotten soaked from head to foot again, after escorting his wife and son back to work and school. The rainstorm still refused to show any sign of stopping. Estimating that Lao Xin would have woken up from his noon nap by now, Cai Shuiqing made a phone call to him, saying, "I don't think this rain is going to stop."

Lao Xin replied, "It's okay, okay. It'll stop soon. You grudge bringing your wife when asked, but you cannot leave home if you don't bring her. Come, just come, and stop grumbling, will you?"

Cai Shuiqing had no choice but to hang up the phone. He suddenly felt rather down, but he could never explain these waves of disconsolation flooding over him from time to time. It was something so concrete that he could almost feel its shape and clear details like its smell, color and texture. Yet, he was unable to describe any of these physical features. The GRE (Graduate Record Exams) had been held already in April, so the results would soon be out. He knew his score would not be great, he could feel it. But in front of Qian Hong's parents, he could only keep up with their expectations of him, saying that the score on his General Test should be "okay" compared with the earlier one he had taken last October, but his Subject Test would "for sure" be better than the previous one. He knew that Qian Hong's parents were trying to seek favors from their friends overseas to help him get out. All of Qian Hong's relatives were trying to encourage him to go abroad, all being confident he would. But, for three years in a row now, the results of his GRE had been disappointing.

In fact, he had scored 639 points in his TOEFL three years ago, but his visa application had been rejected then. Everyone at the office had whispered that the white man behind the left window was easygoing but the Taiwanese American woman behind the right window was awfully arrogant. She basically rejected all the applicants who arrived at her window. Therefore, Cai Shuiqing had been very nervous while standing in line. According to the general frequency of six to seven minutes per interview, however, he felt he would get his turn at the left window presided over by the easygoing white man. However, the mean Taiwanese woman decided to reject the young girl, that Christian convert standing in front of him, in less than a minute. Not even one minute! Before her turn had come up, the young Christian girl had kept telling him her English was poor, so she was praying hard not to fall into the hands of that Taiwan woman. Cai Shuiqing saw her pray with such earnestness that he even felt fearful that God could really help her. And if so, it would mean that he was doomed for sure. However, God did not come to her aid as hoped. Who would imagine she could be rejected by someone in this insulting manner in such a mere instant! Cai Shuiqing panicked right there and then. It showed that God had decided to abandon him, too. He harbored an even more profound fear of that right window, knowing his spoken English was even poorer than the Christian girl's. He had hoped to be able to avoid the Taiwan woman, but how could anyone have guessed that such a pious girl would become so hopeless and have such rotten luck. Now he was thrown into wrestling with the right window. And it was his birthday that day. From very early morning he had been rehearsing in his mind that he would make this special day truly momentous by profoundly impressing the visa official. However, as soon as he saw the girl running out tearfully, his mind turned totally blank and he found himself walking toward the right window like a doomed puppet. His mind was empty and a single voice kept pounding in his head, "I'm doomed. I am doomed with no escape." With these thoughts, he saw the carefully made-up poker-face of that Taiwanese woman behind the window.

That damned Taiwan woman, who would not speak even one sentence of Chinese, had only contempt and viciousness written all over her face, as if announcing, "I see through you! Don't tell me you don't just want to stay in the USA forever?"

According to his earlier rehearsal, after handing over his application form and while the official was still perusing his background information, Cai Shuiqing would say most naturally, "It's my birthday today. I hope I will have your blessing." However, before he could even finish his first sentence, he began to stammer and stutter between every word. He became even more flustered by his own stammering, so the Taiwan woman simply raised her silver-glossed eyelids and replied icily, "Happy birthday."

Cai Shuiqing later discussed the issue in private with Qian Hong, telling her tenderly yet determinedly that he did not really want to go abroad, since he believed their present life was pretty good already. Contradicting him, his wife insisted it was still not good enough, as everyone in her family believed a professional as talented as him must go abroad. Qian Hong's parents were full of enthusiasm about the future of their youngest son-in-law, whenever they chatted with friends in their intellectual circle. Everyone spoke highly about Cai Shuiqing's future. Qian Hong's relatives and their intellectual friends were all in agreement that the academic environment abroad was good for serious studies. Even if he returned home in the future, being an "Overseas Returnee" would be glorious enough. Therefore, Cai Shuiqing had to go through the scheduled list of tasks. In fact, Qian Hong knew that he had used a small cheating scheme to pass the CET-4 English test to graduate from university. She was also aware that Cai Shuiqing's speaking sounded more like English spoken by a Japanese, while his standard Chinese or *putonghua* sounded a bit like that of an English speaker. He seemed to be sort of "language-deaf." Yet Qian Hong still insisted, "Isn't it true that, if there is a will there should be a way?"

But he knew his GRE score this year would be even poorer than last year. Certainly Qian Hong's parents would not say anything harsh, even if his test results were not ideal. They would just comfort him and keep encouraging him. They seemed to be able to maintain their steady comportment in any kind of situation. It was truly extraordinary.

Cai Shuiqing stood before the window and stared at the sky-shattering storm for a long time. Would he have to take the October test again? Yes, he had no choice, just like this endless rain falling before his eyes.

Cai Shuiqing turned on the TV. Although there was nothing to do and no one at home, he still felt guilty watching television. Qian Hong's relatives so clearly despised watching TV, they continually labeled it as an uneducated petty-bourgeois way of life. Then Cai Shuiqing remembered that his mother-in-law had been suffering from some heart trouble recently, so he turned off the television and immediately made a phone call.

"Ma, how are you today?"

His mother-in-law answered, "Oh, I'm fine. Just this storm is so trying."

"The weather changes so dramatically these days. Ma, you and Pa must be careful not to catch cold."

"Yes, yes. It is just that your Papa has a bit of a cough."

"Shall I come over and take a look?"

"Don't run around in such a big storm. Stay comfortable at home. Whenever I say something casually, you become so worried. What a fussy child! Just don't say anything to our Hong. It's nothing serious. Just take care of yourselves, as we have Xiaoli and others with us here."

After hanging up the phone, Cai Shuiqing turned on the TV again. A movie was showing — he did not know the title but it seemed pretty funny. It was a traditional costume drama, a story of a scoundrel becoming a high official.

By 6:00 that evening, the rainstorm was still refusing to stop but only pouring even more fiercely. At moments it seemed as if drummers throughout the country had run out and were all madly beating their drums. Cai Shuiqing phoned his chess pal again to say he did not want to come, but Lao Xin replied, "You would be the only one missing now! Lao Fu and others will be arriving any minute." Hence Cai Shuiqing made a call to Qian Hong to tell her to pick up their son after work. He then left a note to Hong as well as to their son.

Cai Shuiqing's home sits on Singing Spring Hill. The air there is superb and the houses are assigned by the municipal government specifically to talented professionals. It takes fifteen minutes to go down along the winding path amidst the woods, before one arrives onto Park West Road. Many of the exceptional personnel, whom the city has imported from around the country, love to take a walk or chat with one another in the morning or at dusk on this curved hillside lane lined with trees. Cai Shuiqing has never joined them for a stroll. Always hurrying back and forth, he once complained about the traffic problems on the hill. If taking a taxi, one must walk down to the foot of the hill first, which means at least fifteen minutes. To make things even worse, a crossroad on the way remained under construction. Old planks, stones and cement for road repair were always scattered everywhere, making it hard for pedestrians to pass. Cai Shuiqing's umbrella had blown upward right at that intersection that morning. Carrying the fish head, wild rice stems, coriander and other vegetables, he had been trying to quickly jump like a frog around the scattered materials and swelling water pools; by focusing his attention on where to step, his umbrella had been sacrificed.

Cai Shuiqing made a phone call for a taxi but the line was busy. He then made perhaps twenty-five more calls for the taxi but he just could not get through. When it was 7:10, his chess pal Lao Xin called again, "What's the matter? The liquor's been poured into every glass except yours!" Cai Shuiqing replied, "I'm coming. I'm just trying to get a taxi." He had meant to say, "It's inconvenient for me to come and my knees are killing me. Let me come over tomorrow to eat leftovers." However, Cai Shuiqing was just not comfortable using that kind of familiar impertinence.

Lao Fu, Weidong and others had all got on the phone, loud and raucous as "Outlaws of the Marsh." Cai Shuiqing felt too embarrassed.

Cai Shuiqing said, "I'm coming, I'm coming."

But his calls for a taxi just could not get through.

So Cai Shuiqing had to walk down the hill through the pouring storm. It took less than the fifteen minutes before his coat and trousers were completely soaked. There was no taxi to be seen. He prayed all the way down that he would run into a passing taxi but failed to find anything. When he reached the crossroads at the foot of the hill, he was surprised to see the pools of water he had frog-jumped in the morning had already swollen to become a vast lake. As far as his eyes could fathom, he could see only boundless misty water. The hazy headlights of passing vehicles and black streams of rain battled one another in the distance. Cai Shuiqing pondered for a moment, before making the decision to remove his leather shoes and socks. Barefoot, he waded through the cumulated vast water as wide as at least three hundred square meters.

The murder did not occur at this time. Nothing unusual had occurred yet.

After wading through the crossroads, Cai Shuiqing succeeded in finally stopping a taxi. He crawled into the vehicle almost directly out of the water. The taxi driver turned out to be a northeastern woman boiling over with rage and steadily spitting out vulgarities. She used the most obscene language to curse the mayor, swearing, "All the sewers of the f---ing city suffer from the urethral infection the mayor's mother has." The female cabbie kept swearing until they almost reached Lao Xin's home. Finally she stopped cursing the mayor only because she hit a wildly dashing cycling cart delivering goods in the storm.

The two drivers rushed out of their vehicles and grabbed each other's collars. Cai Shuiqing shouted from the taxi, "But this is not my destination yet!"

That northeastern woman jerked her head around, "Get the hell out of here! No charge today!"

Cai Shuiqing received a warm welcome from his pals. Lao Xin's wife tenderly handed him a clean towel to dry his hair. Cai Shuiqing apologized, "Sorry, sorry. The rain is really pelting down." People replied: not to worry, it would be the best to down some liquor into the belly in this kind of weather. The good wife of the host was busy in the kitchen over a pot of lotus seeds and pig stomach. The aroma of the hot soup filled the entire room.

There were indeed three big plates of chive pancakes. Cai Shuiqing knew how to make them too. It was very simple. Just mix flour with water until it becomes a thin batter. Then add salt, chopped Chinese chives and MSG or sometimes minced meat. Pour the flour batter into a frying pan and remove it when done. It was so simple. On the table was also plates of stir-fried spotted clams, fried peanuts, a sautéed ribbonfish, shredded potato in vinegar sauce and shredded dried bean-curd, plus a plate of "three-cup" chicken or duck. As to whether it was chicken or duck, Cai Shuiqing would not remember.

People started to drink more liquor. It was easy to enjoy liquor in this kind of stormy weather. Cai Shuiqing found everyone in high spirits, not at all affected by the foul weather. He began to feel a bit guilty for being so petty. So he tried to echo each topic people chatted warmly about, to conceal the disloyalty he had previously cherished against their friendship. Soon he realized that his chair was wet with water dripping onto the floor. Feeling too embarrassed about it, he also worried that others might misunderstand what it was. Henceforth he spoke less and tried to seize every opportunity to stealthily observe if his chair was still dripping.

Cai Shuiqing wanted to leave for home soon after nine o'clock but felt embarrassed to say so. Around ten o'clock, Cai Shuiqing said he wanted to leave but everybody protested, "It's still so early!" When it was almost eleven o'clock, Cai Shuiqing explained that the roads around his home were hard to get through, so he had better leave a little earlier.

His buddies still refused to let him go, "No way! You were the last to come but now want to be the first to leave. It just ain't right!" Not until the hostess interfered, "It's true, that Singing Spring Hill area is too high. We should let Xiao Cai leave early."

Before the famous lawyer accepted the case, he had read about it in the newspapers. It reported that recently several taxi drivers had been killed. Nine cabbies had been murdered since the Spring Festival, and three had been robbed. The over three thousand taxi drivers from Henan Province were contemplating a one-day strike to express their thorough indignation about the lack of safety. The cabbies guild was trying to comfort the drivers, while sending a coordinated appeal in their name to the municipal government, demanding that the government catch the killers as soon as possible in order to pacify public anger.

Unlike the other eight cabbie murders, this case was solved promptly. The newspapers reported it as: "*48-hour Lightning Crack-*

down / Cabbie Murderer Caught Red-handed," "*Is the Celebrated Talent the Real Killer?*" The famous lawyer usually ignored this type of silly sensationalism. Important lawyer that he was, he rarely touched criminal cases, as their fees were too low. So when the suspect's family members got in touch with the famous lawyer through various channels, he asked for a skyscraping fee of 20,000 yuan. However, even that price failed to frighten the family away. They gratefully wrote a letter of entrustment to hire him.

They kept on pleading, "Please help him. It has to be a false, a totally false charge."

It was on the third day after the murder occurred, at about 10:00 pm, when the police had suddenly descended onto Cai Shuiqing's home on Singing Spring Hill. At the time, Qian Hong had been reading a *Women's Friend* magazine in bed, their son had just fallen asleep and Cai Shuiqing had been brushing his teeth in the bathroom. A small cockroach only a little thicker than a grain of rice was ambling across the snow-white washbasin. Cai Shuiqing spat out some toothpaste froth at it but missed the target. The little roach continued along its cheery journey. Cai Shuiqing aimed at it, spat out again, zapping it this time. The small cockroach was thrown into a panic and struggled desperately until its tiny legs forced their way through the froth. Cai Shuiqing hurried to brush up some more toothpaste froth and spat out once more. The tiny cockroach met its doom at last. It convulsed again, stretching out straight all its legs, thinner than his son's automatic pencil leads. It died in the quaintest posture.

All dressed in plainclothes, the policemen stepped through the doorway. It was Qian Hong who had opened the door, since it had been one of the nearby grannies of the residents' committee who had knocked on the door. At that moment Cai Shuiqing happened to be smiling in the bathroom — he realized for the first time how a tiny cockroach was quite gorgeous. Everything seems lovely when they are young. He changed out of his pajamas and went downstairs escorted by the policemen. He was still thinking of the exquisite posture of the small cockroach with all its thin legs reaching out. He still had the impulse to smile and even relive its desperate choking and coughing in the froth.

Qian Hong remembers his last word as he stood in the living room, "Shish…," as he held his index finger to his mouth, his eyes looking at their already-sleeping son's bedroom.

The famous lawyer did not go to the court to read his client's file personally, but his assistant copied and jotted down quite a quantity of notes. The assistant, freshly out of school, took the case most seriously. He remarked upon returning from the court, "It's so strange! And makes no sense either! He is a respected talented professional about to go abroad soon!" The famous lawyer ignored his assistant. The assistant suspected a case of injustice: perhaps Cai Shuiqing had been tortured into making a confession. However, the famous lawyer became clear about everything after his first meeting with the client. It is not a case of injustice as his assistant suspected, for Cai Shuiqing seems to very well understand the murder he has committed.

Through the other side of the iron bars of the meeting-room window, the attorney asked Cai Shuiqing, "Have you received the indictment?"

Cai Shuiqing said, "Yes."

"Do you have any objection to the charges in the indictment?"

Cai Shuiqing just looked at the lawyer. So the lawyer repeated his question, "Do you find any problem with the indictment?"

Cai Shuiqing said, no. Seeing that the lawyer did not respond at once, Cai Shuiqing said again, "No, I don't have any objections."

The famous lawyer nodded by shutting his eyes. Then he said, "Since you agree to have me as your defense lawyer, tell me what happened that night. Tell me the truth without holding anything back. I must know the whole truth no matter how dreadful it is. Leave everything else to me. I will tell you what to do including what you should and should not say in the court. Now, tell me the truth. The Truth! Only by doing this can we take the initiative in the court, so I can save you."

Upon his first sight of the client, the famous lawyer had felt that his client rather resembles a toiling laborer from rural areas. It seems that he and the relatives who came to the firm to seek help are simply from two worlds. His wife, her family members as well as their friends and acquaintances are all graceful intellectuals moving in respected elite circles. By checking on his client's background, the famous lawyer had concluded that his client must be a bookish, delicate scholar — working in a research institute, possessing academic honors and in the middle of applying to study in Canada.

However, when the lawyer first set eyes upon Cai Shuiqing, he was inwardly very much taken aback. No taller than 1.67 meters at most, Cai Shuiqing is dark and stocky. His hair is not well-patted down somehow, so the wiry hair makes him almost look African. He showed plenty of gray stubble, and he must have had graying hair from his youth. Cai Shuiqing's upper and lower lips resemble two folded pancakes, thick and rather protruding. His nose is broad and each nostril seems ready to flare. His eyes are small, with their heavy, thick eyelids pressing the eyes half-shut. But when those small eyes blink, they reveal extremely long though sparse eyelashes.

Cai Shuiqing nodded calmly and politely to the lawyer on

meeting him. The famous lawyer explained to him that he had been asked by Cai Shuiqing's relatives to defend him. With a slight smile, Cai Shuiqing answered softly, "Such a waste of money." Sensitive to such an answer, the famous lawyer replied quickly, "You could cancel the retainer." Cai Shuiqing smiled apologetically, "I was just making a casual remark, please don't mind me."

It was 11:05 that evening when Cai Shuiqing left his chess pal Lao Xin's home. The storm was still pouring down as hard as before. He waded through the violent wind and rain until he made it to the main road. He tried to get a taxi but every single one was taken already. He soon got wet through again, standing under a tree waiting to grab a taxi. Yet he continued to wait, since it was too wild to walk home in such a storm. He needed a car to carry him through the vast areas under water and up the fifteen-minute hilly path. He also became worried that his knees would hurt too much for him to fall asleep. Would a hot-water bottle help? No use. His aching knees were already killing him in the rain.

As soon as he finally got into the taxi, a strong smell hit him, something like a dish of garlic and vinegar placed in an airtight cell filled with armpit odor. Cai Shuiqing sniffed and glanced at the tax driver who looked to him unpleasantly stocky. When the driver asked where he was going, Cai figured out that the garlic odor was coming from the driver's mouth. As for the sour, armpit odor, it was hard to decide the source, perhaps left by the customer before him.

"Where you going?" the cabbie yelled impatiently. Cai Shuiqing informed him of his destination, but all of a sudden began to feel greatly agitated. He tried to forcefully roll down the car window on his side, but found himself turning the window handle in the wrong direction. So he twisted it again the other way. But the taxi driver abruptly stepped on the brakes and shouted, "Close the window! Don't you see it's raining?"

Before Cai Shuiqing was able to react to his demand, the driver leaned over to roll up the car window. In the short time the window was down, the rain had already splashed onto Cai Shuiqing, wetting his right side. Cai Shuiqing started to roll down the window again, while saying, "Opening it just a little."

The driver grabbed his hand forcefully, "Get out if you're not going to just sit!"

Cai Shuiqing opened the car door to get out, but the storm beat fiercely into the car. The taxi driver was furious, "You mother-f---er, really want out? Real motherf---ers like you not valuing other people's property!" Cai Shuiqing yanked his hand back and stopped trying to get out. It was not that he was heeding the cabbie's scolding as much as he became aware he would never be able to get another taxi in such foul weather.

The taxi driver started his car again, twisting at his steering wheel wildly. "Don't you see this is a new car? I bought it only seven months ago, and its transmission belt has already broken. It cost me 3,000 to 4,000 yuan, so a whole month's work was washed away! Moreover, no one would take responsibility for it, shoving me back and forth. The Technical Supervision Bureau wouldn't give an appraisal of the problem either. All our wages are made by the hour. How can I afford all these problems? But as soon as I replaced the belt with my own money today, I encounter this bitch of a storm! What kind of world is this? Who f---ing sees the value of others' money!"

Cai Shuiqing protested, "The stink inside this car of yours is too much!"

"Stink? Who stinks? Who's the motherf---er that stinks? It's all you people getting in and out of my car, ain't it? I don't smell anything! And if I did smell anything, I'd have to endure it. If you can't take it, get out! Stay away from me! Let me tell you this: all taxis stink. Buy your own *Benz* or *BMW* if you have the money! Don't come squeezing into our stinking cars!"

Cai Shuiqing tried to roll down the car window again with all the intensity he could muster. This time, the cabbie turned around to stare at Cai Shuiqing without jamming on the brakes. Under the dim overhead light, Cai Shuiqing suddenly felt like he was looking into a mirror. Somehow the cabbie's face looks familiar to him, his hair wiry like a wild mane as well as the thick protruding pancake lips. The broad nose, with each nostril trying to stand on its own. But the eyes so small, with heavy eyelids pressing on half-shut eyes. Despite their small size, the eyes shot out beast-like, sharp laser rays. In such pouring rain, the taxi simply became a precious Noah's Ark. You could see people everywhere beckoning at it with such eager and pleading gestures.

Cai Shuiqing rolled up the car window. Scornfully, the cabbie bent to get a rag from somewhere and emphatically rub the fogged glass. Cai Shuiqing felt his knee aching badly. It was the kind of pain that stabs into the depth of your bones though there's no way to touch the spot exactly. Cai Shuiqing rubbed his palms hard to make them warm and then pressed them onto his knees. The taxi moved so slowly that it felt like it was rowing through waves rather than running on a road, like maneuvering a 007 vehicle in a river.

The taxi was too slow. Would Qian Hong go to bed with wet feet again?

The taxi stopped suddenly, "Sorry, get off now. I can't go any further." The way the cabbie said "Sorry" resembled the way the Taiwanese woman said "Happy birthday."

Cai Shuiqing looked outside to find they have arrived at the crossroads at the foot of the hill before the path up Singing Spring Hill. Cai Shuiqing said, "Just go across the intersection. The water is not deep. You can just drive on that side."

The cabbie replied, "Sorry. Please get out."

Cai Shuiqing said, "I walked through here barefooted earlier. The water is not deep at all."

The cabbie exclaimed, "Get out! The bottom plate of my car is low. Once the water enters the car engine, I will not only lose my business, but have to f---ing spend another 3,000 to 4,000 to repair the engine. Out!"

"What am I going to do then?"

"How do I know? Be quick!"

Cai Shuiqing noticed another taxi coming toward them. It was rolling carefully through the pool of water, which reached up to about the middle of its wheels. Cai Shuiqing pointed at that taxi and said, "Look, it has driven through the water. It is a *Santana 2000*, too, isn't it? Let's drive through the intersection like them."

The cabbie replied, "Sorry. Just get out!"

Cai Shuiqing said, "Do you know that I have had three pairs of leather shoes and four sets of clothing soaked through today? And now I have to wade through this large stretch of water again plus a fifteen-minute walk up the hill? Otherwise, why take a taxi? I paid for a taxi just because I have to pass this section of the road. Just take a look at the pouring rain!"

The cabbie replied, "What you say to me means shit! I still have my business to do."

With no way out, Cai Shuiqing opened his bag, a big bag in which Cai Shuiqing can normally carry journals. In the bag Cai Shuiqing spotted the long and thin blue paper package, the knife he had bought yesterday. About seven inches long with tiny saw-teeth, the knife looked like an enlarged fruit knife. The salesgirl had told him it was good for cutting frozen meat and tomatoes. But he had forgotten to take it out from his bag yesterday at home. Hence he spotted the knife while reaching for his wallet in the bag.

"Do you know the *Double-men* brand?" Cai Shuiqing asked the cabbie. The cabbie, thinking Cai Shuiqing was getting his taxi fare, was wiping the window glass hard as he answered, "Don't know. What double men?" Cai Shuiqing replied, "It's a world-famous brand. Germans make the most famous kitchen knives in the world with the best steel. It's of excellent quality and the best workmanship. Although it looks a little clumsy, a set of knives costs over 2,000 yuan. Even a single kitchen knife is 600 yuan. But it's great for cutting."

The cabbie, cleaning the glass, was fairly sensitive. He turned around suddenly on hearing the word "knife." Right then, Cai Shuiqing plunged the knife in between his fifth and sixth ribs, turning the knife once or twice skillfully. However, pulling the knife out was not so easy. He studied the knife under the dim light from the headlights for a while. Yes, it did not leave a bleeding gash.

The storm continued pouring down. Cai Shuiqing took a look at the taximeter. It said "21 yuan," so he had placed the fare on the body of the cabbie, whose head was tilted to one side. He had taken off his own leather shoes, rubbed his knees, and then pulled open the car door and walked slowly into the water.

The lawyer asked, "Why did you want to kill him?"

Cai Shuiqing answered, "The rain was too hard."

The lawyer asked, "Did he say anything?"

Cai Shuiqing replied, "It was raining, everyone was in a bad mood."

The lawyer asked, "Why would you use a knife?"

Cai Shuiqing said, "I had forgotten to take the knife out of the bag."

The lawyer asked, "Why did you stab him in the chest?"

Cai Shuiqing replied, "Perhaps it was handy… I don't know, the rain was too hard."

The lawyer's assistant said, "The victim looks very much like you — did you notice the resemblance?"

Cai Shuiqing said, "I thought it was because inside the taxi, in the dim light one could make out some resemblance. So even you also felt there was quite a resemblance?"

The assistant nodded, "When I saw his picture. You two look just like twin brothers, so alike. Everyone says so."

Cai Shuiqing laughed embarrassedly.

Qian Hong has always been a gentle, peaceful woman. A refined temperament gives her ordinary stature and appearance a sort of pure charm. This kind of beauty would take some insight to discover, not through one glance from boys eager for instant success. Barely a week after entering the university, Cai Shuiqing had set his eye on this serene girl, impressed by her unique radiance. When he later discovered accidentally that she was from a respected scholarly family, he felt so proud of his extraordinary insight.

Qian Hong had also noticed the newcomer Cai Shuiqing early on. Her roommates commented that merely being ugly was not his fault. However, being ugly and crude at the same time was simply unforgivable.

Cai Shuiqing's problem was his vulgarity rather than his looks really. If someone coughed loudly or sucked mucus up through his nose noisily in your face and chose not to let it out but held it in his nose or mouth and then talked to you in a muffled, indistinct voice, he might even talk to you for a few minutes like this and then turn his head to maliciously spit out the yellowish phlegm and greenish mucus. Would you stand it? Other girls said sometimes Cai Shuiqing would talk in this way, but somehow his voice got clear halfway through his talk, so he must have swallowed his phlegm and mucus while talking to you.

Indeed, no one could bear that kind of behavior.

Nevertheless, Cai Shuiqing was ever confident about his talents. After the first year of school and influenced by who knows what artist, he grew his lion-mane-like wiry hair long and forced it into a rabbit-tail hairstyle. Sometimes he played cool and failed to tie up his disheveled hair, so that those fried instant noodles of his made him look as coarse as a toiling ditch-digger at a worksite. And under the unwieldy hair, people could hardly locate where his neck was. Holding high a head a thousand times more unsightly than Beethoven's on his shoulders, he would stride around campus with the most serious and haughty expression. In those years everyone said Cai Suiqing was unbelievably insolent.

Cai Shuiqing began his hot and open pursuit of Qian Hong on campus. The latter prayed that she could flee to the ends of the earth. Qian Hong also felt very scandalized over the reactions around her. Her roommates took it as if Qian Hong had run into a mugger even. However, this was until two things happened, or perhaps when two separate events added up together to help convince Qian Hong. At least they marked a turning point in Qian Hong's rejection of Cai Shuiqing. Since then, Qian Hong no longer refused Cai Shuiqing talking to her.

The first thing was when Qian Hong's foot was scalded by boiling water. During the painful process of recovery, Cai Shuiqing stepped forward and took care of Qian Hong most painstakingly and willingly for a whole month. In the beginning, even the most refined Qian Hong, who would never ever say anything harsh, regarded him as a lapdog. But gradually she began to accept the most loyal and sincere care offered in turn by the lapdog. Then another thing happened right after the new student buildings were completed on the campus. One day, someone had spray-painted huge characters across the sides of all three brand-new buildings: "Happy Birthday, Qian Hong! Qian Hong, I Love You from the Bottom of My Heart!" Furious about the incident, the school authorities swore to track down the vandal. Cai Shuiqing stepped up and announced, "I did it all."

In view of the fact that Cai Shuiqing's scores were outstanding (except in English), the university ultimately decided to give him another chance, after disciplining him severely. Back then, as Cai Shuiqing climbed up so high to clean up public property alone in the wind, he became a hero in the upward-looking eyes of all the female students.

Not until Qian Hong thought she had effectively transformed Cai Shuiqing, did she pluck up her courage to present him to her family. He no longer held thick phlegm in his mouth while talking for a long time. He had learned to prune his nails regularly and keep them clean. He no longer ate with the loud noise of a jolly pig chewing pigswill, nor cracked thunderous, singing sneezes echoing throughout the village like his fellow villagers. If walking with a woman in public, Cai Shuiqing would now take the initiative to walk on the outside to protect his companion against the traffic flow. Cai Shuiqing had learned to open a door or pull a chair and provide other gentlemanly services most naturally and gracefully for ladies. Cai Shuiqing had begun to read English newspapers. He no longer talked loudly, unaware of others in public places. Of course, there were many other advances such as these that Cai Shuiqing managed to attain.

Before taking him to meet her family, Qian Hong emphatically praised Cai Shuiqing's intelligence in her conversations with her parents and siblings. As a precaution, she emphasized to them repeatedly that he was another "Hunch Back of Notre Dame." However, when they visited Qian Hong's family during the first National Day holiday after their graduation, Qian Hong saw how her family members were caught off guard by Cai Shuiqing, even though they tried their best to retain decorum from beginning to end.

Cai Shuiqing had been flustered despite all his careful preparations. He had spent all his savings after graduation for this special visit, on top of borrowing 2,000 yuan from his institute without Qian Hong's knowledge. He bought the best caterpillar fungus, wild American ginseng and some books he had asked others to buy from Hong Kong and Taiwan, as gifts for the visit. However, these special efforts failed. Being such a highbrow family, the Qians were not easily moved by money. As for why Qian Hong did not stop him from buying all the expensive presents, it was out of the vanity of a woman in love.

Qian Hong's parents were very clear in their position. They seized an opportunity to discuss the issue with Qian Hong privately. Without ever losing their geniality, they told their daughter, "It is not that we look down upon his ugly looks or that we despise his pennilessness. However, what we really want to tell you is this: Westerners have always believed in the tenet that to cultivate an aristocrat takes several centuries. The inferior genre of a peasant (what we actually mean here is their sort of coarseness) is impossible to rectify thoroughly by just spending a few years in a university. You must think over the whole thing carefully. After your future life unfolds, you would find a lot of things you will be unable to bear. And it would not just affect you but also your offspring."

Qian Hong's siblings were even more frank than her parents in voicing their opposition. Particularly her elder sister, who simply asked Qian Hong, "Have you lost your mind?" Together with the other siblings, they told her directly, "You won't be happy at all if you marry him!"

As soon as Qian Hong and Cai Shuiqing left after the holiday, Qian Hong's parents, elder brother and elder sisters tried every connection of theirs to get Qian Hong back home, so as to separate the two. However, before they could find an organization in their city willing to accept Qian Hong, Cai Shuiqing received offers from several employers wanting to hire him as a special talented professional, as soon as he had started to look. Consequently, Cai Shuiqing was transferred to their city first. The Qians furtively hated the cluelessness of their own child but had no idea what to do about it. They urgently asked friends to introduce a number of young men to their youngest daughter, but Qian Hong just ignored them, or felt no chemistry at all if she bothered to communicate with them reluctantly.

Cai Shuiqing's academic achievements were outstanding, so the municipal government awarded him a "Special Talent" allowance, along with a red packet containing a 40,000-yuan bonus for his success in converting his scientific research results into a manufacturing project by the end of his first year. Perhaps because Qian Hong was not at his side, Cai Shuiqing wholeheartedly plunged himself into his academic research as well as into his emotional investment, and thus he accomplished both equally well. He often visited the home of Qian Hong's parents. At first, they repelled him curtly and declined all gifts he brought. Sometimes he just stayed put in their living-room for hours though no one would really talk to him. Everyone went about politely being busy with their own chores. However, Cai Shuiqing displayed a methodical understanding of the situation. On the one side, the respected intellectuals keen on their sense of pride, graceful in their manners and daily speech, would never say anything rude to embarrass Cai Shuiqing, not to mention pointing the door to him. So Cai Shuiqing continued his visits, and sometimes on the sofa read a whole magazine from the first page to the last, playing with the cat for awhile, and then saying, "Uncle and Aunt, I am leaving."

About a year and a half later, Qian Hong's mother said to Qian Hong on the phone abruptly, "Xiao Cai is actually very motivated. Country boys are indeed simple and sincere." Following that breakthrough, praise for Cai Shuiqing became more and more frequent, warming bit by bit, until finally Qian Hong's father asked her, if they really felt so good toward each other, why not get married so that she could be assigned back to their home city earlier.

Hence Qian Hong married Cai Shuiqing, and Qian Hong returned to her home city.

Only after returning home, did Qian Hong find a tremendous change in the situation already. Cai Shuiqing had won over the Qian family. Now her parents, elder brother and sisters all took his side if Qian Hong said anything about Cai Shuiqing. Whoever among her relatives who had heard, would also defend Cai Shuiqing devotedly.

Once Qian Hong's father had been hurt in a traffic accident, and her mother had fainted on seeing the blood, right on the spot. All their children happened to be away, so it was "Xiao (young) Cai" who had just got off a plane returning from some work, who rushed to the scene like a firefighter. It just happened that the elevator of the hospital was broken, and the smaller "Xiao Cai" carried the heavier

"Father Qian" up the stairs, step by step to the operating room on the fifteenth floor. Then Xiao Cai, soaked with sweat, ran up and down to register the old man into the hospital and then rushed back to take care of him. When the old man's own children made it to the hospital, their father's operation was almost over. Then Cai Shuiqing hurried back home to cook chicken soup and tasty desserts for the old man, again and again.

Of course these things could be done by others, too. But Qian Hong told the lawyer's assistant, "You don't know. There are many things he did that you just can't imagine. For example, my dad likes hickory nuts, so Cai Shuiqing often buys one or two kilograms of the nuts and puts on a pair of disposable gloves to shell them piece by piece with a set of crab-eating tools. He then stores the shelled nuts in a plastic bag in the fridge to keep them fresh. When he visits my parents, he takes the nuts to my father. My parents would feel indebted to him for what he did, but he would just tell them: Nuts are good for elderly people, but their teeth are not good any more and he happens to love doing that kind of thing. And he just does it like he was playing a simple game."

"My dad must have eaten several dozens kilos of hickory nuts by now. My mom still wipes her eyes when she sees the unfinished nuts in the fridge, 'These are what Shuiqing scooped out piece by piece!'"

"My elder sister, it turned out, had begun to envy me eventually. She said she had come to the realization that no matter what, birth, status, family background, degree of education or looks actually mean little. It is the very person that counts. It is the concrete person you have married. Do you know why my sister said this? Every time Cai Shuiqing visited her home, he always took their garbage out from her apartment to the bin downstairs. Do you know anyone else who would continue doing this? My elder sister swears no one else would do so. Not even the legendary Monkey-king's Pigsy would. You tell me, would such a nice guy kill anyone?"

Only able to blink his eyes, the attorney assistant could not respond, but cried loudly inside, "Exactly, how come? If such a nice person can go around killing people, the world must be going crazy."

Qian Hong had stepped into an unbelievably sweet happy life from the first night she became Cai Shuiqing's bride. At first, she would mention some of her experiences to her female colleagues. For example, once, some of her colleagues began to chat about shaving armpits, so Qian Hong mentioned that Cai Shuiqing once saw a woman passenger in the bus wearing a tank top, and holding onto a swinging ring, revealing her thick armpit hair. Agitated by the sight, as soon as he got home he walked up to Qian Hong, who was reading a novel on the deckchair. Cai Shuiqing raised Qian Hong's arms to check and found her hair underneath was not that thick. Yet Cai Shuiqing still said to her gently, "Let me shave your armpits for you. It won't hurt."

Qian Hong soon realized that the expressions in the eyes of her female colleagues were complicated. It was a sort of disbelief mixed with a bit of disgust, slight envy plus somewhat choked-up feelings. It was hard to describe, but their hesitant expressions made Qian Hong realize that they might be having more discussions and analyses of her stories behind her back. Being an insightful woman, Qian Hong decided not to tell her stories anymore. She had much sweeter stories than those ones but she would no longer share them with others. She came to the conclusion that there are too many lonely wives. Besides, she doubted that anyone would believe her happiness.

Once Cai Shuiqing's mother came to visit them from the

countryside. As an educated woman, Qian Hong welcomed her mother-in-law to stay and told her sincerely to enjoy her time in the city before she returned home. Qian Hong had never visited Cai Shuiqing's hometown. Her husband had told her that his family's old house was haunted for many years. He said he saw the ghost himself twice, the same long-waist woman with two long braids. Truly frightened, Qian Hong told her mother about the ghost story and got her mother scared too. She commented that some corners of rural areas still really had unclean elements. Qian Hong's father seriously criticized his wife and daughter for their remarks. But no one ever mentioned visiting Cai Shuiqing's hometown after this. The truth was, however, that Cai Shuiqing's home village is simply too poor. For example, his family has only one pot to cook both pig feed and their own food to eat. Not owning even a cutting board, the family has to roll up the straw mat on their big *kang* bed, to be able to cut vegetables on it, and then roll back the straw mat before going to bed.

When Cai Shuiqing's mother passed away, Qian Hong had asked him softly, "How about I go with you?" Cai Shuiqing had replied, "You shouldn't take leave from work. It's alright for me to go alone." Always fearful of dirt, Qian Hong felt inwardly relieved as soon as Cai Shuiqing told her not to accompany him. Cai Shuiqing did not want Qian Hong to go with him because, if his wife did, the first thing she would spot would have been the rundown, dank hut leaning towards the right, standing by the paddy field, handed down by his grandpa's grandfather. If it were located in the city, the hut would have been labeled long ago by the department in charge as a "condemned dwelling" unfit for human habitation. As soon as she entered the hut, Qian Hong would have had to step onto the muddy ground inside it, with slushy spots here and there. Next, she would have seen to her right, an earthen stove looking as black as an urban public squat toilet, with some darkened, banged-up pots scattered on it. Choked by the dim and damp strangeness, Qian Hong would have had to seek hold of a thin red plastic twine, as greasy as the dark walls, to turn on the light. The walls have been blackened by nearly a century's grease and smoke. Qian Hong would also see that the family used no dinner table at all, the bowls and chopsticks simply put on an old-style beer crate on the ground. Qian Hong would find to her left a narrow black lacquer cabinet, handed down from no one knows where. Tilting stubbornly on three legs, the cabinet was supported by a rock that acted as its fourth leg. The food on the shelves was the same things the family had eaten for several decades already: pickled green beans, pickled cabbage, leftover boiled eggplants, half a peeled sweet potato, and such. The brightest item one could find in the dilapidated hut was perhaps that last year's calendar of Lijiang River scenery, now placed in the cabinet to line the shelves.

Once Qian Hong walked into the inner room, she would run into a big urinal bucket as high as her thighs. It generally accumulated half a month's output, so a moldy film floated on top. She would be shocked and queasy about it, but this was household fertilizer. Then, she would find Cai Shuiqing's mother's bed, used for several decades already. On it was a tattered grayish quilt, its color already faded beyond recognition. It was never folded, and the mosquito net had hung there from as far back as Cai Shuiqing could remember in his childhood, its original white color long vanished under the black smears. If Qian Hong dared climb the crooked, thick wooden ladder hanging from the ceiling, she would have crawled up into the attic, to find out that Cai Shuiqing and all his siblings had slept directly on piles of straw. With each berth made up with a pile of straw, those left behind by elder brothers and sisters who had set up their own families, married away or gone to school, remained there unkempt, as if tampered by rats.

After his mother had passed away, Cai Shuiqing rushed back home and cried his eyes out. He even kept knocking his head against the wall, which made his brothers, sister-in-laws and sisters feel he were just acting it out for the village to see. However, when they saw Cai Shuiqing pull out 5,000 yuan from his pocket afterward, they shut their mouths at once. But a shrewd sister-in-law still claimed that it meant nothing. Failing to demonstrate any filial piety when their mother had been alive, for whom was he acting after their mother died! It was true that, ever since Cai Shuiqing had entered university, it seemed he had abandoned his village. Rarely sending money home, he had failed to visit even during the Spring Festival holidays. Instead he simply mailed 200 or 300 yuan each time as a gesture. Nevertheless, his mother had still felt so proud of this son of hers.

Regarding Cai Shuiqing as a filial son, Qian Hong also had encouraged him to send money to his family, but Cai Shuiqing would argue that his mother felt content with self-sufficiency, and would not like him sending money home all the time. Qian Hong said, "You give my parents 1,000 or 2,000 every Spring Festival, so you should send your mother at least 500 yuan, shouldn't you?" Smiling upon her urging, Cai Shuiqing continued to send just 200 or 300 yuan home, saying, "Expenses in the countryside are minimal, and they don't really need money. It would be better we invite my mother to come visit and enjoy herself." Qian Hong had said, "Sure!"

So one year his mother actually came. Cai Shuiqing was really nice to his mother. However, the mother discovered the next day that her son waited on his wife on hand and foot. She found him simply too submissive to his wife. If they learned of this back in their village, the Cai ancestors would truly lose face, their reputation dashed to the ground. Indignant, her heart aching at the same time, the mother restrained herself from saying anything. She was indeed fearful of her city-residing son, her city-born daughter-in-law, and of everything surrounding them in the city. Out love for her boy, she tried to do some household chores to relieve the burden on her son's shoulders. But trouble immediately ensued.

She had put Qian Hong's suit, which should have been sent to the dry cleaners, into a basin of detergent and water, and started to rub it with all her strength. The upscale suit was naturally damaged beyond use. That black *Episode* suit had cost Qian Hong 2,400 yuan, as her best outfit to wear on formal occasions, but now it was like dried cabbage leaves left in the sun. Also, her mother-in-law was not used to wearing different slippers, used for the living-room, kitchen and bathroom. She even wore into the bathroom pairs of over-thirty-yuan Japanese medicinal slippers meant for the bedroom, ending up ruining them one pair after another. She often forgot to close the refrigerator door; used the microwave oven as if dropping explosives into it, and mixed up the cutting boards, containers and knives, all meant to be separated strictly for raw or cooked meat. When she went shopping, she would stealthily polish her hair with the vegetable oil in the market, and she also preferred to sprinkle too much salt in the dishes.

There were simply too many problems. Even the well-bred Qian Hong failed to restrain herself at times. For example, when her *Episode* suit had been ruined, she criticized her mother-in-law mildly. With her wrinkled black-yellow face creased into a guilty smile, her mother-in-law kept nodding to show her daughter-in-law that she got the message.

At such times, Cai Shuiqing would knit his brows deeply, but he could not criticize either of the women. Qian Hong was not worried about Cai Shuiqing's frowns, as he would redeem it possibly through longer back scratching or other ways. But his mother was heartbroken seeing her son's knotted brow. Even though showing a stony face, Cai Shuiqing would roll up his sleeves to try to correct the error. Whatever could be redone or compensated, he would do it quietly. Once after he had gotten off work and returned home, he found the rooms filled with oily smoke. Qian Hong and their son who came home at the same time were fanning their hands before their faces, as if they were smelling poison gas. "The fumes are awful!" Qian Hong had complained. Bolstered, their son had shouted, "We're being poisoned! We're gonna choke to death!"

Later at night, Cai Shuiqing had gone to his mother's room, trying to explain to her mildly that she should turn on the kitchen fan when cooking, as it was not like in their village. Smiling uneasily, his mother merely lowered her head and dabbed at her eyes. Cai Shuiqing sat down at his mother's bedside and circled his arms around his mother's shoulders. The mother explained, "Dust got into my eyes." Cai Shuiqing was silent. Then the mother said in a low voice, "I'd like to go home earlier."

Cai Shuiqing shook his head. All that evening, he sat holding his mother's shoulders at her bedside.

Qian Hong had continued acting like a spoiled child, saying, "Why does your mother always have this strange odor?"

"What odor?" Cai Shuiqing had questioned.

"If you had that odor too, I would have never married you."

"What odor?" Cai Shuiqing asked again.

"A sort of... a sort of smell like dog dung baking in the sun...," Qian Hong had said.

Cai Shuiqing turned his back on her for the first time. Being a clever wife, Qian Hong asked, "Are you angry? Wow, so you can get angry, too! I was just teasing. She doesn't have any odor."

Cai Shuiqing had known Qian Hong was not telling a lie. His mother did have a sort of unpleasant odor to her. After hearing Qian Hong's answer, he had turned back and continued to scratch Qian Hong's back, saying, "How could I ever be angry with you?"

Qian Hong is overcome with deep sorrow and utter despair. The attorney just told her to prepare herself, as he might not be able to save the situation. In other words, Cai Shuiqing could be sentenced to death eventually. Qian Hong's tears fall without stop, even after she returned home. The famous lawyer has no time for such sentimental dialogue, but since he has taken quite a lot of money from his client, he asks his assistant to lend her an ear. The assistant is more tenacious. After listening to Qian Hong's pleas, the assistant expressed his viewpoint and reported back to the famous lawyer. He believes that Cai Shuiqing must be suffering some sort of mental problem, so they should obtain a psychiatric appraisal of the state of mind of the defendant. However, the famous lawyer remained deaf to his assistant's suggestion, believing there is nothing wrong with his client's mind. If there was really anything improper, then it is that the defendant was just too good. He had simply been so good that he could no longer stand himself.

The assistant continues to be inspired by his vision of reversing the verdict. Since the famous lawyer has just accepted a commercial case involving about 600 million yuan, he cannot bear to disappoint the assistant, so he allows him to play with the case by himself. At the same time, Cai Shuiqing's relatives unleash all their influence in their circles, and gather many academic experts and officials to submit joint letters to the government. They plead for a reconsideration of the case in their letters, that the authorities should treasure talented professionals and give Cai Shuiqing a chance to rehabilitate himself and turn over a new leaf in his life path.

They succeed in obtaining another mental appraisal of Cai Shuiqing. The lawyer's assistant takes advantage of their prison visits to hint to Cai Shuiqing that he must cooperate with the appraisal. Indeed, many tried to eat feces, drink urine or talk nonsense to weasel out of their criminal responsibility. One fellow even took off his shoe and chewed it appetizingly, as if he were eating a roast chicken. Others would pretend to be the most asinine madmen in the world, chatting with the appraising doctors most earnestly. If the doctor asked him, "How old are you?" one man would say, "I was once 29, but turned 15 later, and now I am 7 years old." Or if the doctor asked, "Why did you kill who-and-who?" the fellow would answer, "But I didn't kill him, I killed a pit viper." Or "I heard people say, if I hadn't killed him, he'd have blown up our new bridge. I have rid our people of an evil!"

However, Cai Shuiqing frustrates his lawyers' schemes, and frustrates everyone who is trying to bail him out. With a most exacting scholar's mind, the smoothest, the most accurate and the best-structured language, Cai Shuiqing helps his psychiatric appraisers to accomplish their task of judging if he possesses criminal responsibility. They have no way out but to come to the conclusion once again that their client is perfectly normal in his perceptions, emotions, desires and reactions. Being one hundred percent logical, his behavior is not controlled by any hallucinations, morbidity or illusions.

The conclusion, "The client bears full criminal responsibility."

After the appraisal is completed, all the experts, who have worked through three mental appraisals for Cai Shuiqing, sign their names decisively on the bottom line, as if they are being chased by wild bulls. Vice-director Lin, of the mental hospital that supervises the appraisal assignment, even ripped the paper with his pen.

A couple of days before the verdict of the second trial is to be announced, the famous lawyer and his assistant meet with their client again. Cai Shuiqing remains as rational as before, maintaining his gentle and refined manner. The famous lawyer has managed to learn ahead of time about the verdict, through his former schoolmates at the provincial High Court. Having accepted so much money from the family of such a celebrity, inwardly he feels a little guilty. Yet this defendant of his seems to think nothing of the murder at all.

Before leaving him, the famous lawyer asks his client two more questions, "Do you feel guilty?"

"From the moment I plunged the knife in, I have felt totally empty," Cai Shuiqing answers.

"Not a bit guilty?"

"Perhaps…, just like killing myself."

"You really had to stab the man at the time?"

"Yes."

The second question comes as the famous lawyer has stood up ready to leave. He then asks, "Do you want me to give any message to your family today?"

Cai Shuiqing smiles apologetically, "Nothing really."

Still standing, the famous lawyer and his assistant take out a red ink pad for Cai Shuiqing to press his fingerprints on, and sign their record of the meeting. It is not really necessary any longer, only to make it look better when they hand the records over to his family.

Cai Shuiqing signs his name but then says suddenly, "There are two words I am not clear about… their meaning. I always forgot to check the dictionary at home. Sometimes I would leaf through the dictionary's pages for fun at home, but then fail to remember what words I had wanted to check. I only now remember them. So would you mind looking them up for me?"

The famous lawyer and his assistant together say, "What are the words?"

"One is *li ge* (farewell song). The other is *ding you* (mourning one's parents). I have not been clear what they really mean for a very long time."

On September 29, 2001, at 9:00 in the morning, Cai Shuiqing is executed. All the people across the country jubilantly celebrate National Day.

(Translated by Ji Hua & Gao Wenxing)

Confidences
in a Hair Salon

—Wang Anyi

Wang Anyi. She was born in Nanjing, Jiangsu Province, in 1954, and the following year her mother moved with her to Shanghai. Since 2001 she has held the post of chairperson of the Shanghai Writers' Association, and from 2004 has been a professor of the Chinese Department of Fudan University. She was elected vice-chair of the Chinese Writers' Association in 2006.

Starting from 1977, Wang Anyi has published writings totaling over 5 million Chinese characters. She became famous for *The Rain Whispers*, written and published in 1980. Since that time, she has won many awards and honorary titles, including the 3rd Lu Xun Literary Prize for "Confidences in a Hair Salon" in 2005; 2nd prize in the national-level 2nd Children's Writing Awards for *Who'll Be the Young Pioneers Secondary Team Leader?*, 1981 China Short Story Prize for "This Train's Terminus," 1981-82 China Novella Prize for *Lapse of Time*, 1985-86 China Novella Prize for *Xiaobao Village*, Top 10 Books of *Asia Week* for *Heroes Everywhere* in 2006, and the 2007 Outstanding Writers Award of the 6th Chinese-language Literature Media Prize for *Enlightening Age*. In particular, her novel *Song of Everlasting Sorrow* was listed among the Top 10 Books of 1996 by Taiwan's *China Times*, and won the 4th Shanghai Literature and Art Prize, the 5th Mao Dun Literary Prize and Malaysian *Sin Chew Daily*'s 1st Huazong Prize for Chinese-language literature across the world.

Many of her works, including *Xiaobao Village*, *Love on a Barren Hill* and *Song of Everlasting Sorrow*, have been translated into English, German and French and other languages, and published in places such as the UK, Germany, France, the Netherlands and Russia. Wang Anyi has been a visiting scholar or guest professor at numerous universities, including Harvard, Columbia, Yale, Cambridge, Hamburg, Waseda, and Lingnan (Hong Kong).

Confidences
in a Hair Salon

The tiny hair salon is in a temporary structure built onto the external wall of another building, intruding on to the corner pavement. Further on, a small noisy lane joins the main road. The owner is a thirty-year-old hairdresser from northern Jiangsu, who left the beauty parlor across the street to start his own business. Actually, he might not even be from northern Jiangsu, but since hairdressers are supposed to originate from there, he has adopted the accent to display his lineage. To go with the accent, he has the pale complexion, and stiff dark hair cut in a flattop with slightly longer sideburns. The country fashion makes him look an bit too slick, but this is counteracted by an unaffected expression of decency. These hairdressers are usually even-featured, with bright eyes under dark brows, and straight noses. Compared to other men, their well-defined looks may seem a bit effeminate, but again, it's really just because they come from the countryside. They tend to be talkative and favor feminine topics, and together with the exaggerated drawn-out Yangzhou modulations, this makes them sound even more like gossipy women, in interesting contrast to their tall manly bodies. Their hands, too, are pale and soft like a woman's, but bigger and longer, which makes them strangely attractive. Such hands have been nurtured by warm water, shampoo and conditioner, and most of all, by the frequent touching of hair, particularly women's hair. They brandish their scissors with a touch of showmanship, up and down and then, with a quick snip, the locks drift to the floor. The comb in the other hand scoops up a strand, the scissors descend seemingly at random and, after a bout of rapid snipping, the pace slows. Carefully the hair is combed, the scissors measure the hair tips, and the blades open. Truly, they know when to move quickly, and when to be slow.

This man from northern Jiangsu, the owner, happens not to be very talkative. He also dresses differently, in a tight black leather jacket that limits his movements a bit. Perhaps he feels that, now that he is the boss, he cannot dress as casually as a mere hairdresser. Also, as he has just started the business, he is naturally a bit nervous, and so must be circumspect. He does the cutting and styling, and has hired two young women to wash and set the curlers for perms. With them around, the salon is a noisy place. They both come from somewhere in southern Anhui, but their accent is hard to place, with some falling tones close to the northern Jiangsu dialect, but mostly from further north. The main difference lies in the thicker sounds. One is just over twenty while the other is closer to thirty, but they look surprisingly similar, probably because of their clothes and hairstyle. Both sport thinned, wispy uneven cuts that raggedly frame their round faces, giving them a slightly wild look. Yet both have direct gazes, and look straight at people like bold country girls. They would even be pretty if not for their slightly blank expressions. Both wear fitting knitted tops with nylon lace at the collar and open sleeves — one in apple green, the other pale red. These are matched with three-quarter-length blue jeans sporting one-inch slits on the legs, and round-toed platform shoes with buckles. These are women who have done manual outdoor work and have developed strong shoulders, arms, back and hips, so the fashionably tight clothes not only make them look constrained, but are also an awkward fit. When both barber chairs are taken up by customers, each stands behind one and pours the shampoo with one hand while kneading the hair with the other into a mass of white lather. Then, they sink both hands into the suds and rub and scratch and tug, moving their shoulders and lifting their arms in exactly the same way as if taught by one master, following the same procedure in unison. While they rub and scratch, they like to watch the customers' faces in the mirror opposite, staring at them as if to probe their secrets. Then they turn to talk to each other in loud voices with clear laughter, quite uninhibited. The owner does not reprimand them. Clearly, he is a silent man, even thoughtful. At this point, they let up a bit and just go through the motions, which usually brings protests from the customers, "Stop the fluff and buff; give me a good rub and scratch." Rebuked, the young women would act aggrieved, "The last customer said my nails were too sharp!" To which the customer would retort, "Sharp or not, what's the use if you just stroke the surface?" At this point, the owner gets up and comes over to wash the customer's hair himself. The young woman walks over to the washbasin, still looking aggrieved, and rinses off her hands. Then she goes to sit on the folding metal chair by the wall, her attitude plainly saying, 'Well then, I'll take a rest!' They have already picked up smooth city ways.

A number of idlers frequent the shop — they live nearby and have nothing better to do than sit here. Customers mistake them for a queue, and often ask as they push open the door, "Is this the line for a haircut?" To which everyone hastily says together, "No, no line!" so the real customers won't be frightened off. Most of these onlookers are women; some come with knitting, while others just sit with folded hands. Though they are idle, they all look a bit groggy and messy, as if they had just climbed out of bed and come straight here. Or maybe it really is not weariness — just a grubby look from the thick secretive atmosphere of the place. And in fact, there have been a couple of times when someone who used to come in disheveled and crumpled, suddenly transformed into a different person with makeup, clean clothes and high heels, strutting by without so much as a glance at the shop, on her way to some engagement. By the next visit, the good times are over and things are back to normal. They recall the previous night's mahjong game, the cheating, the bickering, the wins and the losses; or maybe it had been a wedding banquet, and then the comments range over the bride and groom's looks, their get-up, the food and the decorations, and the status of the guests. It's like the final curtain on a concert. The fluctuations of the stock market, the dispute between the shop owner next door and his employees, the happenings in the nearby lanes, the meanness or good humor of the last customer — all are good grist for the gossip mill. With them around, the two girls from Anhui need never feel lonely or sad — not to mention all the things they can learn. When they get into a tiff with a picky customer, these other women smooth things over. They are all knowledgeable about the ways of the world. You might even find it a bit strange that such worldly people come to this little shop to chat with two girls from Anhui. It is unusual to be so easygoing. It turns out that city people are not nearly as proud as they look, and when it comes down to it they don't have such a strong sense of hierarchy. These women live in crowded places, and they love excitement, and fear loneliness and quietness the most. In some ways, they are not as tough internally as the girls from the provinces. This is probably the result of a sense of superiority born of the fact that their lives are secure, so they need not be on guard all the time. Of course, it's also because they are "pure and honest," though this sounds an unlikely choice of words to describe them. However, in fact it is quite apt, because living a long time in the heart of the city, one discovers after a while that there is also a rustic village quality here. As time goes by, superficialities float to the surface and are swept away, while the more substantial sinks and settles. Such things are not that complicated, but they are what really determine lifestyle. Consequently, few of these idle women have any idea what the two girls say about them behind their backs. As they walk brightly past the glass door, they cannot guess what complex feelings are hidden in the gaze of these two girls.

Every morning about nine o'clock, as the curtain over the glass door is pulled back, the door is unbolted from the inside. The street being a bit crooked, the building does not face squarely in one direction and so, for some reason, the sun shines directly on to the mirror, creating a dazzling light. The two young women arrange the chairs, tidy the dressers, all the while inspecting themselves in the mirrors and tweaking their clothes and hair. It is a bit like preparing the stage for curtain time. Should an early customer push open the door and come in, he or she would find the air stuffy, redolent with many different smells: quilt and mattress odors, body odor mixed with scented face cream, hints of different foods like rice gruel, pickled vegetables, fried dough sticks, and the scent of hot metal from an electric hotplate. The young women live in the shop, and stow their camp beds, bedding and utensils outside the back door, which gives on to the rear veranda of the adjoining building.

Here they have used flattened cardboard boxes to portion off a small storage space half a square meter in size, which they fill with their stuff, and then cover with a plastic sheet. Every household living in this narrow alley has a similar pile behind their place, so this one blends in. A while later, the owner arrives, to check to see if anything is happening, and then leaves. After a bit, he comes back to check again and then is gone once more. He seems very busy with outside matters. Since opening the salon, his appearance has changed. He looks more sunburned, or at least more weathered, as if covered with hoar. The former leisurely expression of the skilled craftsman nonchalant in his casualness has been replaced by an anxious look. His black leather jacket is really quite disreputable: stiff and discolored, it makes him look like a salesman of aquatic products. His black cowhide shoes are dusty and weathered too. After going in and out a couple of times, he settles down, and if there are no haircuts or stylings to perform, sits behind the counter. At his back is a glass cupboard with a mirror, and on the shelves are displayed shampoos, hair perm products, conditioners, and hair dyes. There is a cardboard sign propped up on the counter with rows of numbered hair-color samples. The salon might be small, but it has everything. The owner sits behind the counter, grooming his nails like a woman, which also betrays his true profession.

Sitting with head lowered, he pays no attention to the young women chatting noisily with the onlookers. One might almost forget he is there except that, in a strange way, all conversations seem to be directed at him. It is as if, without him, the talk would become less lively, more desultory and disjointed. After all, this silent person is the owner and the heart of the shop. He gazes at the busy street scene through the glass door opposite, where ordinary daily life goes on. The people know each other, and what they each do. Here, in the heart of the city, deep within these residential streets, there is a cut-off country quality. The waves of the outside world cannot wash in here, only creating a disturbance by beating on the nearby shore. The owner has a faraway look on his face, the look of all those who are just starting out and are struggling to get going, "Is all this worth it?", they seem to ask when they get a quiet moment to themselves. The chatter in the shop is lively, the two girls are excited, their hands moving back and forth on the customers' heads, their bodies jigging about as if in a dance. Soapsuds fly into the customers' eyes and they protest, once, twice, and by the third time, there is trouble in the air. Just as the owner is about to get up, someone slides over and pushes the young Anhui woman out of the way. She lives above the department store down the street; her husband is in business, but she does not work and is a regular bystander in the shop.

Rising from the folding metal chair, she walks up to the customer while rolling up her sleeves, then lifts her arms and, with deft smoothing movements of hands on both sides of the hair part, scoops the suds off the customer's forehead. Quickly she piles the lather up on the customer's crown, then sinks her hands in and rubs and scratches away. She looks back and smiles as if to say, "How am I doing?" Like a child scratching an itch, but also showing that she knows her stuff. Seen from this angle, one discovers that she actually resembles the other two young women a bit! Same round face, short hair, and regular features. All these women seem to have come out of the same mold, though this one is slightly shorter than the other two. Her clothes? A pair of corduroy dungarees with a bear patch on the front, makes her look totally childlike. But on closer inspection, it turns out that she is pregnant, which is disconcerting. Then there are her eyes, which, unlike the other two with their straight bold stares, have a softness that takes in every thing while seeming to see nothing. Clearly, this is no ordinary woman! By now, she is completely differentiated from the other two by her experience, age, skills and origins. In fact, she comes from Shanghai and speaks in pure Shanghai dialect, yet not like those of her age group (twenty-something, thirty or thirty-something?) who like to use in-vogue expressions and unusual pronunciation. Her Shanghai dialect is smooth and a bit old-fashioned, which shows that she has truly grown up in this city.

The customer calms down, but the two young women excitedly ply her with many questions which all boil down to, "So you've done this job too, have you?" She tilts her chin towards the counter where the owner sits, and says, "I had my own hair salon." Before anyone can express surprise she adds, "I sold general goods before, and then I also had an eatery called 'All Good Things'." At this point, no one expresses surprise because they are a bit skeptical. How much time would she need to do so many things, and how old is she anyway? Just look at the smile on her face, like a child full of herself and given to a bit of bragging, blinking mischievously as if to say, "You can believe me or not!" The two young women ignore her and she completes the hair-washing procedure twice before saying, "You can rinse off now!" and returns the customer to one of them, who leads her to the washbasin. She stands beside it waiting to rinse off her hands with her arms raised, and carefully examines the suds on them, piling them into a little spike on her fingertip. A ray of sunlight hits it and reflects on to her face, and her smile seems a little vague in the flickering light. For a moment all is quiet in the shop, save for the soft sounds of water on hair, and the popping of the gas water heater as it switches on and off. The owner sits with elbows on knees and chin propped on hands, rather like a child thinking a child's thoughts.

"My shop was on Anxi Road, you know Anxi Road?" she asks. The young women shake their heads. "It's all gone now, but it used to be a really busy place. Changning District had a well-known clothing street, also known as Small Huating. My shop was at the end of the clothing street, or more exactly, on the other side of the cross street. I know that area pretty well, even though I live near Huaihai Road, but my friends lent me a stall there when I was selling general goods, so I came to know it well."

The two young women turn to her as they listen. The customer finishes being rinsed and goes back to the barber chair, where the owner comes over to blow-dry and style. The one dries her hands with a towel, while she walks over to the empty washbasin, then turns on the tap and rinses off the lather on her hands. She is silent for a moment, but continues to smile. She switches the hand shower back and forth between her hands, directing the spray onto them, and the water gently curls down into the basin in a thin stream. The hairdryer whirrs, filling the shop; the smell of hair wafts in the sunlight streaming through the glass door, a trifle cloying. She finishes rinsing, and one of the girls passes her a dry towel, but she just blots both sides of her hands on it, and returns to her folding chair. "And then?" one of the girls asks, and she looks up with a smile. "Why did you give up the general goods and open a salon?" the girl explains.

"Ah!" she says as if she just understood. "You know, there's very little profit in general goods. If you don't have a special supplier, you're bound to lose out. One deal with them and your appetite's gone for three days!" She breaks off suddenly, aware of nearly saying too much. "A friend had lent me the store on Anxi Road, so anyway I couldn't stay long. After a while, I thought, why can't

I have my own place? But what could I do? When I was at home while looking for work, I decided to go to hairdressing classes with my young neighbor. We used to practice washing each other's hair at home, just for fun. Then I got to be better than her." She juts her chin out as if to say, "You saw just now what I can do."

"So then I thought, why not open a hair salon? Anxi Road was great that way, you can do whatever you want, it's not hard at all, and there was no pressure. I had lots of friends, we all looked out for each other and helped each other out. Our course, the people on Anxi Road were different from those of us who live on Huaihai Road. Here," she says, as she taps the floor with her toe, "the people of Jing'an Temple area are not the same as those in Huaihai. Huaihai girls are just different from others, it's not their looks or speech, well, maybe a bit, but that's not the main difference. What makes them special is their 'style'." At that word she smiles, a bit embarrassed, as if she were lacking in modesty.

"But people in Anxi Road were also very good, they're really helpful, and most important of all, as I said, they make everything sound easy. When you hear them talking, it's sometimes hard to believe. Are they bragging? Even bragging needs some basis! But they always sound real, 'Want to open a hair salon? No problem, I have a friend who studied hairdressing in Hong Kong and styled for movie stars. Need a place? The clothing strip on Anxi Road is going to be extended, and I have a friend who knows the district governor and he'll help out.' Then a third friend happens to be a hair products salesman, and can let me have things at the wholesale price. The trade bureau, the health department, the labor and services office, the police, there are friends to be found in all these places, or friends of friends, all it takes is a word or two. Of course, things are never quite as easy as that or else everyone would be rich. Turns out the Hong Kong stylist really studied in Wenzhou, and only worked for a bit in a Hong Kong hair salon. And he wants exorbitant pay, as well as housing and transportation because he is not really from Wenzhou either but from the rural areas in Deqing. And then, Anxi Road ended up not being to be extended after all, but actually pulled down because a number of prominent residents, people's congress representatives and the like, had been complaining about it. You know, the area used to be a really quiet neighborhood with lots of foreign houses. As for the shampoo salesman, he used to come to my stall every day when I still sold general goods. He brought a briefcase with him that was full of little pigeonholes with samples, just like a Chinese medicine shop. They all looked pretty good, but they were all fake, concocted in an underground workshop near the station and sold all over the place. The moment you have anything to do with these people, all sorts of problems appear, and then it's so hard to get rid of them. I started out half in fun, but then it became for real, and I really got into the spirit of things. I had to do this! So my salon really did open on the cross street, just when city policy was a bit more lax, partly to provide more jobs and partly to increase neighborhood revenues. But then things got tight again, and my shop was the only new one. It was in one of those long lanes, with the door facing inwards towards the opposite side."

As she was speaking, two new customers have come in one after the other, a man and a woman. The owner gives the man a shave, and then starts on a tint job for the woman. She ponders the color samples on the board for a long time before choosing one. The two young women are still listening enrapt by the former salon owner's account, and no more distracted from their jobs than if they were themselves chatting. Indeed, listening gives them more focus, quiets them down so that they become less sloppy. The owner still says nothing. He really is a quiet man, and even communicates with customers mainly through gestures such as nodding, shaking his head or pointing at a photo. If he must speak, he does so in the shortest sentences, in a soft voice. She, on the other hand, speaks fluently and clearly, moving lightly about the shop, amongst the clippings from the scissors, the streams of the water from the hand shower, and the soft words between the owner and the customer.

"So was business good?" asks one of the girls. She does not answer directly but continues along her line of thought. "On opening day, my friends from the clothing strip all came to light firecrackers. Amongst them was one who everyone called 'Old Monk'." She pauses and skips over this part, to be dealt with later. "You ask about business," she eyes the girl who had asked. The question has broken her recounting and she needs a slight pause to find her rhythm again. "Well, business was so-so, mostly hair-washes, and at least half were friends, who 'chose' me." She smiles a bit shyly after the use of the vulgarism. "My kind of shop was a bit neither this nor that. Most people were still used to going to the state-run shops; inside the residential area was a hairdresser run by the district where a wash only cost five yuan. Those with money liked to go to beauty parlors, style specialists, shops run by Hong Kong and Taiwan people. Then there were other 'salons' on the edge of town, where outsiders liked to gather. They call themselves hair salons, but the girls didn't even know how to wash hair." She pauses and decides to skip over this topic. "Most of my customers were teenagers in high school who had just got into the fashion thing. Their parents wouldn't allow them to go to a real beauty salon, so they came to me. Most had dead-straight hair falling down their backs, still with some light fuzz on the temple. They would come with their own bottle of shampoo, sit in the chair, call me 'aunty' and ask me to give them a good scratch. Young they might be, but they had already acquired the mannerisms of white-collars: complaining that I scratched too hard, or not hard enough, that they would get dandruff from the wash, that the hairdryer was too close and would give them split ends. They did not really know anything about hair, but were quite sharp-tongued. I could not be tough on them and had to just 'kid' them along." After using another colloquial expression she chuckles to herself. "When you spend most of your time on these young things, you are a bit put out when someone who wants a real style comes along. Of course, most customers who want a perm are elderly women for whom a set and blow-dry are just fine. Even for something more fashionable, I was not worried because my stylist was properly trained and had worked at the Violet Hair Salon before. The trouble was if someone who wanted something really out of the ordinary showed up. But of course, the more you're afraid of something, the more it happens. One day, a man came in." She stops suddenly, unlaces her hands that had been folded in her lap and thrust them into her dungarees pockets, which makes her chest and stomach protrude even more. She presses her legs together, points her toes and continues, "He wanted his head shaved."

"He had originally had all his hair shaved off, but it had grown out a bit and he wanted it shaved clean again. This is how he came in: he pushed open the door and, standing half in and half out, asked, 'Do you do head shaves?' In an uncertain, inquiring tone. My hairdresser started to chuckle and was about to say, 'Go find yourself a street barber' — though actually no one saw those anymore, it's just a figure of speech. I don't know what came over me but I jumped up and before the hairdresser could say anything, I said, 'Yes, we do!' When I think back, I realize this had been no simple impulse but there had been a special reason: I felt this was somehow no ordinary clean-shaven guy." She laughs, and the two young women laugh too, "Why did you say that?" "How to explain...," she pauses a moment, a short pause but a very noticeable one in her fluent, flowing account, as if many things had bubbled to the surface.

Then she takes up the story again, "If it had been an old man, or a worker or a farmer, or someone poorly dressed... you know, the kind of person who usually shaves his head, I would not have offered to do it. But this one was youngish, about thirty. He was wearing a black woolen jacket with an upright Chinese collar, in those days when it was not fashionable to wear Chinese-style clothes again like today — and it resembled a monk's tunic. He wore black slacks and a pair of round-toed cloth shoes. His bag was also very strange — guess what it was? A washed-out white canvas satchel with a five-pointed star on the top, an old military bag. He looked pretty weird, very out of the ordinary, really unusual."

"I invited him in, sat him down and draped the nylon cape around him, and fastened it snugly at the neck. Then I went to my box to fetch my instruments. Everyone watched me, wondering how I was going to deal with this. I stared at my hands, picked up the electric razor first, then exchanged it for the long scissors, then took up the small scissors. The moment my fingers closed over the small scissors I knew I had the right thing, and I knew what to do. That's the way I am, I go by feeling, and the feeling is in my hands. That's why for many things, I have to actually do them first.... I act first, then think. Before I act I know nothing, but as soon as I do I know it all. When I was young, all the girls in our lane used to be mad about crocheting and always exchanged patterns. There had also been books with pictures of different stitches. I had never looked at them. All I needed was a crochet hook and thread. A couple of twists, and once started I could do all the stitches. Everyone says that I have great hands. So what does that mean... well, just this! I went back to the customer with the small scissors, and lowered the chair a bit because he was pretty tall. He looked at the scissors but said nothing. I don't know whether he thought I knew what I was doing or not, but I felt I knew. Afterwards, my hairdresser asked me where I had learnt to do it, because from the way I held the scissors he felt I knew. Actually, I had never learnt how to cut so closely, nor had I ever even seen anyone else do it. I just knew that I could not use an electric razor or even a hand razor — that would really be like going to a street barber! After all, we were a hair salon, and with a customer like that we had to keep up with the times. Once I held the scissors I did not hesitate, I started from the hairline and began to snip towards the back, bit by bit. With small scissors and short blades it's easy to cut close and not leave any 'angles.' That's the most important thing, no 'angles,' really 'round.' This customer had a really good head, nice and round. You may laugh, but you should know, after all the heads you have touched, is every one round? Of course not! Most heads are not round, or rather, not round all over, but have bumps and dips. But this guy, perfectly round, no bumps, and even more unusual, he had no bald spots or scars. If you shaved everyone's head, you would find that most people have bald patches and scars. But he didn't, that was why he could shave his head. Not everyone can get away with it. I cut for an hour and a half, and the bits were as fine as powder. I was totally focused on his head, but I knew he was staring at me in the mirror, watching my every move. Later he told me that all his previous shaves had been with an electric razor by his girlfriend. They were both in the drama academy, where he was a teacher and she a student. She was out of town working on a TV series and so he had come to find a shave. He had walked down several streets and asked at a number of salons, but they had all declined until he came to mine. He and his girlfriend were renting a flat on Wuyi Road, not far from Anxi Road, and after that he often dropped in. He told me all this later too."

The story has reached an important point and there is a palpable sense of tension in the shop. It is around two or three in the afternoon, when business is usually slow. The two young women are now sitting down on either side of her, the owner dozing behind the counter, indifferent to what she is saying, but not interfering in the chatter either. He really is different. Usually hairdressers love to chat and gossip, but this one remains quite disinterested. The young women wait for the story to continue, but she suddenly changes the topic.

"Remember I mentioned 'Old Monk,' one of our friends selling clothing on Anxi Road? He was called 'Old Monk' not only because of his age, already forty then, but also his experiences. He used most of his experiences not on doing any business but for gabbing. The moment he started talking, bosses would forget about business and gather round to listen. When he used to be inside, the people in charge of his case would even forget about crossexamining him." She pauses, and blushes because she has let the cat out of the bag. Then she smiles calmly, "Well, anyway you probably know without my saying, at least half the bosses on Anxi Road had been in the clink." This time she does not stop at the slang, though her blush deepens and spreads, and she looks a bit defiant. "When he came out he couldn't find a job so he went into business. Old Monk got caught because of his big mouth: for fraud! He duped people by saying he was an overseas Chinese with a rubber plantation in Southeast Asia, and had come to Shanghai to find a wife. He claimed Shanghai people have good blood. You know, he seemed to know everything and to have been to every corner of the world.

He said Shanghai people were of 'good stock,' and the women were better than the men; the moist climate of the south nurtured the *yin* element. 'You read *A Dream of Red Mansions*?' he would ask. Jia Baoyu said women are made of water, that's what he really meant. Shanghai women are made of water. The soft moist air breeds a certain smoothness in the bones and in the skin, everything is in balance and well proportioned. Take faces, for example, northern types are mostly of Mongolian stock with wide flat cheekbones, broad jaws, wispy eyebrows, eyelids without folds, short noses, shapeless mouths and dull expressions. Southern types are of Yue stock, like folk from Fujian, with large round eyes with folds, but too deepset, and they have pug noses like a monkey, most unrefined. People from south of the Yangtze have features from both north and south, and Shanghai folk have melded the bloodlines even further. They have what the water and soil gave them, and also added something from industrialization. Seen the calendars from old Shanghai? A beautiful woman in a traditional *qipao* with a Western-style fur coat, brocade high heels, and sitting on a high-backed Western chair with a carved coffee table beside her, and on it a gramophone with a gaping loudspeaker and a branched lamp with a mother-of-pearl shade — now that's what industrialization added to the mix. Old Monk, dressed in a Western suit and carrying a latched briefcase, would sit in the lobby or the bar of a hotel, and hold forth with group after group of guests. Come mealtime, naturally someone would invite him to the dining room, and then order crystal shrimp, sweet-and-sour fish, chicken. And then he would start talking about food. They were a continuous stream of mostly sweet young things, barely in their twenties, some from really good backgrounds, too: daughters of high officials and doctors, some were college graduates, teachers, and there was even one movie star. So he would get to know them and after about a month, he would ask to borrow money. Actually, he didn't even have to ask — they would offer it to him, saying, 'Changing money is a real pain, queuing at the Bank of China and filling in all those forms, here take this Renminbi to use, no need to stand on ceremony!' He would take from Peter to pay Paul, just like a bank, very smooth, and no loopholes. Old Monk is pretty ugly — well, not really ugly, just strange-looking. At first glance he doesn't seem to have a chin, but if you look closer, he actually does, it's just that it disappears into his neck. Then he doesn't have any shoulders. Well, of course he has shoulders, and they are really wide and his neck is really thick too, and he has big shoulder muscles, so his shoulders seem sloped down. Third, he has an odd twist to one arm, particularly when he turns his palm up. You might say that his appearance is pretty unpromising, but he is redeemed a bit by his hands and feet, which are all small, quite out of proportion to his height of one meter and seventy-eight. That, too, is something really strange about him. So there he is, twisted and crooked, with just his glib mouth to attract bees and butterflies." At that, she laughs because the analogy just doesn't fit with Old Monk's looks. There is derisiveness in the laugh and just a hint of pity too. Her face is still flushed, and the rosy color has spread so that her formerly pale features now appear quite pretty.

"Then one day, someone introduced a young woman to him, and she came to see him with a whole group of friends and relatives. One of them had seen him at work, and recognized him as a salesman for the district food company. Another even knew his name. And so they reported him to the police. One by one, all those he had duped spilled the beans and it turned out that there had been twelve of them, a round dozen. Old Monk denied nothing and took it all on himself, saying that he was solely responsible. A real man doesn't try to wriggle out of things he has done. The investigator in charge of his case took a liking to him and during the nightshift, when he got tired, would take him out of his cell and get him talking. Then they would both have a big bowl of pork-rib noodles as a midnight snack. He was given a light sentence of three years' labor because he had admitted his guilt. At the Baimaoling Labor Farm, the authorities also had taken a shine to him and made him group leader. There's a hierarchy in labor camp too, you know, and swindlers are at the top. After all, they have the highest IQs, and Old Monk's was the highest of all!"

A woman then comes in wanting a wash and a perm for a wedding banquet that night. She wants things done carefully, so the story is interrupted, as one of the young women does the wash. The other pulls over the plastic basket with the curlers and opens the elastic bands, placing them to one side ready for use, and she asks, "And what about the guy with the shaven head, how come you got into telling us about Old Monk?" The other one doing the washing turns towards her too, "Yes, what happened to him?" She smiles without answering, asks for a disposable plastic cup from the owner and goes to the water dispenser. She drinks slowly; no one dares to hurry her so they wait patiently. Activity in the shop slows to its regular pace, back to the tranquility of storytelling and listening.

"Old Monk spent two and a half years at the labor farm, with the last six months of his sentence cancelled," she continues talking about the "Old Monk." "When he got back, he rented a stall on Anxi Road and sold women's clothing. His business was so-so, which simply shows his experience. He would often say, 'We are all in the same boat, why should we try to outdo each other?' Some people on Anxi Road pulled a lot strings and started to expand, renting out their stalls, and went to Hongqiao Road to start clothing shops; some opened factories, went to South Africa, even Argentina. But not Old Monk, he stayed put. He often said, 'What's the use of lots of room, you only need several feet to lie down on.' So he did business in a free and no-pressure way. When he got new stock in and we liked something, he would say without hesitation, 'Take it!' He was really good to us young women, not only generous, but also taught us many things. He often said, 'A woman doesn't have to be a great beauty, it's just fine if she has regular features without any big blemishes, the important thing is to be smart, to have intelligence. An old saying goes, 'Beauty is short-lived,' which also means that it does not guarantee good luck in life, right? Another saying, 'Clever face, stupid guts,' but what does that mean? Why set those two things against each other? Because a pretty woman often forgets to learn, and so the other saying, 'Beauty is short-lived' ends up coming true. China's famous 'Four Beauties' actually weren't that gorgeous. Everyone's heard of Imperial Concubine Yang, the one who was the favorite of the Tang Emperor and for whom he nearly lost his kingdom. The army demanded the Emperor kill her or they would not fight for him anymore to recover his throne. But it's said Concubine Yang had strong body odor and always wore fresh flowers around her neck; that's where 'shame the flowers' comes from in the expression 'Hide the moon and shame the flowers.' So you see, she won the Emperor's favor not by looks alone. What did he see in her? Figure it out yourself. Then look at Wang Zhaojun, you think she was that beautiful? Would the emperor have sent someone really beautiful to the barbarians? All she actually had was the status, someone from the imperial household, which was more than enough. But she had also been truly clever. Here she was ordered to go to that freezing place where she did not know the language, made to live in tents and eat mutton, but she didn't kill herself, instead did as she was told and went. And what happened? Her name is in the history books. As for Xi Shi and Diao Chan, they were even smarter. After all, they were actually spies sent into the enemy camp. How could they do all that if they had not been really sharp? Now looking at it from another angle, a clever woman has a natural beauty, if not in looks, then in spirit and character."

As she says that, she cannot help smiling again before she continues speaking. "Take Xi Shi, an ordinary girl chosen from the village of Zhuji. Why was she not sent directly to Fu Chai, King of Wu, but instead given to the scholar Fan Li to coach? Train her in what? How to walk, raise her arms, speak, and look at others. And how does one learn these things? By being smart. The way a person walks gives them style. We talk about attracting attention, yet how does that happen? On a crowded street, who has time to notice facial features, skin or height? So what attracts attention is how a person walks, or their deportment. Old schools for girls of the aristocracy, China-West High School for Girls for example, all had deportment classes. Girls had to learn to walk, bend, go up and down stairs with books balanced on their heads. What were they learning? How to lift the chest, but not too high like marching a soldier; and how to hold the head up, and keep the gaze straight, without overdoing it. Once the chest is lifted, the back and neck all straighten too. The strides should not be too short, not the small quick steps used in operas, which are too mincing, yet too long strides are too masculine. Have you noticed that the *qipao* in old movies are slit to just below the knee? That allows for just the right stride, to be used to the full without overstretching. These new *qipao* today are slit all the way up to the thigh, really vulgar, you could even run in them! When business was slow, Old Monk would teach us deportment. I'm not kidding, I can always tell when someone has been trained by him, just by their walk. There were several of us who got along with him really well — you could see there was something special there. But all knew that nothing could happen, because they either had husbands or boyfriends, or just wanted to have some fun with Old Monk, not marriage. Old Monk himself was already over forty, and used to say he was not interested. He said we all hung out together because of the good company, and no one wanted trouble. He also used to warn us not to sleep around with young men because one might get too attached and get hurt."

The customer has finished having the set and is under the dryer. She flips through an old magazine with curling pages. The owner and the two young women are all taking a slight break. The sun has shifted and is now shining through the nylon curtains, lighting the storyteller from behind. Her face is in shadow but only by contrast with the bright sun, so it is still quite visible and even soft looking. She smiles and squashes the plastic cup between her fingers, like a final gesture, but then adds:

"Maybe you didn't guess, but Old Monk is now my husband. Actually I was not one of his favorites, but I wanted to marry him. He said, 'That's where you are smarter than the others.' He used to say this before too, but then he only meant that I had style, the style of a girl from Huaihai Road. She smiles proudly and a little shyly, stands up and walks towards the door.

"What about the shaven-head one?" the two young women jump up and follow her.

"Dead!" she replies, as she pushes open the door and walks out. The door swings back and forth on its spring, flashing sunlight on the disappointed faces of the two girls.

A slight pause, and they launch into a lively discussion about her age. She looks in her twenties, but when you list all the things she's done that would not be enough time, so she must be in her late thirties.

Suddenly, the owner spits out one word, "Tart!"

This is the only word he has said all day, and both the word and the tone are harsh. The two young women suddenly break off their chatter and fall silent.

(Translated by Shi Xiaojing)

Say, "Qiezi"

Dai Lai

Dai Lai. Born in October 1972, in Suzhou, Jiangsu Province, Dai Lai has in recent years published fiction of varying length, totaling over 2 million Chinese characters — in literary periodicals such as *People's Literature* and *Harvest*. Her novella and short stories have been included in many journals and anthologies, with some translated for readers abroad. Her fiction collections are *In or Out* (Changjiang Literature and Art Press, September 2000), *I'm Not Here* (Baihua Literature and Art Publishing House, May 2001), *A Fleeting Flash* (People's Literature Publishing House, October 2002), *Shut the Door* (New World Press, June 2003), *Are You Ready?* (Shidai Literature and Art Press, November 2004), and *A Twist of My Waist* (Qunzhong Press, January 2005). Her novels include *Someone Is Peeping* (Baihua Literature and Art Publishing House, September 2001), *Handsome Nose* (Huayi Press, January 2002), *Practice Life and Love* (Writers' Publishing House, October 2002), *Falling in Love with a Friend's Girlfriend*, *Love Quadrangle*, and *Shattered ·Abyss of Time*.

In 2002, Dai Lai was conferred the Spring Literary Prize.

Say, "Qiezi"

The distance from home to the photo lab is roughly only two bus stops. Even when strolling slowly, it only takes about the time to smoke two cigarettes to get there. Old Sun habitually lit a cigarette and let it dangle from his lips, as he double-checked the doors and the gas before locking up to go out. After walking one stop, he would almost be finished with his first cigarette, so he lit another one halfway through toward the second stop.

Three months ago, Old Sun had rented the photo lab: a store of only thirty square meters consisting of only a Kodak enlarger, a shrewdly covered antediluvian couch, and some irregular customers. These were all the assets of the store, save for two pots of nameless plants that Old Sun did not recognize and some miscellaneous photos left behind by customers. The former owner of the lab, Old Niu, could hardly wait to be rid of it. He was a hard-working fellow, with more good traits than can be counted on ten fingers. But he had one lethal indulgence — gambling. It was this sole indulgence that

* "*Qiezi*" (eggplant), is the Chinese equivalent of saying "cheese" to smile when a picture is being taken.

caused Old Niu to ultimately lose, along with his family, the photo lab that he had worked so hard to build over the last ten years. At the zenith of his achievements, Old Niu had owned six photo labs, monopolizing almost one third of the photo-developing market in the city. Old Sun vividly remembers the day when he handed the money to Old Niu who, with quivering hands and a shaggy moustache, handed over his blood and sweat of the last ten years, and drowned himself in emotions which only he could identify.

Actually, the store has been rented for Xiao Long, Old Sun's son. Xiao Long was approaching twenty-seven, without a decent job for a long time. All he has ever cared for is fun and games: computer games, handheld games, even some punk ideals. Fortunately, Xiao Long has never caused Old Sun any real trouble, and for this Old Sun is grateful. Qiang Zi, the neighbor's son, who is the same age as Xiao Long, had already completed a doctorate. Qiang Zi's parents simply could not stop flaunting his accomplishments, until one day a police wagon stopped in front of their house. Who would have thought someone so close, and one so learned, could be a rapist! Old Sun thinks that bringing honor to the family is merely secondary to not disgracing the family.

Old Sun had faith in Xiao Long, but reality has proven him somewhat overly optimistic. His hopes that his son would become something only produced utter disappointment; as his hopes of spending the rest of his life with his wife, now ex-wife, turned out to be even more devastating. The harsh realities of life have taught Old Sun to resort to now lowering his expectations, because lower expectations mean less disappointment.

Before he could finish his second cigarette, Old Sun arrived at the photo lab. He unlocked the door and took off his jacket as he stepped inside. He boiled some water in the kettle to prepare a cup of tea. While waiting for the water to boil, Old Sun grabbed the cheesecloth under the counter to wipe clean the counter. At one corner of the counter was a pile of pistachio shells, which must have been left discarded there by Xiao Long's plump girlfriend Mei Zi. Mei Zi was a sweet girl, though a bit silly at times. She was somewhat stout in stature and slightly overweight. Old Sun had the urge to speak to Xiao Long about this issue on several occasions, but restrained himself it due to the awkward nature of the matter.

Old Sun sat down and habitually picked up the box that contained all the photos awaiting customers to pick up. He gingerly opened an envelope, and saw it was a family portrait of a large extended family of more than a dozen people: the family's elders and youngsters are in the front row, the man standing in the middle of the back row donning a patronizing smile, as if he has made it; the woman beside him smiling reluctantly, and contorting her face in a way that made her look like she was crying. They are probably a couple, Old Sun thought, a couple who had reached the terminus of their marriage, yet still holding on to it desperately.

Old Sun opened another photo envelope, which contained pictures from two rolls of film. There were a myriad faces scattered through about sixty or seventy photos. Appearing the most frequently were two couples, who seem to be good friends on holiday together. Everyone in the photographs feigning naturalness, though after looking at a few snapshots, Old Sun thought he has figured out the peculiar relationship between the two couples.

In the innermost crevices of the box was an envelope that no one had come to pick up yet from a long time. Old Sun removed these photographs from the box, photos he had viewed countless times. Beside the "Name" column on the envelope, only "Fei" had been written. There were altogether thirty-seven photos in the envelope, all amateur self-portraits. All thirty-seven photos were of a young woman with a youthfully dressed but not-so-young-looking man. The shots were taken in one single room, in various intimate poses, demonstrating a rather amorous relationship between the two. To add to the mystery, Old Sun had made a shocking discovery a few days ago, when he received a roll of film for development.

The customer's name was Mu. Old Sun had thought his countenance looked rather familiar but could not remember where he had encountered it. When the photos were developed the next day, many faces appeared in photos of what seemed like a family event, and Mu was in the pictures with a woman his own age and a young man in his twenties. They seemed like a normal nuclear family, when suddenly Old Sun realized that Mu was the same man who had been in the pictures with the young woman. It was apparent that the earlier roll of film with the pictures of Mu and the young woman had not been brought in by Mu, or else he would have picked them up when he had dropped off his new roll of film.

Old Sun tried to resolve the relationship mystery between the man and the two women; it seemed obvious enough, but was it really so? Nevertheless, the two sets of photos had become part of Old Sun's daily education, and his attempts to untangle the relationships between these people grew quite interesting. Old Sun was content with the conclusions he had reached, and after days of viewing and contemplation, he truly believed his suppositions.

A few minutes before eleven o'clock, Xiao Long walked in to take his shift at the lab; and Old Sun went home to make lunch for the two of them, and then brought the food back to the store to eat lunch together with Xiao Long. It was the only occasion when the father and son ever spent time with each other. Old Sun had been introduced to a woman two years ago, and had some notions of moving in with her. Taking the opportunity, Xiao Long had moved out.

Business being slow lately, Xiao Long spent most of his time watching videos on the small television sitting at the side of the counter, or pointlessly staring out at the street while plugged into his earphones. During these moments, Xiao Long's brain would go empty.

Xiao Long maximized the volume. It was the strangest song he has ever heard: two different songs penetrating each of his ears. One song bright and cheerful, the other slow and somber. Both songs seem to want to overpower the other one, but in reality they were just singing their own separate songs.

Through the glass doors, the street and buildings across the street were clearly visible. The flamboyant "Push" sign beside the door handle had been put up by Mei Zi, who defined it as "art." Mei Zi encouraged Xiao Long to grow long hair in order to look artistic, despite the fact that he was by no means any kind of artist. She loved everything in the name of "art," and Xiao Long always had the feeling that she would leave him for an artist, thus romanticizing and justifying a breakup at the same time.

Xiao Long picked up the photograph box, and pulled out two sets of photos. He had discovered the relationship between the two sets of photos long ago. Three days earlier, when the man's face had come up on the developer, Xiao Long felt so much shock that he had almost screamed. Seeming inadvertently, he asked his father about the man, and his father only answered the man was in his fifties, clean-cut and appeared educated. Xiao Long did not share his findings with his father, deeming it unnecessary.

This man, the man who aroused some sort of faint curiosity and jealousy in Xiao Long, who could this fellow be? Upon closer examination, Xiao Long discovered that the man's facial expression was different in the two sets of pictures. In the pictures with the younger girl, his smile was sincere, even with a bit of shyness; while in the other set of pictures, he was feigning his smile, a smile of conformity.

For no reason, Xiao Long was convinced that the girl in the picture would eventually come and retrieve the photos. The girl had extremely long hair, and was frail-looking and seemed vulnerable. There was one picture of the girl holding onto the man's arm that gave Xiao Long a vivid impression. She was holding on to the man's sleeve rather desperately, resting her head on the man's shoulders, and there was a look of destitution in her eyes. Maybe it was a momentary expression, but it had been captured by the camera.

Xiao Long was almost sure that it was a typical extramarital tale, but he wished to see the people in the pictures, especially the girl. He thought the girl was special, not beautiful, but the desperation in her eyes attracted Xiao Long. After staring at the picture for some time, Xiao Long even felt a kind of pity for the girl. That's a girl in need of help, Xiao Long said to himself. Maybe she was tired of life, maybe she's trying to leave that man and change her life, but that takes courage. Xiao Long thought maybe the girl seemed to be just looking for someone to pull her life together, and that "someone" had now come along — and was him of course, Xiao Long.

Xiao Long made extra prints of the pictures featuring only the girl and her heart. He had placed them in his room, but shortly after they were discovered by Mei Zi. Mei Zi demanded an explanation, but what was there for Xiao Long to explain?

On the envelope with "Fei" written across the "Name" column, the date read "February 7," more than two and a half months ago. Xiao Long constantly tried to call the number written on the envelope, but no one ever answered. After a while, Xiao Long assumed that the no one would ever pick up the phone. He envisioned all the reasons as to why the phone was not being answered, and shuddered at the thought of any mishap befalling the girl.

Whenever Xiao Long was bored, he would dial that number, because he was almost positive that no one would answer. But this time, a female voice said "Hello" at the other end of the line, and without hesitating, Xiao Long hung up.

When Xiao Long was preparing to lock up for the day, Mei Zi showed up. She lived in the nearby Taihe complex. Mei Zi liked photography and, to be honest, she was photogenic. She knew how to capture her best looks on camera. Moreover, she was rather over-confident about her image.

In the two months after Xiao Long had taken over the photo lab, Mei Zi became a frequent customer. Her rolls of film, her friends', her neighbors', her extended family's rolls of film, all encouraged her to frequent the little store and produce the effect that the shop was popular. In the third month, she became Xiao Long's girlfriend.

Whenever Mei Zi was in the store, Xiao Long felt the space in the store getting smaller and the temperature rising. Xiao Long thought about this situation but never came up with a solution. One day, while Mei Zi was bending down to pick up something from the ground, her plump bottom aroused an epiphany from Xiao Long. It could not have made more sense. Her oversized physique struck Xiao Long as that of a sex symbol. Mei Zi was extremely conscious of talking about her weight, just as middle-aged women are of talking about their age. If Xiao Long mentioned the weight issue even by accident, Mei Zi would turn unhappy, even to the extent of walking out on Xiao Long. According to Xiao Long, Mei Zi's weight must be between 130 and 140 pounds, which would be considered obese for a girl of Mei Zi's height of only 161 cm.

Before becoming acquainted with Xiao Long, Mei Zi's pastimes included reading detective novels and watching videos. She loved to read detective novels under the covers in the middle of the night. The more intense her fear was, the more she was drawn to the book. Her only solution to the fear was emotional overeating, and that was how a fatter Mei Zi came into being.

Mei Zi worked as a cashier in a grocery store, standing at the cash register every day, greeting customers with "Welcome" and "Please come again." Xiao Long began to wish that someday she would speak those words to him, but not as her customer, of course. Xiao Long began to fantasize countless times that he would hold her tight, bury his face in her hair, stroke her back, and then cut to the chase and fondle her more sensitive parts. This fantasy became part of Xiao Long's daily routine before bedtime, and sometimes he would give the fantasy a location, which was in his room; and if he had to specify a part of his room, it would be his bed.

Mei Zi had come to offer Xiao Long two DVDs she had recently rented: Ewan McGregor's *Trainspotting* and *Nightwatch*. Xiao Long had wanted to say that he had seen those films before, and not only these two, he had seen almost all of Ewan McGregor's films. Instead, he applauded Mei Zi's choice in choosing the most classic works of Ewan McGregor.

Mei Zi, obviously delighted, blushed slightly. She consciously or subconsciously leaned towards Xiao Long, and Xiao Long felt a rasp of hot air coming towards him, therefore he shifted slightly in the opposite direction. Mei Zi leaned towards him again, and it was definitely conscious this time because she had a playful smile on her face. Xiao Long extended his arm around Mei Zi's shoulders, as if without any intentions, but surprised Mei Zi with this movement. To cover his embarrassment, Xiao Long said he wanted to go outside for a smoke.

Across the street were two beauty parlors: "Cherie" and "Lacey," typical beauty parlor names. Those two beauty parlors were only separated by a grocery store, so competition was conspicuously fierce. Cherie was bigger and had more business, and also more promotional sales, while Lacey's business was slower. Whenever Xiao Long was bored, he would lean on the counter and watch people come and go from across the street. Suddenly, Mei Zi hollered Xiao Long's name, and shouted, "Who's the person in this picture?"

"I don't know," Xiao Long answered without turning his head.

"Who is this?" Mei Zi was screeching now.

Xiao Long suddenly realized who Mei Zi was referring to, and froze silently. He tried to remember how he got away with it last time, and tried to come up with an answer for this episode.

After dinner, Old Sun opened the lock on the drawer and pulled out a thick envelope, taking out a photograph envelope from it. He donned his reading glasses and turned on the lamp on the table. He separated the photos into two rows, six pictures in total. The top three were of the girl and the man, and the bottom three of the man and his wife. Old Sun had printed these additional copies surreptitiously. The thick envelope contained other privately developed photos as well, but mainly of middle-aged women. These women gave Old Sun room for imagination, and served as filler to his monotonous life.

There was also a slip of paper in the envelope with three phone numbers written on it. Fei's number started with a "5," so it should be near the photo lab. Mu had written a landline number first, before crossing it out to leave a mobile number. Old Sun remembered the man, tall and lean, wearing rimless glasses and looking kind. The photos were to be picked up three days ago, but they had still been there when Old Sun left for lunch.

The girl was around the same age as Xiao Long, maybe even younger, yet the man was old enough to be her father. How did they meet and develop such an illicit relationship? The man did not seem wealthy, so what did the girl want from him?

However you might look at it, their figures (although what it was Old Sun could have put into words) did not divulge the illicit nature of the relationship. But if it were not illicit, why would they take such a plethora of photos inside their home and not outside? Then the fact that the man had dropped off pictures of his family only served to prove Old Sun's conjecture. The man was already married, and had a family. Old Sun juxtaposed the man with his own ex-wife, who had abandoned a stable family life. "Motherf---er," Old Sun said out loud. After the vulgarity was uttered, Old Sun felt shocked that he had actually said it. His voice seemed even more cacophonous in an empty home.

Old Sun stood up and turned on the television. He was used to having some noise in his house, and noise made him feel better.

Old Sun sat down at his desk again and placed a picture of the girl and the man embracing under the lamp. They seemed so happy together, the girl with her huge smile. Old Sun let out a sigh, feeling that the man was definitely lying to the girl, telling her he was either single or going through a divorce for her. If the girl knew the man was happy with his family, what would she think? "You should know the truth," Old Sun solemnly said to the picture of the girl. "You deserve to know what kind of person he is." Old Sun felt provoked, and with the slip of paper in his hand he went over to the phone.

"Hello?" It was the voice of a young woman.

"I'm from Xiao Long's photo lab. I'm looking for Ms. Fei?"

"That's me."

"Great. The pictures you sent in for developing were ready almost three months ago. If you don't retrieve them, we'll have to dispose of them."

"Oh, I'm sorry. I was out of town. In fact, I'll come now. Oh, but I don't know where I put the pickup slip. I don't know if I can find it."

"Are you the person in the picture?"

"Yes, I am."

"That's fine then. Can you come tomorrow morning? I'll be in the store. And...."

"What?"

"Never mind. Please come tomorrow morning, and we'll talk."

After much explaining, Xiao Long still could not convince Mei Zi that he had nothing to do with the girl in the picture, so he gave up. Mei Zi kept a look of disdain on her face. The two of them just stood frozen there, until Mei Zi compromised and said she would renew the relationship if Xiao Long promised not to see the girl anymore. Xiao Long stared up at Mei Zi and shouted, "Why should I? Who do you think you are?"

Mei Zi left the store angrily and slammed the door behind her. Xiao Long did not chase after her; instead, he just watched the "Push" sign on the door swing to and fro before it came to a complete stop. Xiao Long was surprised at his actions, knowing he had not needed to be that harsh. He might not love Mei Zi, but he had feelings for her. No other girl had ever relied on him like Mei Zi did, and it boosted his male ego. Xiao Long lit a cigarette and took a few prolonged puffs. He continued to organize the pictures on the counter, so the one on top was the picture of the girl alone, sitting on the couch with a cigarette between her fingers. She looked frail, and upon close examination, her fragility also belied a hint of impatience.

What was she so tired of? Was she happy with the man? Did she know the man was married? Why was she attracted to the man? Status? Money? Sexual prowess? Why had she not picked up the photos after all this time? Had she forgotten? Had she left the man? Xiao Long reached for the phone and pressed "redial." He took a deep breath before the line connected.

"May I speak to Ms. Fei please?"

"Yeah, that's me."

"Hi, I'm from Xiao Long's photo lab."

"Oh, yes, I've been looking for the pickup slip."

"Well, the photos you sent in to develop have been sitting here for more than two months. According to our regulations, we're obliged to throw them away if the customer doesn't come pick them up."

"I know, you told me earlier. I'll be over tomorrow to pick them up."

After hanging up, Xiao Long still had trouble processing the information, since he had not said anything to her about having called earlier during the day. Xiao Long wondered if it was his father who had contacted her.

Old Sun could see the big cardboard figure of the Kodak girl from the distance. Had Xiao Long forgotten to bring it in the night before? As Old Sun approached the store, he saw the front door open, with Xiao Long sweeping the floor inside. Old Sun thought, Xiao Long must have gone crazy, because he never wakes up before ten in the morning, and certainly Old Sun has never ever seen Xiao Long with a broom. Nevertheless, Old Sun, still displeased with the lackluster way Xiao Long was sweeping the floor, snatched the broom from Xiao Long.

"Why you up so early? I thought you never wake up before ten."

"I woke up early today and had nothing to do, so I came over. You can go home, I'll watch the store this morning."

"No," said Old Sun, straightening up, but immediately realized he was overreacting and explained, "I've got nothing to do either if I go home, and you know it. So, just let me stay, you go."

Xiao Long, neither saying that he would leave or not leave, instead took out a cigarette and also handed one to Old Sun. After a while, Xiao Long walked outside the store.

After sweeping the floor, Old Sun also wiped the counter, then sat down and watched his son smoking outside. He felt that Xiao Long was acting abnormal today, and looked as if he had something on his mind. Could he be waiting for the girl as well? Old Sun looked at the photo box, and the girl's pictures were still there. Due to constant viewing, they looked slightly old and dusty.

He watched his son finish the cigarette, and light another one, then walk back into the store. Old Sun grabbed the washcloth to vehemently scrub at a nonexistent stain on the counter. Xiao Long came in and sat down on the sofa and stretched. Old Sun sensed he had something to say.

Since Xiao Long moved out, father and son rarely had any chances to talk. Not as if they had talked a lot before. When Xiao Long was young, Old Sun had always scolded him while he just listened silently. As Xiao Long had grown older, he started talking back, and gradually they had nothing to say to each other anymore.

For five whole minutes, the two just sat there smoking on their own. It was awkward, but Old Sun became sure that Xiao Long was trying to say something to him. He was also sure it had to with Xiao Long's mother. After the divorce, Xiao Long still stayed in regular contact with his mother. Old Sun had wanted to intervene but did not, considering the fact that she had left the boy to him.

"Have you seen your mama recently?" Old Sun decided to initiate the topic himself. Over the years, he had got some details out of others. She had another son, and her new husband treated her well; their son went to university. But Old Sun had found this information merely superficial.

"Yeah, I saw her."

"Well, how is she?"

"Same as before." Xiao Long seemed unwilling to talk.

"What do you mean, same as before?"

"It's what it is. She's doing not bad."

"What do you mean by, not bad?" How could she be doing well? Old Sun pondered this question. A woman who spent six years with a man and raised a child with him, suddenly marrying another man, how could she just forget her ex-husband and child? If the heart cannot forget, how could she then be doing "not bad"?

"It means, not bad. She has a house and a car, and their son is in university, what else is there? Pa, what is it you really want to know?" Xiao Long seemed impatient, and got up and walked outside.

"Are you thinking about living with your ma?" Old Sun yelled to his son's departing figure.

Old Sun closed the store before six o'clock. He felt exceptionally tired that day, and yearned to just go home, lie on his bed and doze off with nothing on his mind. But how could he clear his mind of everything? His argument with his son had made him uneasy. Part of it was due to Xiao Long's description of his mother, but what made him most uncomfortable was Xiao Long's attitude. Also, the girl who came up to pick up the photos made Old Sun uncomfortable, too. She had stayed in the store for no longer than two minutes, and she looked even younger than in the picture. Her immature appearance gave Old Sun a sense of unavoidable responsibility. Old Sun believed that if the girl's parents were to find out about the situation, they would try and stop it as well.

After walking home, Old Sun splashed some water on his face and fumbled in his drawer for her telephone number.

"Hi, I'm from Xiao Long's photo lab. We met this morning?"

"What is it now?"

The girl's impatience confused Old Sun. Just this morning, the girl had been polite, and thanked them for their service.

"Oh, it's something I meant to tell you this morning, but it wasn't a very good time. However, I feel obliged to tell you…."

"I know," the girl interrupted him, "You don't have to tell me. Someone from your store already told me. I really don't get it. How come everyone in this industry is so absorbed in their customers' private lives?"

"Young lady, this is for your own good! I have pictures of the man with his family. If you saw these pictures, you'd know what kind of person he is!"

"Why don't you just do yourselves some favors? I can see you are all sick!"

Old Sun wanted to tell her, "If you keep on this way, you'll regret it one day," but she had already hung up on him. Old Sun's hand was still pressed against the telephone, angry and confused. The girl's attitude and the girl's answers shocked Old Sun. How could girls nowadays just treat their relationships like this, with no moral standards, as if, as long as they are happy, they don't have a care in the world.

It was almost seven o'clock, and Old Sun still had not started cooking dinner yet. Being single meant looking after himself more. Old Sun's three meals each day were typically punctual and well prepared and balanced. Old Sun got up and walked towards the kitchen. Because he had rushed through lunchtime, the dirty dishes were still in the sink. Staring at the greasy mess, Old Sun lost his appetite.

As if in conflict with himself, Old Sun stood for awhile in the kitchen. Old Sun felt like vomiting. He returned to his room, sat down at the desk and stared at the three telephone numbers written on the piece of paper. He just could not figure how that girl could be like that to someone who was only trying to help her, someone with a good heart and good intentions toward her expecting nothing, as himself, and how could the girl suddenly just say he was sick.

Despite everything, Old Sun already found himself involved in this ordeal. He felt as if he owed himself an explanation, as well as an explanation to the man's wife. Old Sun thought of phoning the woman and telling her what kind of person her husband is. A woman his wife's age probably would not be as unreasonable as that girl.

Old Sun was not sure if the number that was crossed out was the Mu family phone number, but he dialed it anyway. He prayed while he waited for an answer.

"Is this Mr. Mu's house?"

"Yes, who are you?"

"Are you Mrs. Mu?"

"Yes, who are you?"

"That's very good, just great. Listen, I can only speak to you of this matter. I don't know if Mr. Mu is home, but he must not know about his. I'm from Xiao Long's photo lab, your husband sent in a roll of film to be developed a few days ago."

"I know."

"The problem is, about two months ago we received a roll of film, but it wasn't picked up. After your family's film was developed, I discovered that your husband was the same man as the person in the unclaimed film. That roll of unclaimed film was full of pictures of your husband and a young girl behaving in an amorous manner. Do you get me?"

"Yes."

Her calmness was something Old Sun had not expected. Because of that, Old Sun thought the woman was not an easy character. After a short moment of silence, the woman calmly asked, "What do you want from me, having told me all this?"

"I don't want anything!" Old Sun yelled in denial, "Do you think I want to extort from you? If I wanted to do any extortion, I would've called your husband's cell-phone!"

"Sorry, that's not what I meant. Could I see those pictures?"

"Sure, come over tomorrow morning, I'll wait for you in the store."

"Can I come today? I'll come right now."

Even though many days had passed, Xiao Long still thought about the girl. Every time he thought about her, he could see her desperate look. He still did not know her name, age, or occupation.

After the day the girl had picked up the pictures, Xiao Long had called her and asked if she wanted to see the pictures of the man and his family. She rejected his offer, saying that she was neither interested nor did she care. She also said it was none of Xiao

Long's business. Xiao Long had retorted he had no ill intentions except to let her know the truth. He asked her in return, "You really don't care?"

The girl's voice kept rising, and rising louder, as she said she simply did not care, really she did not care about anything, until the girl had yelled at him that he was a maniac.

When looking again at the girl's desperate eyes, Xiao Long could not believe that the girl did not care. An apathetic person would not look at the camera that way. He was convinced that he could talk the girl into starting a normal life, though whether that new life would include Xiao Long was another issue.

After that, Xiao Long called the girl again, and the girl became so annoyed. She even asked, " Is it that you wish to hook up with me?"

Xiao Long never spoke with the girl again. Sometimes he would dial the number and after the girl answered, he would hang up. He did not know why he became so obsessed with calling this number. Maybe he needed to hear the girl's voice. Just like that. After awhile, the phone was disconnected. The girl had probably moved or changed numbers.

In the few days after the National Day holiday, the photo lab had very good business, and Xiao Long came earlier and left later each day. Watching faces appear on the machine, and watching everyone's life flash in front of him, Xiao Long laughed. Everyone seems so accustomed to feigning a smile in front of the camera, "One, two three, *qiezi*...," snap. The moment is captured, but is it real?

When the married couple walked in, Xiao Long was working on the developer machine. The woman called out, "Hey there." Xiao Long turned around and stared.

"Where's the older technician?" the woman asked.

"Oh, he went home, he's usually here in the mornings."

"Then let's come back on Saturday morning." She asked the man, "How's Saturday morning?"

"I'm busy on Saturday morning. You can come alone," the man seemed uneasy because Xiao Long was staring at him. He pretended to be looking around the store, while his arm was tightly clasped by his wife.

"Sunday morning then," the woman spoke firmly, "We'll come together."

From beginning to end, the woman held on to the man's arm, even when she was taking out her wallet to pay. She held on as if making a statement, but it looked unnatural. Xiao Long believed that these two people would appear the same way in front of his father on Sunday.

It was nearing nine o'clock but Xiao Long had not had time for dinner yet. When he had been with Mei Zi, she always came to the photo lab after work and helped Xiao Long out, so Xiao Long could eat. Honestly, Mei Zi was a good girl, and Xiao Long felt some disappointment at not being able to work it out with her. He remembered that Mei Zi swore that she would eventually find a boyfriend who is better than Xiao Long. Now, she had a new boyfriend, who has long hair and looks like an artist. Mei Zi and her new boyfriend had gone vacationing during the National Day holiday, and their vacation photos were now in Xiao Long's hands, straight out of the developing machine. Xiao Long flipped through them: Mei Zi had lost some weight, and Xiao Long assumed that she must be working hard at her new relationship. Nevertheless, there were huge smiles on both of their faces. By reading their lips, Xiao Long could tell that they were saying over and over again the same word: "*qiezi*" or "chee-se...."

After looking once, Xiao Long looked again, and then stacked them into the envelope and put them back into the box.

(Translated by Lian Wangshu)

The Great Masque

Wei Wei

Wei Wei. Born in 1970, she began writing in 1994. Wei Wei was conferred the 3rd Lu Xun Literary Prize, the 2nd Chinese Fiction Society Prize, the 10th Zhuang Zhongwen Literary Prize, in addition to a number of other prizes.

Her major works are *My Memories of Weihu Sluice Gate*, *A Different Summer*, and *Big Lao Zheng's Woman*. Her works have been translated into several languages, including English, French and Japanese.

The Great Masque

1

Ten years ago, Jiali had still been a poverty-stricken college student. Uncommunicative, inarticulate and slow-paced. She was not at all bad-looking, but neither was she attractive. Like many girls on her campus, she wore thick glasses.

Jiali never realized how beautiful her eyes were: big, calm, lively, and often glowing with spirit. One day, a male student told her that her eyes shone. She said, "Don't everyone's eyes shine?" The student looked at her, smiled, and then said, "I meant your mind. Your inner mind gives off this light."

Jiali had felt embarrassed. Now she realized what he was saying. Jiali used to be generally very quiet. She seldom drew attention to herself — just a mediocre student who did not study very hard or even paid much attention to love or her appearance like most female students. All day long, strange little thoughts or ideas would fill her head and then rise like little bubbles, until they burst into new thoughts and new ideas. These must be the light the male student was referring to. They were like ghostly fires, flickering like soulful blinking eyes, deep and bottomless. They were the sound of buzzing mosquitoes, circling around her life, which she could never swat away. Sometimes these thoughts and ideas scared her, to the point that she was afraid that they could drive her to behave strangely, to surprise people by accident. Other times, she seemed to enjoy them, allowing herself to plunge into the sea of exquisite joy and excitement they brought her.

Four years of college life had gone by uneventfully. Nobody seemed to know what she was thinking about, and, thank goodness, she had not done anything foolish.

In the autumn of her final year at college, Jiali had been sent to an intermediate court in a neighboring city for a half-year internship. It was during that brief period that she had fallen in love and slept with the director of the unit where she was interning. A certain Mr. Zhang, in his thirties; a spirited and competent judge, married, father of an eight-year-old boy. A family photo on his desk made it obvious that he had a pretty happy family: a middle-aged couple with a child, sitting on a spring lawn. They seemed to be looking at a void, calm and smiling wanly. For a long time after seeing the photo, Jiali had felt a strange sadness.

It was under such circumstances that Jiali had begun her incurable journey of love. She had felt awkward, disoriented, and sorrowful. She had not had a chance to experience normal love, love with any of the numerous young men around her at college. Somehow, she had been able to resist them all, but not this man. Her desk had been right across from his. There were times when their eyes would meet accidentally for fleeting moments, and then immediately tear apart. Jiali could not bear to look into his eyes. They were much too full of serenity and grace. With a pair of wire-frame glasses perched on his face, he looked a bit younger than his age. He was mild-mannered, handsome and elegant all at once.

One Thursday afternoon, an unexpected rain had begun to fall. Everyone in the office was out on his or her respective duties, except for Jiali. She was flipping through an old newspaper, clutching her hands on her cold shoulders from time to time. Suddenly, she had heard a voice from across the desk.

"Chilly?"

Jiali could not feel too surprised. Unflustered, she smiled widely. Evidently, he had just come back from a banquet. His hair was slicked with water and he smelled of rain and alcohol. He stood by the desk, fiddled with some papers, rearranging them somewhat. In one instant, his eyes seemed to glance at Jiali. They seemed dull and lifeless. He started walking toward the wash basin to grab a towel, but stopped when he got near Jiali, and asked her how work was going. She rested her elbow on the desk, allowing her open sleeve to fall, revealing a slender porcelain-white forearm. She did not look at him, but she knew that his eyes must have landed on it, like ants crawling inch by inch up her bare skin.

She had wearily let her arm fall on the table. He walked up, touched her sleeve, and whispered, "You really ought to wear more clothes." Jiali was shocked. It felt like he was moaning, biting her earlobe, and gently blowing his breath into her ear.

Two days later, they had had their first date. It was a weekday. Dusk had just fallen. He had come to her dorm, a stack of documents in his hands. He appeared to be in a hurry, saying a rushed "Hi" to every colleague he ran across, and hastily exchanging idle pleasantries with them. After he had stepped into the dorm, however, he became silent. He sat on a chair, stared at Jiali, and did not utter a word. It had only been two days since they had last seen each other, and he looked dirty and weary, his beard unshaven. He told her he had not slept well. Jiali's heart tightened. She knew the answer but she asked anyway, "How come?"

He had looked down, and then stood up. Snatching her into his arms, he crushed his lips to her ear, and whispered something inaudible.

They both knew this was going to be a hopeless love affair. Besides, Jiali did not have long to stay there. She was to go back to school in two months and get a new job. When they were lying together, he would often count with his fingers, forty-three more days ...thirty-two more days. It seemed to be driving him insane. Sometimes, he would calm down, and gaze at her as if he never knew her, as if he wanted to inhale her into his body.

"Jiali," he said.

"Yes?"

"Jiali," he spoke again.

Jiali fondled his hair, smiled, and said, "What is it?"

He murmured, "I just want to say your name."

Jiali's eyes had welled up with tears. At that moment, she had realized that this man loved her. When they were lying together, when their bodies touched, she *knew* he loved her. He began talking like never before. He poured his heart out, talking about gossip in the workplace, who was friends with whom, who and who were not on good terms, how he rose to the position of section director, coming from a lowly family of meager means..., how his wife had courted him, how everybody seemed to like her, and how he detested her. They had been married for fifteen years, but for the last seven years they slept separately.

He had very rarely slept with Jiali. There were simply no opportunities. Even though they were together every day from dawn to dusk, there was not a single moment for them to be alone together. They could only sneak at peek of the other's hand, a strand of hair, half a face, or a corner of the other's clothing. Occasionally, he would seem so suffocated that he would suddenly lift his head and stare at her, holding back his wildest impulses with all his strength, without regard as to whether people around him might notice. At such moments, Jiali would immediately lower her head. She did not dare respond, thinking he must be crazy. Another time, he had pretended he needed to look at a document by her side. He walked over, talking, pointing at the document with one hand, while his other hand prowled to find her palm, grasping it tightly, massaging it desperately as if slaking a terrible thirst. Looking at all the people in the office, a frightened Jiali broke into a chilling sweat. Many years later, Jiali would remember that men could be at times so ferocious.

Yet all he ever wanted was simply to sleep with her. He was always busy, agitated, and fearful. People surrounded him around the clock: his superiors, his peers, litigators, friends, his wife and child.... He had very little time for Jiali. When he managed to find a moment to take Jiali to a hotel, he would only have time to have a meal with her, hastily embrace her, putting his face to her breasts, then off he would go. There had never been any moment of respite for him. Jiali could only sigh. Because she loved him, she had to oblige him.

Jiali had not really understood what pleasure there could be in a sexual relationship with a man. She loved him for such minute things, things which usually escaped other people's attention: his hair, his attire, his dusk-like eyes when he had a quiet moment, his childlike temperament, his misbehavior toward her when he was drunk; including when he bad-mouthed his peers, or when he banged on desks, his serious demeanor when he was in front of people.... One night, he had suddenly burst into tears when he was

with her. He said his life was a mess, that he was a big failure....
That if his mind was clear, and if his wife did not shout at him to
come home, he would let Jiali know all of his grief. But, he had left.

That night, Jiali had realized what she loved about this man was
his pain, the side of his life that no one else shared. One afternoon,
they had been standing in front of the windows of a high building.
He had wrapped his arms around her from behind, laying his head
on her shoulder like a child. She felt a lump in her throat. He did
not say anything. Instead, he covered her eyes with his hands, and
wiped her tears that were slowly falling down her face, one drop at a
time. Then he had turned her around, and said in a tone filled with
deep regret, "Jiali, I cannot give you anything."

Jiali, tears in her eyes, had shaken her head ever so slowly and
said she did not need anything. This became the most beautiful
interlude in her life. She had been twenty-two. Her body in full
bloom. Many years later she would remember these moments. She
would remember this man. This man who had been with her when
she was blossoming.

Jiali had been very poor. She had lived on the scanty money her
parents mailed to her through the post office month after month.
She had a younger brother who was a sophomore at college. Both
her parents were ordinary workers. They took out heavy loans for
her and her brother to go to college. That was something Jiali would
never forget. One summer, she had been staying at a girlfriend's
house for a few days. Her friend was much bigger than she was. The
friend's mother gave her a few pieces of old clothing her friend had
outgrown. Jiali had declined. The mother had said, "You see, these
are all old clothes. They are not worth anything."

Tears had poured down her face.

She could not forget the fact that she was poor. Poverty to her was more important than anything. She constantly reminded herself that she must eat the simplest food, wear the plainest clothes, that she must live life with self-respect. Sometimes, Jiali would ask herself what she loved most in life. Was it men? Or, was it some feeling that would be eternally engraved on her heart? No. It was actually the fact of how utterly poor she was. She was sure that when she became old, and when death approached, the one thing she would always recall would be those dark days during her four years at college. She was more sensitive than anyone else. She was easily hurt. She was bitter. She hated poverty, but she loved it too. She was afraid that she might never be able to liberate herself from the word.

During her internship, Jiali had gone in and out of some big hotels with the director. He had taken her to the most luxurious dance halls in the area. He spent money like water. Of course Jiali knew he was not spending his own money. He did not have any of his own money, and he seldom gave Jiali presents. There was only one time when he had traveled out of town. Upon his return, he brought a ring for Jiali. For the life of her Jiali would not accept it. She was used to being poor. She did not need a ring. It would not feel right on her hand. She did not know much about gold. But she did know that one of her aunts had bought a ring once, bigger than this one, of very delicate craftsmanship. They said it had cost almost a thousand yuan. Jiali had estimated this one would cost at least four or five hundred yuan. So she felt even more determined that she could not accept such a ring.

The section director had felt dejected. He said, "Jiali, I just thought this would be nice. I didn't mean anything else by it."

"I know," said Jiali.

He had taken the ring out and placed it on her finger. Jiali slid it off, smiling. He jammed it on again, and she simply repeated her earlier action. Upset, he had sat down, ashen-faced and speechless. Jiali felt a pang of sorrow as she watched him; but this gift could not be accepted, for it was a ring. To buy a ring required a great deal of money, which was simply something Jiali could not accept.

After a long while, he had spoken, "Jiali, my love for you is true. I can't give you anything else. This is all I have…. I don't know how to be good to you."

In the end Jiali had accepted the ring. Ever since that time, he never mentioned gifts again. But now and then, he would still give her some clothing, for Jiali truly paid too little attention to her appearance. She had always worn very plain clothes. One time, he could not help himself and said, "Jiali, you're actually very beautiful."

"Actually?" Jiali chuckled.

"Well, you only need to dress up a little bit."

Jiali became silent. This was her sore spot. Who in the world did not like to dress up? Who was born to be against pretty clothing? Looking at those beautifully dressed women…. No, she did not want to look at them. She despised them, hated them. After all, it was still *money*.

A few days later, he had gone to a department store and selected a few pieces of clothing for her. Afraid of being turned down again, he had sighed before he said, "Please let's not fight this time. Just take these." Reluctantly, Jiali did. She did not really like these clothes. They were not in style and were rather gaudy…. Suddenly casting doubt on the price of the clothing, she felt an unsettling nervousness. In the end, unable to hold back her doubts any longer, she had gone to the department store. What she found out really saddened her — the clothes she had received were the cheapest ones in the department store. He loathed spending money — only *once* giving her clothes, while she had slept with him for half a year. Needless to say, he was stingy and miserly when it came to money.

Jiali had taken out the ring, pondering whether she should take it to a jeweler to get an estimate, but sneered and decided against the idea. What for? It was not really the money. He did not love her. That was it. If he had shelled out some money on her, he still had got more than his fair share out of the deal. Even prostitutes cost money. She figured, during the six months they were together, the total amount of money he had spent on her was not even enough to pay for three visits to a prostitute. Three? How many times had she slept with him? Jiali cried. She was worth less than a prostitute.

She could not forget the single time she had mentioned marriage to him. Seeming distressed, he had smiled faintly, gently stroked her hair, and then said firmly that he could not divorce his wife, because a divorce would mean the end of his career. Finally, he had added softly that she was a good girl, and he knew she would understand and that, even if his wife was totally worthless, still....

Jiali had wiped her tears as swiftly as she possibly could, while more streamed out from her eyes. Grief overcame her. No, no one would ever love him as she did, and she loved him as she loved her own life. But all he wanted was to sleep with her.

On the day she was to depart, they had slept together again. It was still early by the time they had arrived at the train station. He stored her luggage in a locker, and then they had wandered around by the train station until they finally arrived at a small hotel. Jiali would never forget that dirty little hotel. Her heart had sunk as they trudged up the shaky staircase, full of spider webs and filth. She wondered how she had ended up loving a man like this, no romance, only sex. The room had been painfully empty: only a shabby bed, the sheets baring the splotchy stains from the couples that had slept there previously.

Jiali had wanted to talk about something else, but he looked at his watch and grinned.

"Come on, there's still time."

Jiali had clasped him in her arms and swiftly stripped the clothes off him, almost as if in desperation. Outside the grimy window, it was spring. Jiali's eyes fell on a delicately blooming oleander. There, in such a desolate environment, flowers survived. Who would ever expect it!

When they had finished, with a sigh of a great relief and delight, he had said, "Wow, it's been a long time since I've had such great sex." Feeling embarrassed by his own words, he pretended he needed to wipe his glasses. He slid them off his face, blew some dust off, and then pushed them back up his nose without wiping them. A strange feeling suddenly seized Jiali, distancing her from him. She felt as if she never had never known this man, and she never wanted to see him again; even a feeling of disgust for the city began to seep in. She had lived here for only half a year, and she had already been tarnished and soiled.

He had looked at Jiali, holding her face in his hands. During that long moment, he seemed overcome by true feeling. He was silent for what seemed like an eternity, eyes looking pure and melancholic, his glasses reflecting the sunlight from the westerly window. He had said, "Jiali, are we never going to see each other again?"

Jiali shook her head.

"I will find you," he had said.

Jiali had listened to these words he enunciated one by one from between his teeth, as if they came from a different world. He had suddenly embraced her, biting her ear, her hair, her neck, her fingers, and her clothes…. In that one instant, Jiali was suddenly overcome with confusion. She felt genuine love between them, that they were capable of it. He could be tender when his needs were satisfied. Now she would rather believe that she had been wrong. She had not understood men before; she had been too closed-minded. It had been *her* fault. Men were the strangest kind of animals on earth. He was bestial and ferocious, he was not good at expressing himself…, nevertheless he loved her.

Appearing to have remembered something of utmost importance, he then quickly produced three hundred yuan from his pocket, stuffed it into Jiali's hand, and said, "Take it. Buy something for yourself."

As if somebody had just woken her up, eyes wide open and speechless, Jiali could not believe what she had just heard. She had never expected *this* to happen. He was *paying* her, for having just slept with him! Slowly, she had started sobbing.

Not understanding what he had done wrong, and panic-stricken, he had blurted out incoherently, "The money… Jiali, please take it. I know you can use it. As soon as you get back to school, you will forget about me."

His voice had softened, faded and humbled as he said, "I'm very sorry… this money is nothing," with a quaver in his voice."

Jiali had jumped out of the bed abruptly, hands covering her ears, and let out a wail so sharp it pierced the whole neighborhood around the train station.

2

Life had not been bad for Jiali over the last ten years. She found a job in the same city she had gone to university in. She had changed jobs many times, until she and her partner had jointly opened a law firm four years ago. Later, her partner withdrew, so she took over the entire firm. The last two years, the firm had witnessed great progress. She was able to hire several staff members, rent office space in the golden downtown area, and drive a black *Audi* to and from her villa in the countryside....

Jiali did not really know why she was living a life like this... extravagantly and superfluously. Yes, she had money, and could afford it. But many other rich people who also could, instead chose to live simply and hold back from spending too much. Not Jiali. She indulged herself just for the sake of indulgence. There were even times when she enjoyed a fine meal at the penthouse of a five-star hotel, rotating hundreds of feet above the bustling metropolis; eating quietly, squandering six hundred or seven hundred yuan on a lunch, where it did not matter if anyone knew her.

Yet Jiali was not happy. She found herself wondering, why was it that money became totally meaningless when it fell into her hands? Had she not been living for just this all these years? Contrary to what she had expected, she felt bored and purposeless. Deep down she was still a simple and honest child. She had been well-disciplined in her younger years. She frequently talked of how she used to be poor, and nobody looked down upon her — but that she had once been very poor was an undeniable fact. One night, after she got back to her villa, it suddenly dawned on her that, in her thirty years of life, she had dated a few guys but they had all left her, gone. She remembered her college years, remembered that girl named Xu Jiali, whose eyes often shone, with her head full of fantasies.

What happened to those bizarre and incomprehensible fantasies? They had disappeared without a trace, not a single one remained. All of a sudden, Jiali felt as though her soul had escaped from the confines of her flesh. She fought the urge to cry. She plopped herself down on the sofa, then slid down and crawled onto the floor, painfully curling herself into a ball.

One day, at noon, Jiali got a phone call. She picked up the receiver and heard a voice on the other end.

"Hello."

She knew immediately who it was. Even though it had been ten years, even if he had died and been burned to ashes, she would still recognize his voice. She only wondered how he had got her phone number. Over all those years, if she was to name one thing she was proud of, it had to be the fact that she had successfully made a clean break from him. She had already turned a new page.

In the first few years, it had been hard. She would often think of him: deep in the night she would abruptly sit up in her bed; on her way to work; at the entry to a small alley early in the morning; at a noisy and crowded bus stop; or next to a shoe-repair stand on the street curb at dusk.... Tears would stream down her cheeks. Many people would see her cry, but they never knew why she cried and whom she cried for. She had never called him.

One year, during Spring Festival, he had called her at her parents' home. Jiali remembered she had given him her parent's phone number. He had said "Hello," briefly talked about how he was doing, and then out of blue, he had sighed and said, "Jiali, I miss you."

Filled with sorrow as well as annoyance, she had been unable to utter a word. Her parents were standing right by her, watching, baffled. So she had simply hung up. Later, she asked her parents not to give anyone her contact information. Perhaps they had forgotten, for he had still called her once or twice a year, always managing to find her, with that sorrowful tone of his.... Until Jiali had decided it was time to change her phone.

The last time they had talked was six years ago. She had blatantly lied, saying she was married. Silence. After a long while, he had said, "How are you doing?"

"I'm doing well," said Jiali.

After that, he had nothing else to say, and never called again.

Jiali decided this time to see section director Zhang, since he was already in town. Over the phone he said he was here on business, and that he had never been able to forget her and thought of her often over all those lonely years.

It had taken him a lot of courage to make the phone call, he said. In fact, he traveled to this city often. Whenever he was on the street, he had always harbored hopes of running into her, or hearing a voice calling him, or to getting a tap on his back from behind. Then, abruptly, he said, "Jiali, have you changed much?"

Jiali lowered her head, thought about it, and then murmured, "I'm old."

"So am I."

At this, the pen in Jiali's hand froze in midair. She did believe that he had become old. How cruel she was. They were both old now. She had given him the best time of her life, her youth, yet she did not even seem to remember or care anymore. Her heart softened and she said, "I am divorced now." Again she lied.

She heard a kind of melancholic sigh from the other end. Soon, they decided it was not convenient to talk over the phone. They would meet in the evening.

There were still four to five hours before they were to meet. Jiali thought she would have enough time to go to the hair salon to have her hair done, or perhaps go to a nice boutique to select a few items of new clothing, and then go home to rest a bit. She figured it would be inevitable that they would sleep together that night. For one thing, they had not seen each other for ten years, for another, she was "divorced." No matter what, sleeping together was a must, or it would not seem right.

What happened subsequently was purely coincidental, all because she walked by a secondhand shop. She opened the door gingerly and walked in, blushing. The owner was a rather plump woman. It was obvious that this was the first time she had ever seen such a stylish woman in her store, for she started humbly following Jiali around. From some of the old baskets, Jiali selected a few out-of-fashion college blouses, a pair of heavy, bulky and worn shoes, and a loose black sweater. She tried them on in front of a mirror and smiled satisfactorily.

Now she knew exactly what she was going to do. She was going to masquerade as someone else, as Jiali of ten years ago: dismal, self-abased and poor. She would become quiet, gray and dusty-looking again. No one else in the world would remember her Cinderella period, that time of shame, and the sensation of the pain that only those who had been gnawed by such a bug could have known: subtle, yet embarrassing. That's right, no one, not even her parents or her brother remembered those days anymore, except herself, because that was all she had.

She was overcome by a feeling of warmth and tenderness; she began trembling at this strange sensation. She sprang into action with all her heart. She discovered for the first time that in the thirty years nothing excited her as much as this plan. As her car zipped home along the country road, she felt the refreshing wind on her face and relished the spring leaves, the new green wheat plants, and the golden yellow mustard flowers. How long had it been since she had last noticed these colors of life? Now she saw all of them as she sped by, smiling and sighing.

Jiali spent the whole afternoon to touch up until she was finally satisfied. She stood in front of the mirror, and contemplated her new self — it was perfect. The woman in the mirror looked like someone in her thirties. She wore a pair of thick glasses (the ones she wore ten years ago, which she had packed away), her eyes looked hesitant and expressionless, and her face was yellowish and dry. When she managed a smile, wrinkles crawled around her eyes. But her clothes were clean and neat. You could clearly see that she had carefully matched them, but it was also obvious these were the kind you could pick up from street vendors. You could infer that she must be meeting someone important, because she had put on some lipstick as if for the first time: hesitant, uncertain, and repeatedly, until the color took on a very unsettling shade.

All in all, she became a woman you could find by the dozens on the street: she was mediocre, so-so looking, and by all accounts she looked humble and of lowly stock. She... she was poor.

Poor again! Jiali felt a shiver jangle her spine. Who knew the pain of a poor person? Those endless dark days had depressed and aggravated her so much that thinking about them now made her eyes wet. Now, looking at herself in the mirror, she truly believed one thing — that she had changed back. Time itself had just turned back ten years — ten years of her striving and struggling had just all vanished into the void. The glamorous Xu Jiali of three or two hours ago had just morphed into a dream.

Suddenly, sadness seized her again. She leaned against the wall, staggered into the living-room, and slumped down on the sofa. From there, she scanned the huge room and everything in it: beautiful light fixtures, elegant bar, huge projection TV, glass staircase... and then her eyes moved toward the green lawn outside her huge bay windows: neighbors' children and a dog, a rolling ball, and a ray of sunlight chasing them.

She gazed at all these longingly, as if one day she might lose them. These belonged to her, and she must always in her heart remember them.

Jiali stepped out of her villa, looking back at each heavy step. She drove her car to an underground parking lot downtown, and by the time she came out of it, it was already dusk. The sun was setting, announcing the rush hour. Many people were scampering on the streets like fallen leaves dancing across the ground. Jiali, standing on the curbside, felt lost for a moment in the midst of the huge crowd.

At that moment, she saw a man walking from across the street toward her. It was Li Mingliang, owner of a stock brokerage company. Two years earlier, he had had some brief interactions with Jiali because of a lawsuit. Jiali helped him win the case. They had seen each other a couple of times afterwards. He appeared to have an attraction to her, because he would call occasionally just to say hello. Not long ago, he invited her out for afternoon tea. There was an air of ambiguity between them, even when all they talked about was work.

Jiali had not expected that she would run into someone she knew on her first outing in disguise. Now, he was walking toward her, could almost see her.... Jiali's hair was standing on end. Her first thought was to turn around and run. She wanted to avoid all people, known or unknown.... Then, she heard him say "Huh?" No sooner had she lifted her head, he was already standing in front of her.

She stopped breathing. They glanced at each other with mutual looks of puzzlement. But, he smiled dismissively and said, "Sorry, I thought you were someone else."

Yes, someone else. Quivering, Jiali clutched the lamppost next to her for support. The man had gone. Now, she realized that nobody would ever recognize her again, neither her friends nor relatives.... One of these days, they would all abandon her.

Jiali wept. Now she could not wait to see the one person, the only person who would recognize her, even if she were old and ugly, even if she wore ragged clothes, or had become a beggar.... He was the only person who would believe in her: as long as she stood in front of him, whether she spoke or not, he would know she is who she is.

Hesitantly, she set out to take a bus (really, she had even forgotten she could take a taxi). On the way to the bus station, she walked like a thief: head lowered, and cautiously watching the pedestrians around her. Everyone seemed to be in a hurry, walking with a cold look in their eyes. Jiali began to contemplate the world around her with a different set of eyes for the first time: those men in suits and those young women with heavy makeup who had just come out of their office buildings.... Ordinarily, they would have exchanged looks at each other, some scale in their heads weighing each other's looks, status, and salary... but not today. Today, no matter how she looked at them, they refused to look back.

Jiali suddenly felt intimidated by her surroundings. She withdrew to a corner, far away from the crowds. These people despised her, despised all poor people. An indescribable envy and hatred enveloped her. What was this? Just what is it that gives these people such rights? These little employees of those big companies, standing under a bus-stop sign, having such self-centered and self-assured airs about themselves, which made her envious. She sneaked glances at them now and then from the corners of her eyes. Even at that moment, she still could not get over another feeling, that in reality she was superior to all these people put together. She spit at them in her mind: "Who do you think you are? Your bosses kiss my ass!"

The bus arrived. She squeezed herself into the milling crowd and was pushed up into the bus with her feet just brushing above the ground. The air in the bus reeked of rancid sweat, a smell once so familiar to Jiali. Overwhelmed by a feeling of nausea, she freed one of her hands to hurriedly cover her mouth. Hordes of people, countless faces: yellow, nervous, and distorted.... Somehow, Jiali felt a natural affinity to them. She had once been part of them. But now, she had distanced herself from them. Only she knew how these years of profligate lifestyle had betrayed her roots and her people.

Leaning forward, one of her hands traveled over the multitude of heads until it caught a circular handle. Her face was beet red with excitement. The bus conductor was announcing repeatedly, "If you just got on, please buy a ticket. Next stop, An Hua Li. Please buy your ticket." Jiali squeezed her body deeper into the crowd, and came upon a mental conclusion. Today, she would be a freeloader.

Yes, she was going to play a freeloader today. One yuan was nothing to her. But to a poor person, it meant a bowl of pork wonton soup, three *shaobing* buns, or a haircut; a couple of times of freeloading, and you would have saved enough to buy a pair of tennis shoes, or some trendy T-shirts and shorts.... To her, that was a whole new lifestyle.

Jiali had never done this before. She buried herself in the crowd, her ears vigilant, listening to anything, any movement around her; her back first arched, and then straightening. She now stood tall, and looked out through the windows of the bus as if nothing had happened. The bus was moving along jerkily, and then it took an abrupt turn. In that sudden thrilling moment, she heard her own sharp intake of breath, and wondered where this bus was going take her....

The bus screeched to a halt. Jiali tried to move out with some other passengers. The conductor was checking tickets, and Jiali suddenly felt icy nervousness balling up in her stomach. She looked at the front door, and then the rear door, and then at the front door again.... During the brief moment that the conductor had turned his head to the front door, she dashed off through the rear exit before even realizing herself what she was doing. She pushed aside the crowd, hopped off the bus like a rabbit, and then ran like crazy through the alley. Many people stopped to look at her in astonishment, but Jiali did not care. She knew her darkness had fallen.

3

By the time Jiali finally reached the hotel where the section director was staying, she was already late by more than an hour. A hotel attendant in a gray uniform was standing at the door. He leaned forward slightly, one hand behind his back, as the other opened the taxi door for a customer who was about to leave the hotel. For whatever reason, Jiali caught a glimpse of him, and he glanced back. She then gave him a friendly smile, and was about to walk in, before he called and stopped her.

The handsome young man looked in his twenties. He took a good look at Jiali, his young face giving away restrained suspicion, and then he asked where she was going. Jiali was stupefied by the question and instantly blushed. Oh, this was not a place for *her*! But she was not going to let this young man stop her from going inside. So she kept on going. The young man suddenly blocked her with his arm, and asked in a calm and cold tone of voice, "May I ask whom you are looking for?" This was truly irritating. Jiali raised her eyebrows, took a long stare at the young man and said, "And just what are you thinking?"

He lowered his eyes, with both hands down, and replied politely, "I don't know."

"Well then, why did you ask?" Jiali raised her voice a good octave, which immediately drew many people's attention from the lobby. A man who looked like the manager at the lobby rushed over and asked what was going on.

Jiali burst into tears. What had happened today? What had become of her? The manager and the attendant whispered to each other for a moment, and then the manager said to Jiali with a big smile, "Sorry for the misunderstanding...."

"Misunderstanding?" Jiali exploded, "You shameless little suck-ups," and pointing to the other customers in the lobby, shouted, "Why don't you misunderstand them? Huh? Look at yourselves in your own piss. Who do you think you all are? I'll sue you, you sons of bitches. You just wait. I'm an attorney...." She suddenly bit back her harsh words. What was she talking about? Oh god, she, an *attorney*?

Someone in the crowd started laughing. It was only then that Jiali noticed there were some people around her: janitors, receptionists, along with some customers in suits.... They were looking at her with strange looks on their faces, as though waiting to see what other nonsense she would conjure up now. Two tough-looking security guards stood on both sides of Jiali. They seemed to have run out of patience, signaling the manager with their eyes, waiting for him to give them the go-ahead to arrest the madwoman.

Jiali began to realize that she had gotten herself into big trouble, and this was really not the right time for her to be in a sticky situation. She had come today to meet her old lover, an important mission to accomplish…. Choking, she swallowed her anger, and blurted out the name of the director and his room number.

Like a shadow, Jiali wobbled toward the elevator. Right before the door was about to close, she turned back and gave the crowd a long acrimonious glare, before leaning her head against the ice-cold elevator wall. She hated these people. As she closed her eyes, a stream of clear tears fell through her lashes, down the sides of her nose, all the way to her mouth. Now it became clear to her that she hated this world, and she hated all the people in it.

The director had become old. From the moment he opened the door, smiling at her, Jiali had felt her own disappointment. She should have known. She had envisioned him many times as a gray-haired old man with a cane and a hunched back. In reality, he was far from being that pathetic. Instead, he seemed to just look his age. As a forty-six-year-old man, his facial skin loose, he had sagging bags under eyes, and he had put on some weight. How unfair, it had only been ten years, and look at this creature! What had happened to the romantic and handsome young man?

He was wearing a navy blue suit. Standing by the door, with his hand grasping the doorknob, he gazed at Jiali with such earnestness that it seemed that he was trying to compensate for the long and lonely ten years apart. He exhaled and murmured her name.

"Jiali."

Jiali felt a bit embarrassed. She slipped inside the room, and they sat down face to face. For a long time, they were both unable to talk, unable to even look at each other. Ten years... all had been destroyed: their looks, their love, and their life. For a brief moment, Jiali felt as if she was hallucinating. It couldn't have been ten years! How did she live those ten years? She shook her head, for she could not seem to remember anything.

He extended an inviting hand across the table, and Jiali grabbed it appreciatively. In response, he tugged her hand earnestly, and Jiali's head drooped onto his wrist, and without thinking, she let her body slide around the table, as she knelt in front of him.

He plunged his hands in her hair, stroking it while asking, "Jiali how have you been all these years?"

Jiali felt a lump in her throat. She was about to cry.

He bent over, put his face against Jiali's hair, slid down from the chair also and then embraced Jiali with all his might.

Jiali buried her head in his chest. Just then, she caught a whiff of his odor. It came out from his V-neck wool sweater, from within his body, his limbs, his chest and his nose. This was what people called, "an old man's odor."

He was only forty-six years old. Had the odor not come a bit too early? Jiali frowned, and felt a little nauseated. She quickly glanced at him, thinking she would not be able to bear sleeping with him today.

Then Jiali began to talk. This was the whole reason why she was here today. Taking two deep calming breaths, she told him these past ten years had not been easy. Her tone of voice was placid and sorrowful, and she spoke as if she were recounting something from long long ago, her attitude resigned.

She told him that ten years ago she had been assigned a job at the legal department of a state-owned enterprise. Her husband was a union leader at the same company. At that time, all the state-owned enterprises were already suffering from low benefits. The two of them decided he would quit his current job to start an ornamental horticulture business of their own. Well, he did not make any money, but instead got himself involved with many women, and she divorced him soon afterwards. Two years ago, her factory had gone bankrupt. So now she was an unemployed citizen, in other words, she was a *"xia gang nü gong,"* or a woman worker who had been laid off.

Upon the words *"xia gang nu gong,"* Jiali paused. She pressed her chest, trying to suppress the lust creeping up on her, until she was on the verge of losing control of herself.

While she was talking, the section director would interrupt to ask after certain details. Jiali had plenty of these for him. With the old accustomed expressionless and dull look on her face, she kept on telling her made-up old stories. Occasionally she would shoot a straight glance at him, unblinking, or sometimes she blinked.

The director sat on the carpet against the bed, hands on his chin, deep in thought. He was listening seriously.

"Jiali."

Jiali replied by lifting her head to look at him.

He hesitated for a moment, but asked anyway, "What kind of man was he?"

Jiali tried to figure out what he really wanted to know: he probably did not want to linger on the issue for too long; two men who had extramarital affairs, two different outcomes. He probably did not want to put himself in an awkward position. It just so happened that she had no interest in "Jiali's divorce." So, she shook her head, signaling that she was not willing to talk about her ex-husband, and went on talking about her own impoverished life.

Jiali seemed to be interested only in that topic. Upon touching the word "poverty," her body quivered, her eyes glowed, and her breath quickened, so much so that she had to stop to catch her breath and to cough loudly. She said that she had worked as a private tutor and as a legal counselor at a private company, but she had been fired and, at her most difficult time, she had not even had enough money to take the bus. Her remaining thirty cents not even being enough for the bus, she had had to turn to a friend for help…. She had thought after four years of hard life at college things should become easier, but who would ever have thought they could get worse?

She took a deep breath, and could not bring herself to go on any longer. She depicted such a pathetic picture of herself that it had the effect of actually hurting herself. The director went to hug her, mumbling for what seemed to be eternity, but without being able to come up with any proper words to console her. It was only after a long time that he finally said, "Jiali, how did this happen? — how did this happen?" Jiali gazed at this face until it showed itself fully in her eyes…. She threw herself on his shoulder, and cried the most heart-wrenching sobs of the last thirty years.

He took her downstairs into a small restaurant. He did not say much during the meal. Instead, he kept on putting food onto her plate, saying, "This is liver. Eat more of it. It's very good for you."

Jiali felt overwhelmed with gratitude. There could not be one single person in this world who could possibly be kinder to her than he was. He respected her, and he loved her. In an instant, she even felt she was in love again. She was ready to put the past ten years behind her. There never had been any real reason for her to hate him. So, he had spent some money on her. But have you ever heard of any man not spending any money on women? It was only natural. She should not have minded such petty things. In the old days, she had simply been too poor to face anything related to money. The three hundred yuan he had stuffed in her pocket at that tiny hotel remained intact. That became a souvenir of her past, the money she earned with her "blood and flesh."

After a couple of drinks they went back to the hotel room. Jiali felt a little drunk. So she swiftly took off her sweater, lay on the bed, and stared at him longingly. She thought he would rush to her, but no. Instead, he sank into a chair by the window, one leg propped on the other, as he smoked.

He seemed to be thinking, his face pinkish. Suddenly, he lifted his head and looked at Jiali. Jiali knew those dark eyes of his held something that was not quite right. After a while, he extinguished his cigarette, walked over by the bed and sat down right next to her. He started talking about some unrelated things at first, and then, nonchalantly, asked, "Jiali, what did you live on these years?"

Jiali had not anticipated that question, so she thought for moment and then said with a smile, "What else? Working all kinds of jobs, help from friends, and sometimes taking small loans."

He asked smilingly, "Help from friends? Male or female friends?"

Jiali abruptly sat up from the bed, looked at him seriously for a long time, and then laughed and said, "Male friends, of course."

He laughed along, meaning he did not care, and then asked from between his teeth, "Many?"

Even if Jiali would have had the best disposition, this pushed her over the edge. She jumped out of the bed, threw her clothes back on, and was walking out the door. He stopped her nervously, clutching her body tightly with his arms, and said, "Jiali, let me explain."

Jiali pushed him away, stumbled backwards a few steps to lean against the desk. There was no more room for grief in her heart. How many times had she cried today? How many times had she been disappointed? How many times had she been humiliated? It was all over now.

She called out his name, and told him, "Don't worry. I don't have any venereal disease. I just don't have any medical certification, although you don't have to believe me."

He sat at the end of the bed, thoroughly distressed. Nevertheless, he wiped his forehead and said, "Jiali, you didn't understand. I was just joking."

Jiali looked down at this man, and felt like spitting at him. He was not a bad man. He was just filthy, cowardly, and full of nonsense. She asked, "Do you have… those diseases?"

He looked at her, shocked, and slowly shook his head. So now the same fact emerged in both of their minds, but neither would state it — that all these years she had been living as a prostitute, and tonight she was selling herself to him.

Jiali turned around and headed to the bathroom, slamming the door behind her. The decision she had made to play prostitute had come so suddenly that it made her a little dizzy. She gazed at herself in the mirror and was deeply disappointed by what she saw. She was getting old. She had never considered herself pretty. But, with these old peasants' clothes, she looked hopeless. Ten years ago he had fallen for her because she was young — and now? It was only then that she recalled when they first laid eyes upon each other in the doorway, and now she could tell that he was disappointed no matter how hard he had tried to conceal it.

Jiali, who had been leaning against a desk, now pulled herself up to sit on it. Things were beginning to make sense now. She recalled that, as she was giving her account of her miserable past, his demeanor had become strangely shady. He had looked up, as if thinking about something. He must have been thinking about money — thinking about how much he needed to pay her, for it to be just right.

He must despise her and hate her. In those long and agonizing ten years, he must have pictured Xu Jiali as a glamorous young woman, with a great career and a happy family. It was not entirely beyond imagination that he had come to see her because he still believed in their old love affair. But most likely, he had come because he believed he could draw some pleasure out of their meeting. How many men visited women because the latter were broke and desperate? He had probably been hoping to take a walk with her in a park, to have a little tea in a tearoom, to chitchat and, if he was lucky, to sleep with her. But the reality of the day had crushed him. She had crushed his long-held dreams of ten years. He must have been disgusted by the vulgar attitude with which she had spoken; he must have felt embarrassed for her, and threatened by her: she had threatened him that he had to pay her.

It was only after a long time that Jiali came back into the room, so they chatted a little longer. Now the toughest thing facing them was probably the word *money*. Up until now, the word had never been brought to the table, even though its presence between them was ubiquitous: it had concealed itself when the two of them talked, but it now spoke when they were silent.... It barely seemed to be there, but it was everywhere; so thick in the air you could almost touch it.

For one moment, Jiali felt sorry for him, thinking she should just leave, go home, have a good sleep, and the next day she could be back in her nice dress suits and be a lawyer again. Oh, just let this nightmare end! Just pretend that nothing had happened. She must have gone crazy today! Why had she felt that she had to put on such a great masquerade, watching people fall into her trap, exposing their ugly nature, and, embarrassing herself amongst them? What was the use of letting the dark side of human nature be exposed?

The section director cleared his throat and began to talk. His lips shuddered before he spoke — even after thinking long and hard, it still seemed very difficult for him to let out what was on the tip of his tongue. He told her honestly that he had not brought much money with him, and after staying in town the last few days, he had already spent most of what he had brought, so there was not much left.

Jiali looked at him, and asked softly, "How much do you have left?"

He frowned, hardly concealing his surprise, and asked, "How much do you want?"

"What do you think?"

"I don't know."

"Have you been to a brothel before?"

He shook his head.

Jiali sneered and said, "You are a good man!"

He gave her a cold look and said, "I don't visit prostitutes."

Jiali said, "Right. You have to pay for a prostitute. But you don't like to spend money."

He exploded before she could finish, thrusting his face up against her, blue with anger. He glared into her face for a long time and said, "But I did spend money on you. Don't forget that." Then, lifting his hands in the air, he said, "I don't owe you anything."

Jiali did not say anything. She quietly undressed herself and got under the covers. It was now deep into the night. Noises from outside the windows were subsiding. Occasionally, there was the shouting of street vendors selling wonton soup, and gradually those dimly discernable sounds faded as well.

At midnight, he also crawled under the covers. In the darkness, Jiali's eyes were wide open, but her thoughts were murky. She was exhausted, and soon closed her eyes again. He left early in next morning. Jiali had not slept all night, but she pretended she was asleep when he was leaving. The moment he had slammed the door behind him, Jiali got up to see if he had left any money. He had not. Jiali did not try to chase him down. He must have deemed this had been a visit unworthy of his money, or had it only been the most humiliating experience of his life?

Now, Jiali was wandering through the streets, as daylight was creeping over the tops of the buildings, and pedestrians were beginning to fill up the streets. A gust of wind forced her to hold the tattered clothes tightly around her body, shivering like a stray, homeless dog. She was walking up an overpass when she saw a beggar in his torn coat, crouching by the railing, waiting for people to walk by. He looked at Jiali coldly, scrunched his nose, uninterested, then lowered his head and went back into his own world.

Jiali leaned heavily against the railing of the overpass, as more people and cars started scurrying about below; she looked at them in a trance, her body sinking down, just looking at it all.

(Translated by Zhang Xiaorong)

Paperclips

Zhang Chu

Zhang Chu. Born in 1974, he now works for the Luannan County Office of the State Administration of Taxation in Tangshan, Hebei Province.

Since 2001, Zhang Chu has published novellas and short stories totaling 300,000 Chinese characters, including in periodicals such as *People's Literature*, *Harvest*, *Dangdai*, *Shanghai Literature*, *Youth Literature*, and *Chinese Writers*. Of these stories, his "Paperclips," "Long Hair," "Story about Yingtao," "Hive," "A Woman Running in a Nightgown" and "Let's Go See Li Hongqi" were included in over 20 journals and anthologies, including *Selected Stories, Pioneer Writing, 21st Century Chinese Literature Series*, and in the yearbooks of *Selected Chinese Short Stories* and *Chinese Contemporary Literary List*. "Paperclips" won the 2003 Prize for the Top 10 Literary Works of Hebei Province, and the 10th Literature and Art Rejuvenation Prize of Hebei. "Long Hair" was awarded the 2003 Prize for Top 10 Literary Works of Hebei and the 2004 Short Story Prize sponsored by *People's Literature*. *Story about Yingtao* was conferred the Dahongying Literary Prize by *Chinese Writers*. Zhang Chu's novella and short-story collection, titled *Story about Yingtao*, was selected by the Chinese Writers' Association to become part of the 21st Century Literary Star Series. Hebei awarded him the 2nd "Ten Outstanding Young Writers Prize" of in 2005, and the 2007 "Youth Culture Contribution Prize."

Paperclips

1

The snow this winter seems to be going crazy. One after another, big bursts of fluff blast in almost hysterically, the next hardly before the previous flurry has ended. *"The snow ends up wrapping the earth / just as through a honeymoon night / as man enwraps woman through time."* Zhiguo remembers the poem from many years ago, as he reclines on a sofa in the hotel lobby. He is obviously a little surprised by verses popping into his mind from nowhere, so he chooses to tilt his head to peep again at that girl at the reception. Still talking into the handset, the girl has a face dotted with heavy eyebrows and large eyes. The zits on her forehead appear in a greasy motley under the parlor light. Zhiguo feels it is a mistake for the hotel to place her at the front reception. Moving endlessly like two wriggling leeches, "Her upper and lower lips touch each other 69 times a minute." It makes Zhiguo extremely uncomfortable. If he had a Browning pistol in his hand, he would prop her mouth open gently with the pistol to see if she has one tongue more than everyone else.

At his side, Daqing releases a snore in his sleep every now and then. The best qualification this guy has is that he can fall asleep as sound as a dead hog even if he is thrown into a dog hole. The strong stench of the instant-boiled mutton they just ate makes Zhiguo a bit sick, forcing him to stand up and go for a stroll out of the hotel. The plump snowflakes whirl into his eyes and drive him back inside. At that moment, his cell-phone starts to ring its musical jingle. The call is from Su Yan. He glimpses at the number displayed on the cell-phone and immediately turns it off. She has been frantically looking for him these days. Putting the phone back in his pocket, he says loudly to the receptionist, "Miss, I'll pay the bill now."

The girl puts down the handset in her hand somewhat reluctantly. Taking up the bill, she begins to punch on a calculator. She looks uglier when she frowns. It suddenly occurs to Zhiguo that he has never ever dealt with such an ugly girl before, as he asks, "How much are the service charges for those two girls?"

The girl at counter answers, "Fifty yuan for one and one hundred for two. We at reception are not responsible for the tips paid them."

"Would you like some chocolate?" Zhiguo pulls out a *Dove* chocolate bar and waves it in front of her.

Showing no reaction at all, the receptionist takes a look at him and says, "Uncle, pay the bill, please."

She calls him "uncle." Zhiguo asks, "Those two guests of mine, when will they finish?"

The girl replies listlessly, "How do I know? Both so big and fat, they don't seem to be quick gunslingers." The girl's reply shocks Zhiguo, as he had not expected her to say such things. All of a sudden, he begins to loathe her. The revulsion rises in him so fiercely that he doesn't even hear the special ring-tone on his cell-phone when it rings again.

"Mister, your phone is ringing," the girl says, "Your ring-tone's nice. It's Wang Fei's *You're Happy So I Am Too*." She then says with a sort of sadness, "Wang Fei is doing a solo concert at the Hung Hom Coliseum in Hong Kong next month. When will I ever be able to fly to Hong Kong to attend her concert?"

"You're happy so I am too?" It sounds like a summing up of the lovemaking of men and women. Are those two northeasterners and the two Sichuan girls happy? It's almost thirty minutes since they disappeared into their cubicles. He visualizes one of the northeasterners. Huge and robust, the young man trafficking in train rails, on his left arm has a tattoo of a lizard, and on his right arm is an image of the boxer Holyfield, who almost had his ear bitten off by another boxer.

"Let me sign the bill," Zhiguo says.

"We do not allow credit here."

"You must be new then. I am Li Zhiguo. Get your boss over here," Zhiguo says, "Go get your boss for me."

The counter girl moistens her lips with her tongue, "Our boss's kid is sick. He's at the hospital."

"Get your landlady here then."

"We have no landlady," the girl answered and started to punch the phone buttons.

Not pushing the issue further, Zhiguo pays the bill with cash. He wonders when those two northeasterners, the two fellows trafficking train rails in Russia, two guys from the cold northeast wearing necklaces around their necks and spitting f-words out of their mouths all the time, would finish with the two middle-aged yet still attractive Sichuan prostitutes. Heavyhearted, he glances at Daqing who is still sleeping as sound as a baby, and gives a light cough. Just at this juncture, a man and a woman walk into the hotel from outside. The man is quite young and the woman is not that old either. They take a glance at Zhiguo and their eyes look searchingly at the furnishings by the cashier counter. They then amble towards a sofa next to the one Daqing is sleeping in. When they brush past Zhiguo, he smells the soothing aroma of the woman's perfume. Zhiguo flashes a glance at the woman especially. Her perfume gives off the delicate fragrance of oranges. Zhang Xiuzhi uses this brand of perfume too. Before going to work every day, Zhang Xiuzhi, exhaustion written all over her face, would spray the orange-scented perfume onto her neck, hair, armpits, wrists and skirt hem as if in a fit of pique. Then she goes to work holding onto that obsolete handbag of hers on the bicycle. Through her many years of makeup and splashing perfume, Zhiguo feels that bit by bit she has dried up gradually like a fresh apple eroded by time.

2

On Zhiguo's way to the hotel, he felt as if Su Yan's calls were almost bursting his cell-phone. Zhiguo has been chastened into a patient temper with this hot-tempered woman. "A quick fire burns a pig head and a slow fire brews delicious pork." Zhiguo often lectures her that anxiety will spoil everything. While trying to educate her, Zhiguo always keeps his fingers moving. He always has in his pockets a number of silver-color paperclips. He often takes out his paperclips when listening to others talk. Once many years ago he saw a beautiful photo in a magazine. It showed miniatures that Louis Jude, a US artist, had made with paperclips. They included an hourglass, a woman's breast, a ballet dancer with stretched arms balancing on one leg and a trumpet. Admiring the works greatly, he had never experienced before such a high respect for people in the US. A lavish ideal inspired him that he could also bend and fold a lifeless paperclip into various shapes of artwork in a few seconds. He had never expected himself to become an artist like Louis Jude. Yet, he wished he could do it.

However, those cold, hard steel wires were so stiff once held in his hands. He was unable to bend them into the tiny likenesses he visualized in his mind, not even the simplest shapes of a rose or an abstract tiny house. Instead, the half-finished works between his fingers looked like nothing at all. In other words, even he himself could not figure out what they really resembled. Fortunately, after many repeated attempts, he has finally turned himself into an amateurish paperclip artist. At least now he can bend a paperclip into a shovel or a girl's silhouette in a few seconds.

Once when he was making love with Su Yan, his fingers folded a paperclip into a shovel, instead of caressing that fat, bulging woman, his eyes shut amidst her gasps. During the final burst-off, he grasped the glittering silver-colored shovel tightly in his palm without a sound. Su Yan crawled over him sobbing softly, muttering that she knew he no longer loved her. After she gave birth to a son, she had turned into a pile of trash in his eyes. "You always look so absentminded. Is it that you have other women?" Eventually she reached over to his hand and threw away that misshapen paperclip. "Is that girl who had an abortion still clinging onto you?"

Now at the hotel, with his fingers groping in his pocket as usual, his eyes keep glancing at the man and the woman until he made out their faces clearly. The woman looked very attractive. In other words, you can hardly find anything improper about her facial features. Her makeup is done nicely. She uses rose-pink lipstick. It is said that it has a very pleasant name — "Hot Kiss Leaving No Trace." It makes her lips look like a half-ripe but plump cherry, dreamy at a distance. She seats herself on a sofa, takes out a mirror and glosses her brows with an eyebrow pencil. Her slender legs and buttocks are wrapped in a clinging long woolen skirt that easily glues the eyes of the man by her side. With his eyes often wandering all over her body, the man says something to her now and then. The woman looks at the man's face and smiles at him from time to time, too. Zhiguo knows what type of words said by the man would move the woman most effectively during such a night. Then, the man walks toward the cashier until he stands almost shoulder to shoulder with Zhiguo at the counter. Zhiguo hears the man say, "Is there a room available?"

A john and a whore, Zhiguo tells himself, while continuing to finger his paperclips calmly. If his guess is correct, another sex deal will be struck. They must have agreed on the price already. "I am always more sober after drinking," thinks Zhiguo. "I haven't drunk too much. Why can I never get drunk?"

Zhiguo drank three bottles of *Wuliangye* liquor with the two northeastern customers. Through the years dealing with those who had grown up in colder regions, he has slowly cultivated a respect for them. They never wince or bargain about how much each must drink. It not only shows their inherent capacity for alcohol consumption, but also convinces Zhiguo that it was better not to play games with these guys when doing business. The best way is to be frank, hitting the nail on the head. Just take this train-rail business, for instance. They hadn't mentioned the price at all, even when they drank together, but Zhiguo is sure they will give a most reasonable price. Of course he has his own scheme for this deal. He feels his body shudder momentarily as his scheme shoots across his nearly paralyzed brain.

"Sorry, all our cubicles are full," the counter girl puts down the handset, "Please take a seat and wait a moment. We should have rooms available in just over ten minutes."

Being far from the downtown, quiet and safe, this hotel sits at a good location. Customers flock here for this advantage. Zhiguo hears the man sigh and say to the woman, "Shall we go to another place? This place is booming, you know. Damn, it's always so full."

It seems that the woman has known no other expression but a smile. The best trick these hookers have is to smile foolishly all the time like a Mona Lisa. Zhiguo's fingers keep busy, moving all the time. He has slender and fair fingers and his ring finger is longer than the middle one. No one would be able to tell that these are the hands of a steelworker. He cast tens of thousands of *Wolf* brand shovels in a state-owned plant with these hands, as well as caressed the breasts of nine women. Now he uses these hands to do his private business. Although his shovel factory has not been doing very well recently, he is sure he can handle this major contract successfully. The medicine costs for Lala have been a bottomless hole that he has had to keep feeding paper money into. What else can he do but pour paper money into that hole?

When Daqing wakes up yawning, he is at first a bit startled by the pair sitting next to him. Then he shouts at the top of his voice, "Miss! Gimme a pot of tea! F---, I'm dying of thirst! What? They've still not finished up yet?"

Zhiguo ignores him completely. He holds the paperclip in his hand. It becomes a woman's silhouette. Her nose sinks in a bit and her lips are half open as if uttering the most soothing words. But her chin looks a little abrupt so it resembles a stiff arc of a blade and the sheath of an opened knife.

Is this woman... Zhang Xiuzhi? Su Yan? Or that tight-mouthed counter girl?

None of them, thinks Zhiguo. It is his daughter, Lala, his pale, living-upon-medicine-all-day-long Lala, his daughter Lala suffering from mild depression and autism. Lala. Poor Lala. His 16-year-old Lala who loves *Dove* chocolate and *Green Arrow* chewing gum. With congenital heart disease, her left and right atriums' blood flows slower than normal, while her left and right ventricles often skip a beat. Lala. His only Lala. His own Lala. Lala.

3

Before the tea Daqing has called for arrives, steps ring out from upstairs. A woman is running down the stairs, crying desperately under people's startled stares. Her leather skirt is not zipped up so the white superfluous flesh at her waist glows greasily. "I've never seen such a kinky devil!" the woman's voice trembles, "What's wrong with being a whore? Isn't a whore a human, too?" She scuffles into her spongy shoes, pulls her vest down just in time, and then deftly wraps herself with an overcoat. Only then does she notice the curious looks. "I'm leaving now." She smoothes her disheveled hair and says to the counter girl, "When Mary comes down, tell her I left early. Tell her to watch out. What sons of bitches!"

She pushes open the door and runs out of the hotel. Then Zhiguo sees one of his two northeastern customers walking down the stairs. Red-faced, he waves to Zhiguo as soon as he spots him downstairs. He hands a cigarette to Daqing, who accepts it and asks dumbly, "What's wrong? What happened?"

"Nothing. I've never seen such a weakling before." The client puffs at the cigarette fiercely and then puts his mouth by Daqing's ear and says something. Daqing cracks an awkward chuckle and then looks at Zhiguo. He is in awe of this mild and experienced boss of his. He wonders if he should ask the boss whether they should find another girl for their client, since he's been their biggest supplier so far. Yet apparently the boss is a little annoyed by what has happened. Even if he did not hear what the client just whispered to Daqing, he still seems annoyed. But the boss generally laughs uncontrollably when he gets really angry. Daqing watches his boss put something shiny into his trouser pocket and grin at their client. "Let's get another one," Zhiguo pats the customer on his shoulder, "Don't you know that a watched pot never boils? Take it easy and you'll enjoy it even better. You don't need me to give you lessons, right? Ha-ha."

Now Zhiguo has to deal with the phone-addicted counter girl again. Obviously the girl harbors some resentment towards them, as if she has never encountered a customer who's scared away their girls. "We don't have any girls available now," she says, bending over an abacus and fingering its beads, "I'm really sorry. Why don't you check the other hotels?" Then she gestures toward the man and woman, "We've a room available now. Do you want it?"

Zhiguo's cell-phone rings again with the tone *You Are Happy So I Am Too*. Zhiguo only just discovered the song's name. The ring-tone was chosen by Su Yan. What trifles does she have? What does she have at all? He turns toward the client and says smiling, "Just a minute. Your sister-in-law's calling."

The northeasterner replies, "Forget it. I'm going back to my hotel now. It's so f-ing boring here. The girls in our northeast are much more exciting than yours here."

Zhiguo pats him on his shoulder and turns around to look at the man and the woman. They are now quietly strolling in his direction. Turning off his cell-phone, Zhiguo waves to the woman. "What is it?" the woman asks Zhiguo, surprised.

Zhiguo asks, "How much of a tip does this gentleman pay you?"

The woman says, "What did you say?"

Zhiguo says again, "How much does this gentleman offer?"

The man pulls the woman aside as her chest heaves fiercely. The man asks Zhiguo, sneering: "What did you say just now? Say it again if you've got the guts."

Zhiguo says reflectively, "I'd like to hire this lady.... So how much money did you offer? I could give you double the money, okay?"

The man smiles at Zhiguo, "Just what do you think we're doing? But okay, give me a thousand yuan. For a thousand yuan it's a deal."

Feeling he has never ever met such a shameless man, Zhiguo finds that the several bottles of *Wuliangye* liquor he had drunk earlier are now starting to work their power. Under the hotel lights, Zhiguo realizes that the man is not actually that young and his upper lip is quite short. In other words, a normal part of the strip between his nose and mouth is missing. This is why, when the man speaks, a kind of disdain seems to expand his thick lips endlessly outward, so it affects all the other symmetrical features on his face, making them appear abnormal too. His meaty lips seem to fill Zhiguo's view and his hunting-dog kind of cold aura plus the orangish perfume on the woman all mix together, and push Zhiguo to the edge of puking.

"Are you sick?" Daqing spits out at the man, "You... Are you mother-f---ing mad? For what would we pay you a thousand yuan?" Zhiguo pats Daqing on the head. Somehow he never can quite like this minion of his, who gets unruly after several shots of alcohol. If not for the fact that they had been coworkers in the steel plant for fifteen years, and the guy has an out-of-work wife and a long-paralyzed father, Zhiguo would have fired him long ago.

"That should be fine." Zhiguo pulls out a handful of cash from his pocket and offers the money to the man, "Count it." Then he turns to the woman, "Go with our friend now."

The woman's face twists under the light. Zhiguo has no idea that a woman's facial expression could become this dramatic. He repeats a little impatiently, "What? The price is not a problem. After you finish, I'll pay as much as you ask."

Just at that moment, the woman's hand hurls out. Zhiguo is stunned that her hand can slap his face so nimbly. While the dry pain burns faintly on his cheek, a pair of icy cold handcuffs clasps his wrists before he realizes what is happening. Daqing and the northeasterner, along with that counter girl burbling into her handset, all look on dumbstruck. They have never witnessed such a near-perfect action by such a man before. They even failed to see how the pair of handcuffs had been whipped out like in a magic show. The handcuffs, like a toy, lock Zhiguo's wrists together. Daqing sees a curved paperclip fall from Zhiguo's fingers. Showing no signs of fear, Zhiguo just quizzes the man, smiling, "I'll sue you for illegal detention. Your joke's too funny, isn't it?"

The woman is patting Zhiguo on his cheek. Her fingers give off that kind of orange-scented perfume. He hears her announce proudly, "We're not joking with you. We're police."

4

It turns out that the policeman and the policewoman had stopped their vehicle — not a police car — at the end of the alley next to the hotel. As they hustle Zhiguo into their car, Zhiguo struggles to shout to Daqing, "Take care of the guests!" Then he curls himself obediently into the backseat of the car, feeling the warm tiger-skin mat under his buttocks. The man drives the car and the woman sits next to him. The car smells sort of like burnt rubber, so Zhiguo cannot help coughing. He now turns more and more sober. He peeks and sees the woman lean over to whisper with the man. Suddenly Zhiguo realizes what rotten luck he has had today.

They are not driving a police vehicle, so that means they are not on-duty police officers. The intimate expressions on their faces revealed their shady relationship. If Zhiguo has not got it wrong, this male police and this so-called female police were just out on a date. From the moment they stepped into the hotel lobby, their expressions indicated they were not out on a mission. Instead, they had come out on a date like other sweethearts on this cold night. They had even tried to book a room in the hotel! Zhiguo smells the strong liquor in his own nostrils.

When the car reaches an abandoned railway yard in the city, the woman pushes open the car door and jumps out like a kangaroo. Zhiguo hears the man's gentle voice, "Take a taxi back. Do you have pocket money with you?"

The woman's face is clearly reflected in the car window. Zhiguo sees her smile at the man. She pulls out a handkerchief to wipe her lips gently. Is she trying to wipe off her lipstick? It is of a rosy pink hue. In Zhiguo's mind, all those women who love this rosy pink are stupid.

The man drives the car around through the streets, as if he is not too eager to get back to the police station. He puts on some music on the car cassette player. When the first notes of *Hothouse Girl* start up, Zhiguo is slightly startled, because he would not expect a policeman to like Cui Jian. Following that song, comes *False Roving Monk*. Then, *An Egg under the Red Flag*. On such a night, with snow flurrying about, being escorted on one's way by a policeman to a police station accompanied by such frenzied rock songs, Zhiguo can find no explanation but only absurdity. Thus, the policeman and a shovel factory boss who has just insulted a policewoman are conducting a seemingly endless trip amidst the noise of an electric guitar, bass drum and *suona* trumpet. Zhiguo realizes that the car has already just passed nearby a police station. Soon the signboard of another police station flashes through the bright headlights of the car. Zhiguo's head hurts more and more severely. He is at a loss as to what trick the policeman is playing with him. When the music tape gets stuck, Zhiguo can longer control himself but asks, "Which police station are you from?"

The man just turns around and smiles. Then he inserts another tape into the cassette player. It is a foreign melody this time. Zhiguo hears a woman's beautiful voice sounding as if heaven were flowing about in the car as in a church. "Do you like Enya?" the man asks, "You should enjoy Enya."

Zhiguo shakes his head.

"I know you," the man seems to be thinking aloud to himself, "Your name is Liu … Liu Zhiguo, isn't it? Your nickname is Thumb. Yes, it's Thumb."

Zhiguo nods, perplexed now. His wrists are starting to ache in the tight handcuffs. He has been trying to get hold of a paperclip in his pocket, a total of thirteen attempts, but though his fingers manage to touch the small exquisite paperclip he just cannot pull it out, hands trapped within icy cold shackles.

"I know you for sure," says the policeman, "You used to work in a steel plant and you're a poet. I've read your poems. Now you're a private entrepreneur, am I right?"

Zhiguo's head hurts again. The man continues, "I once even bought a collection of your poems in my high-school days. There was even a murky photo of you on the inside cover of the book. You look older now." He mumbles a bit sadly, "I would read a poem or two of yours before going to bed every night in those days. I couldn't fall asleep if I didn't." He has his face turned away, so Zhiguo could not see his expression. "Yet, if not for those poems only lunatics care to read, I would have damned been enrolled in a top university long ago!" He seems to be consulting Zhiguo now, "I wouldn't have to be making the rounds at these wee hours if I hadn't gone to that rotten police school. You think it's easy being a policeman?"

Zhiguo is no longer shocked by anything this policeman says or does. "Really?" he answers wearily, "Where are you taking me to?" Hearing no answer from the policeman, Zhiguo sighs disappointedly as his cell-phone rings sharply. It must be Lala this time. She calls at ten every night. She just cannot fall asleep if Zhiguo is not home.

"Can I answer a phone call?" Zhiguo asks.

"No," the policeman announces, "I don't like criminals answering phone calls."

Zhiguo falls silent. He finds the car has furtively returned to the deserted railway yard again. Built before liberation, this section of the railroad has no trains running through her anymore. When Zhiguo used to drive his own car here regularly, he would look at the railroad extending her rusty arms into the distance. He never understood why the local government had failed to tear it down.

What puzzles him even more now is that the policewoman has appeared again. She is standing by the roadside and waves in their direction. Then she gets into the car, and Zhiguo realizes only then that she has changed her clothes. That long woolen skirt clinging around her slender thighs has been replaced by a pair of slightly loose trousers. And her body is wrapped in a fluffy red down coat, making her appear rather bloated. Zhiguo hears the policeman ask her, "Is everything set?"

The woman answers, "Yep, let's go back to the station now."

Escorted by the duo, Zhiguo arrives at the Luxi Police Station. He gives a sigh of relief on seeing the sign of the police station.

The man and the woman drag him out of the car and push him into the interrogation room, which is fairly warm. Zhiguo asks, "May I make a call using my cell-phone?"

The man knits his brows and takes the cell-phone from Zhiguo's pocket. After holding it in his hand and glancing at it once or twice, he throws the phone on the cot beside him. The woman sits down on a chair, expressionless. Zhiguo finds that the woman in her down coat now appears much older than when she was wearing the wool dress. Her lips look a sort of cold dark red, and the sweetness in her eyes has gone too. On the contrary, the sharp, searching look in her eyes reminds one of an aged vulture. She looks more like a cop now.

The woman asks Zhiguo about his name, occupation, gender and nationality. Zhiguo starts to feel sleepy, listening to her simple, almost dreary questions. With no warning at all the liquor's powers begin their attack again. Zhiguo's eyes begin to throb painfully. He licks his dry lips and says, "My cell-phone is ringing. Shall I just answer it?"

The man cracks a vague smile. His meaty nose, like that of an executioner in cartoons, jitters when he smiles. "Are you still writing poems now?" he asks.

"Could I answer my cell-phone?" says Zhiguo.

"Your old poems are really good. I can still recite quite a few of them."

"Can I just answer the phone?" asks Zhiguo.

"*Let your tears fall on my toes / Let the blood of your ventricles / Flow onto my soul.* Ha-ha, great poems!" The man winks at the woman, "How come even poets can become so shameless!"

"Let me make a call with my phone, okay?"

The man and the woman look at each other, "You want to

contact a whore?" the man laughs, "It's too late. All the whores have been f-ing sold by now."

"Does Liu Qiang work here?"

The woman eyes Zhiguo hesitantly. Zhiguo tells her, "We were schoolmates at high school."

Then Zhiguo says once more, "Could I use my cell-phone just once?"

The expressions on the man's and woman's faces have changed. They apparently had not expected Zhiguo to have such a relationship with the chief of their station. The man said, "I could make the call for you. But as it's so late now, he's probably gone to bed already."

Hearing the man's voice pounding in his head again and again, Zhiguo feels his head about to explode. He cannot tell what the policeman is talking about, but just feels this tiny goose flesh creeping on his skin. His eyelids close gradually in the relatively warm air from the air-conditioner. His cell-phone bursts again agitating his sleepiness. The man's farfetched laughter and the woman's tender voice are stirred with another kind of empty, ambiguous sound. He finally hears the man saying, "It's easy to resolve this now. We'll just give him a nominal fine. We wouldn't have been this angry if he hadn't taken Xiao Xia for a prostitute! He even had the nerve to try to drag her off to entertain his whoremongers! Yes…. It was originally Xiao Zhang and Xiao Wang on duty today. But they had other things to do so they changed shifts with us. Who'd imagine we'd run into such a thing! Okay… okay. I know how to take care of it."

The man hangs up the phone and undoes Zhiguo's handcuffs, "Our Chief Liu says you're exempt from the fine. He urges you to go home right away and not to drink again." The policeman jeers, "He says he doesn't want you giving him any more trouble after getting drunk."

Zhiguo ignores them. He walks out of the police station with his cell-phone gripped in his hand. Then he holds onto a plane tree and starts to vomit. Finally he hears someone's voice as his cell-phone rings again. It is Su Yan's icy voice, "Your son is sick. He's been three days in the hospital already. He's got pneumonia. You'll not see him again if you don't come!"

Without replying, he turns off the phone. He has never got it cleared up whether that two-year-old boy named Yali is indeed his son. Once a popular prostitute, Su Yan was unbelievably slender and coquettish at the time. God knows why she should set her eyes on a forty-year-old, slightly impotent, small factory boss with not much cash in his pockets! What was it that made her fall in love with him? He understands Su Yan is waiting for Lala to die. She feels sure he would divorce Zhang Xiuzhi once Lala is gone.

He begins to call home. His fingers get busy again as he makes the call, holding the phone between his head and shoulder. Zhang Xiuzhi answers the phone and she doesn't show any surprise at his blurred, shaking voice, "You're with that woman again? What do you want? What do you really want?" Her breathing becomes more rapid as she grows more agitated, "If not for Lala. If not for Lala's sake...."

"... ..."

She sobs, "I talked to Doctor Su again today. He said, Lala... Lala...."

"... ..."

"Lala ... may not survive this winter. You've long expected her to die, I know it. You're such a brutal monster, an ungrateful wolf. I know. I know everything. What is there I do not know?"

"I don't have the strength to fight you," Zhiguo says, "I don't want to fight with you at all."

Zhang Xiuzhi falls silent for quite a while. He knows she is shedding tears again. Her tear pouches have become withered over the years, so even if she cries, there will not be the salty, wet liquid creeping along her nose to her lips any longer. Whenever he sees her sad face, it reminds him of her youthful complexion. He still remembers when they had settled in the countryside as urban youth, harvesting rice. Zhang Xiuzhi seemed to be a born expert at rice harvesting. She used to move by to his side quietly, her blue-veined bare feet showing below her rolled-up pants. She was so thin then, with her hair tied into two small pigtails. She would leave him far behind in a short time, then she'd straighten her back and laugh with a wheezing sound. Her bulging breasts would heave up and down.... In fact she looked very ugly when laughing. She never knew how ugly she was when she laughed. She has never known that he loved her unsightly appearance.

"I'm very tired," she lowers her voice. "I cannot hang on anymore," she sighs, "Telling you the truth, I can't hold on any longer."

Zhiguo says nothing. The paperclip held between his fingers is instantly bent into a girl's silhouette. He rubs her lips but she cannot speak. How he wishes she could say something. His eyes become moist from wishing so hard.

5

Zhiguo spots the woman at the mouth of the alley next to the police station. Wrapping herself in a wadded overcoat, she leans against the wall, smoking under the mottled streetlight. She seems to be waving to him, so he walks up hesitantly. While walking towards her, Zhiguo finds the woman's facial features varying with the changes in the streetlight. For a short time, Zhiguo feels as if he is walking toward many women. When he gets closer, he notices her small eyes and lips trembling in the cold air. He even smells her slight underarm odor. She nips off the cigarette and abruptly grasps Zhiguo's lower parts, "You're cold, right?"

Zhiguo makes love with the woman for a long time. He was tempted to take her to the two northeasterners, knowing how they preferred playing around together with a single woman, but he soon changes his mind. Before he took off his clothes, the woman had bent to roll up the bed-sheet and jam it under the sofa seat. He did not even make out much of her looks. She takes off his pants and socks and begins to kiss the ribs on his chest. "You're so thin," as her furred tongue stiffly glides down his belly. Then he begins to get aroused. The woman had not expected him to be so forceful. He holds her tightly from behind and enters her dry body almost fiercely. The woman seems bored. "I don't like this posture. Let's change to another one," she orders, "I hate doing it like dogs. I mean it!" Before he can respond, the woman throws him onto the bed like a judo master, and then sits on top of him. She looks like she is enjoying the action greatly. Her lips are purple. She resembles Su Yan so much, even in their postures of lovemaking. His hands start to move restlessly again. He grasps the bed-sheet. Where did she throw his clothes? Then his hand touches a roll of newspaper. As he unfolds the newspaper bit by bit, the woman's face flashes through those seemingly wriggling characters. Then he feels the woman turning into a flail, colorless figure in a shadow-puppet show. Her arms and supple thighs are pressed into pieces of skin by a truck, pieces of skin without blood, flesh or bone. Amidst the puppet's madder and madder movements and skillful groaning, Zhiguo reads the news in the newspaper.

English Army Special Forces Narrowly Miss
Bin Laden in Sudden Raid "A Heartbeat Too Late"

(London, England) – An English news report claimed that soldiers of a special unit of the English army missed Osama Bin Laden by "half a step" while searching a cave where Bin Laden was suspected to be hiding, during a surprise raid in the mountainous regions of southern Afghanistan.

The Sunday Post reports: Intense fighting erupted between a small airborne English special forces unit and Bin Laden's cohorts at a Taliban hideout in a cave in the mountainous area southeast of Kandahar. Four British soldiers were wounded.

Only when the battle was over and English troop questioned their captives, did they find out that Bin Laden had left the site a mere two hours before they arrived. British forces believe that Bin Laden escaped in a hurry, the moment he learned about the onset of the battle.

His cell-phone starts ringing as he turns over the page of the newspaper. The woman seems to wake up only now, "Are you in difficulty?" Zhiguo looks at her face, "Keep going, just keep doing it." After letting loose a couple of weary grumbles, the woman continues to rock her body. Zhiguo's eyes return again to the swaying characters.

Super Inflatable Doll

Made and imported from the USA, this product is made with special material, simulating a real virgin, with great features such as being able to tremble, massage, vibrate and suck, plus many other combinations. It will plunge you into real pleasure. The doll is equipped with a vagina that vibrates and massages with freely adjustable frequencies until you attain satisfaction. On being inflated, the doll appears lifelike. It also decorates your room as an exquisite work of art that instantly lights up your home. Unit Price: 1,680 yuan.

He scrunches up the newspaper and throws it away, as he asks the woman, "Finished?"

Only now does he see that she has already put on her clothes and curled up at his feet, looking him searchingly. "You're suffering from some sickness," she announces but then tries to comfort him, "You should go see a psychiatrist." She seems really worried about him, "Your thing has been hard all this time but you behaved as if it were not yours. You don't feel any pleasure?"

"How much?"

"Up to you."

Zhiguo begins to get money from his pocket, but then realizes that he has already given all his money to that policeman in the hotel parlor. "Sorry. I don't have any cash on me."

"What?" the woman asks.

"Yep," answers Zhiguo.

The woman sneers, "You are sick. Are you an escapee from the mental hospital?" She straightens herself up and moves to his side. Then she grabs his lower parts at once. She shouts into his ear, "You're f---ing sick!" He would not have expected such a woman to slap his face, but she suddenly gives him a slap. This is the second time he has had his ears boxed; in one day he has suddenly taken two slaps! "I've never seen such a shameless guy as you!" She shrieks, "Why do I keep running into such lowlifes? All I wanted is to have money to go home for the new year! But you guys won't even pay me just for a train ticket!"

Zhiguo begins to believe this woman may be suffering from some slight mental illness, but then he is stunned to see the woman starting to rummage through his clothes. Her practiced behavior starts to infuriate him. So when she pulls the chain of transparent glass beads from his shirt pocket, he gives out a roar, "Don't touch that! You hear me or not!?"

The woman looks at him as if in a trance, but then she gives a quick smile and inserts the beads into her sock. Zhiguo, naked, dashes toward her. Before the smile disappears from her lips, Zhiguo catches her slender neck. The woman pushes him away, and his bones and muscles don't seem to match hers. She must have been an outstanding boxer before she became a prostitute. When her second blow hits his nose, he smells a strong whiff of liquor. He even feels the fine liquor made from sorghum creeping out of every pore of his body, even spilling onto the woman. It has inflamed the coordination of his bones and muscles.... He discovers, after throwing the woman back and forth onto the floor like a toy, that a pool of black blood is sticking to her yellowish hair, and for a time is shocked. He had thought he was just trying to scare her. Now she must really be scared. Her lifeless body collapses at his feet like a snake with its spine peeled off. Her hand grips the glass beads, though he has no idea when she took them out from her cotton sock that smells of scented soap. No one can take away gifts not meant for them, not even if it is a four-yuan item bought from a street stall. He blows the dust off the chain and licks off the blood stains on it. It was a gift from Lala. He was surprised that someone dared to so shamelessly steal the gift Lala gave him.... He kicks the woman's buttocks, but she seems to have turned into a fish on sleeping pills.

She will never kick and splash again. He experiences a moment of mournful reflection. Perhaps she will never again crawl onto men to perform her vertical pistol movements.

6

He had not expected to see the policeman and policewoman after walking out of the woman's room. Maybe they have found him out? Zhiguo feels as if the man is waving to him. Or maybe it is not them at all. Lovers do not come out for strolls at so late a time. They must have been making love somewhere in the police station around this time. Or are they doing anything at all? Who knows?

Zhiguo exhales. He stares at the vapor of his breath, finding it as thin as the color of snow. Those two northeasterners are so lucky. He had meant to kill the two robust fellows tonight. No one would have noticed it if he killed them. In fact these gangsters are foolish suckers. They passed by his city accidently, signing a huge deal with him for no reason and paying him 200,000 yuan in advance for his products. It would have been a good bargain for him to bury them in this snowy winter. At least he would not have to worry about more girls being abused with beer bottles. Having already contacted some gangster bosses in the city, he had even paid them a deposit of 30,000 yuan for the job.... But he now wants to do nothing. He has no desire to do anything at all, he tells himself. It is not that he can not, but that he just does not want to. Just like that.

He turns on his cell-phone. Then he leans against a bare tree and squints his eyes. He always feels so tired. A taxi cruises by slowly. It sounds as if someone is asking him something, but he pays no attention. Nothing he wants to hear now. He puts his ear close to the silver-plated cell-phone. Now he hears the soft greeting, "Is this Papa?"

He utters nothing. The girl's voice sounds fuzzy to him, "I know it's you, Papa."

His tears flow freely.

"Please come home soon. Mama's fallen asleep. You find it more comfortable staying out there than coming home, is that it?"

He had not shed any tears for many years. He hears his daughter's soft breathing, "I love you, Papa. Mama loves you, too. Papa, you love us too, right?"

He mumbles something, but he discovers he has already switched off the cell-phone. He starts to rummage around every corner of his pockets until he finds altogether fourteen misshapen paperclips. Except for two clips bent into the likeness of shovels, the rest are of a girl's skinny silhouette. "Why can't I ever curve any of them into a rose or a ballet dancer?" His fingers immediately become nimble. He orders his hands to turn themselves at once into those of Louis Jude. He is convinced that his fingers have become Jude's, because these paperclips seem to have bent into tiny, exquisite likenesses: a dog, a rose, even a dancing child. "Good," he thinks, "I am Louis Jude!" Laughing to himself, *ha-ha*, he then spreads open his palms and stares carefully at those paperclips. They look like nothing.

Afterwards, when he puts the fourteen paperclips into his mouth, he forcefully curls his tongue around them. Their icy cold taste is similar to the taste when he kisses Lala. What surprises him slightly is that he has never realized in his life that his teeth could be that sharp. He thought they had been eroded by cigarettes, strong alcohol, wolf-like businessmen, women's fluids and the nonsense poems he recited many years ago. However, he feels as if those paperclips have really been chewed into a kind of soft, sweet malt sugar by his teeth. As the hard metal cuts through his throat, his fingers keep nervously searching in the corners of his pockets. He believes if his luck is good, he can find one last one in his pocket while those roses, dogs and girls dancing on one leg jump crazily in his stomach. His luck has always been good so far.

(Translated by Ji Hua & Gao Wenxing)

The Great Typhoon

Wang Xiaoni

Wang Xiaoni. Born in Changchun, Jilin Province, in 1955, Wang Xiaoni once went to live and work with a production team in the countryside, and in 1982 graduated from the Chinese Department of Jilin University. She lived in Shenzhen, Guangdong Province, for 20 years, and now works for the College of Humanities and Communications in Hainan University.

Wang Xiaoni writes poetry, informal essays and fiction, as well as all kinds of sketches. She has published collections of poems, informal essays and novels, numbering over 20 titles.

The Great Typhoon

1

B eads of sweat stood out like ant eggs on Ah Jin's nose.

Ah Jin had just got a call from his clients. They wanted to fly over to Shenzhen to sign the contract. Very anxious, Ah Jin dearly wanted to shape "his own design company" in the shortest time.

Ah Jin made a phone call, "Do you have a decent office to rent?"

A real estate agent replied, "We have both offices and residences. What size do you want?"

Ah Jin said, "I want to rent it for just two days; it's an urgent matter. Tomorrow would be best."

The agent said, "Hmm... a two-day deal. You'd better try Skinny. Here's his phone number."

Ah Jin asked, "Skinny? Is he legit?"

The agent replied, "Who cares, sir. Very few people rent offices for two days, when who knows who such a tenant might be. But doesn't everyone have to earn money for a living, sir?"

Now Ah Jin was on the heels of this man nicknamed Skinny.

They rushed along the busy street, one following the other. To outsiders' eyes, the two of them appeared as if they had nothing to do with each other, as they squeezed through the crowd like two eels moving forward at the same speed.

In the sky, the sun could be faintly seen through a hazy veil. The clouds were floating unassumingly. The storm had not yet arrived. The eye of it was still over the Pacific. Before the approach of a typhoon, very few people take notice of the forecasts about it. City blocks are too dense to allow view of any vast space of sky overhead. Anyway, nobody could divine the propensities of the weather. Ah Jin came to a standstill and cast a glance at the time showing on his mobile. Then he resumed walking on the double to catch up with Skinny. Small fruit shops stood along the roadside. A large split jackfruit looked like a hunchbacked beggar squatting on the sidewalk. With thorns all over, it smelt sweet as well as stinking. The one walking in front was really quite a scrawny fellow. The clothes on him were absolutely superfluous.

Skinny spoke, "This is the back street; the good views are all at the front."

Skinny spoke again, "My real estate company is called 'Left Wing,' not 'Left Bank.' There are too many 'Left Banks.' The name became tedious and vulgar long ago."

Once again Skinny spoke, "It's not to your profit, sir, renting the office for only two days. It's 500 for one day, 1,000 for two days. I'd let you have the suite on a one-year lease at 4,500 a month. It's a distress price, a bad bargain for me."

Ah Jin said, "One year for what? I just need it for two days."

The regular coming and going of pedestrians on the street had made the brick surfaces sticky. The slippers on Skinny's feet squelched monotonously forward.

Ah Jin exclaimed, "It's so stuffy. What weather!"

Skinny said, "Watch your head!"

The two went under a sunshade awning temporarily propped up by a sugarcane-juice-extracting vendor. In the sky, a plane flying silently north to south was making a turn. Its oblique wings reflected the bright sunlight, resembling a weapon hidden in the sky. The plane reminded Ah Jin to check the time on his mobile. He kept doing it continuously all along the way. He never cares about weather. Whatever the weather, he has to work because it is his own business. The address of the office on his calling card is his home.

Skinny announced, "Here we are."

Just at that moment, a guy of a medium height suddenly cleared the iron fence of a lawn. He rushed over with a loose robe in one hand while murmuring something in a Hunan or Hubei dialect. He said to Skinny, "Want a casual laborer, boss?" Already tired of him, Skinny quickened his steps instead. The guy caught up with Skinny and kept asking, "Any job for me, boss? I can take it on right now. Once I start working elsewhere you won't get another hand."

The guy with the robe glimpsed at Ah Jin, and then fixed his eyes on him somewhat in surprise as if he knew Ah Jin from before. Meanwhile another guy strode over the fence and bluntly asked Ah Jin, "Are you Mr. Huang?"

Like shooing away live fowls, Skinny shouted at them, "Get away!"

Skinny said to Ah Jin, "Here we are. My suite is on the twenty-ninth floor of this block, with the best view."

Skinny bent down to open the burglarproof door while complaining that the last tenant had badly renovated his suite. He said, "He knocked down all the walls, leaving only several ugly bare columns. It's difficult to rent it out now. If not for him, a nice office like this would've been long rented out."

The door opened to reveal an office that was not as dim and dull as Ah Jin had imagined. It was spacious. Surprisingly, the hundred-and-forty-square-meter room was all wide open, not a single wall left. There was nothing to use as partitions in the wide space. Skinny pulled open the shutters. It seemed that from the four windows you could see in all directions. Sunlight shone into the room, and the space abruptly became genial. Furniture of white, gray and red divided the room into several parts. The first thing Ah Jin noticed was the L-shaped desk standing in a recess of the room, with a rattan curtain hanging half to one side.

Skinny escorted Ah Jin to a big window with a view of the intersection below. The vehicles waiting for the green light looked as small as a pile of toy bricks down below.

Skinny exclaimed, "My suite has the best view on this floor. Look, it's Hong Kong's Fen Leng right in front."

It was difficult to catch a clear sight of Hong Kong, separated by a river. Masses of gray clouds were pressing up from the direction of the sea.

Skinny said, "Look, what a nice suite; what a deluxe apartment. They've turned it into a big studio or what? If you want to rent it for a year, boss, I'll rebuild the walls and partitions."

Ah Jin took a fancy to the room immediately. It did not look like a discarded room. It seemed as if the tenant had just gone out and would come back to retrieve something at any moment. Some white porcelain coffee cups were still set out on the big table in front of a red sofa.

Skinny said, "If you're satisfied with it I'd call in some odd-jobbers to clear away anything you found unnecessary. I guarantee to get the room cleaned in two hours."

Ah Jin said he wished to retain everything here as it was. Then his mobile rang. He moved to the window to take the call. He said, "I'll see you at the airport car park at six thirty in the evening." Then he turned to Skinny, "That's it. It's settled."

Skinny said somewhat reluctantly, "I rented it on a one-year lease."

Ah Jin replied, "One thousand yuan for two days — you're getting the price for a presidential suite."

Ah Jin counted out the sum, "Here's five hundred yuan. In two days I'll be here at four sharp in the afternoon. I'll pay you another five hundred when I return the keys to you."

Skinny said, "There are so many things here. They are also property."

Ah Jin said, "What use is any of it to me? Would I take away this desk other people have used? Or the old sofas used by other people to sit on?"

Skinny took the money as he pondered something over. After a few minutes' hesitation he put the keys on the wooden table and left.

When approaching the lift, he turned back and said, "We're going to have a typhoon today. Mind you close all the doors and windows properly. This is the twenty-ninth floor. The higher the floor, the stronger the wind."

Ah Jin said, "What typhoon?"

Skinny called out at the entrance to the lift, "The 'wind ball' signal has been raised. You can check it on Pearl TV."

Ah Jin closed the door behind him and put down the laptop he had been carrying in his hand. Now he began to unhurriedly examine the office.

After settling in, he heard the hubbub around like the even

snoring of a colossal beast. Ah Jin walked across the room and found that the noise came from the outside. It was the noise of the city, not from a single car or any individual but from the congregation of all the noises, loud, heavy and oppressive.

Ah Jin came back to the front door and looked around the room for two minutes with the eye of a client from the north, before saying, "Well, okay. It looks like an art design shop." Then he scanned the room again for another two minutes with the eye of a common employee and said, "Not bad. It's got some taste." For the third time, he examined the room again with his own eyes. He had five years' experience in advertising design. If he could get his own company to such an appropriate status as to keep up appearances, he would be confident of getting decent design orders.

Ah Jin said as if chanting an incantation, "A 200,000-yuan contract. It'll be entered into my account for sure!"

The sky was much gloomier than when he entered the room. It did not stay high above but pressed down to a level parallel with the bay windows. There were darker clouds sandwiched in the gray.

Ah Jin inspected all the posters on the walls. He felt astonished, as if the one who had rented the room before had been he himself. The tablecloth on the table at the corner of the wall was of pure linen. The tableware was made of coarse ceramic. The PC monitor on the desk had been unexpectedly left active. The cloth-upholstered sofa could easily swallow up a two-hundred-kilogram guy. Ah Jin sat down on the sofa and thought that he had not enjoyed himself so much for so many years.

Two hours later, Ah Jin would go to meet his clients at the airport. If things progressed without hitch he would contact two of his friends in the evening. They would act as his employees when the moment comes. The next morning he would invite the clients to visit "his design company." It would be best if they could sign the contract, the most important one in recent years, in this office. If things went smoothly, the preliminary down payment of 200,000 yuan would be deposited into his account.

The phone on the desk rang. Looking at the black *Siemens* phone, Ah Jin did not know what to do. It certainly could not be for him. It would be reasonable to ignore it. But it kept ringing; the other end would not give up.

Ah Jin picked up the receiver. A female voice came on, very quick in tempo. She told him her name and invited him to the seashore to watch the typhoon. Ah Jin told her she had contacted the wrong person. He was about to explain but the caller seemed to refuse to hear him. She said that in one hour they would meet at the crossing by the mountain. If she could not meet him then she would go by herself. Ah Jin wanted to explain again. The other end asked, "Aren't you Huang?" Ah Jin said, "Huang?" She hung up.

Ah Jin said, "Crazy!"

Back on the sofa Ah Jin felt he had never felt so sleepy. After setting the alarm on his mobile he curled up on the red sofa and soon fell asleep.

2

Xiao Lan got out of bed. For her afternoon nap every day Xiao Lan always stays in bed until she tires of it. What should she do after getting up? Sitting or standing was only an alternation of a posture.

The TV had been left on. This is a habit Xiao Lan has when she is at home. The information on the typhoon was at the lower edge of the screen rolling reasonably from right to left. In Hong

Kong, a typhoon warning is known as the *fengqiu* or "wind ball." All citizens are familiar with this Hong Kong expression. But Xiao Lan did not notice the scrolling information, so she had no idea of the approaching typhoon before she went out.

Clouds were pressing down very low. The air was suffocating. Sometimes there is no wind when a typhoon approaches land. Even thin and transparent curtains stay still, as if every thing was suffocating.

Xiao Lan lives on one side of the city where houses are built halfway up a hill, one layer upon another. Long and narrow, the city faces the sea and backs mostly on hills several hundred meters in height.

On the TV a man spoke in a very low voice. Xiao Lan walked to and fro in front of the TV but never turned her eyes to it. She wants the TV to serve as an unquestioning obedient man, staying in a corner and talking earnestly to her alone. Compared to a little cat or dog, the TV is a dumb animal that most easily breeds. Xiao Lan dimly saw a black Western male jacket hanging in the study. She never has books or anyone in her study. It is nearly empty. However, the jacket in the corner always gives off the appearance of some figure.

A few minutes after getting up Xiao Lan completely came out of her trance. Things around her became stereoscopic and authentic. She found the flowers in the big pot needed a change of water again. Something adrift in her mind during sleep had vanished or hidden in some corner of the big suite. She spent more than half an hour on makeup and changing. Finally she walked to the door with a long gown in her hand while making a mobile call, "I'm coming down."

Xiao Lan never uses desktop phones. She is fond of talking

while walking.

Every afternoon, Xiao Lan walks along the road repeatedly, staggering down the winding steps to the shopping street in the estate. The stretch of sea several hundred meters away is the lead-colored bay resembling a mire or shabby dump constantly repaired with asphalt. No travelers, no fishing boats, no seagulls, no wharfs, it is an expanse of sea on the verge of death. The excessively built high-rise buildings of the city skirt along the bay, too dense to let in any wind. The incessant din of traffic around the clock composes a steady sound that only lulls people to sleep.

Xiao Lan let herself down, each step lower than the previous one. Now she could see the boutique run by her friends as well as the olive-green parasol at the door of the shop. They had been employees in a bank. Later they got married. Their husbands had long gone to Hong Kong, coming home only on weekends or public holidays. They had hated very much wearing uniforms and their jobs where they had to force a smile when meeting anyone. So they had resigned together and moved to the building with the sea in front and hills at the back. Gradually her friends, no longer able to stand the idle life, opened the small shop. In addition to the fashionable clothing brought from Hong Kong, they often display and sell clothing from their own wardrobes. Many of them they had been bought and tried on, then remaining untouched in their collection. They display them in this shop. Hence the shop sells only woman's clothing and each and every one is a single piece. It is like a boutique transit station.

The boss of the shop was trying on the gown Xiao Lan had brought and asked about the price.

Xiao Lan replied, "The bottom price is four hundred. I bought it at three hundred and eighty."

The boss said, "It can be sold easier at a cheaper price."

Xiao Lan said: "Who cares. If nobody buys it, I'll take it back for myself."

Then they started to grind coffee beans.

Many an afternoon they ground coffee beans together like this. Then they made coffee while looking at the bus stop outside the window. Sometimes they witnessed motorcycle thieves in the act. Other times they could see cars cutting lanes and colliding, or a mass of passengers pursuing a bus — pushing, shoving, pulling and dragging along at the doorway. The large windowpane is a special channel for them to watch reality shows.

The boss said to an employee, "Fetch us more ice cubes."

She and Xiao Lan have kept up the habit of taking the hottest coffee and the coldest soft drinks. The most exciting thing they do every day is to have something to drink.

Xiao Lan said, "I went to the Big Square yesterday. I saw two people there, don't know whether they were doing performance art or just begging for money. One of them acted as a pure black cat and the other looked like a kangaroo — two animals or wooden statues perhaps. They each struck a pose but couldn't stick it out. They moved before long."

The boss of the shop had been fixing her eyes on the bus stop in the distance. A bus was pulling in. Passengers always chase after the door. A girl dropped her slippers. She got off the bus to retrieve them.

Three months ago, Xiao Lan had encountered a street artist in Paris. Garbed in a silvery suit of armor he had stood atop a half-meter-high platform shaped like an ice cube. It was almost dusk as Xiao Lan had followed halfway behind her tour group to visit a white cathedral. The white knight of the Middle Ages was probably ready to knock off. Suddenly he moved, bent down to take off the white helmet. The dense and long brown hair betrayed the fact that this "he" was a very young lady. Xiao Lan deliberately walked at a slow pace to watch the lady collecting the small platform. It had turned out that the "ice cube" could be folded. At the back of her mind, the idea that it was amusing to be a street artist, had stuck. Back from the tour she had repeated the idea to the boutique keeper several times.

The latter asked, "Would you put a hat on the ground to collect money, too?"

Xiao Lan replied, "Of course I would."

The woman shopkeeper then asked, "Don't you feel the money you collect would be dirty and shabby, and smell bad? I can't even bear it to think of it."

Over several extended afternoons they discussed how they would spend the money they had begged. What type of costume and paraphernalia would feel unique to spectators.... It was an everlasting subject, a discussion that would have no end. Before that they had discussed how to flee for their lives if they committed a capital crime, in case they would have to flee far from home. The woman boss said they could purchase fake passports and flee to Tonga. Xiao Lan, however, believed it would be much safer to escape to Inner Mongolia and herd sheep on the grasslands. Xiao Lan has never been to Inner Mongolia. She imagines that people there are herding white sheep on the vast prairie.

Just at that moment a salesclerk said, the TV had forecast that a typhoon was brewing.

The TV had stopped broadcasting regular programs to flash special information concerning the typhoon.

Xiao Lan said, "Let's go watch the typhoon."

The woman boss said, "A storm is a storm. Nothing

exceptional."

Xiao Lan said, "It's a typhoon, it's best to watch it at the seashore. Storms come in from the sea."

The boss said, "It's dangerous at the shore. Last year, three people went missing during a typhoon. Human beings can die very easily. Do you think people are so strong?"

Xiao Lan said, "I really want to go."

The boss said, "What's so interesting about a storm? Better to sit here watching the street."

Xiao Lan said, "Didn't you used to experience power-cuts at night when you were young? At midnight your eyes grow accustomed to the darkness, when suddenly the electricity comes back on. The strange light overhead would be too dazzling to look at. Didn't you ever think to touch the light?"

The boss said, "What light? We're talking about a typhoon."

Xiao Lan said, "I'm going by myself. I'll try to get a sense of the storm from the nearest point."

Xiao Lan went home at a run. A security guard stood by the road adjusting his belt. An estate caretaker switched off the lawn mower and fanned himself in the shade of a tree. They were rather carefree, completely ignoring the typhoon gathering momentum in the South China Sea. Xiao Lan said, "We're going to have a typhoon!" The guard responded with a professional smile. After Xiao Lan went past, he resumed attentively fiddling with his belt.

There was a grassy fragrance. By now, a gale was blowing. Slivers of grass freshly mown were still alive and green, swirling in the wind from one step to another.

When Xiao Lan opened the door of her home she thought of someone. Months ago she had met this guy in an audio-video shop downtown. It so happened that as she had been asking about *The*

Death-Call Code, and a guy behind her said that it was a nice film. Xiao Lan could not recall his appearance but she was still impressed by his voice that sounded so solid. Xiao Lan had said she had by chance rented *The Death-Call Code* and felt that she should keep a copy of it to replay any time. While the shop attendant looked for the film, they had chatted about several Hollywood disaster films. The guy recommended her *The Day After Tomorrow* and said that the US had made the disaster film into "disaster art." Xiao Lan was fonder of the blue gray Paris remolded by the French, with carriages floating strangely in that color....

Xiao Lan had said, "What can I get you to drink? Wouldn't you like some pearl tea?"

The guy had replied, "You'd better invite me to watch a typhoon."

Xiao Lan said, "What?"

The guy said, "I mean it, *taifeng* ('big wind')."

Xiao Lan said, "I've never heard of inviting people to see a typhoon."

The guy said, "Actually, I don't care much if its fine or cloudy every day, I'm too busy to attend to the weather. But I like typhoons a lot. When there is a forecast of a typhoon, please call me. I wish to live by the sea and watch typhoons hitting land."

Xiao Lan had said, "Are you serious?"

Afterwards, the guy had written down his phone numbers, bending over the cash counter.

Xiao Lan now walked up and down in the room. She switched off the TV and packed her things in a plastic case.

Ten minutes later, Xiao Lan decided to make the call. The mobile on the other side was shut off. Perplexed, Xiao Lan carefully checked the number she had just dialed. The first several figures were the same as her own. It indicated the number had been used for nearly ten years. Users generally do not change numbers at will. She dialed the office phone number the guy had left her. At the other end was a man, but he said she had dialed a wrong number. Xiao Lan checked time and again the number stored in her mobile. It seemed that the lump of plastic in her hand had made the mistake.

Standing before the bay windows for a while, Xiao Lan finally said, "It'd be better to go alone anyway. More carefree."

She called a seashore holiday resort to book a room.

The other end hesitated, "There is a typhoon!"

Xiao Lan said, "How talkative you are! Don't you know there are people who do *want* to see a typhoon?"

The sky lowered like an immovable congealed metal plate pressing over the city.

Xiao Lan put the plastic case in the car and said, "The winds have started. What does it matter if there's one person less?"

3

Two men were squatting on the lawn behind the rear door of the Hao Men Restaurant. The gap between them was slim, though they did not say a word to each other.

Old Liu, the elder one, gazed at the street dozens of meters away as he did every day. His gaze was serious, not giving off a sign of anything. Young Zhang, the younger one, fixed his eyes on the lawn. He was rubbing the grass with his warped old rubbers as if he was fed up with it. Workers in the restaurant are fond of the two men, because they are amusing, giving others lots of cheer. They call them the "Rabbit Men," as the pair each step by turn into an exaggeratedly large robe to act as a rabbit, standing at the door of the restaurant to solicit customers each day.

The robe was now held in Rabbit Man Zhang's arms. He rose to his feet to sun the robe.

Rabbit Man Liu said as he straightened up, "What's that guy carrying?"

The hauler turned out to be a sanitation worker. He was carrying a fallen leaf of a fake betel palm. The leaf was four meters long, rustling when pulled along.

Old Liu felt frustrated, burying his head between his legs. However, he never shifted his eyes from the street. They were like spy holes, scanning and filtering every thing bit by bit. The head waiter of the restaurant staggered over.

The head waiter said, "Who's first on duty today?"

Old Liu replied. "He is."

Staring at Old Liu, Young Zhang said, "Me again?"

The head waiter said, "Don't look so muddled. How come you're so absolutely clearheaded when you collect your pay?"

Young Zhang said, "The robe's too smelly. It smells of his sweat. Please tell the boss to make another one."

The head waiter said as he walked away, "What an idea! One for each of you? You'd pay the bill?"

Young Zhang said, "Me? If I had such money, would I come to work here?"

The head waiter had gone.

Old Liu said, "Why blame only me? Don't you sweat, or are you made of wood?"

In that instant Rabbit Man Liu suddenly stood up, leaped over the fence to block the path of a lanky man, "Need some casual help?"

Rabbit Man Zhang also saw the two passersby. No sooner said than done, he also jumped over the fence.

Rabbit Man Zhang rushed straight over to stop the one at the back and asked, "Are you surnamed Huang?"

Both of the passersby gave no reply but proceeded directly into the apartment compound.

Young Zhang asked Old Liu, "Isn't he the one who jumped from the block? The one surnamed Huang? I think it's him."

Old Liu looked absentminded for a while. He jumped back onto the lawn and said, "Nonsense, that Huang is dead!"

Old Liu said again, "That's funny; he looks every bit like that guy!"

The two Rabbit Men appeared at a loss for a few minutes.

Old Liu walked past the pitch-dark back door of the restaurant. He recalled in his mind the guy who had jumped from the building about ten days back. The noise then had not been that loud. It sounded like a cotton-padded quilt falling to the ground. Not until the dough-kneading chef had stepped past the place did he realize that the fallen object was a man. At first no one dared approach the spot. They just stayed around and watched. No blood could be found nearby. The body had first fallen on the bicycle shed. Somebody had heard the hollow sound from the vinyl-coated steel shed. The guy now lay on the greasy ground by the back door of the restaurant. It seemed that the fellow had been drunk or in a trance. The police came and bustled about for some time. Finally they had said, "Come on, come on. Who'll give us a hand?" Rabbit Man Liu was the first to step forward. He had grasped hold of the guy but failed to get a proper hold on the slippery arms. In the end, Old Liu had carried the guy half on his shoulders and thus managed to shove him into the police van. It is said that a dead body feels stiff, but as a matter of fact, Old Liu had felt that the body was quite soft. That aroused fear in him. After laying the dead guy down, he had still felt that there was something clammy on his hands and back. He had shaken his hands around madly, and washed them under the tap, but whatever it was just stuck there. He would not tell anybody, especially Young Zhang, about the feeling of having handled a dead body in his arms.

Constantly needled by Old Liu's perspiration, Young Zhang said, "Who's ever heard of two persons using the same skin?"

Rabbit Man Liu imagined he should have got paid for helping the police to carry the dead. You could get a hundred-yuan fee from a report to any media. However, when Old Liu had put the corpse down and gone to the police, they did not even as much as turn their eyes toward him. The police had closed the door of the van with a bang and driven off. There were no bloodstains on the ground. Someone still pulled out a hose to wash the place down for ten minutes. It seemed as if nothing had happened.

Nevertheless Old Liu's arms felt bad, not aching but droopy.

Rabbit Man Liu was forty years old, while Rabbit Man Zhang was only twenty-two. But no one in the restaurant seemed concerned about the age of these two guys. They were only happy to see them banter in the course of using the same rabbit robe. Particularly, just at the point when one of them stripped down to the waist and bent down to step into the rabbit robe, they would come up and ask, "Does the robe stink?"

The rabbit men distributed flyers about the restaurant on the sidewalk, attracting young passersby or children.

The head waiter always thought they did not work hard enough. He said, "Get a move on. Get hopping! Don't stand like that all evening. Who knows what's at the back of your mind?"

The two Rabbit Men almost had the same thought at once: "Who's any different? Who does not want to make money?"

Rabbit Man Zhang squatted down and leaned against the only tree on the lawn. He felt restless thinking of the cell-phone hidden all the time at his waist. He had once spoken with the guy who jumped from the building. The guy's name card was still tucked under his pillow. He knew the guy was surnamed Huang. One afternoon Young Zhang had fished out the pincers he hid in the crook of the tree. With it he turned on the faucet on the lawn. Then he had taken a shower with only his underpants on. He did not care about being seen, even if the entire city came to watch him shower. At that moment the guy surnamed Huang had come up to him with an extra-large portfolio. The guy had asked, "How much you get for a month as a Rabbit Man in front of the restaurant?"

Young Zhang had looked at him and said, "Eight hundred yuan, in addition to room and meals."

The guy said: "Want to work for me? One thousand five hundred, no room or meals."

Young Zhang asked what the job was. The guy asked Young Zhang whether he had ever been to the Big Square. He wanted Young Zhang to join his company as a walking "Adman." The guy had seemed in a hurry, saying he would contact him again, and then made tracks.

After that, Young Zhang had gone to the Big Square to watch the performances: roller-skating, mini-biking and street-dancing. There was a group of people in bright colors with wooden placards in their hands, promoting mobile phones. Threading through the crowd they moved as finely as at a dance. Rabbit Man Zhang liked jobs involving performance. In the Big Square he had also seen a guy daubed in black greasepaint standing motionless to disguise himself as a black man. Young Zhang considered it to be a good job, interesting but not painful; he could decide the work hours himself and probably make more money than acting as a rabbit every day.

He had grown eager to meet Huang again as he grew more tired of his current job. He really hated to get into that rabbit robe stinking of Old Liu's perspiration. It had started getting warmer. When the guy had jumped off the building it was on a warm afternoon, the kind of weather that makes some people feel drowsy. It looked like something not very big dropping onto the ground. The chefs and security guards of the restaurant recalled hearing the mobile phone singing on the guy's body, the ringing in harmony. They did not know whether the singing was a result of the fall, or if there had been a call for the guy. They said, sounding regretful, that the mobile phone was nowhere to be seen after the guy had fallen to the ground. Young Zhang had picked up the cell-phone unnoticed, as the others were shouting, "Check whether he is still breathing!"

They said, "Why take things too seriously?"

Young Zhang had felt more scared than the others, but he never uttered a word. When the police had come, he grabbed the rabbit robe and went back to the dorm with the phone wrapped in the robe.

At that moment Rabbit Man Liu was walking across a pedestrian overpass. A bell was chiming in the distance. It was five sharp in the afternoon. Old Liu often wandered onto the bridge at that time. The day was particularly sultry. Old Liu stared at the distant high-rise buildings. With their tops mantled entirely in dark clouds, the buildings exposed only their lower parts.

Old Liu did not care about the other Rabbit Man Young Zhang's reproaches, when he scolded him for the bad smell. He completely filtered everything right in front of him. There remained only he himself and money in the world. He had come to this city to make money and send his earnings back home to the village. He concerned himself only with reward announcements or notices looking for missing persons. Sometimes he picked up a newspaper for that same purpose. In his eyes, the ten million residents in the city were nothing to him provided they did not fish money out from their pockets and count out sums for him.

From the bridge Old Liu could see some people playing cards on the lawn; they were gambling. One guy had even climbed up a tree to watch the game. A fellow wearing a tie was asleep with his portfolio as a pillow. A young man took out a brush from his handbag and started shining his shoes. Old Liu saw someone promoting something to the drivers while their cars waited for the traffic signal to change.

Old Liu ran down the bridge and found two persons selling a large roll of paper to a driver. Old Liu thought, why is it people pay for anything at a discount? Is a mess of rolled paper worth ten yuan? He wanted to make out what type of paper it was, but the two sellers refused to let him take a look.

The light turned green, and all the vehicles moved off. The cars began tearing past, so suddenly that the three guys could hardly keep their footing.

Old Liu said, "There's no harm in taking a look at your goods!"

One of the rolled-paper sellers asked Old Liu to first break a twenty-yuan banknote into small bills for them. Old Liu presented four filthy five-yuan banknotes before he could take a look at the roll — world maps. The entire world printed on them.

Old Liu went back onto the bridge. He fumbled to pull out the twenty-yuan banknote and felt it with his fingers. The more he felt it the thinner he sensed it was. It did not resemble a real banknote.

Old Liu leapt down the bridge like a madman. The map sellers were nowhere to be seen. Instead he found a newsboy hawking the evening paper. Old Liu grabbed hold of the boy and asked him whether he had seen the map sellers there only a moment before. The boy hummed and hawed to indicate that he was dumb and could not speak. Finding no other outlet, Old Liu gave the boy several kicks and wrested a few copies of the paper from him.

A car slowed down, and the driver opened the window and shouted, "Good kicks!"

Rabbit Man Liu retraced his steps, his arms feeling very heavy. The dead man had brought him rotten luck. Somewhat vexed he ran to the lawn and tried to switch on the tap to thoroughly wash his hands. However, there was a sanitation worker in a fluorescent vest standing nearby. They probably noticed that someone had been stealing water there and started patrolling the place. Old Liu could only sit down and thumb through the newspaper.

Old Liu saw the typhoon warning. He laughed very calmly. Rising to his feet, he patted clean his trousers right and left. Before his eyes there seemed to be a stretch of shining water. The area by the back door of the Hao Men Restaurant was the lowest point in the city, so the surface of the road would always get flooded. When a typhoon had hit the previous year, three pedicabs had appeared on that road to specially convey the ladies who were in a hurry to go to work but could not cross the road. Old Liu decided to borrow a pedicab.

Rabbit Man Liu met Young Zhang in the dorm. He told Young Zhang, "The typhoon's coming again!"

Young Zhang asked, "Who's coming?"

Old Liu said, "'Da feng,' the wind, the great wind."

Young Zhang said, "What wind? You take over my shift in a bit. I've got something on. Next time when you're busy I'll take over yours."

Old Liu said, "No way. I've got something to do right now!"

Young Zhang said, "You? How could you have anything urgent!"

4

Hardly had Xiao Lan taken out the key to start her car when the mobile in her pocket rang.

Xiao Lan said, "How come when you're offered business, you won't take it up?"

The seashore holiday resort replied, "They cut off the power today. We don't have any capacity to accept guests. Don't you know, miss? There's going to be a typhoon."

Xiao Lan said, "Of course I know. Would I want to stay at your place without the typhoon?"

The seashore holiday resort repeated, "Very sorry, miss, but we are experiencing a power-cut."

Xiao Lan said, "What do you mean by 'sorry'? Tonight I wanted exactly to stay in a hotel without electricity!"

This reminded Xiao Lan that she should take with her several candle-stands and candles in different colors. She went back to her room and spent ten minutes searching for things.

Through the bay windows she could see the wind gaining strength. As if poisoned, the magnolia tree shuddered vigorously. The light in the room immediately grew dimmer. Xiao Lan's shadowy figure overlapped with those of the magnolia tree and the bay, all swaying on the screen of the turned-off TV. Xiao Lan was entranced with the image of herself as the leading actress in a soap opera on TV with an electrifying plot. In the end she set off with a telescope, towels, toiletries, a raincoat, apples, pistachios, instant coffee, candles and candle-stands, all packed into her car.

It was hard to tell now whether Xiao Lan was late for the action or the storm had changed its speed. The wind was accelerating its pace. It was raining by the time Xiao Lan made it onto the main highway. Everything before her eyes was wet; the whole city had become imbued with darker hues.

At first the wind was not too strong. Then the rain turned heavy in an instant. The windscreen wipers swung crazily. Xiao Lan had to pass through the entire constricted city before she reached the open seaside she wished to go. The sandy beach there faced the endless waters of the Pacific. In no time the road was submerged in torrential rains. The car felt almost as if it were drifting. The wind suddenly gathered momentum. The city outside the window appeared to quiver. Xiao Lan felt in a mood to loudly sing a certain song.

Xiao Lan could hardly see anything on both sides. She had no idea of her exact position, only following the tail-lights of the car in front. She managed to make out a small section of the road ahead by leaning forward, but the seatbelt kept pulling her back. Not until red signal lights appeared again in the miasma could she relax for a moment. She imagined that when she returned from the seashore the next day, the road would not be passable for traffic. Over ten years ago, she had just started to work at the bank, when one morning after a severe typhoon she had come across tree trunks fallen all along the road. She had been like a village lass collecting firewood in a forest. The city was rather small then. Now it had developed from a transparent youngster to a big chap with a tie gripping at its throat.

A short distance ahead, the road completely vanished. The front of the car suddenly sank into deep water.

Xiao Lan exclaimed, "My heavens, it's become a submarine!"

Full of curiosity Xiao Lan now had it in mind to see other drivers' facial expressions: distressed or excited? Traffic had obviously become sparse on the road. In front of her there was a red *Polo* car with its hazard lights flashing all the way. Xiao Lan stepped on the accelerator, intending to get closer to it.

All of a sudden a black object moved near her window — a widely spread hand banged on the window. The sound was muffled as if happening underwater. The moment the hand touched the window it looked deformedly huge.

Xiao Lan thought to herself, did I hit somebody?

She went on, "Blast! I have."

She could see nothing from the rearview mirror.

Flustered now, Xiao Lan rolled down the windowpane. The strong wind found its way in through the open gap, so the car felt on the verge of blowing over. Xiao Lan flicked her eyes toward the rear of the car, where she saw only dark curtains of rain. The back wheels were submerged in water. The accumulated water was swirling away. She was aware that there was a drain somewhere.

Now she had to shut the window tightly, so that she could be safe in the small space. No matter how big the world was out there, it had nothing to do with her. She found it difficult to calm the palpitations of her heart and the trembling in her legs. She still felt as if there was a hand stuck on the windowpane. At that point she did wish there were another person sitting by her side, a person, a her or a him she could talk to. Now she saw only the shadows of the nearest cars moving along like ghosts. She simply could see not a soul around. Another person did not exist. There was a river on the other side of the road. The river level was likely rising. The stink of the water flitted into the car.

A traffic policeman appeared right in front of her windscreen, a policeman seemingly molded with flowing fluid. There was the blare of police sirens.

Xiao Lan murmured, "The police!"

The police did not block Xiao Lan's car. He was directing all the traffic along the road to make a turn in the direction opposite to the usual course. She could sense the waving arms of the police. The arms kept giving instructions, waving repeatedly. Xiao Lan's car was at the closest spot to the turn by the riverside. She noticed a taxi floating in the river, the vehicle roof rising then falling, like a buoy.

Xiao Lan said to herself, "Go home!"

It had become entirely dark, except when incessant flashes of lightning lit up the horizon of the city. It was like a magic show, tearing up a sheet of black paper and then rapidly joining it together again. Even though everyone knew that the city with all its lighting equipment was still standing in its original location, all one could see now was only the wind, the rain and the lightning. After getting down from the car Xiao Lan simply stood on the spot for some time. Not far away, somebody holding an umbrella was struggling ahead through the teeth of the storm. The canopy of the umbrella would bellow and bulge. In no time it bent outward, and finally got free of the holder, shooting off into the darkness.

Once out in the storm Xiao Lan faced the head wind. She was quickly carried completely by the wind, with her body slanting upward. She felt as if she were going home by cable car.

When she made it back home, Xiao Lan stepped in gingerly, turned on all the lights, took a bath, made tea and changed her clothes. She did all this making as little noise as she possibly could.

No sooner than Xiao Lan had sat down by the window, all the lights suddenly went out. The power had been cut. She did not rise to search for candles, but remained in her seat.

The woman owner of the boutique called, "I saw you going home drenched to the skin."

Then the owner spoke again, "I bought all the candles from the convenience shop, and just lit twenty of them. Now I'm not scared."

The owner went on, "Why are you keeping silent?"

Xiao Lan replied, "I'm watching the wind."

At the moment the rain had abated, but the wind had only become even more severe. She heard the sound of glass breaking. The magnolia tree by the window bent down into the muddy water, leaving only a vast view of this black curtain that had never been seen in front of the window.

Xiao Lan thought to herself: Did I knock anybody down?

If she had, the man would have bled and fallen into the dirty water, crying out or perhaps dying. After sitting down, Xiao Lan felt even more frightened. The wind at the moment only heightened her fear all the more. On such an evening it might be better to have many people gathered together. However, a person is an individual. For instance, if you have knocked down one person, you cannot say it was two.

The phone rang again. The storm had already cut the power off, but surprisingly phone calls could still be put through.

At the other end was a male voice, "Excuse me, did you dial the number I'm now using? I received a call this afternoon. You might have been trying to call the former tenant in this place."

Xiao Lan asked, "What do you mean?"

The man replied, "I want to know about the man you were looking for. Who is he?"

Xiao Lan said, "It's none of your business."

The man said, "Sorry, but I think I should tell you that the man you were looking for was perhaps in an accident."

Xiao Lan said, "Could you speak louder?"

At that moment Xiao Lan sensed that the bay windows were bulging inward. It resembled an elastic, wet and transparent belly pressing toward her. The wind suddenly became stronger. All the things in the room were rattling, on the verge of shattering. Something was swirling close to the window. Phone in hand, Xiao Lan thought she should try to prop up the windowpane.

Xiao Lan bent forward, stretched out her hands, but out of the blue, the glass broke. She felt as if she was falling into glittery flames, which seized her tightly before she fell into it. The flames were crystal bright, icy cold and powerful, while she was only a flattened, extinct object.

Xiao Lan found herself sitting on the floor with nothing around her, apart from the glass fragments and the wind that filled the entire room.

5

Ah Jin had been awakened by a noise. He soon realized that it was not the alarm on his mobile. Displayed on the phone was his clients' number.

At that time the clients should already be on the plane. Ah Jin had an ominous presentiment. New problems were cropping up… some sudden change of mind or they simply had not taken the flight. Ah Jin anticipated various evil possibilities in the several seconds before he picked up the call. The clients said their plane had landed in another city because of the typhoon. They could probably come the following next noon.

Ah Jin heaved a long sigh, thinking that he should not have to be so wary. Such wariness may be reasonable for beasts or fowls, but not for human beings. Ah Jin's clients were arranged to stay in a hotel in the other city a hundred and twenty kilometers away. Now Ah Jin felt he could relax, and he longed to sleep again. The sofa in the office was more comfortable to lie down on than his bed at home. The preset alarm in his mobile rang just at that moment. But he noticed the noise was even louder outside the window.

Ah Jin rose to his feet, recalling the typhoon that Skinny told him about. It was entirely dark; black clouds were surging and the storm would hit at any moment. Outside the window, lights had come on — a large pink character for *Hao*, composed of rapidly flashing neon lights. Shifting his eyes downward he managed to see another character, *Men*."

The typhoon had disrupted Ah Jin's plans. The clients, for whom he had strained every nerve to make this deal with for the past three months, had ended up being held up by the unexpected typhoon several hours before they were to sign the contract. There was no guarantee that the twenty thousand yuan would arrive in his account the following day. Ah Jin could not help but sigh. At present he had nothing to do; he had never enjoyed such leisure. Anyway, the office was being rented at a high price. He should occupy and use it. It was a waste of money leaving it idle for even a second. In view of that, Ah Jin lay down on the sofa again. He decided not to go home that night. Shortly afterward, he began to feel hungry again. He thought, what a nuisance to live alone.

When Ah Jin went down the building, he found the elevator was small and the apartment was close to the Hao Men Restaurant, with its rather grubby yet ostentatious signboard. A security guard followed him for a short distance. Ah Jin turned his head, and the guard ducked away. Ah Jin disliked living in such types of high-rise buildings. They always had a sense of swaying, somewhat unreal, as if one were hanging onto a ladder. The dorm he had rented to serve as his real office was on the ground floor with a yard. He could see sturdy gardenia and hibiscus blooming in turn, as well as flies and mosquitoes freely flying in and out. He could also see his neighbors escorting their children to and from the kindergarten. The kids were growing little by little.

Ah Jin went back up to the twenty-ninth floor, and looking under the desk he kept coming across different name cards, including one of his own. He immediately pulled it up. It was one he had used the previous year. He wondered if he had earlier known the former tenant of the office.

He switched on all the lights and searched all the corners of the room. There were some back issues of a geography magazine. In the wastepaper basket were paper scraps hacked by a shredder. With no photos, or any characters he could make out on paper, he could find no trace of the former dweller of the room. There was a white board by the phone. Someone had casually jotted down dozens of phone numbers and some entirely unrelated words:

Simple life

Half past six

Right now

OK

Ah Jin asked himself: Do I know the guy?

Ah Jin called one of his friends.

The friend said, "He lived on the twenty-ninth floor? I don't remember."

Ah Jin said, "He was engaged in design."

The friend said, "You know how many people live off this business in the city?"

Now Ah Jin was playing the role of private detective. Under the desk he discovered half a cardboard box of white sheets of paper torn in half. There were several sealed bottles of coffee beans of different brands. Ah Jin thought he should ask Skinny.

Ah Jin asked, "Who was the former resident here? What was his name?"

Skinny answered from the other end, "Mind your own business. You're only renting the office for two days."

Ah Jin said, "Perhaps I know the guy. I want to know who he is."

Skinny said, "You know the rules, don't you? I have to maintain confidentiality about my clients. We have letters of commitment. I can't casually divulge private data."

Skinny then added, "Check the doors and windows for me. Make sure they're properly closed. Otherwise the room will get soaked when the rain pours in."

Meanwhile the room was suddenly thrown into darkness. The typhoon had cut off the power supply. The storm was obviously growing even more violent. Even the blocks on the opposite side of the street were no more than a blur. Curtains of rain were mantling the windows. Only the shadows of the streetlights and the neon lights of the restaurant could be faintly seen. The cracking of glass was heard, perhaps from where windows had been left open.

Ah Jin could smell a scent of ill omen in the air. He opened the door just as the beam of a flashlight caught him.

A security guard for the block said, "Who goes there?"

Ah Jin said, "I live in 29 C."

The guard said, "What? Who are you?"

Ah Jin said, "Who are you?"

The guard said, "You live here?"

Ah Jin said, "This is my office."

The guard said, "What do you mean?"

By now the guard had come closer with the flashlight almost pressing on Ah Jin's face.

Ah Jin said, "I'll report you!"

The guard turned around and shouted into his walkie-talkie. Ah Jin for the first time discovered that human's eyes could also flash in the darkness.

Some security guards dashed up the stairs and simultaneously ordered, "Show us your ID!"

Ah Jin produced his ID card and driver's license. The guards thumbed through each of the identification and then shone the flashlight in his face again.

Finally one of the guards said, "Sorry, we've made a mistake. That guard's a newcomer; he was too nervous. There were some incidents in 29 C very recently."

Another guard said: "The landlord rented out the room so soon!"

Ah Jin questioned them closely. The guard said that ten days before the tenant had fallen down from the twenty-ninth floor.

They even took Ah Jin round the corner to a wide space. Pointing to a small window one of them said, "He fell down from there."

Ah Jin asked, "What did the police say?"

The guard said, "That the guy had jumped, committed suicide. The police have too many cases of murder to investigate, and don't have time to worry about other cases."

Another guard said, "They didn't say 'suicide'; they said, 'fell down from the block'."

Ah Jin went back into the room but he left the door open. The wind blew in ruffling the surface of the rug. Ah Jin could imagine that the guy surnamed Huang had devised a meticulous scheme to cover any traces before he jumped down unhurriedly. He protected himself very well at the end, leaving no sign for others to determine the truth of his suicide.

Ah Jin looked at the sofa that had no longer had anything to do with comfort. He called Skinny again, "I know the facts now. He committed suicide, surname Huang."

Skinny said, "Perhaps he was surnamed Huang and perhaps he was not, or maybe he used a false identity card. Who knows! Is anything real nowadays? I didn't mean to dupe you. It didn't happen in my apartment after all."

Ah Jin said, "I know it happened over the hanging garden."

Skinny said, "That's right. Nothing happened in my apartment. You can rest assured."

For quite a long time Ah Jin, like other people, was used to living a plain and simple life, never thinking too much or being sensitive. However, the night of typhoon had suddenly changed him into a kind of animal with tentacles all over his body.

Ah Jin thought about the woman. He dialed back the call made to him that afternoon. Ah Jin said, "Some accident happened to your friend."

The other end felt very cold, and then the line was cut.

Ah Jin went downstairs using the fire escape. There were emergency lights along the stairs, but few of them functioned. His first idea was to go to the lobby where he could talk to somebody. The storm would probably subside in a bit and he might be able to go home. Noise reverberated very loudly through the stairway. There was a disturbance below. Many people were shouting at the same time: "The neon lights have hit somebody!"

6

Rabbit Man Zhang hurried into the mobile-phone repair shop after it had started raining. The shopkeeper had just come back in himself, with rainwater streaming down from his bald head.

Young Zhang said, "I want my mobile repaired."

The boss said, "Let me have a look. Repair this? Why don't you sell it?"

Young Zhang said, "Sell? Okay."

The boss said, "Has it been dropped? If so, I don't want it."

Young Zhang said, "You repair phones, don't you?"

Staring at Young Zhang, the boss said, "Repair? You'd better go see someone else."

Young Zhang was about to take back the phone, but the boss did not loosen his hold of it. He knocked the phone on the edge of the counter. Young Zhang said, "You'll break it!" The boss did it again, and then took a look at the mobile before handing it back to Young Zhang. At that moment two people came into the shop at the same time. Both of them took out a mobile phone each, and put them on the counter. The boss flipped them over and put them under the counter without a word. He began to quietly count money out for the two sellers.

It dawned on Young Zhang that the shop was a fence for disposing of spoils. The boss said from behind him, "How about 1,500?" Young Zhang walked away, pretending not to hear him.

The storm had lessened the number of pedestrians out on the street. Someone ran by, braving the rain. Young Zhang was not afraid of rain. What should a Rabbit Man be afraid of? Rain is a natural substance, much better than Old Liu's stinking sweat. Now that he had with him a mobile that was worth 1,500 yuan, he would not expose himself in the rain. The sum for the phone was as good as two months' pay for him. He evaded the rain for a while in the doorway of a convenience shop. Now Young Zhang recalled what Old Liu had mentioned. It was a typhoon that could not be evaded in any short time. He bought a white rice dumpling to eat and found an excuse to ask for two plastic bags. He wrapped the phone layer upon layer before going back to take over the shift from Old Liu.

Young Zhang pulled off his galoshes and tugged them under his belt to protect the mobile phone pressed to his skin. Rainwater had submerged the street. Young Zhang intended to race across the street ahead of a car, but the car did not slow down. It shaved past him, and splashed him all over with water. Young Zhang pounded the car with all his might. Generally he did not do that, but now he had this pricey thing on him. He had suddenly become daring. He was worth good money now.

It was Young Zhang's first time to touch the windowpane of a car. It was not what he had expected, it was very strong, not made of ordinary material. It could not be broken easily. He saw very clearly that the driver was female. She also looked at him somewhat panicked.

Young Zhang sensed the shaking of the mobile phone under his belt. By then he was nearing the restaurant. Hiding himself quickly in a supermarket, he saw the tiny green light was blinking. That meant the mobile phone had not broken down. It still worked and blinked. How could a broken phone cost 1,500?

Young Zhang said, "I've made a pile!"

A long zipper was fixed on the belly of the rabbit robe. The Rabbit Men had to bend down to get into it. Old Liu was a bit taller than Young Zhang, so it was more difficult for him to get into it.

A flower girl squatted by the roadside selling a few sprays of roses. She fiddled with them for quite a long time. Old Liu showed up, pulling the rabbit robe halfway on, and said, "You'll spoil them that way. How will you sell them later!" The girl raised her head and gazed at Old Liu. A slip of a lass, of about seven or eight in age, she revealed an unexpected look of nonchalance and scorn. Old Liu was reminded of his three daughters in the countryside. Usually he was loath to think about them. He did not know why he had to bring them into this world. Moreover, he was unwilling to mull over himself, making money by acting as a silly rabbit in the street.

Rabbit Man Liu soon got the upper part of his body into the robe again. He set to propping up the rabbit.

Rabbit men are not allowed to stand there loafing. They have to hop and bounce perpetually and do all types of lovable postures to attract customers. Old Liu felt that he was just a fool. Rabbits, hens, geese and whatnot were never so foolish. Rabbit men were the most foolish of them all.

A kid passing by said, "Look, a rabbit. How cute it is!"

The child spoke again, "I'd like to touch the rabbit's red eyes!"

Finally he said, "I can't jump that high! Hold me up, hurry!"

Rabbit Man Liu saw the child suddenly coming up and stretching out a hand. Old Liu's left eye became dark, and then both eyes went dark.

The child cried out, "I didn't touch them, no, I didn't!"

When Old Liu regained his sight, the head waiter was coming toward him. He said, "You should jump and jump and brace up. Business is slack today. Work harder and keep an eye open. You're a rabbit, not a man."

Old Liu grumbled in his mind that it was not he who was to be blamed. It was the typhoon. But in the robe you are unable to say a word. You cannot be heard from the outside. The moment you put on the rabbit robe the lining sticks to the skin. After several minutes the lining slips off the skin and the whole body becomes slippery. Perspiration seals all the crevices of the robe.

The head waiter left and Old Liu kept on bouncing aimlessly. Through holes much smaller than his eyes, he paid close attention to the pedicabs passing by in the street. A fellow making a call almost bumped into Old Liu.

He said, "It landed right in front of you, right in front.... Are you blind!"

Young Zhang stripped sluggishly, trying to avoid Old Liu. He did not know where he should hide the mobile phone. There being only one thing that belongs to him — his body beneath the white light of the fluorescent lamp. He could be rest assured only after he tucked the mobile close against his body.

Old Liu said, "Last year during the typhoon, it cost fifteen yuan for one person to be carried across the street. They spent only a few minutes doing it by pedicab. You've held me up from borrowing a pedicab because you're late."

Young Zhang usually gave a scolding when he put on the robe Old Liu had just taken off, but not that day. Young Zhang behaved very quietly.

Old Liu noticed one of Young Zhang's thin legs was wet through the trouser leg, while the other leg was bare. The hair on the lower leg all stuck to the skin like leeches. Meanwhile Old Liu was naked, standing unperturbed at the door of the dorm. His body moved right and left following the swaying of the fan. It was a big industrial fan about one meter in diameter. The simple blades of the fan vibrated vigorously. Old Liu believed it was the best way to cool himself, without clothes on. Neither Old Liu nor Young Zhang was afraid of people seeing them naked. Old Liu always said to any passersby in the distance: "Feel free to look. If you can take a piece of my flesh that way, you should pay me for it." It was strange that Young Zhang now was turning away to change.

Old Liu said, "What's up?"

Young Zhang said, "I came back late."

Old Liu knew it was a pretext. He did not ask anything more. Old Liu said, "Just now I saw that guy again."

Young Zhang said, "Who?"

Old Liu replied, "The guy who looks like the one who jumped from the apartment. But I found out they are not the same person, for certain. He carried a lunchbox with him, a normal person."

Young Zhang said, "Well, you don't know why that guy jumped from the building."

Old Liu said, "He had taken things too seriously. Everyone comes across trouble."

Before the storm arrived Old Liu had indeed looked over the guy with the lunchbox. He had been in the rabbit robe then, so nobody could tell if he was fixing his eyes on them. Old Liu had contemplated the fellow as if he could get rid of any ill luck by doing so. He had followed the guy for a few steps and affirmed that he was the same one who had walked past, but he and the building-jumper did not look alike at all. Old Liu had felt very relieved. He looked up at the sky. It was a reddish yellow. In his mind's eye the sky was as beautiful as the sandy soil that was good for growing peanuts. Old Liu's arms felt normal again. He tested moving them. The hands that had carried the dead body did not feel slack any longer.

The head waiter appeared and sent Old Liu to deliver some takeout food. At the sight of naked Old Liu he said, "You look like a naked pig. A pretty sight that way?"

Old Liu said, "Nothing matters, except that I feel cool!"

The wind had become like a mad dog seeking revenge. It swept over the street. Many things were rolling by and toppling over: newspapers, water bottles, tree branches, umbrellas, underwear, shoes, street awnings, plastic bags, and so on, were all fleeing like defeated soldiers.

At about nine in the evening Old Liu managed to borrow a pedicab. Now the storm had become extreme. But the boss of the restaurant refused to stop doing business. In the hall there were only two customers sipping tea, to take shelter from the rain. Old Liu asked the cook for a slice of fat; it felt very greasy in his hand. Old Liu said, "Country folk have become infected by the bad habits of city dwellers." He added some oil to the pedicab. Afterward Old Liu fumbled through all the corners of the restaurant, including those filthy places customers do not know about, looking for a bicycle lock. He found one after half an hour. Old Liu sat down and thought: I'm waiting to collect money tomorrow.

The entire restaurant felt cozy. The waitress, still dressed in white simulated wool cloaks, was talking and laughing teasingly with the head waiter behind the door. They were all at ease and relaxed. Young Zhang, an umbrella in hand, was the only one out on the sidewalk trying to drum up business. As a matter of fact no one could see the sidewalk through the gloom of the rain and wind. Even those sitting behind the windowpane in the restaurant were barely able to make out the blurred moving figure of Young Zhang. One of the attendants said, "How pitiful Rabbit Men are!"

Young Zhang did not feel it. He stuck to his post in the wild storm, feeling mighty and splendid. A Rabbit Man holding a big umbrella looked like a small animal huddling under a mushroom. A taxi pulled up at the roadside. The driver thought that Young Zhang had wanted to flag down a taxi for customers, while Young Zhang took it that there were customers getting out of the taxi so he had gone up to greet them. The taxi suddenly sped off. From the shape of the driver's mouth, Young Zhang could detect curses.

Young Zhang tried to keep the umbrella steady in the wind but it was very difficult. The moment he slackened his grip, the umbrella blew away with the wind.

Right at that moment the large neon light of the restaurant collapsed and fell down. Young Zhang felt no pain but instead saw something blazing, too dazzling to look right at. He simply turned his eyes to one side; he could not look. The neon light, tens of meters high, broke in pieces here and there once it touched the ground, but the power had not been cut. The characters *Hao Men* were still leaping.

Old Liu could not see why the door of the restaurant was suddenly so bright. He guessed that lightning had struck the door. He walked through the hall, finding the glass door no longer there. It had been smashed by the neon light.

Old Liu saw the rabbit robe on the ground. He tried to pull Young Zhang. The light tubes pressed into Young Zhang's body were still blinking. Under the neon tubes there was a steel frame. One could not stand up underneath such a steel frame. Old Liu could not see the face of Rabbit Man Zhang. He tried to drag the man inside but in vain.

With rainwater all over his face, Rabbit Man Liu was then blown backward by a blast of high wind. His hands were still pulling at a glowing tube of light.

Old Liu shouted, "Young Zhang, Young Zhang, Young Zhang!" Rainwater poured into his mouth. In circumstances like that, the shouting of a single person sounds incredibly weak. Old Liu made it close to Young Zhang's body. He felt something bulging out.

Old Liu said, "It's a bone. He's got a fracture somewhere."

(Translated by Kuang Wendong)

Last Tango in the Square
One Midsummer Night

—— Xu Kun

Xu Kun. Born in Shenyang, Liaoning Province, in March 1965, Xu Kun holds a doctorate in literature from the Graduate School of the Chinese Academy of Social Sciences and the professional title "first-ranked writer of literature." As a premier literary writer, she is now a member of the Beijing Writers' Association and on the National Committee of the Chinese Writers' Association.

Since 1993, she has published fiction and prose totaling 3 million Chinese characters, including such well-read short stories as "Encountering Love," "Bird Droppings," "Kitchen," and "A Foreigner in China"; the novellas *Vernacular Chinese, Pioneer, Hot Dog, Shenyang*, and *Young People Gather Together*; and the novels *Twenty-two Spring Nights, Love for Two and Half Weeks*, and *Wild Grass Roots*; as well as the drama scripts *Silver Fox* (adapted from Wang Meng's novel) and *Men and Women in Love* (staged by Beijing People's Art Theater in 2006). Some of Xu Kun's works have been translated into English, German and Japanese; and some have received prizes for outstanding fiction from the periodicals *Chinese Writers, People's Literature, Selected Stories*, and *Fiction Monthly*. She was given the 1st Women's Literary Achievement Award by the Chinese Association of Contemporary Literature in 1998; and the 2nd Feng Mu Literary Prize, the 2nd Lu Xun Literary Prize and the 9th Zhuang Zhongwen Literary Prize, respectively, in 2000, 2001 and 2003, by the Chinese Writers' Association.

Last Tango in the Square One Midsummer Night

1

The ground lights on the square are blindingly bright. With each displaying four halogen bulbs, these square lights reach their horizontal heads out of thickets about a foot high from the ground. Forming an angle of thirty degrees, they blindly shine upward from various directions. The lights catch her two ever-spinning white legs — with hardly anything special except their shiny pallor. Well, somewhat reluctantly, they may also be deemed slender and well-proportioned.

Certainly the legs are also long, at least longer than normal lengths for Beijing women. The stripes hanging down from the top of her thighs are flying and rippling along with the swaying of her body, like a century-old wine-shop's sign banners in the wind. The stripes are actually part of a most fashionable tutu, shockingly short yet elegant. When the dancer spins her body, the skirt opens up *"sola sola"* to reveal her long and slender white legs. With another *"sola sola"* swirl the flying stripes reveal silk underpants of a netting material with floral lace. These are scarlet red underwear, not flaming, dark red or tangerine, but scarlet red. Set off by the green tutu of a white floral design, the scarlet panties jet out a ferocious sense of sexiness.

A crowd of migrant laborers watching the scene from the sidelines cannot stand it anymore; they look about to burst out into a collective nosebleed. Standing or squatting on the grass or along the cement sidewalks on the square, their jaws have dropped open, and they are breathing heavily. Their fire-blazing eyes are staring at that vicinity beneath her tutu, shooting out one after another heated and red-hot spotlights following her swirling skirts.

The rest of the crowds on the square, however, regard the female dancer rather disdainfully. These are the upright residents of the city, coming to dance in their loose summer vests and big shorts. In twos and threes, they hold onto their partners' arms, dragging their legs and feet idly following the music of the "Beijing four-step," while shooting haughty glances at the pair — he and she — two bewitching yet vulgar strangers intruding onto their space. They try to pull away from the two as far off as possible, as if to let them make fools of themselves under the bright limelight on the square.

Nevertheless, the man and the woman seem to ignore the atmosphere around them or simply do not care. They seem to intentionally seek the limelight with their bodies, exposing her legs in the illuminated square without a trace of reservation. The woman is still spinning and swirling swiftly. Actually she not only spins quickly but tries to catch up with the quick tempo of the music by shifting her feet so her short skirt flies open as much as possible. Her partner, the man always wearing black tights, is capably agile and slim, with everything on him tight and hard. He reaches his arms out, kicks his legs, turns and twists his hips around her flying stripes. Looking from behind, the perfect shape of the man's buttocks and legs are those of a professional dancer. His Latin dance moves are up to standard, too. His moves of shrugging, shaking, clinging and rubbing are well composed, with every detailed pose in place. However, when observed more closely, you would find plenty of wrinkles on his face. He should be in his late forties or early fifties at least.

The woman looks not young either. Even as she is busy raising her long white legs in the limelight, the lamplight of the night fails to provide any luster to her body. Instead, it ruthlessly exposes the sagging state of her thirty to forty-year-old skin. Although her transparent silk stockings hold up the loose flesh on her legs —oh no, she does not seem to be wearing stockings at all. Her legs are bare and her sockless feet are clad in a pair of flesh-color, round-mouth leather shoes strapped across the instep with half-high heels, about one to two inches shorter than real dance shoes. Her dancing skills perhaps amount to just have completed a training class in social Latin dancing.

But does it really matter? The woman just uses a fashionable tutu of stripes, two big white legs and scarlet panties flashing through her open skirt to attract the eyes of everyone, bewitching them, making herself the absolute star on the square. Certainly profiting from her, the man becomes the leading male partner here, too.

2

The square is a gathering place for middle-aged and elderly idlers in the city. Young people despise coming here. What they love to frequent are the bars, the discos or the discount KTVs, which are noisy, lively and costly. While the rich and the powerful middle-aged residents go to the foot massage parlors, sauna houses or hot-spring resorts in the suburbs to relax and seek entertainment. They have no reason to swarm to the free open square! Only the old lower-income citizens air themselves in such an open space as a city square all the time, doing their morning exercises, playing card games, dancing, walking their dogs or strolling to kill time and give vent to their desires.

Let us now focus on the dancing people in the square tonight. The dance starts punctually at eight every evening. By eight o'clock every evening sharp, always on time. After watching the CCTV-1 "Network News" and "Focus Interviews" (Beijingers care greatly about current events, so these two TV shows are watched in every household), cleaning up the dinner tables and turning off the TV sets, these square-frequenters then check their clocks and hurry out the door towards that brightly lit space. There, the exciting dance music has just begun!

The management office of the residential district has arranged special people to connect the cable and player to broadcast the dance music. A bald janitor bicycling from the office arrives early to where people are gathering to dance in the square every evening. There are sixteen magnificent colonnade pillars of a baroque style standing around the space here. They hold up a number of huge green air balloons that remind one of those round domes atop Russian Orthodox churches. Actually these are no more than a sort of useless architectural decor. One after another, flocks of white and gray pigeons fly in and out among the pillars and leave pigeon droppings everywhere. The large vacant space nearby can comfortably hold over a thousand people to gather and dance. It is also where the pigeons play and seek food in the daytime. When dusk falls, it becomes a recreation center where middle-aged as well as older men and women dance in pairs, holding each other with ambiguous expressions, while stretching and loosening up limbs and bones.

Every evening the bald janitor pulls out the extension cord from a small shed in the square, to plug it into an old cassette player. The shed was formerly used by a pigeon breeder. After the pigeons returned to their nest every evening, the pigeon breeder used to carefully clean up the droppings on the cement with clear water. The washed ground would always waft off a vaguely pleasant fragrance.

Just think about it: although the square is located in a "economical housing" district in northern Beijing — a new term coined during the urban construction of recent years — to be frank, it is just a residential district built for lower-income citizens. Even so, its environmental planning and construction are by no means much inferior. The designers reserved a large space, which could have housed more than ten residential buildings, for a giant square, and named it "Promenade Park." The square has various sections, eye-catching extensions and cascading spaces. The tiered cement flowerbeds and waterside pavilions resemble stadium seating. When blown dry in the winter, their mottled beaten appearance reminds one of the weathered amphitheater of ancient Rome, offering a rather shocking sight at first glance. Several pigeon huts with small red steeple tops were built in the western corner of the square. Italian-style iron grills provide windows in the back of the pigeon huts. The fountains, ponds and statues have been erected in a fine pattern, loyally following ancient Greek fashion. That cement statue of a hunting goddess often has her head squirted with pigeon droppings. Even the pigeons may not know why love to relieve themselves on the heads of statues.

All sorts of exotic styles and flavors have been flung together in imposing and fastidious efforts by its designers. Nevertheless, the mixed arrangement looks rather tumultuous and vaguely indefinite. Visitors coming to the square for the first time would often joke about where on the earth this place could be. "Other than China, this could be any place in any country around the world."

Only after some time do people learn that this residential district was built by a company from Heilongjiang Province, who had simply moved their Russian architectural style in Harbin over to Beijing!

Ah, no wonder! People sigh in admiration. The developer should simply convert all the slums of Beijing into those of Heilongjiang or the former Soviet Union, so that people living here would feel as if they were living in Harbin!

Let us now see what that bald janitor is doing. He has set up that old cassette player, as big as an old black-and-white television, in an out-of-the-way corner by a colonnade pillar. Then he pulls out a cassette from a big bag full of music tapes and inserts it into the cassette player, before the arrival of the square's dancers. The world has long entered the digital age by now but he is still using that cassette player to play dance music! Just think about it, must it not be that, in a city slum everything is still retrograde? The songs he broadcasts are also the old ones familiar to the middle-aged and elderly. His wide collection ranges from the old songs sung by Guo Lanying, Wang Kun, to Deng Lijun, Fei Xiang, Mao Amin or Peng Liyuan. The dancers in the square are not picky about professional dance tunes. So long as there is a song or something resembling one, they start moving their legs to the tempo.

One thing to note here, however, is that there is no Sun Yanzi, Zhou Jielun, Dao Lang or Liu Ruoying in the air for sure. There are not even songs by Wang Fei, Sun Nan or Na Ying. The collective memory of the square regulars remains in the 1980s and 1990s, or even the 1950s and 1960s, in the past century when songs of the former Soviet Union were in vogue. The dancers here cannot follow these postmodern singers and their songs, as they sound unfamiliar and their tempos do not groove with them. They are just unable to harmonize to such beats.

As soon as the music starts playing at eight o'clock, people gather in the square from all directions, locate their partners and get ready to step into the circle.

Ah, what a wonderful feeling! On a midsummer night, bathed in the silver moonlight against the vast world, the cool breeze spreads a serene atmosphere under a tranquil sky and on the earth. The holly, cedar, clover, rosebush, redbud, weeping willow and lo-cust trees in the square, nurtured by the rich nutritious soil, compete secretly to impart fragrance throughout the night. These are faster-reproducing species, so they have flourished around the Promenade Park Square to decorate it with luxuriant leaves and waving boughs, all in a short time of less than two years. It is said that the square sits on a former garbage dump, so the soil here is extremely fertile, and also that its groundwater is good for plants.

Those who come here to dance are mostly local residents. Rather careless about their attire and acting very casual, the men only wear loose vests and short pants, with some of them even dragging slippers on their feet, not much different from when they are roaming in the vegetable market. The women coming to the square are equally casual in their dress, wearing no makeup and no bras under loose blouses, simply unable to shed their homely hab-its. Their dancing could also better be called "strolling" more than dancing, except they do their ambling in pairs. Some of the pairs are of a man and a woman, but others are of two women holding onto each other (although you won't see any pairs involving two men here). While holding, touching or caressing their partners' hands, either deliberately or unwittingly, the dancers kick, move or drag their feet. Despite the furtive and turbulent passions surging and whirling between them, the expressionless faces of these dancers show little emotion, as if in public men were not men and women were not women. Just looking at their ambiguous manners, you recall those mass movements of the past century, of say, group Yangge dances or Taiji exercises, collective movements resembling injecting chicken blood or drinking black tea fungus. Why not! You may lose your chance to share in this if you wait too long to jump in.

Pigeons cluck above your head. Dogs run around your feet. The working people's mass self-entertainment movement is ongoing and lively in the big city, against the curtain of the summer night, monotonous as pond water yet enduringly peaceful and unfailing present.

3

One day suddenly, the square spawned the glamorous couple from among the crowds, disturbing and shattering the former tranquility. Their pungent, showy performance stuns everyone else and drives them to gasp for breath. The two occupy the smoothest and most-favored spot in the circle and steal the limelight of the entire place. Although the other dancers still move about to the beat, their attention and interest are away from themselves, blown away by this pair in their center.

Where are they from, these two? No one knows. What is their background? What is the relationship of the two? Why do they dress like that and dance so wildly? No one has the slightest idea, or can understand it at all. This is but a mass dance in the square amidst a cool summer evening. What necessity is there to put on those formal, coquettish costumes? Just look at that woman, what kind of trashy dress has she put on? Already in her early forties, she bares her shoulders and back, bends over and kicks her legs high, so shameless and shocking at her age, under the stares of everyone. Look at the man shaking that big bottom of his as if he were in convulsions. It is not a social dance competition on TV. There are no cameras focusing on you. Why whirl and twist so vigorously?

That woman's efforts to spin, in particular, just make no sense at all, as it is neither necessary nor meaningful. She seems to love spinning especially, that kind of senseless swirling. For instance, when the song on the cassette player sings *"Really miss you/ you're in my dreams,"* it is probably referring to an army spouse missing her husband serving in the border regions. But when those words are sung, what necessity is there for her to spin five times; so it is 360 times five turns into 1,800? Or at the start of the song *"When the year 1997 ushered in its spring/ an old man in China drew a circle by the South Seas on the map,"* when she spins merrily, her two feet shift so fast with heels following toes, that her body turns endlessly like a senseless top.

Most awkwardly, when she spins, her short skirt opens up completely right before the upturned faces. If not totally defenseless, you may call her utterly shameless.

The upturned faces belong to migrant laborers from rural areas working in the residential districts. The workers with dirty faces and disheveled hair are smart, as they have chosen a wonderful angle by sitting on the ground so their heads are at the height of the lights shining out of the bushes. It provides them the best expanse for keen observation. Sitting on the cement ground most peacefully and orderly, they forget the mosquito bites or the cold dampness under-neath their bottoms. Turning blind and deaf to everything else and holding their breath, they wait for those magic moments when she spins — much like a peacock unfolding its tail.

What do they care that a female peacock doesn't open up her tail and only a male one does? Whenever those scarlet underpants show through the skirt's stripes, they feel a thunderous explosion in their ears, all their blood surges into the head, and their opened mouths start watering. Gawking at the woman dancer, giving her their undivided attention, they then turn into stone statues.

This type of free underwear show is just also much safer, more attractive and fascinating compared to other types of recreation such as stealthily watching adult tapes in underground video parlors or hiring secret prostitutes at pedicure clinics.

It makes the onlookers wonder if she is spinning so hard just to be able to reveal her panties to the rural laborers. It at least proves that exhibitionism and voyeurism are capable of delighting each other in a perfect exchange. Though many in the surround-ing crowds perhaps cannot help but feel contempt toward both the dancing duo and the peasant audience.

The square community figures that the unidentified pair appears not to be husband and wife. They are seen riding bicycles to the square from different directions every evening, meeting at the square after leaving their bicycles against a pillar. The woman rides a twenty-six-inch bicycle, as does the man. Both vehicles are pretty old, carrying bottled mineral water and towels in the bicycle baskets. Apparently the dancers dress up at home for the occasion, rather than coming to the square first and then changing into their cos-tumes.

It is rather hard to imagine that woman, dressed in her short ballet skirt, riding an old twenty-six-inch bicycle parading to the square. It is equally hard to visualize how that man, dressed in his tights, presses his chubby, constrained buttocks onto that rusty, stiff bicycle seat, clunking all the way to the place. Quite a number of *Mercedes*, *BMW*, *Land Rovers* and other expensive cars park in the public parking lot next to the pillar where they leave their bicycles. Their bicycles stand proudly by the expensive cars without showing the slightest embarrassment or inferiority. One bike leans against the other intimately, with great accord and contentment.

Now, with the lights in the square turned on, the curtain of the dusk is drawn and music fills the air in the square. The man and the woman stand at attention in the center of the square to declare their presence. Then they raise their arms high to strike a dramatic pose. Their formal foreplay has wilted away all the other dancers, who have just humbly slipped out to form a circle with hunched backs and shoulders, after the man takes the hands of his female partner. Look at our star duo! After their striking posing, they immediately plunge into their explosive dance, wielding limbs and widely shaking hips. Entering soon into a state of ecstasy, they seem to forget everything else around them, as if there were just two of them between the heavens and the earth. It is as if they are prince and princess of this open square. No, more than that, they feel like they have become the king and the queen of the square. They seem to hear nothing and see nothing, except their own dance for the moment. Neither the disdainful looks of the onlookers nor the obscene peeping by the rural laborers, nothing else exists around them any more. They seem lost in their world of dancing from head to toe.

Enjoying their own dancing wholeheartedly, the two seem to care nothing about the rabble, turning up their noses at everyone else, confidently self-sufficient and musing to themselves through their own dance dialogue. They dance among the vulgar multitudes and are elevated by their own intimate body communication. They whisper to each other only and stare at each other tenderly, beyond others' comprehension. Actually, they don't really talk or look at each other while dancing attentively. Rather, they talk to and look at each other using their dazzling body language. He is the controller of her body as he uses his fingers like a magic wand, animating wherever he touches on her body. When it is time for her to spin, he just gives a light push with his left hand while holding high his right hand in the air, and she dutifully starts her wild spinning. The touch is often done with one finger rather than his entire hand. Then she starts her swirling in abandon, with skirt's stripes flying, on the axis of his finger as if not to lose her orientation.

They hold each other's fingers lightly, sometimes tightly and sometimes just touching, as if secretly to flirt with yet also to reject each other. With words becoming unnecessary, the dance is their magic language of communication, so they push out their bottoms and shake their hips all the more dramatically. When the quick rhythm of the *Blue Danube Waltz* is played, the man holds the woman's waist, spinning her with such mad speed that the lights around the square must turn into flashing flares in their eyes. The night becomes timeless and the years eternal. They look as if they are floating off the ground at times, both elevated into a dreamy dizziness.

The two are about the same height, so the bulge below the man's waistline just reaches her meaty belly (a physical feature common to amateurish dancers). She feels his occasional rubbing and uncontrollable erection but chooses not to dodge it. Except for blushing inwardly, she only feels more excited and their movements become even more provocative. Their turning, bending, touching and parting just become more abandoned.

They enjoy their physical caressing concealed under the public cloak of their social dancing.

Through their very public and eloquent mutual embrace, the two carry out the mission of their dance to the end.

4

The power of habit is tremendous. After a few times watching the pair dance, the crowds in the square begin to get used to seeing them around. Besides snatching the limelight from all the others, the two have not really bothered anyone else, but instead have manage to attract more and more onlookers and made the dancing on the square at night increasingly popular. Whenever they show up, the excitement of the square's populace reaches a crescendo. More migrant workers gather around the dancing people. Even the bald janitor becomes more professional in handling the music. He has somehow collected a large number of dance music cassettes, so dances in the square become much more colorful and complex than ever before.

An inexplicable eagerness ripples in all directions of the square as people anxiously await eight o'clock in the evening. Inside each mind are held expectations to see the pair, as if looking forward to the appearance of two stars onto a stage. Gradually, people even get used to the couple's gorgeous costumes and spectacular poses. More than that, the fancy dances of the two seem to transport them straight to the Vienna New Year's concert or a live show of some international social dance competition on TV, those being simply too spectacular and far away. Well, isn't it great that the two have brought such magnificent spectacles right before their eyes right now!

Nevertheless, you have to admit that the special pair has obviously had some professional training, as they indeed outdo all the other dancers in the square. Someone claims that they are sure they saw the man act as a judge in some sort of international dance competition on TV. According to the latest conjectures about the relationship between the man and the woman, someone announces that they are most probably a dance coach and his student from one of those fashionable Latin dance classes in Beijing. The man is surely a coach, but that woman must be a spare-time student, with too little muscle on her legs and not enough height about her instep to be a dancer. She has mastered only basic-level dance steps or at best, just above intermediary. However, she is deft enough, impressively energetic, perceptive and atypical. In particular, the creamy color of her skin is invidious. It is so white you are reminded of cream cake. And look at that willowy waist of hers! It is not easy to retain such a good shape at her age at all. As for her red underpants, people have stopped feeling nervous after getting used to them. After a while, the square crowds even feel that the green ballet skirt has always perfectly matched the scarlet panties from the very beginning.

Sometimes the other dancers cannot help but try to stealthily imitate some of their moves. They not only start to stride over some basic "Beijing four-step dances" following them, but also try one or two poses from their "Argentine Tangos." However, the latter is so difficult that people find it hard to make such wild poses. A man can get a crick in his neck if he turns his head too fast, or a woman may hear her knee crack when she kicks a little too high. Hence people sigh inwardly: not all the middle-aged and elderly can deal with the Tango — a type of expertise that makes an issue out of the female body. Feeling gradually convinced, with a secret admiration brewing for the pair, the dancers in the square begin to feel attracted by the duo. While dancing, their feet uncontrollably drag them towards the two in their center.

The man and the woman seem to sense nothing around them but just dance attentively within their own small radius of activity. Through the slow three-steps and four-steps to the Rumba, Samba, Knight, Cha-cha and Argentine Tango, the duo's dancing becomes more and more advanced as the square becomes their public stage to trot out their techniques. Their bodies get closer, their shoulders rub more intimately and their hips swing even more dramatically. Given to abandon yet at the same time ambiguous, they dance together by touching and caressing, enjoying each other through their mutual plunging; their bodies in communication where the public eye doesn't detect. Surrounded by approving sighs and the admiring looks of the onlookers, they soar higher, burning and blossoming boundlessly. They are simply uninhibited and bursting free.

Their desire spurting, their bodies join each other into one.

In the midst of the rustling night breeze, the unfolding show entertains the crowds in the square throughout the hot summer and chases away the stifling summer heat.

5

Then, all of a sudden, the pair stop coming to the square, without a word or a trace. On the seventh day of the seventh lunar month, the two just vanish.

The crowds in the square feel like they have been fooled. Confused and unused to the absence of their stars, people seem to lose something suddenly, yet fail to define what they have really lost.

Everyone who comes to the square to dance and finds the center in their circle vacant has the same disappointed expression on their faces.

Believe it or not, the seventh day of the seventh lunar month in that year also takes another bizarre turn. Long before the date arrived, newspapers drum up a report that a certain national committee member of the Chinese People's Political Consultative Conference (CPPCC) has proposed to convert the seventh day of the seventh lunar month into a Chinese-style Valentine's Day. Not only is the suggestion conveyed through all levels of government, but a public mass poll is carried out to test the popularity of the proposal. The management office of the residential district treats the issue most seriously. It even sends ballots to every household for residents to fill out. Reacting to the issue with big laughs, the residents comment, "It's rather funny calling our seventh day of the seventh lunar month 'Valentine's Day'! Isn't it the day the Cowherd and the Weaver Girl, husband and wife, reunite by crossing the bridge of magpies? Why call a married couple sweethearts now? How many pairs of sweethearts do we have in our land? Are we being encouraged to go around and seek out sweethearts?"

Then there were rumors that "such and such a member" of the CPPCC national committee must be representing certain business interests. For example, some merchants trying to market red roses, lovers' watches or diamond rings have bribed some committee members to submit such a proposal. "We will raise both our feet to applaud," they would've joked.

Sweethearts or not, it is true that the pair did vanish from the square with no warning or even a note. Their mysterious disappearance, like their uninvited advent, simply made no sense. At once the space where people are dancing has turned gloomy and spiritless.

Everyone began to feel listless and discouraged. Their dance steps become sluggish and sapped, as if the former lackluster atmosphere had somehow made a cunning comeback.

However, can the old order ever be restored after being destroyed?

Those who frequent the square have nowhere to complain to nor would they even know what to complain about, since no one can define what they are really missing in the square. Even the migrant laborers, who so enjoyed watching the dancing, have stopped coming to the square. The rural laborers, with their dark complexions and long disheveled hair, yawn and leave resentfully, after glancing at the elderly uncles and aunties in loose blouses and pants shuffling in the circle. What await them would be either the stuffy, hot video parlors or the loneliness of their sheds throughout the long summer night.

That bald janitor has also lost much of his enthusiasm for playing dance music. Often he even gives up playing any dance music, but simply shows some documentary films such as how to guard against AIDS, war films commemorating the sixtieth anniversary of the war against Japanese aggression, or others. A yellowish, shaky piece of cloth is hung between two pillars. Waving big rush-leaf fans and squeezing both in front of and behind the cloth screen, the dense crowd watches the films rather absentmindedly. It seems to at once throw one back to those scarce and outmoded years of the 1960s and 1970s. Both the blurry images moving on the screen and the panicky insects darting between the bushes seem to test people's patience. The calm blood of the middle-aged and elderly provides a tasty feast for the mosquitoes, looking for those who sit still during such a hot summer night.

After the two dancers vanish from the square, some others do step forward to try to fill the vacuum and seize the starry crown. However, it is all to no avail. All efforts are simply useless. One time, a pretty young girl with big eyes and raddled makeup steps in, wearing three-inch high-heels, a tiny suspender vest and a bright pink knee-length pleated skirt. Her flashy entrance on the scene attracts one man after another to invite her to dance. She accepts each of them and starts whirling, kicking and flying showily like bird under the halogen lights. She imitates that woman dancer also, by spinning whenever there is a chance, whirling senselessly until she makes her own head spin. She also twirls so hard as to also let her skirt fly open to reveal her youthful, jade-white legs and her underpants — a pair of pure white ones.

Pretty well she dances, really not bad at all. With all the male partners who get to steer her, she cooperates with each companion skillfully, well coordinated and flirtatious. She also lets her skirt flare open, flashing a bit of underwear from time to time. Her light pink skirt is equally dazzling under the bright lights of the square.

However, it just does not work. No matter how hard she tries, the right kick is just not there. Even if she tries her best to preen, stretch and charm, something is simply not right. What is it that's wrong? People can't seem to pinpoint it. The migrant laborers can't clearly say. But their hearts are crystal clear. They have been conditioned and given their approval to the first pair — the fixed one man and one woman style, their implied sexual flirting and mutual teasing, passionate romance and pure inspiration. They tacitly accepted their red flashing and green swirling, their obscure making of eyes, one-on-one explosive swan songs, their brilliance and the flaming final pitch.

Yet that pair just kept to themselves, caring or concerned about no one else around them.

One-to-one may be the most beautiful, admirable, enviable and romantic pattern of human emotion. Whereas those who could go with just anyone are considered no better than sluts, cheap and without value. Although the migrant workers might not understand nor be able to express it clearly, they comprehend it clearly enough in their hearts. After experiencing that special pair, they have a model of impassioned spectacle already in mind. Their appetites are set and heightened. Subsequently, whoever arrives and however much the newcomers try, they are just not accepted.

6

The vanishing of the special pair lasts about two weeks, which is a long enough time for the square community, given the summer in north comes and goes at a wink. How many fine weeks could they afford to lose?

When the pair appears on the square again, everyone livens up at once — the dance circle here badly needs its stars! Whatever the size of a place, as vast as a country or as small as a residential square, it needs leaders to command the populace. Such leaders are eagerly expected to inspire and illuminate the multitudes with their charisma, their dedication and passion.

The migrant workers excitedly file back to the bushes and sidewalk. They again align themselves with the level of the ground lights again, eagerly waiting, with orderly yet bubbling anticipation, to enjoy their familiar underwear show. The other dancers, bored for a long while already, await the performance with equal anxiety. They voluntarily make way for the center of the square, so the star couple could have the smoothest cement, the best-lit space to themselves. They are awaiting the return of the stars to the stage in their own hearts, too.

The pair steps in. They get into the circle now. They raise their arms and start to dance as before.... However, somehow, something has changed. How come their raised arms, dancing steps and bending are no longer the same as before?

Although they have returned to the square, kicking and dancing as before, clearly something is not right. Yet no one can really define what it is. Anyway, you feel that something is no longer the same as before.

They are dressed exactly the same, the woman in her green tutu with a white floral design, and the man in his black tights, his hair as mousse-polished as before. However, something strikes the onlookers, that they have somehow changed. Yes, they are dancing, but their muscles are way slacker, and both of them seem to be preoccupied, absentminded and uncertain. Their bodies seem to be filled with much exhaustion, as if after their respective codes have been deciphered by each other. No longer is the woman lithe, or the man aroused. They move their feet flatly and effect much less spinning. Even when the woman turns, she does it reluctantly and awkwardly. Turning with such clumsiness and heaviness, she whirls so badly, as if she may stumble at any moment. The man's finger signaling for his partner to spin also looks rather listless now. Wriggling his hips lazily, he throws his head and neck back casually. When sometime they happen to touch each other, the woman no longer trembles with excitement. Indifference is written all over her, as if she has just touched a club. Her wooden reaction and lack of excitement seems to depress her partner too. He looks just as discouraged and uninspired.

They rather resemble two exhausted beaches swept empty by a tsunami, with devastation everywhere.

Even details, like the woman's scarlet underpants look obviously discolored. The scent emanated is no longer provocative, and the laborers, aided by their male animal instincts, seem to smell a sort of tainted odor of sexual unraveling.

How could there be such a dramatic change in just half a month? What has happened in those two weeks? Two rainfalls and one threat of a typhoon named "Maisha" passed over the area, with the bad storm deciding to progress along the edge of the continent to wreak havoc on the coast of Dalian by the Bohai Sea instead. So across the city it had merely bequeathed a few symbolic light drizzles. Once the sky had cleared up again, the wild wormwood grass shot up more than a foot. Lawn mowers start humming diligently to cut the grass, sending whiffs of grassy fragrance around the square. The nice smell of green grass remains the same, yet somehow the spell before or after the rain has bestowed on people a sense of regret, of loss.

How could the people's mood change so quickly? In only two weeks, their clothes had become soaked by summer sweat, so they could hardly wear them again after those several days due to the perspiration stains. Even when they try to wear them outside, the clothes have somehow lost their style and shape, looking discolored and wrinkled, with a shabby feel to them. Those who had danced on the square merely half a month ago are so soaked by the days of heat and humidity, already showing traces of summer exhaustion.

All the pairs are dancing as they did two weeks ago, yet they all look a bit bored now. Both the men and the women look sort of helpless, while also seeming to hold onto some kind of anticipation as well. They are killing time while waiting and wasting away, wasting time but no one appears to know how to end this pointless process. Their bodies are clearly spent and every dance seems to be a swan song before a finale. They still come to the square and drag their limbs reluctantly and listlessly each day. The onlookers should have realized the dissolute mood in the square, but they soon also get used to the situation. Humans cannot just do what they like and dance as they wish all the time. Sooner or later, they will tire and fall into a hopeless resolve. But no matter how people feel, so long as the two continue coming to join them in the square, they still feel fine about the whole thing.

What is different now, nevertheless, is that the masses around the two have lost their shyness along with their worship for their stars. They have cultivated enough courage to dance with the two at the center of them. By imitating their poses and moves, the masses have learned a great number of complicated steps too. Having lost their former brilliance, the two are no longer the absolute leaders at the center of the square.

7

Autumn arrives in the twinkling of an eye. Being the most beautiful season in the city, the fall has its mild winds coming in from the southwest, lifting the sky so much higher above. All the leaves on the trees glisten in the clear sunlight, and the city is bathed in a bright and crisp mellowness. The nights have already become cold and windy, so the people dancing in the square have donned woolen skirts and thick coats. However, the star duo, the man and the woman, still dress in their unaltered summer attire. Somehow their tight costumes look a little stingy in the autumn lights now. No, not just stingy, they simply look pathetic and miserable.

The Mid-Autumn Festival in September happens to fall on a

Sunday. The management office of the residential district makes an exception for the holiday, allowing people to revel in the square and dance until midnight. Generally the office enforces the regulation that the dancing in the square should be over by ten pm, to prevent the din from disturbing nearby residents.

The holiday is destined for mass revelry according to folk tradition. When dusk falls, the square is packed with visitors enjoying the full moon, walking dogs, strolling after dinner, dancing, or simply sharing in the excitement. The merry clamor uplifts the square toward the sky. A supermarket is peddling discounted leftover moon-cakes near the thickest crowds in the square. Dogs are barking animatedly. Pigeons, startled, circle overhead. The moon moves behind some layers of dark clouds, as the clouds roll happily above the square. A folk saying goes, "The mid-autumn moon is at its fullest on the sixteenth day of the eighth lunar month, rather than the fifteenth." The saying is best illustrated in the Beijing area due to its latitude.

The dance music rings out at eight o'clock as usual. Pairs file into the circle to dance. Becoming ill-mannered and pushy, the dark crowds of dancers and onlookers start to hustle and shove, scratch and jostle. Small quarrels and bodily collisions occur from time to time in the dense throngs of people. Several veterans of the square cannot help wondering about that couple and start to throw glances at the bright halogen-lit center, looking for the explosive ballet tutu and those two familiar white thighs. Only up until the leading stars make their appearance are all the other dancers able to attempt to show off who is better and who is worse.

Too bad... nowhere to be seen. The vast mass revelry, like a dragon without its head, is but a chaotic blur without its leader. There is not even one spotlight or a pair of lovely thighs in sight.

Hours seem to pass, and by half past nine the star duo has still failed to arrive. The veterans and habitués in the dancing circle can no longer control their disappointment. Everyone is asking inwardly if the two will play the game of abandoning them once again.

It's okay though. The two finally show up, better late than never. At almost ten o'clock, the mass of the dancers have warmed up and are in full swing already. Once the two appear at the site, the eyes of the crowds light up, their backs straighten up and a new climactic tide sweeps over the space immediately. Not expecting such a saturated square tonight, the two are motivated at once and plunge into the dancing circle with a declarative pose, without hesitation, and are soon confidently occupying center stage. For the first time the woman has changed into a diamond blue dance skirt for this night. With a tight waist and long ruffles, the skirt is decorated with lots of glitter. When she is spinning, she seems to be flying with a golden smock, which dazzles everyone's eyes! Before their appearance, the bald janitor in charge of the music had almost dozed off. Now, as soon as he spots their arrival, he seems as if infused with a great deal of chicken blood. He presses down the "stop" button on the cassette player at once and pops in a new cassette with more complicated performance tunes.

What a grand sight, this thrilling collective dancing! The sky transforms into a surrounding theater curtain as the earth becomes a colorful stage. The two lead the dance in the brightly lit center, as multiple layers of dancers revolve around the pair in growing circles. As if rehearsed by a choreographer beforehand, the multitudes are suddenly transformed into mannerly and disciplined dancers. Starting with the slow three-step and four-step social dances, the crowds concentrate their enthusiasm in their feet, their passion pouring into their hips. With the crisp and clear autumn wind, and under the peeping silver moon, they dance with all their heart, accompanied by the swaying tree branches and ever louder chanting of autumn insects.

The pair dances perfectly tonight. Elegant and touched with special grace, they seem to find their initial spirit once again aflame. A soft romance and even a feeling of dreamy tenderness seem to dart between the two tonight. They look at each other lovingly from time to time, as if their body language is insufficient so they need to add tender gazes too. The mood of the crows is also fired up, as if enchanted and inspired to follow the light steps of the duo. However, in that moment, who could have known, not even the two stars themselves... would have been able to guess that this is to become their swan-song performance for their public dance career on this square.

By and by, the duo changes their steps into the quick rhythms of a sailor dance, rock, then rumba, samba, jazz, and eventually the tango. The tango is the best display of their dazzling dancing techniques. Only a small number of dancing partners can follow them now. The big space turns into their solo performance again. Without any complaint about being flung aside, the crowds around them watch the two in their mutual pleasure. After all, it has been a long time since seeing their stars dance so blissfully. They feel contented, even having to be onlookers on the sidelines.

During the last tune of a tango melody, the woman seems to enter a state of ecstasy. Perspiring and heaving fiercely, she turns all the cells of her body toward resounding drumbeats. In wild abandon, already beyond herself, she flings her head around almost hysterically, swinging her hips exaggeratedly and pressing closer and closer to her dancing partner. Incited by her wild moves, at the same time the man becomes more excited too. He dances with trembling limbs as if he had stepped on an ignition switch, and every joint of his begins to jiggle dramatically to the musical rhythm. They are in a stage of ultimate oblivion, as if everything around them has become natural and instinctive. Now the woman places her abdomen against the man's body and wags her bottom dramatically, imitating body-to-body friction. Without warning, the woman turns bolder and bolder, more and more excited, until she becomes completely hysterical. All of a sudden, by placing all her weight onto her left leg and lifting her right leg, she wraps her big white thigh around the man's bum!

This move is rather too abrupt, simply too wild! As a stunning move in the tango, such an act can only be executed before competition judges in a TV show. How could she ever make such a brassy reality-show move before the innocent, defenseless masses in the square!

First, you hear a chorus of *"oohs"* ringing out from the crowds. Then a hush falls around the entire place. Everyone holds their breath and stares with wide eyes, waiting for what is to happen next.

Unprepared for his partner's move, the man is also startled. However, he tries to reach his arms out to respond through pure instinct. He makes his best effort to hold the woman's waist with his right hand, meanwhile raising his left arm to complete a standard pose. He must have thought that the woman would let him go, so their dance could reach its finale in a few seconds. Who knows why the woman refuses to let go but instead moves further to bend her body back, throwing both her hands out and kicking her left foot high in the air. Hence she drops all her weight onto her thigh that has wrapped itself around the man.

How can this be borne! Who could expect such an outrageous move! Utterly shocked and unprepared, the man is totally stunned by the woman's act. Shocked inside and going stiff all over, he not only fails to hold the woman up but even loses his own footing, too. In an agony of frustration, he cannot help but let his partner fall solidly onto the ground right on her back. Worst of all, as her leg is still enwrapped around him, it drags him down with a loud thump as well. So he crushes her squarely into the ground.

Oh, too awkward! Too disgraceful! Two big grownups falling on top of each other at the brightest-lit spot on the square. Fortunately, helped by his basic training as a professional dancer, the man jumps up swiftly in barely two seconds, as if nothing has happened at all, before everyone figures out what is going on. And immediately, he reaches out to try to pull the woman up from the ground.

But the woman seems to be in great difficulty and takes much longer before she can get up from the ground. It is obvious that her fall was really bad. By bending both her legs to try to sit up, she tries hard to get up slowly, with a most pained expression on her face. Seeing her twisted facial features, the man hints to her to control herself, so she quickly restrains herself, to put on an appearance of calm. Then, she manages to stand up with great effort and some help from the man's supporting arms.

Both having put on such a brave face, the two do not comfort each other before all those eyes. The man holds the woman's waist as if he is propping her up from behind. Together they are walking slowly toward the nearby pillar where they had parked their bicycles. People watch the two people, as they walk towards their bicycles leaning on each other slowly, as they unlock their bicycles, then push them, saying not one word through all this, as the duo together leave the square early.

Watching them walking away so slowly, all eyes in the square

are following their backs. They push their bicycles away in the same direction and the woman seems to be limping hard. By following their steps now as they walk, the usual crowd is shocked to realize that those are, in fact, two old and tired backs! They have not been young for a long time now. Actually people knew that they were not young for quite a while already. But somehow, the crowd had chosen to forget their age when the two rejuvenated their youthful spirit in that midsummer square. When the lackluster place was lit up by their headstrong passion, people had just completely forgotten about their age.

They walk farther and farther into the distance, and the dance music draws to its denouement bit by bit too. The dancers in the square can continue no more. Their enthusiasm wanes rapidly, after witnessing the scene before them. Gradually the reveling masses drift away. The midnight bell tolls across the square. This is the moment of disillusionment, when the crystal shoes change back to bare feet and the beautiful princess returns to be once again Cinderella. Finally, the moon pokes its head from behind the clouds and, at once, a layer of coppery red metallic moonlight sprinkles across the vast earth.

(Translated by Ji Hua & Gao Wenxing)

Meeting Xiao Fang Again

Chen Xiao

Chen Xiwo. Born in Fuzhou, Fujian Province in the 1960s, Chen Xiwo once worked as a secondary school teacher and then as an editor of a literary periodical, before he went to Japan for further studies in 1989. He now holds a doctorate degree in comparative and world literature, and teaches at a university in China.

Chen Xiwo mainly writes fiction, informal essays and studies. His representative works are the novels *Exile*, *Scratching an Itch*, and *China*; the fiction collections, *Our Ignoble Existence* and *Offensive Book*; the novellas, *Meeting Xiao Fang Again*, *Endless Shows*, *Cover*, *Happy Hero*, and *Vow to Heaven*; the informal essays, *My Regrets* and *Snowy Cherry Blossoms*; and the monograph, *Study of Literary Masochism*. Chen Xiwo has been awarded numerous prizes, including the People's Literature Prize, and has also been nominated many times for the Chinese-language Literature Media Prize. His works can be found in many anthologies and top lists. Some of his works have been introduced to readers in France, Japan, Taiwan, Hong Kong SAR, as well as other countries and regions.

Meeting Xiao Fang Again

1

What the hell did the woman want? She didn't have a mike, and had to type, she said.

We were chatting on NetMeet. She had a mike, and I knew it. I had adjusted my audio and the indicator for speaker volume was flickering. "You have a mike, and you're lying," I said.

Why had she lied? She refused to voice-chat, but only typed. Typing is like castration in the face of voice. Technology today has made everything possible, so why get castrated? She at last issued some voice, "Hi."

"How are you?" I asked.

"Just fine."

"But I can't see if you're fine," I said.

"I don't have video," she said, "sorry."

"Lying again," I said, "you have video, but didn't switch it on."

"How do you know?"

"Not really. I'm only trying to draw you out." She laughed. And I heard her. The laughter was her true voice. "How do you know?" she asked.

Of course I know. "Cos I know more than you do about the Internet," I said.

She went hush. "I don't know much about the Internet," she said. "*Ding*," she went offline. Dumb. I got up to pee. I live in a company dormitory, and my dorm-mate was just leaving the bathroom, in a hurry. He nodded at me. I knew he was rushing back to his room, since he also liked to chat with women online. I nicknamed him "Sohu" (Seeking Foxes), not that he actually searches for them, just that he more often than not refuses to be disappointed, even if he finds himself chewing tasteless chicken ribs. But Sohu stopped short, as if realizing the fact that nobody is waiting for him, even if he stayed inside. He murmured something to me.

He asked how I was getting on with my refurbishing.

I was moving into my own home soon. Planning to get married, I had bought the new apartment with a mortgage and was refurbishing it. "Another month to go," I said.

"Alas, one real person added, one virtual person less," he sighed in a queer voice. I knew what he meant. Another person similar to him would disappear.

"More is not necessarily good, while less not necessarily bad," I replied. Just then, NetMeet buzzed in my room. Who could it be? I rushed in. That woman again.

I replied. Again, she had not switched on the video.

A little annoyed, I felt an irritating pressure in my bladder. A feeling of being wronged.

"I got disconnected," she explained.

"Yeah," I said.

"I'm a real novice," she said, resuming the topic.

"You sure?"

"Yes, but I like chatting."

"You sincere about wanting to chat?" I asked. "Or what's the point? Better not to chat. Switch it on."

She finally switched on her video. The camera was not pointed to her, but at a wall and a plaster statue nearby, that broken-arm Venus. "Boo, you not a Venus. Still hiding. Especially when I reveal myself all the time. You are unfriendly, when I've shown myself," I said.

She giggled. "The costs are different for a man to reveal himself than for a woman," she said.

Sure enough. Was she a hag? "I'll cut off unless you appear," I said.

At last, there appeared an arm, which was fleshy. Expectantly, I asked, "Where are you?"

"Shanghai. And you?"

"Me too," I replied.

"Wow," she cried, sounding pleasant, "What are you?"

"A boss," I said.

I was also lying. In fact, I was a mere chauffeur for a boss. I liked calling myself boss, at least feeling sweetly intoxicated as if oozing through chocolate liqueurs when I spoke.

I suddenly realized that I had left the door open behind me. Sohu was standing in the sitting-room. Fortunately, my camera was very close to me, making it impossible to include him. I moved the camera away and turned back to close the door. I heard him sneering outside: "Boss."

I blushed. What a bloody nuisance! Wasn't it the same with him? But I was doing better than him. I traded stocks, so I had a girlfriend.

But since I did have a girlfriend, why should I still be seeking women on the net?

When I readjusted the camera, that woman said, "You're handsome."

2

I was shopping for a bathtub with my fiancée Ying. Girls are all shopping maniacs, who can be easily overwhelmed with mere money.

Ying was talking about the massage tub. I said it was no good, not conducive to her health. She asked, "How do you know?"

"Just think, there are tall and short people, but the massage points are fixed on the neck and waist. If it works okay on me, won't it work on your buttocks?"

"So sweet of you to curse me!" Ying screamed in reply, ready to pinch me.

She is shorter than me by half a head. I was right to say so, but I knew I was only shirking responsibility, for I was hard up. A massage bathtub would cost at least five thousand yuan, but had I sunk money into the stock market. Eastern Realty, where the house I bought locates, was an empty shell company, into which I had invested all my money. Of course, that money came from the market itself, slipping into my account in a flash and leaving all at once, all of a sudden. No longer my own money. Stock trading was like this, dreamlike. I had attracted Ying with the quick money, but she did not realize that it was only temporarily deposited with me. I dared not tell her that, or she would have flown away. Who would follow a pauper? I had to hide it from her. And get married first. I knew that a married couple could get divorced, and marriage was no longer a binding force, but I could do nothing but keep on going.

I then pretended to run away, and she followed. I quickly led her out of that damned massage bathtub shop. She caught up and said, "Do you mind my being short?"

"How could I? And you are not really short. One meter sixty, is that short?"

She is quite a beauty. And I said so. "Not beautiful at all!" she said, "Getting old. You keep me from staying young."

"Who keeps you from staying young?" I retorted, "I just think your pretty body should be kept in that tub."

I pointed to a wooden tub in front. It looked crude, an enlarged specimen of the wooden basin I used as a boy. Nowadays, people were so queer as to reproduce such things. I took hold of it, assuming it would not be very expensive. Sure enough, Ying jumped at it happily and strode in. She did look beautiful in it, like an exquisite toy. "Come on in!" she cried.

"How can I? It's so narrow," I said.

"So squeeze in!" she screamed. "Why, don't you want to squeeze in with me? Don't you like me even before getting married? A girl becomes an old lady after marriage, but you boys will be young, will always look handsome," she said.

Handsome I was indeed. Didn't the woman on NetMeet say so, too? But it was no use being handsome. I used to be a racing car driver, but ended up as a chauffeur because I was a failure. I only deserved a wooden bathtub such as this. I took a glance at the price tag. Ten thousand yuan! I was shocked.

The salesgirl came over. "Sir, miss, do you like it?"

"Such a toy?" I said.

I caught sight of Ying staring at me in surprise. She did not understand why I had changed my mind again. "This is a thing that country folk use," I added.

The salesgirl said, "Sir, you are mistaken, this is called 'Return to Nature'."

Boo! To hell with Returning to Nature. "What ails modern folk?" I said, "If this is 'Return to Nature,' my grandpa could've returned to nature fifty years earlier."

"Right," the salesgirl said, "That's exactly why we say, 'Return'."

I went speechless. Ying giggled, "It seems you didn't finish elementary school. You got a fake diploma, hah."

"Boo," I said. "What's not a fake nowadays?" I said.

"Then you're a fake to me?" she screamed.

"How could it…?" I stammered.

"Then pay for it!" she shouted. Almost an order. "Either you are a fake, or you don't love me!"

Of course I love you. But what do I have to own to love you? I said to myself. I'm hard up. But how could I yell that out to her? Hey, just pay for it if I have to. At worst, on credit. We'll have to pay back the debt together. If she wants a divorce, she will have to carry half of it.

It was almost cruel, to consider divorce before marriage. What made me so hard up? What made me bankrupt? What made me trapped by that damned public company? So I paid up my earnest money, and she kissed me outside the shop. I bit her tongue, experiencing cruel love. Was this our love?

3

That woman, I met her online again. She called me. She always seemed to have a lot of leisure.

"What do you do?" I asked her.

"A company."

"In a company, CEO eh?" I asked. I was only sneering. I hated rich people, I was poor.

"Aren't you a boss, too?" she asked. Sure enough, she was a boss. I was at a loss, suddenly remembering I had told her I was a boss. "I'm a small boss, and you're a big one," I said, maybe out of a guilty conscience in front of the real thing.

"How do you know I am a big boss?" she asked.

"Of course I know," I said.

"Speak up!" she sounded anxious. I perceived she was hooked like a fish, pulling at the hook and unable to leave. "Because I know it," I kept on.

"Out with it!"

I saw her arm. With such a fleshy arm, how could she be a small boss? "Because I saw you," I said.

Her arm jerked away, out of the frame. I laughed.

"You didn't see me at all," said she.

"I did."

"What did you see?"

"I saw you were afraid."

"Me afraid? Ha, ridiculous!" She generously showed her arm again, as if saying, why should I be afraid? Why should I hide?

"Why do you only dare to show your arm?" I said.

"What more do you want?" She asked. A jerk of the camera showed her face. It did not seem ugly. But her neck suggested that its extension might be fat. "Do you dare to meet?" I asked, out of sheer provocation.

"Then let's meet!" she replied.

Really!

We made an appointment at a café. She showed up. Fat for sure, very fat. When a woman is fat, others' impression of her slumps, so that nobody analyzes anything else that might recommend her. That included my original impression of her quite passable features.

I could not even discern her age, perhaps forty.

She was apparently uneasy, incessantly calling out to the waiter for this or that, as if trying to distract. Suddenly she seemed to find herself ordering too many dishes, only reminding others of her obesity. So she said, "Let's go."

"Where?"

"For a drive," she said, pointing to her car outside the window. It was a *BMW*, a good car fit for women drivers. I often saw women driving good cars in the street, and some of them were young and pretty, but I knew nine cars out of ten were not their own, or not bought with their own money. Certainly, women who really owned their own cars would be hags. I always feel a bit cheerless at the sight of such women: those cars appeared to be like the thick cosmetics they apply to their faces.

I suddenly remembered to mention my own car. A boss could not be without a car. I said, "My car broke down."

She smiled.

"Why do you smile?" I asked.

"Mine hasn't," she said, "What make do you drive?"

"A *Benz*," I lied. But not an outright lie, since I do drive a *Mercedes*, belonging to my boss.

"Good for you," she said.

"Nowadays a *Mercedes* is just so-so. You see, mine broke down," I said.

She gave me a ride. She seemed to have squeezed into her car, sideways. That big belly especially, I was afraid it would break open. Why on earth were there such fat women? But then she owned a car.

How good it was to own a car! I remembered a big trader at our stock exchange, who used to come with a *BMW* for some time. He said he had bought it with his first bucket of gold made on the market. We were so envious! Then he no longer came. He had reputedly made more money and opened a big company. Why didn't fortune smile on me?

"How did you nab your first bucket of gold?" I asked her.

She was shocked by my straightforwardness. Yes, nobody would ask such a rash question, especially to a woman, and a woman boss at that. But it was precisely because the woman was ugly that I could punish her so.

"Do you think it's because I slept around?" she retorted.

What a statement. Just take a look at yourself. Who'd care to sleep with you?

When people see successful pretty women, they think they must've slept around. She said, "When you see successful ugly women, what do you say? Look, such an ugly woman also made it because she slept around!"

I was taken aback.

She laughed. "It was pyramid marketing", she confessed.

"You weren't caught?" I exclaimed.

"Almost," she said, "It was exhausting!" She had really taken part in pyramid marketing. She said, "During a cadre meeting, they had been informed of a police check and relocated to the thirteenth floor in the opposite building. Walking downstairs from the sixth floor here, and climbing to the thirteenth there…."

"You climbed too?"

"We had to," she said, "but I was young then, capable of climbing." Wasn't the present size. She even eyed her own fat body. A resistant self-mocking. This woman was so conscious of her own appearance. To tell you the truth, which woman is not conscious of her own appearance? I was at a loss what to do. It seemed an offence to look at her ugliness. "It's good to be young," I had only this to say, "When you are young, you make lots of money."

"No, more often than not, when you are young, you don't

make lots of money," she said, "When you make money, you are no longer young."

It sounded like a tongue-twister. I too laughed. She switched on the CD player and music drifted out. That pop song, Li Chunbo's *Xiao Fang*. It was popular only among that particular age group; as for me, I was indifferent. The lyrics and music were simple, mediocre, but to them sounded mellow wine. Perhaps after long brewing.

"And then?" I asked.

"What?" Almost nervously, she was kind of startled. Actually, I was only asking casually, for I could not find the appropriate words. I immediately explained, "I was asking about your next business."

"Real estate," she replied.

Wow, the business that had ruined me! I had invested in real estate shares. I hated it, even though that public company had had nothing to do with her. "Real estate is good. You can buy and sell shares in property. Trading frantically until one side is bankrupt and the other eats its full to become fat...."

"What do you mean?" she asked.

I knew what she meant, but I didn't want to shut up. "Isn't it good?" I responded.

"It is," she admitted. She could not deny it. Nor could her spongy body conceal her original form that she had absorbed.

"You can keep eating!" I said.

"Why?" she said.

"Why not?" I said.

"What's the need?"

"It's always possible to eat more!"

"I've eaten too much," she said. She again peeked at herself. "I'm fat enough," she said smiling.

I felt in a bit of a daze, as if my first attack had been rebounded by her fat flesh. But I would not let it go at that. I said, "What does it matter? You can go and work out! Go sell the car, and walk it off. Share the money with the poor and I'm sure you'll lose pounds!"

"Right," she said, softening.

"I can't do without the car," she continued in a hoarse voice, as if whispering into my ear. I was suddenly touched.

"Nor can I," I said, "I can't go without my car. These days, with my *Benz* broken down, I can hardly move."

She laughed. "You don't have one," she said.

My heart was suddenly dashed. I had not expected her to be so straightforward.

"You don't need a *Mercedes*, like this coffin," she continued, "You can still move about, able-bodied. You don't need a coffin." She was hammering at the steering wheel. It honked. We both were surprised. There were no policemen about, but she made haste and stepped on the accelerator.

"How could this be a coffin? You see, it honks," I said. My humiliation was obliterated, perhaps just because she called her car a coffin.

She laughed.

"You see, it runs so fast," I continued.

"That's good of you to say so," she said. "Heard this piece of news?"

"What?"

"About a Yankee. A fat guy who couldn't rise from his couch, until it collapsed. He lay on the ground until he died. People had to undo the door to move his body out."

I felt like I had heard about it, but I wondered if it was the same story. There are so many stories like that, and obesity has become a major topic in our time. Someone had even estimated that, if one day our world was full of fat people, the Earth would not be able to hold itself up.

"Obesity doesn't matter much," I tried to comfort her.

"Then I'll shift it onto you?" she said.

"Okay," I said, "I don't care."

"Of course, you don't care," she said, "It doesn't matter if a man is fat."

"Only if he is not sick," I said, "Aren't you sick?"

"Is that important?" she responded.

"Sure, health is the most important thing. If only one is not sick and feels fit...."

"Are you speaking your mind?"

"Why not?" I said.

"Men don't want women's money," she said, "They only want their beauty."

I was startled. That was true. This seemed to be a constant truth regardless of human evolution or changes in world situation. I asked, "Are you married?" My question might be too forward.

"Was."

"You were?"

"Yes, and divorced."

"Sorry to hear that," I said.

"Nothing to be sorry about," she said. She stared at me, almost a challenge. I felt perplexed. "Why..." I asked vaguely.

"Because he couldn't stand it," she said.

Oh!

"Because he didn't want money from a woman. He would not take a penny, and left. At that time, I was already quite rich. My business was flourishing and my body was fattening. Progress is a paradox for a woman."

I was puzzled at the word.

"Isn't that so?"

"Maybe," I thought.

"You can never stay balanced," she said, "Unless you are dead."

She suddenly sped up. I was taken aback. She was relentless, as if ready to face death itself. I felt myself flying, in a critical moment. I used to be a car racer, but I had never felt like this. Perhaps because someone else was at the wheel, and it was her. I wanted to catch her. I felt we had been bound together. That experience was weird.

4

I had been thinking of her for the last few days. But she had not appeared on NetMeet again. Could she have changed her ID? We did not know each other's names even. I blamed myself for having not asked for her phone number or QQ username.

I could never get rid of that weird feeling. Perhaps because it had something to do with death; it touched our fundamental weakness. Who would not die? We are actually prepared to die anytime, whether we are scared or ready for death, whether we are hopeful or desperate in living.

Death connects us all together, or the discourse of death does. A transcendental discourse. When people get into this discourse, they share a weird world as companions just back from a journey to Hades.

It was a week later when she appeared on NetMeet again. I called her. I demanded where she had been all these days, as if she had broken her promise and she ought to belong to me.

She said, "Busy at the company."

Oh yes, she had a company. I just remembered, her major role was company boss. What she should be busy with was her own company, not me.

"Keep busy then," I said, "I'll sign off."

"No, no," she said, "I'm free for now."

"You come to me only when free?"

She laughed. "I don't care now even if there is anything," she said, "These matters are really boring."

"All bosses say so," I said. "But you wouldn't just give up your business, put up the shutters, go to bed or go out to play. We only want leisure. But that's an obsolete remedy."

"Right you are," she said, "I'm giving up today. Care for a drink?"

We went to a bar on Hengshan Road. It was extremely noisy there, with a band playing, making conversation difficult. A waiter told her something, which she could not hear. Nor could I, and only his open hand was to be seen. She then gave him a wad of bills, she was rich. The waiter counted it and left.

Liquor was served. She should not have drunk it. According to books, liquor makes one fat. But she did. She also ordered pickled turnip. They say pickles can reduce fat. This should show her rational side. But isn't she afraid of the carcinogens in the pickles?

Cheers. A boy with dyed brown hair was singing hysterically. She suddenly started talking to me. I couldn't hear. She bent close and I smelled the scent of her mouth.

I bent close to her ear to reply and smelled her perfume.

A noisy place, only fit for drinking and behaving crazily, but not fit for chatting. Perhaps I was distracted by the boy singer, who was singing Elvis the King's *Don't Be Cruel*. People were swaying with the song, letting themselves be led by the song, letting it fill their hearts and empty themselves.

The music ultimately toned down, and some people started dancing. "Shall we?" she asked.

"I can't," I said.

I really couldn't. On such occasions, one was ashamed not being able to dance.

"Too bad, you have a good body," she added.

I reacted. "Is it really good?"

"Of course, you look just like an athlete."

She was good at sizing people up. "You are wrong," I said, "I'm only a chauffeur."

"I know," she said, "Now a chauffeur, once an athlete."

How did she know all this? "Am I right?" she asked.

"How do you know?"

"Look at your arms, so graceful," she said.

"So," I admitted. "I was a racecar driver," I said.

"Admirable," she said.

"What's to be admired? Only fatigue," I said.

"It was exercise."

Ha, it was exercise. "I hate exercise," I said. I had been forced to get trained. I had to reach the preset results and find my way out, like a princess ceaselessly dancing in her red shoes, until death. In the end, I had no way out but to work for someone else and remain hard up.

"What's annoying is often useful," she said. This was fatalism. "As you get rich, you inevitably become fat."

She had brought up fatness issue again. "Ha," I said hurriedly, "That word again, no big deal."

"What's the big deal?" she retorted.

"No big deal? You deem it no big deal because you are a boss?" But I cannot say it.

"Yes, when you are a boss," she said, "you can show up on various occasions. You participate in business conferences and people say, 'that's a lady.' When you are doing extraordinarily, they say, 'this lady is terrific.' What does she look like?'"

I was stunned. Why, I hadn't noticed that. Perhaps this was the inescapable fate of women.

"Yes, look like?" she said, mocking herself. "So I look like this. It's no use, however successful you are. The more successful you are, the more you attract the eyeballs, making people more aware of you just 'l-i-k-e' this! No woman can avoid being criticized for her looks. No escape. You can't even if you wished to run. Once I donated money to a village school, ten million. I held a red cardboard printed with the words 'ten million' on the stage. When a pupil presented me with a bouquet, I reached out a hand and could no longer hold the heavy cardboard with the other hand. The host helped me with the other side immediately and kept praising me. A man," she said.

I nodded. I knew why she had made a point of mentioning the anchorman.

"How happy I was," she continued, "I felt on top of the world. How beautiful the world was. I bent down to kiss the bouquet boy, who happened to have a runny nose. My cheek was stuck with something warm and slimy. I smiled. I didn't feel filthy, but blew at his nose instead. The boy said, 'Auntie, your hand smells good'."

Her hand? I looked at her hand.

"Is that so? I laughed intensely," she said. "'Auntie, your hand looks pretty,' the boy continued. I looked at my hand. Was it really pretty? Perhaps it was only a boy's viewpoint. Mostly because of my present role as philanthropist. Or a giver of money. So good to have money. This hand is like that of the Goddess of Mercy. Though isn't that Guanyin quite plump? I would have been willing to donate another ten million.

"...The host told me to make a speech. I said, 'I'll just sing a song, *Contribution of Love*.' People began to applaud. I sang. Standing at center stage, I held the mike. There was musical accompaniment. Everybody listened to me. I sang, feeling I was Wei Wei herself. I was moved to tears. I was self-intoxicated. Suddenly, I heard something in the audience. It was like water splashed on violin strings. What was that? I did not hear it clearly. It was a male voice. I did not know where he was. Or I knew but would not admit it.

"…It was a mere whisper. I didn't have to listen, but I could not but hear it. I wondered what he was talking about.

"…That voice was saying: 'You see what she looks like!'

"…My heart was thrown to the bottom as if pushed by a stick."

I was startled. How could that guy say such a thing? "So mean!" I smiled slightly, fearing she would sense my concern.

"You smiled," she said.

"No, no, not that…," I hastily explained. "How could I?"

"You would," she said, "You're a man, too."

Perhaps…. I am also a man. No man does not care about a woman's looks; an ugly woman is always a loser.

She began to drink. One glass after another. The music had drifted to some sax, nobody knew when; it was subdued, spiraling down, down, to the bottom. She dipped her lip in the liquor. Her face behind the glass was immersed in water.

I reached out to remove her glass. "You'll get drunk," I said.

"Wouldn't it be better?" she retorted. "When drunk, there's no difference between reality and dreams. How miserable if you never got drunk in your whole life," she said.

5

She was drunk when we came out, staggering. It was autumn, late at night.

She did not go to the driver's seat. It seemed she was still sober, though she could not control her own movements, like a regular drunk. She pushed me into the seat instead, saying she lived far away in the southern suburbs.

I drove her car. Passing the bus terminal, I realized I would have to spend money on a taxi. Surely I couldn't drive back in her car. I calculated my pocket money, for I was poor.

There we were at her house. A pretty three-storey house. She said, "Come in."

I said, "No thanks."

"Sorry to have troubled you." She continued, "I insist, at least come and have some water. I just can't let you go."

Since I wanted like to have a look at a rich home, I agreed.

Spacious rooms, quite splendid. Walls covered with leather, giving a sense of affluence. I smelled leather, the smell of luxury. The interior of my boss's car was filled with this smell, which was suffocating sometimes, almost bullying, as if testing whether you could bear this luxury, whether you were born for it.

Nobody else was inside. I remembered that she was divorced. My heart felt pulled tight, like the leather on the walls. Nobody else. The room appeared more than vacant. "You see, such a big house, for me alone," she said.

"Can you fill it?" I said.

"There's help for me," she said.

"Who?"

She smiled. She took me into a room, where there was an exquisite mahjong table. "Fully automatic," she said. She closed the door. "These things help me." She opened another door. This was a large room, filled with fitness equipment, like a machinery room. Heavy. It made you tired just looking at it. "So many machines," I said.

"But useless," she said.

"Why useless?"

"For losing weight," she said.

"Oh," I said.

"Useless even if you go hungry," she continued. "But you lose consciousness."

I know.

She suddenly seemed not to be so reconciled and went to the running machine. Stepping on it, she pushed the button and began running. She was soon breathing hard, but the machine kept her running. This reminded me of my cycling to work every day, a long range of going up and down slopes; working myself to the bone for someone else. But she worked herself for nothing at all. There were huge differences between people. The poor did not have enough meat to eat, but the rich wanted only pickled radish and cabbage.

I tried to turn off the button, but she would not let me. She could not run any longer, as if dying. At last, she retreated, very pale. She did not sit down, or stand still, but kept moving. She said she could not stop. I knew this. Sudden death could follow abrupt stoppage of violent exercise. Your heart cannot stand it. "You must keep walking. Walking! Walking!" my coach always yelled this at us during our stamina training. The more tired, the more you must walk. The secret of life is movement. What a shame....

She finally breathed again. And was normal again. What was her normal state? Being fat. She seemed to realize that, and started moving again. She entered a large machine, which looked hideous, like a tool for torture. I had never seen such things. She said it had been newly developed. The researchers must have been in a hideous state of mind, in a rage, without which it would have been impossible to invent such a device.

She pushed her arms into two long barrels, leather barrels. Their sudden wringing made her shudder. But she did not back away, and blinking she persisted. Then her legs were in cuffs too. The machine was turned on, giving off savage noises. She was totally suspended, horizontally. Now it was too late for regrets. Impossible but to be at the mercy of the machine. This could not have been the first time she experienced it; she must have known the result. She willingly submitted herself to the torture.

I saw from her face that her arms and legs were being violently squeezed. But she inhaled as if welcoming it. Was this to counteract suffering, only by welcoming it?

The barrels loosened a bit, but the machine whirled again. Soon I could no longer see it, but felt it like a breeze. Her body began to shiver like mad, as if electrified.

Through her shivering, the clothes on her belly shrank. A really terrible belly.

Suddenly a strip whipped her belly. *Crack!* Before I could see clearly, that strip had tightly bound her belly. A leather belt. Her belly was twitching underneath the belt, but when the belt was detached it followed as if infatuated. The belt moved away regardless. When the belly flattened despairingly, it jerked back and whipped again. It was a scheme of tightening reins after false release. The belly was constrained, quite deeply, almost touching the spine it seemed. It promised to solidify.

She laughed sadly. Beads of sweat oozed from her forehead.

Her waist was also sweating. She said, "I must have lost some weight!"

I doubted it.

"Sweating will cause a loss of weight," she added. She climbed down and stood on the scale. "Lighter, you see," she said.

I couldn't tell, not knowing her original weight. To console her, I nodded yes.

"But it returns after drinking some water," she said.

"How so?" I asked.

"The problem is the fat," she said, "That of rubbing it out, releasing it." She said through clenched teeth, "Only through an operation!"

"An operation?"

"Liposuction!" she said.

Oh. I knew about that.

"They just make a cut in your body, and your plastic surgeon inserts a probe into the body and then liquefies the fat before extracting it," she said, her mouth sucking, evoking a sense of terror.

"…You can see the suction tube swimming under your skin, like the point of a transfusion needle going for the right position. But that's not the case; when the tube finishes its job in one place, it is moved to another for extraction. You feel the tube working here and there. Your skin seems to be transparent, so that you see the tube end protruding, it looks light blue. Sometimes you find the tube piercing out…."

I felt the pain; not a pure pain, but an indescribable sensation. I felt sick. But she laughed. "Fat is extracted, yellowish, no, orange, since it's mixed with blood and water. Heap by heap, it comes out," she said, her hands smoothing down her own body. She smiled, as though seeing the results of the liposuction.

Why did she torture herself? Just for survival? Why should she? I remembered playing with a goldfish when I was a boy; the fish swung, sometimes showing its belly, obviously dying. Someone said that it would survive if we poured urine on it. We pissed. Sure enough, the fish was alive and kicking after the stimulation.

"Looking good is only a sensibility," I reassured her, "You are not so fat after all."

"Really?" she asked.

"Really," I replied. I thought she believed me. Women are animals easily persuaded.

"Thanks," she said, "You flatter me."

"Me, for me, what's the point of flattering you?" I said. "I don't plan to borrow money," I said, laughing to myself. Why did I say this? Simply a pet phrase.

She laughed too. "Sure, how much do you need?" she said.

I laughed. "If I don't borrow money, then I will tell the truth."

"Who knows," she said, "Saying nice things to your face, that's available everywhere."

"Hardly so," I argued, suddenly finding myself in possession of excellent reason. "You forgotten? The man who spoke about you at the donation ceremony."

"He was not a man," she said, "But a beast."

I was startled. That guy, he was a beast.

What he said had indeed been right. But she said, "He was not a beast. I am one instead." After saying that, she jerked up her shoulders, so that her body was as round as a bear. Her fat nape was hideous to look at. Her movements were almost vicious. Why should she ravage herself like that?

Unable to stay with her, I said goodbye.

"Wouldn't you like to have a look upstairs?" she said.

Upstairs? I raised my eyes. The staircase was dim. "No," I said.

"Just take a look," she said.

I looked up again. Normally, it should be her bedroom. She was drunk. I said, "No thanks. It's late."

"Go up and I'll show you something," she was insisting.

"You're drunk," I said, ready to leave.

She came up to grab my hand. I dodged, but she grasped my arm, tightly holding it in her arm. "Don't go!"

Her arm was fat indeed, like a huge rope. Her eyes were red, like those of a hungry wolf. I struggled to get free, but that body, extraordinarily clumsy, almost pulled me down. I finally shook her off. She sat on the ground, patting herself and crying, "I am drunk! Too drunk to go upstairs. Are you just going to leave me here like this?"

My heart sank. But I left alright.

6

I knew what she wanted. A single woman, a woman nobody wanted, a woman who could not be saved by torture, a desperate woman.

Besides, she was so rich. She thought she could buy it. I felt mortified. What was it really worth, her wealth?

But wealth is a big deal. In this world, people are all busy, and who is not busy for money? The stock market is frenetic. Eastern Realty proved to be an empty shell and its share price had just bottomed. I went to the stock exchange while my boss was absent. People were cursing, and weeping. An old man had fallen on an automatic terminal and was hammering the machine in a bid to rescue money from it. The security clerk came to stop him, but was hit. The clerk called 110. The man was taken away with dry fists and wet lips. He yelled, "This is my money! All my hard-earned money!"

I had a securities newspaper in hand, feeling dreamlike, as if unaware what had happened. Was all this real? There were only a few hundred words on the paper. Then the money displayed on the screen disappeared. Another fit of turmoil. People were rushing upstairs, saying that someone had climbed to the top of the building. They suddenly turned back, for the man had already jumped down.

I looked out of the window, as if on the brink of an abyss. The man was lying spread-eagled in the abyss, facing me. He seemed to be smiling at me. I shrank as if stung.

I could have imagined that. But I had been imagining they were only rumors, not true. But rumors were often true. I could not face up to it, hoping chance would reverse itself. I was still kind of keeping her company, keeping my links with a rich woman. How ridiculous it was that I had comforted her, sympathizing with her.

I hurried back and my boss asked me where I had been. I was at a loss what to say. I used to be good at finding excuses, but that day I was unable to.

My boss said, "You can quit if you don't want to stay!"

I could not quit. All I had left was only this salary. I felt as if I had been driven to a single-log bridge across a deep canyon. I ducked and crawled, clutching onto the bridge.

When I came off duty, I dared not go to my girlfriend's. I did not know how to tell her. If I told the truth, she would surely turn on her heels. I went home, and Sohu said, "What's the matter with you?"

"Why would anything be the matter?" I said. I did not even want to tell him. The world worshipped the strong, instead of the weak. I was strapped.

Sohu was still playing with his computer. Poor guy, he did not have a girlfriend and had to make do with virtual reality. He played the boss, to attract admiring female eyeballs on the Internet. But that woman was not his. She could not be snatched away. Technically, she was only some graphic on the glass screen. He did not have a girlfriend. I would join him soon.

"Ying came for a visit," Sohu said, "She said your phone

wouldn't connect."

I fished out my phone. Out of battery some time ago. No wonder my boss had not been able to reach me. As soon as the battery was replaced, Ying called.

"You know?" Ying said.

"What?" I asked. What did she know?

"Eastern Realty."

Did she also know? I felt as if I had just been condemned to death. "What, Eastern Realty?" I said.

"Stocks," she said.

"Oh, what has that to do with me?" I said.

"Didn't you invest a bit?"

"Who? Who invested?" I lied.

"Didn't you say you invested in Eastern Realty?" She also hesitated.

"Who said that!" I said, "What did you hear? I invested in Eastern Pearl. You see, you never listen carefully. How will you manage our future purse strings!"

I felt ridiculous myself. Having her control our future purse strings? What was there to be controlled anyway?

She giggled. "I don't want to control them! You'll be the banker, and I'll just cash in." Ying then said, "I have a LCD TV set in mind, extra-high pixels."

"How much?" I asked, almost hysterically.

"Twenty-seven grand."

Unexpected. "Too expensive, eh?" I said.

"No, people even pay fifty-plus grand. So goods in stock are limited," she said.

Who are such people! I almost blurted out. But I swallowed it. If I had said that, I knew, she would have left immediately. Nowadays, women are so realistic, especially pretty women. Why should pretty women marry paupers like me? Why should I be a pauper?

7

"Hi!"

"Hi!"

I was back on with that rich woman again on NetMeet. Rather, she searched for me. I knew why.

She did not hesitate to show her whole image in the video. No longer necessary to conceal. Her fat body was poised to break the video frame.

"How are you?" she asked.

"Not great," I said.

"What happened?"

"Nothing," I said.

"Out with it. Perhaps I can help you."

"You?"

"Not able?" she asked. Her body bent forward in the video, as if bearing down on me. I backed away in alarm. But I still felt crushed.

Able. She was indeed able. She was rich. But before this realization, I had only felt myself sympathizing with her.

She might have seen through my frailty, as she laughed expansively. Her body was shaking with laughter and the video showed heaps of mosaics, whirling with her wriggling body. My heart seemed to be whirling too. I became annoyed.

"I could indeed help you." She added, "Don't you believe that?"

"I do," I said.

"Then, could you tell me?" she said. Her body was fixed, quietly waiting for my reply. Perhaps she would indeed help me. Perhaps she had already guessed. Such a big event. Within her own industry too. Somebody had even jumped from the building. Though the jumper was not me. In this unfair society, the weak will always encounter unfair events. A weak person suffers, which means that other weaker persons would suffer the same. Why should I hold out on her?

"Of course I believe you," I said. I obeyed her from the bottom of my heart. "I have no money," I said.

"That's it," she said. "I thought it was something serious," she said flatly. Of course, she was so rich.

"Is anything more serious?" I asked. "Like disease?"

"What does disease matter?"

"Cancer?"

"Only cancer," she said.

"Than death?"

She laughed.

"Than gaining weight?" I said. Simply vicious. I wanted to irritate her.

Her smile suddenly stopped. "Why did you say that!"

She had taken it to heart. I had touched a raw nerve. I experienced the delight of turning from passive to active. What does this matter? I imitated her tone, "Why are you afraid of gaining weight, since you are not afraid of death?"

"Don't you speak to me in this way!" she said, "You must apologize!"

She almost screamed. What a rare state of affairs, being afraid of obesity rather than death. Can a sense of beauty exist when the human body is destroyed? Maybe she deemed it so. She thought this way, because she was far from the possibility of being destroyed

physically; she was not sick. She might pursue the spiritual, as a
luxury, from a purely aesthetic perspective. But I was far from such
attainments. I was penniless. I was starving. What does a starving
man care?

"Okay, I apologize," I said.

"You have nothing to be apologetic about," she said abruptly.

I was surprised. "Thank you for your constant consolation,"
she said, "Can I help you solve the problem?"

"I wouldn't want that," I said. I became recalcitrant.

"Don't be so deadly determined to save face," she said.

I suddenly felt sad to hear that.

"It's really not that," I insisted.

"Don't be bullheaded," she added. "I know you are proud. And
you are a gentleman?" she said. I seemed violently shaken by that.
I smiled. Still a gentleman? Am I a gentleman? "All right," I said,
"Could you lend me some money?"

"Just say it, how much?" she said.

"Twenty-seven grand," I said. Maybe I could have mentioned a
larger sum, as backup, but I was too shy. Not confident enough.

"A small case," she said. "Come to my place for supper today."

8

Why should she lend me money? We did not even know each
other in a strict sense. We had just met once. She knew hardly
anything about me, nothing about my name, address or company.
What she did know was I am a man.

She said once, "Men don't want women's money; they only
want their beauty." But when a woman is rich, and a man is poor,
the reverse may be true. "You are a handsome guy," she once said.

Come to my place. She was calling for me, and I must go on call.

Why should I go? As I sat in my dormitory, Sohu forced his way in and asked, "Haven't had lunch?" He held in his hand a bowl of instant noodles. With a pauper-like smell of steam.

I did not reply.

He asked again.

"Can't I do without it?" I cried out. I was thinking of her supper: "Come to my home for supper."

Sohu was puzzled. What's wrong with me? "I only asked a question," he said.

Nothing wrong with him. Nor with me. What is wrong is that you are a pauper and I am a pauper. Paupers can only be herded together in disarray, never in order.

"Sorry," I said.

He stood, as if with something to do. He always came to me if something happened, since I was the only one he could come to. "What's up?" I asked him.

"I wanted to ask your opinion," he said. He became pitiable. "A girl, she wants to date me."

I smiled, something real finally.

"But I told her I ran a company," he said.

That must be true. We always pass for the boss online. Why had he not planned ahead? If nothing could come of it, what was the point of lying? Perhaps it was only for psychological gratification, even if he drew cakes to allay hunger.

"Then you just stick to what you said, a company owner," I said.

"But I am not a boss."

"You could be, go and open a company," I said.

He laughed, "Easier said than done. You go and open one to show me."

"You think I cannot?"

"What do you open a company with? Where's the money?"

Money? Why? Where was the money? I was damned in want of money. Just then, Ying called me. She demanded I accompany her to buy that LCD television set that evening. She was afraid it would sell out. How could I have the money?

I said, "I have something to do tonight."

"What is it?"

What was it? Could I tell her? "With a friend," I said.

"What friend? Then the friend is more important?"

"It's not important, but we have something to do."

"What is it?" she kept nagging me. It's something to do with you, I said to myself, a bit annoyed.

"Something is something!" I said.

"Then it's something you're hiding from me?" she cried.

Could I not hide it from you? Well then, I won't hide it. When I do tell you, would you let me? Aren't you concerned about money? Don't I know you? Now I knew why I still liked to have girls online though I had Ying. What did reality mean? Nothing at all. "Who hides anything from you?" I had to say that.

"You don't? Well then, tell me."

I couldn't. Poverty is something strictly unmentionable. Poverty is the biggest secret.

"Can't tell me?" she cried, "Great, you've been hiding something from me. Out with it! What is it? Who is she? Who is this woman?"

This woman? How did she know? "What?" I said, "Why do you think so!"

"You think you're rich enough to have a woman here and a woman there?" she cried.

Am I rich? I thought. Am I rich enough to keep women? Why,

she is right! Rich men can keep women. And rich women can keep men. I am hard up and have to be kept by someone else! Don't you know that I am a pauper to be kept by someone? This is the logic of this world! I cried: "Yes, yes, I'm keeping someone!"

"You, you are evil!" she screamed on the phone.

"I am evil!" I cried. "I am evil. You can do without anything, except for money! I am mean, contemptible...."

She threw her cell-phone down. I heard the rattle on the ground. It stopped abruptly before silence fell.

Finished, I knew. Even if I was willing to criticize myself, it was impossible. Irreversible. I might not be able to find her again. I knew where her home was, but her family might turn a deaf ear to me. Once, after we had quarreled, I went to her home to look for her, but her mother had simply said she was not at home. In fact, she had been upstairs.

Our relationship was so weak. Even if we had gotten married, could you have maintained it? Nothing could be kept.

I suddenly felt extremely tired.

I do not remember how I got to the rich woman's home. She came out to meet me, in her lingerie, very loose, like the fall leaves now. She stood before the setting sun, so I got a faint glimpse of her body beneath.

She said, "Let's eat first." Of course, after a full supper, things would go easier, even more forcefully. That was logical. That was the reason for so many dinner parties. Banquets might not be just an excuse after all. I said, "Yes."

She arranged my seat in the sitting room. She was cooking in the kitchen, and I could hear the dishes rattling and smell the aroma of stir-frying. It reminded me of my mother, the same aroma I used to smell when I played near her cooking stove as a boy. But now I was not playing, and instead I heard the fighting between knife and chopping block.

"Dinner's ready," she beckoned me over. A fabulous dinner. I had not expected her to be a good cook. Why, she was a woman.

She had not opened any wine bottles. I had thought she would. She said, "We'd better go without wine. No good getting drunk."

No good getting drunk? What did that mean? Because when drunk I would be hard to order about? Even so, didn't she need to be drunk? Would it be convenient for her not to be drunk? But why should it be inconvenient? And why should she be ashamed? Not drunk, and she could be clear-headed to enjoy fully her possession of a boy. I understood.

If she did not allow it, then you could not drink. She did not allow you to get drunk, so you could not. You must be clear-headed in order to serve her. But then, was it so bad to be clear-headed? I could be clear-headed to bargain with her, to get my value back, and maximize my benefits.

She said, "We won't drink, because wine is not healthy."

"Why is it not healthy?" I asked.

"Makes you fat," she said, and laughed.

Why did she speak of herself as fat again? Did she mean to underline her obesity as a confirmation that her real self was dominating me? An ugly woman who possessed a handsome guy like me? What a pleasure! If I had been rich, I would have liked to do likewise.

"I am not fat," I said. "Besides, I'm not afraid of being fat."

"I know you are handsome," she said. She spoke of me as handsome again, as expected. "Do you know? You hurt me," she said.

I was alarmed. Unexpectedly.

"Because you are so handsome," she said, "I feel more and

more hideous after I saw you. You were displayed before me so close, making me feel worthless. After all these years, what have I gained? I've made money, but what of it?"

This is the typical logic of the rich. When rich, one allows one's fancy to run wild. But I was not rich; I was only handsome, only young.

"I too was young once," she said. "I can show you old photos. I was once young and pretty," she said.

I thought she would go and get the old photos, but she did not. I did wonder how she had looked in the past. "Could you show me your old photos?" I asked.

"I'd rather not," she said.

"Why not?"

"Why do you want to see them?" She stared at me. I felt her piercing my heart.

"I don't have ill intentions."

"I know," she said. "But better not, if you saw, you'd make comparisons."

I saw.

"That would be totally wrong," she added. "Two photographs, one old, one new, juxtaposed; one pretty, one ugly. Okay. The old pretty photo is meant to relieve the present ugliness, but the reality is more real. You can't erase it. It is visible, tangible, out there. The past beauty would almost be telling you, gone are the days of all that was pretty. Look, how ugly you've become!"

I hadn't thought of it that way.

"I had committed this mistake," she added. "Right on the night of our meeting. With those two photos put together, you could clearly see the evolution of all parts of the body, almost a process of uglification. Look at the waist, grown from how many centimeters to how many centimeters. Also this belly, originally flat, with nothing there, but now has this much proud flesh, which is full of fat, like a cancer."

I was terrified. I could not see the fat on her body. I saw nothing. I only knew that she had gestured. I imagined, trying to figure out the cancer cells in the body of a patient.

She had gone too far.

"Then there are the bags under the eyes," she continued, "and the corners of the eyes. That one is smooth, and look at this one, one, two, three lines of crow's feet… crawling upward. So obvious, such a piercing contrast."

"Piercing!" I was surprised at her wording.

"…One line after another…," she went on.

A mischievous boy had made three cuts on the door of the pretty *BMW*, making a split face. How cruel!

The same person, this woman, not another woman. "This is how it came to pass, my present appearance," she said.

I had nothing to say in reply. Everybody comes to this stage, a time when you are old and ugly. I suddenly became afraid, found it hard to breathe. "Actually… it is not so fearful…," I said. I was comforting myself as well as her.

"You don't think so?" she asked.

"I wouldn't," I said. I did not say I did not, but said I would not. "Really," I added.

"Now you're not entitled to say so," she said, "You are borrowing from me."

I was taken aback.

She laughed. But that laughter soon solidified. "I already look like this. Isn't it sheer hypocrisy to talk about the past and things like that?" she said.

"Am I not right?" she continued to ask me, almost interrogating.

She put her plate and chopsticks aside, and stopped eating. I looked at her. Her actions somewhat resembled floating in water. She let herself submerge, sinking down. I was not able to rescue her. She was so clear-headed, and it is impossible to rescue a clear-headed desperate person. Why would she so harshly keep herself clear-headed?

I also stopped eating. She said, "Let's go." Her voice was cold, as if not coming from a living body, but from a corpse. I felt disconcerted.

We saw the gym room again. Her tone got somewhat more cheerful. She said, "You want to go and work out?"

"Me?" I was surprised.

She nodded.

"No thanks," I said, "You go ahead."

"Why should I do it?" she said, "All this is useless for me."

I know.

Always hope for the best. "But every time I tried, I only got more disappointed. Let me see you do it," she urged again.

I did not know why she wanted me to, but I immediately realized I could not refuse. I was asking her for something. I should be clear here in this room, who she was and who I was. You see, you always get muddleheaded. You took pity on her again. You should have pity on yourself instead.

I entered and lifted the dumbbells. She said, "That's not the way. Take off your jacket."

This was also something I could not refuse to do. I took it off. It was fall, and I was only wearing a thin tank top. I picked up the dumbbells again. She clapped her hands, as if patting me on my naked body.

"Strong and handsome," she said.

I was strong, I knew it. But this was not a bodybuilding competition. I was selling myself. She was not appreciating me, but dallying with me. She kept praising me: "how strong!" "a standard gentleman!" "you see that deltoid, men's exclusive," "a real gentleman," "a standard gentleman," and "a typical gentleman!" I knew why she said so. She wanted to feel herself as faced with a typical gentleman, a man of all men. All men were being played with in her hands. Her fat palms were clapping hard, almost ready to punch me flat. I brandished the dumbbells angrily. But I knew, the more forcefully I waved my arms, the more obvious were my bulging muscles and the more she was satisfied.

This was my destiny.

But why could I not satisfy her? Why should I be determined to resist? What the hell should it mean to bow under the skirt of a rich lady? You must be qualified even as a hustler.

I started to move briskly, through various compulsory exercises. This was not hard for me as an ex-athlete. I began to laugh. I simply took off my tank top, too.

She could hardly help letting out a squeal.

"Could you try the leg muscle stretcher?" she suddenly asked.

She was cautious. I felt her heart trembling, too slimy to catch.

I tried. I soon understood her intentions. I had to take off my trousers to get onto the stretcher. Of course, it was out of the question to go topless alone, with legs covered. Male bodies above the waist can be seen everywhere; it is valueless since there are no secrets involved. Now real secrets were requested, real value. It had thus begun.

My hand was raised to my waist, and I touched the belt. I found her a bit nervous. I knew clearly why she was nervous. But she did not say anything, neither approving nor stopping it. I unfastened my belt buckle, loosened my trousers, letting them fall down.

She remained silent, which was quite normal, because I still had my briefs on, even though they were small. My thigh muscles greatly squeezed the rather small briefs.

Her eyes widened.

This might still be a bodybuilding performance. She was only watching. I touched my briefs, pulling up the rubber band and bouncing it, as if plucking a violin string.

She shuddered. She made as if to speak, but she did not. Could she say anything? Could she take the words out of her own mouth? Did she need to say anything else? I knew what I should do. I dashed toward her, snatched her in my arms and threw her down on the ground. I found her quivering all over, as if cramping. Her need was obvious. I pressed her down. I was a gentleman. Don't you need a gentleman?

Suddenly, she started to struggle, to my surprise. She tried hard to break away from me. Wasn't she wanting it? Isn't this what she meant? Why did she have me come to her house? She, such an ugly woman, who nobody wanted. How could she reject me? You, a regular gentleman. Hadn't she said so?

I let go my hold. She lay prone on the ground, wailing like a cat. The sound came straight from her heart, very touching. I had never seen people like her crying, a successful woman of her age. She had totally lost the reserve of a strong woman.

Maybe I had been too rash. Women do not accept rashness, as an article on the Internet had advised.

9

I sat on the ground stupefied, almost in a posture as if I had been pushed down.

She also stayed there, prostrate. She had stopped crying. It was quiet outside; I heard the falling leaves.

"Are you gentlemen all like this?" After a period nobody knew how long, she continued.

"…There was a gentleman, right here in this gym, who had done this to me."

She went on.

"He said he loved me so deeply that he would marry me. He was a mere employee of mine. Of course, I did not look down on him; what am I indeed? I was only in the right place at the right time, taking advantage of loopholes in government policy. Speculative buying and selling, everybody is capable of that. I actually cherished his love. But before we could get married, he ran away with a big sum of my money."

Did she take me to be like him? Why she was reluctant to give me money.

"…I realized it only later on," she added, "Why he had done this to me in such a place. Because he always did it in such places, or in the bathroom, in a car, even on the sidewalk. I was not accustomed to that. Why did he avoid the cozy bedroom? I had a house, okay. A big one at that. I owned several more villas of this kind. But he never did it indoors. He ordered me to pose in this way or that. All these unusual postures. My begging-dog posture was his favorite. He said it was stimulating and he needed the stimulation. I realized that he hated me and he had to treat me as a dog and regard such things as rape. What he really loved was my money.

"…There were a few others later, who were just the same. They all were aiming at my money. Almost all of them avoided making love to me, because love cannot be faked. They were incapable of that. Nothing cannot be made into something. They did not love me at all. They did not even want to touch me, a mere heap of sow meat, let alone hug me. Women are animals who like to be hugged.

"Did you know that? It feels so good, that at that moment you can do without your feet, feet usually bound in shoes — do you know that women like the feeling of taking off their shoes? — most of all, those burdened by body weight. The whole body floats up. Once, I asked a man whether he could hug me. He said, 'I am unable to embrace you'."

I peered at her thick waist.

She stood up, went to the jogging machine and pushed the button. The machine began to run. She then turned to the riding machine and also pushed the button. A huge shape began to push and swerve about in the room. The rowing machine made threatening gestures, and the multifunctional weight-lifter warned of a falling sky. The whole gym began moving, like a huge factory, with all kinds of noise, clattering and pounding. The lights and shadows were dazzling. You could not tell how they came and went. You truly had to marvel at them. Right in the midst of this wonder, she was being tortured.

She was frenetically shaking her head, as if tearing at herself. But this was futile, for she was who she was, still the whole thing, still so fat. Finally, she fell down dejectedly.

"Could you come upstairs?" After a long while she spoke.

"Upstairs?" I was surprised.

"Yes, would you?" She said it in a tone that was negotiating, or rather imploring. I could not refuse her.

I knew what was upstairs. I suddenly became aware of the reason why she wanted me upstairs. The first time I had come to her house, she asked me upstairs. According to the basic layout of a house, there should be a bedroom upstairs.

Women cannot bear crude behavior; they need tenderness and refinement.

I nodded. "Come on," she said gently.

I followed her up the steep stairs. She led the way. Her body was so limp that she looked as if she were collapsing inward like melting cream. She could endure no longer, I thought.

After the second-floor landing, she kept on climbing. It must be on the third floor. It was better to position the bedroom on the highest level. On the third floor, we turned into a hall, which was dim and long. I had not expected such a long hall. Though she lived in a separate house, which belonged to her alone, I could not imagine why such a space had been arranged.

Perhaps because of the smooth turning, it was growing dimmer. The night outside must be quite advanced. I smelled something, something about an ancient house, a wooden house. I had not smelled this for quite some time. Recently I had gotten accustomed to leather, paint or metals, which exclusively represented modernity and luxury.

I touched the wall along the hall and was chafed by the coarse wooden surface, as if electrified. It was not even painted. It was unthinkable that they had decorated such a luxurious house with unpainted walls. Was it intended as Return to Nature? A philosophical idea. A practice of the rich. Going back to eating wild herbs when they had had enough of delicacies.

Finally, we reached a room. She opened the door and switched on the light. It was strangely a pull-switch and a primitive incandescent light-bulb, covered with a sheet of paper. It was exactly the same as my childhood home. The room was filled with unpainted crude furniture, including the bed and table. The style was not the latest fashion of Return to Nature, but an old makeshift type from a decade ago. Sheer shabby specimens. Pure country style. From a time when no Chinese were rich.

Why did she use such furniture? The dim incandescent light made everything look like an old photograph. Perhaps it was nostalgia? Nostalgia was also fashionable. Who says the things from that era cannot become fashionable again? Isn't it fashionable now to go to a restaurant fashioned in the style of the old re-educated youth using military satchels?

But there were no photographs on the walls. No old-time photos, nor of course any of her present photos. Hadn't she mentioned it already? Too piercing a contrast.

Nothing but a coarse environment. Perhaps she had used such furniture when she got married. And had she loved her husband on such a bed? I realized that she wanted such an effect: returning to the good old days, and making love to me.

I waited. Sure enough, she began. She opened the wardrobe. What did it mean to open a wardrobe in front of an outsider, especially a man? I smelled camphor balls.

She produced a pair of panties and laid it out on the bed. Then a bra. Those things seemed very old. I knew what was next. I even peeked around for the change room.

But she did not take off her coat to change into them. She only laid them out on the bed, in the form of a body. The skeleton of a woman appeared before me. To tell the truth, a woman is mainly these parts. When they appear, a woman shows up.

But after all, that is not the real thing. No flesh, no body temperature, only a shell. When did we start to play virtual again? We had passed from her invisibility to her image, to dating and transaction. When the real person is here, why should we play virtual?

Perhaps she wanted to inform me of her past figure? Without

photographs, she had still tried to do so. After all, those were fine old days.

"Your past?" I asked her.

"No way!" she denied. "How could that be me?" she said, "You see my form."

"I meant the past you!" I said.

"Don't you talk nonsense!" she said, greatly angered, as if by talking about her, I had defiled the lady before me. "What do you think I look like!" she cried. She jumped up abruptly, pulling off her layers. She had on a corset. She had been quite fat even with the corset on all the time.

She stripped off her corset too. When she pulled it over her head, I saw her belly, undulating looking just like a frog.

When she resumed her normal posture, her belly became more protruding, layer upon layer, like the neck of a Chinese Shapi dog. Before this, I had not seen her naked belly vertically — which was, together with the flesh of her body, pressed to her bra and panties. The strings of the bra and the panties looked almost about to snap. She poked at her bra, "Look, is this the same size as that?" She pouted her lips at the lingerie on the bed. "She is she, and I am me; I am me and she is she. What is the connection?!"

She suddenly began to pull at her belly, folds forming into unsightly flat mouths. "Do you think this woman pretty, in this fashion?" she cried. "This body is only fit for an artificial device. And this offal is only fit for the consumption of a dog. No, even dogs won't eat it. It is only fit for burial!"

No woman should punish herself so, it surprised me. Even though she had proclaimed herself ugly, that was only mouthing words, which you could regard as mockery. Even, if honestly revealed, and totally exposed, could one ever be so viciously vilifying.

What was the matter with her? Even if they did not belong to her, and I had been wrong about it, did it make sense for her to behave like this? Could that girl be more important than herself?

Who was she? If not herself, then who?

"Sorry," I had to say it.

"You don't have to apologize," she said, calming down, or rather she was sensing a certain success. She had succeeded in separating that girl from her. She sounded a victor's cheer. "She is Xiao Fang," she said.

Xiao Fang?

"Who's Xiao Fang?"

"Xiao Fang just is Xiao Fang," she said.

Is that Xiao Fang from the song? Or someone she had invented? But it could have been she herself. I did not in fact know her name, nor she mine. Might it be her pet name? Fang is a commonplace female name. But so many people are called Xiao Fang, I could not place the name. Maybe it was her maiden name.

"What do you think of her?" she asked.

"I don't know," I said, "I know nothing about her."

"Figure it out," she said.

"I can't."

"You're so alienated," she said, "How did you survive on the network? Use your imagination."

Yes, why had I suddenly lost my imagination? It might be her presence just in front of me. Her presence was a barrier.

This girl, how could she be the same as the ugly fat woman in front of me? Look at that lingerie. How slim she was! You cannot cheat that! I imagined: a good figure.

"Not bad looking," she said.

"Should be," I said.

"Can you give her three dimensions?" she asked.

Three dimensions? I knew what they meant, but I had never pondered them. I did not even know Ying's measurements.

She opened her drawer and fished out a measuring tape. Unfolding it, she handed it to me. I knew that she was inviting me to measure. I did. I accidentally touched her bra, becoming electrified and not knowing why. Not that I had never touched such a thing. I was going to marry my girl Ying, whose body was real.

Bust: eighty-three centimeters. Better than Ying's. Exquisitely well developed, while Ying's was rather wizened. The bra was round, and pointed as well.

"Measure her waist," the rich lady said.

Fifty-eight centimeters, a slender waist.

"Tell me your feelings," she said.

"Would break if handled," I said.

"I think so," she said.

I really thought so. I had a deep desire to possess it. No, a desire to grab a hold of it and throttle her, totally possessing her.

I measured her hips. "Don't forget, clothes are flat and the person is round," she reminded me.

"I know."

She held the panties open for me. Puffed out, the panties looked extremely thin, almost transparent. I seemed to see the world beneath that thin material, cylindrical, right down into it.

Eighty-eight centimeters. Pretty! I thought.

"Is she pretty?" she asked.

I nodded.

"Want her?"

"Yes," I admitted.

"But you can't catch her," she said, "For many people are in love with her. She is surrounded by men, like flies. Those men like to buy her clothes. Since she can't afford to buy so many clothes, she readily accepted them. Those men said she looked pretty in any kind of clothes. When they found something pretty, they would like to put it on her. Friends and colleagues, they all took her for their model. They kept saying, 'You must wear it every day you come to work'."

She said laughing, "Indeed, they all had wished to possess her. Many of them wanted to trap her. Even so, didn't it feel good? You see, you ran and he pursued, and there were even fights over your favor. How amused you were to see them quarrel and fight among themselves!" she said. Her eyes glistened with tears.

"Do you know who trapped her in the end?" she asked.

"No idea. It must be the man who had excelled most."

"No," she said, "The man who was the most capable of cheating her. He said he was rich; a rich man for a pretty wife." She laughed. "Maybe he was excellent, in knowing how to cheat," she said.

"...In fact, he was very poor and the gold necklace for her wedding had been borrowed. After the ceremony, people came to take the furniture from the bridal chamber, everything but an unpainted bed and a broken desk. She had wept."

I took an abrupt look at that bed and that desk. Might they be those? Couldn't be. I did not believe it either.

"...He just knelt before her, begging for her forgiveness," she continued. "He said that he was determined to go and earn money, to make it up to her. He wept. He embraced her and she felt her bones were going to be crushed. Grief and tenderness penetrated the marrow. This feeling would not have been there had she not been cheated, or had he not embraced her in repentance. She wept again. She said, let's go and earn money together."

"...They started a business. They got rich. Actually she became rich, for she was far more successful than he. They bought a house, complete with brand new furniture. They threw away the old furniture, just like markers of poverty.... We were no longer impoverished! They were no longer needed! She no longer needed others to buy her pretty clothes. She could afford whatever clothes she liked, including the latest expensive fashions. I owned myself. But that...."

"What's that?" I asked.

Surprised, she stopped talking.

"People need some outside power, don't you know?" she asked.

I was puzzled. "Don't people say that it is better to have it than to see others having?" I asked.

"It was different at that time," she said.

"At that time? What happened after that?"

"What do you mean after?" She was startled, as if awakened from a dream. "This is just about now."

"Now?" I was surprised.

"Right! Look at her," she pointed to the lingerie, "She is looking at you."

She spoke so vividly. I fell into a trance.

"She is asking you whether you like her or not."

"I like her," I said.

"You love her?"

"Yes."

"Thank you," she said. I did not know why she thanked me; was it on that woman's behalf? I really did not know....

"Could you hug her?" she asked all of a sudden.

"Hug?"

"Women are creatures who like being hugged."

"Yes," I said. I hugged her. I fell in love with her.

The rich lady trembled. I felt it clearly. She wept. I did not know why she was crying. I really did not know.

She opened another drawer and produced a stack of money. At the sight of money, I remembered the reason why I had come. They were all hundred-yuan bills. I was surprised to see so much money kept in such a crude drawer. She casually picked out a sum for me. I fingered it, obviously more than twenty-seven grand. She unexpectedly then put the remaining money in my hand, too.

"I don't need so much," I said.

"Take it," she said.

I took it. This was the money she was buying me with. She gave me more, to increase my price, I thought. How the devil did she want me to serve her? She seemed to make a sudden decision and turned to the drawer to get a stack of bank deposit books. Why did she do that? Did she mean to give me all her money? She did mean that. I would not accept it. I could not afford to. I was even a bit afraid. What did she want to do? She stopped, and said, "That's okay. It's all kept in this drawer. I will write it down that this money belongs to you."

Did she want to die? I thought. What would she write? A will and testament? How could she write it without knowing my name? Ha, lip service.

"You gave me so much, how can I return it?" I asked.

"No need," she said.

I was surprised.

"You may go now," she said.

Go? Things had not started yet. I looked at her, nodding at me. She really wanted me to go.

I dared not.

"You may leave," she repeated. "I don't feel so good."

Why, she was just allowing me to leave for the time being, to be called back. I must be at her beck and call, to be available anytime as a call-boy. That was within my power. However, wasn't she afraid that I would leave for good? I had gotten the money. Or that I would just be halfhearted in front of her, like all her men before me. Why did she trust me so? Wasn't she afraid of being cheated again? I kept looking at her.

I suddenly felt a little sad, as if I had intended to cheat her. I needed money, which was the world. That had been my whole intention. But she did not seem to understand it. She was so simple and innocent, a weak woman.

"Aren't you afraid of being cheated?" I asked. I wondered why I said these words.

"No," she said. "Thank you for your cheating. Go immediately! Leave, just leave!" she cried, "Go quickly!"

10

I was practically pushed out by her.

It was past the midnight hour. I looked back at her house: the lights had been extinguished.

The last bus had left, and there were no taxis either. I walked a long distance, before hitchhiking a ride on a truck delivering fresh vegetables. "So early!" I said, trying to strike up a conversation.

"Only the early ones get a good price," the driver returned.

Oh, money. I clutched the money to my bosom.

I returned to the downtown area and was reconciled with my girlfriend. She did not ask where I had been that night, because I bought the LCD TV set for her. Nowadays people are no longer so pigheaded. We also bought furniture, set aside money for the wedding and took the most luxurious wedding photos with the remainder. We were ready for marriage.

But I became indolent, as if marriage was not my aim. I often fell into a trance. Perhaps I still remembered that girl, Xiao Fang. I never knew whether she had been a real person, and was unable to confirm it. Even if she existed, was she such as that rich lady described?

That lady never called for me. One day, I went to her house. The gates had been locked and sealed by the police. There was a notice on the side asking for clues. She had died, a suicide, though the possibility of homicide was not excluded. The date of her death was the same day I had left.

I went to the Public Security Bureau. They said she had left a note. A will? Did she really will me the deposits? But no. Of course, she could not have willed me. There was only one sentence on the note:

After your embrace, I am ready to die.

And what about her?

"She's referring to you?" the police asked.

"Yes," I admitted, "But I didn't do anything to her!" I defended myself. "I only hugged Xiao Fang…," I was surprised.

"We will need to clarify that," the police said.

They were unable to, but there had been no weapon. She died in the simplest way. Jumping from the house. Simplicity meant speed. That was why she had hurried me away. She could not wait. She could not even wait to get pills, to get a knife, to find a rope. Just made one jump from that window.

The scene of beauty had thus been set in a freeze frame.

(Translated by Wang Zhiguang)

Traffic Jam

Ye Meng

Ye Meng. Born in Hebei Province in 1976, Ye Meng graduated from the Accounting Department of Yanshan University, and now works for a power enterprise. His fascination for film and literature began during his years in middle school, when he dreamed of becoming a playwright. He began his literary writing career after graduating from university.

Since his first publication in 2002, Ye Meng's works, mainly short stories, have appeared regularly in various periodicals, web magazines, nongovernmental publications and compilations, totaling over 100,000 Chinese characters. His representative works are "Lao Zheng Is a Dog" (published in a special issue of *Lotus* for works of writers born in the 1970s, and in *Short Stories of 2005*, 21st Century Chinese Literature Series); "Traffic Jam" (Issue No. 6 of *People's Literature*, 2006); *Past*; and *Desperado*, adapted into a film script under the same title, with Ye Meng's authorization. He is currently compiling a short-story collection for publication, entitled *Lao Zheng Is a Dog*.

Traffic Jam

Zhu Wen always says that sooner or later everyone becomes just another wheel. I've never doubted this and I even hold that it's a good thing — at the very least it would save some gas. This feeling has only grown stronger in me, especially with oil prices on the rise.

Sometimes I even think that if the world would only listen to Zhu Wen, then everything would be alright. I know that's impossible, though: everyone knows that it's 'The Lord on High' who calls the shots. If you suddenly let someone like Zhu Wen have a go, then you'd have a lot more to worry about than rising oil prices. Besides, these days people don't even listen to the Lord on High, never mind someone like Zhu Wen. So because of our delusions and our sad exploits, we put off advancing in the direction Zhu Wen has mapped out. That's why I just spent a hundred bucks on half a tank of gas, and even with half a tank of gas I'm not going anywhere.

It was then I started to feel someone was laughing at me, and I had an idea that that someone might be Zhu Wen. Zhu Wen laughs whenever people get caught in traffic jams.

I told all this to Old Li after we'd been sitting in a traffic jam for an hour and a half. Old Li was in the car just behind. He was about forty and didn't speak much, but what he said was quite forceful. We started talking half an hour ago and now found ourselves walking ahead to try and find out the reason for the jam. When we had passed twenty cars we found out that it was because of a pileup. When we had passed forty cars people were saying that a ten-ton truck had suddenly blown a tire. After sixty cars people were saying there had been a head-on collision. Most people went with the last reason, but they differed when it came to the details. Some said it was because the driver traveling northwards had been kissing his girlfriend when he was driving through the intersection; others said it was because the driver traveling westwards had started hallucinating; still others said it was because the drivers were trying to avoid a white pig crossing the road. I preferred the third explanation — it seemed the most humane. After we had passed one hundred cars someone with a non-local accent pointed a finger at *us*, saying it was because we had put the management of the city in the hands of a fool. Enraged I said, "That's right, things would be better if Zhu Wen was in charge." The man then threw me off guard when he asked, "Who is Zhu Wen?" I told him Zhu Wen was the guy who'd lost the election. As we walked back we found the rumors had changed and had become like miniature novels in their level of detail. When we finally got back home, Old Li sighed and said, "A straight line might be the shortest distance between two points, but it can be the longest too."

When I use the word *home*, I actually mean here, our traffic-jam homes, our homes on wheels. Old Li had three people in his car — he, his wife and his daughter — so his traffic-jam *home* was a little crowded. Since I was living alone I invited Old Li over to my *home* to sit for a while. We got on pretty well. I did most of the talking but every now and then Old Li would say a few words to neatly sum everything up. We heard the real report about the traffic jam on the radio. It had already been classed as the worst in recorded history but still they were not clear about the reason.

By half past four the traffic jam had been going for almost two hours. Peddlers started appearing outside my window selling drinks, food and newspapers. I bought a newspaper and had to pay five *mao* over the cover price. This is normal in my experience. I mentioned to Old Li that he had better take the opportunity to buy some food — for the price would surely double in a while. But I told him he shouldn't buy instant noodles because they charge for the hot water to go with it. Old Li looked very moved. When he bade goodbye he invited me over to his *home* whenever I was free.

After dinner Old Li knocked on my door. He said it was true what I'd said and that he had gotten proof. I told him that there was no need for proof — it was true even without it. He asked me if I wanted to go for a walk. His wife would stay behind to watch the cars. She had inflamed joints and didn't like going out in the evening breeze. We crossed the road through the gaps between the cars and went down the main road to the sea. Old Li's daughter came with us. I hadn't expected her to be so grown up. She was every bit the young woman. The way she clung onto Old Li's arm was enough to fill anyone with envy. She called me "Uncle." She said it very naturally, but I felt a little uneasy and didn't know what to say, so for a long time said nothing. Luckily the evening sun was very beautiful and so there seemed no need to say anything. Soon the sun had sunk down into the sea. I could dimly hear a creaking sound. The moon still had not risen so it was quite dark, and we listened to the endless conversations about the traffic jam, occasionally punctuated by a few flirtatious words. "Why aren't you two saying anything?" Old Li's daughter said, "It's so boring. Uncle, why don't you tell us a joke?"

I was at a loss for words, but luckily just then I saw a golden neon "M" up ahead. I suggested it might be better to go and sit in there for a while. The girl gave a little clap in assent. The whole way we kept our eyes focused on that "M." The girl said it was like tonight's moon. The whole street was strewn with rubbish. When we were crossing the road, Old Li's daughter put her foot in an old noodle carton and got her shoes dirty. She was so angry she burst into tears. When we got to the McDonald's, without any qualms, she lifted up her leg and wiped her shoe. Old Li didn't pay any attention to this so I didn't either.

When we got back *home*, Old Li's wife was enthusiastically chatting with her neighbor through the window. Almost all the women were talking in this manner. It was virtually a wide band for gossip to be communicated quickly. It was a time of rare happiness for them. A Pekinese dog stuck its head out the window. I turned to Old Li and said, "Why don't we go back to mine for a drink? I have some beer in the car." Unfortunately just as we got in the door, my cell-phone started ringing. It was He Feifei. She asked where I was and whether or not I could come keep her company. I couldn't easily refuse, so I could only apologize to Old Li. Old Li quickly said his goodbyes, then got up to leave. I called after him, "Old Li, hold on. You can stay here tonight if you want." Before I left, I patted him on the shoulder and quietly told him that he could have his wife over, too. His expression was almost completely impassive but revealed a slight smile. I smiled myself as I left. The whole way I wondered why it was that people make fun of simple, honest people.

Feifei was in the traffic jam on Jianshe Road South. It wasn't very far — only a couple of blocks. On the way I received two more phone calls. The first was Li Chuan asking me where I was in the traffic jam. The second was Li Chuan again, telling me how lucky he was not to own a car. I told Feifei about this. She laughed, saying how charmingly silly Li Chuan was. It was nine o'clock, a time when no one was ready yet for bed, so we went to look for a place to have a drink. As I expected, all the bars were full because of the accident. Eventually we passed a Baolongcang supermarket and got something to drink there. We decided to go to Qian Wang's house to drink it, as he lived pretty close by. We didn't warn him in advance because, no matter what, he'd always claim he wouldn't be in. When we made it to his house we waited awhile, but no one answered the door. We gave him a call — he said he was stuck in the traffic jam on Dongxiang Road. He asked where I was and whether he could stay over at my place tonight. On our way back we kept making and receiving calls. The first thing everyone asked was, "Where are you in the traffic jam?" We figured out that most people were stuck in the south. They had all got together and were making a party of it. It was only us two left to wander about. "How amazing that it's only us left out," said Feifei.

"It's fate," I said.

"It is fate. *It is*. We should just get married. Tonight. Right now. Without a second thought. What do you say? C'mon, what do you say?"

This sort of thing would take most people by surprise, but not me. It's not because I'm not most people; it's just that I've been through it before. I stayed quiet and counted thirty seconds, then exclaimed happily that I would. Feifei smiled sweetly and said I was too late.

In theory you can do everything a married couple does when

you're not married. You only need a good reason and a place to go. Right now there was every reason but nowhere to go. We went to Feifei's *home* (her pink QQ hatchback). We had a few drinks and listened to some nondescript music. The windows didn't let in much light and the music was a little distorted. It's not like we didn't try, but in the end my leg kept banging on the gear stick and Feifei's head kept banging on the door. "It's just too small!" I said.

"Well, that's spoiled the mood!" she said.

At midnight we went out to look for a wider space. I had firmly rejected Feifei's suggestion that we kick Old Li out. My reason was very simple — he is a simple and honest man. By this time there were already a few hookers out on the street. They scraped their brightly colored legs along the sides of car doors, and every now and then bent down to get inside. I was positive that the air was starting to smell more and more sharply of perfume. The scene became a mixture of that smell and the groaning of the wind and the waves. I suddenly started to feel a little depressed. "Why is it only us left standing on the street like fools?" I said, "You can't say that's fair, can you?"

Feifei glared at me and pointed to a violently shaking QQ, "Other people cope, so why can't you?"

"Fine," I said, "We'll do it on the car roof." She told me to go to hell.

And where could we go? By then we had been walking for over an hour and were completely exhausted. I didn't want to walk any further. Feifei used the last of her energy to jump onto my back and I could barely move. With this not exactly slender body on my back, I trudged through this bog of iron and steel. I felt like I was about to die of exhaustion amidst this pile of scrap metal, like someone who dies of hunger in search for some bread. No! Forget all of that. My *home* was just up ahead and then I'd just kick Old Li out. But when I got closer and saw Old Li sleeping soundly, I knew my conscience had not yet decayed to the point where it would let me chase Old Li out. I kept on walking. When I passed Old Li's *home*, I couldn't help peeking in. I saw the mother and daughter sleeping, one in the front and one in the back. I crossed the road onto the promenade. I threw Feifei down onto the sand. The force of it made her breasts bounce up and down like volleyballs.

The moon had come out now and there were a few stars. The sea breeze drove away the heavy smell of perfume hanging in the air. Feifei fell asleep. So did I. In my dream I saw a girl. She used to work in the hair salon on my street. We used to be in the same unit. Her high heels always made a wonderful sound. She liked to wear her hair up to stretch the skin on her forehead till it shone. She painted her face very white. In the light it looked like a layer of wax, and in the dark it was protection against mites. She has a big wide mouth and well-formed white teeth, which were occasionally smudged red by her lipstick. Her arms were well rounded and when she lifted them her armpit hair would poke out. She always left a couple of buttons undone on her uniform, revealing a bit of breasts. She started twisting her body, and slowly became a snake wriggling on top of me.

At daybreak Feifei had already gone.

When I got back, everything and everyone seemed busy. No one was busier than the peddlers who filed back and forth across the road. The relevant departments had sent food and water but it was just a token amount — it didn't stop the peddlers taking advantage of the situation to raise their prices. Old Li and his family were eating breakfast. As soon as they saw me they called me over to eat with them, but I politely refused. Compared with yesterday, the rubbish had really started to pile up. In front of my *home* were instant-noodle cartons, plastic bags, toilet paper and mineral-water bottles. I kicked the rubbish away from my car and immediately incurred my neighbors' displeasure. They asked me how I could just dump my rubbish like that. The implication was that no one could have dumped their rubbish by my door, so it must all be mine. I can't bear being wrongfully accused, and was about to launch into a fight to the death when Old Li talked me out of it. He said that just that minute he had gotten into an altercation, but when these things get started they always get out of control. "It's so vulgar!" he said. I told him it was these last words that got to me. Though I may be a damn vulgar person, I have no wish to play up to the crowd through my vulgarity.

I put on my Buddhist *Sacred Mantra* CD and began to feel much calmer. Feifei called and said she had gone home — she had given her car to someone else to look after. She asked where I was and why there was someone reciting sutras in the background. I said I had converted to Buddhism and I kindly requested that I not be bothered further by some layperson. She told me I was nuts. After I hung up the phone I was able to catch some sleep in a rare moment of peace and quiet. When I woke up, all the peddlers had gone and had been replaced by people rifling through the rubbish. I opened the window and asked some guy to help me get rid of the rubbish. He didn't pay any attention. "I'll pay you for it," I said, "I promise."

He looked at me and said, "Forget it. Why bother about the rubbish? It will pile up again anyway."

He was right. Seeing this I took out a can of beer and handed it to him. "Keep it," he said. "You need it more than me."

Old Li's daughter came around for a visit. It was her first time at my *home*. I quickly took out a bag of watermelon seeds and plums and offered them to her. She sat in the backseat, drew her knees together and rested the food on top of them. While she was eating she said, "Uncle, don't you like snacks?"

"Not really," I replied.

"Who did you get these for then? It can't have been for me."

"Uh... It was actually. I bought them to offer guests."

"So you're saying that you often have girls in your car, Uncle?"

"Uh, sometimes, sometimes."

I gulped down a mouthful of saliva, making my Adam's apple bob up and down. It made a rumbling sound. This made me look like a chump. The girl smiled furtively and said, "Where did you go with that lady yesterday?"

Trembling all over I stuttered, "Uh... ah... What lady?"

"Come on, Uncle, I'm not a little girl. Just tell — don't be so boring."

I swallowed another mouthful of saliva. "How old are you?"

"Sixteen."

"What year of school are you in?"

"Senior, year One."

"Oh right. Of course. But I still don't even know your name."

"Li Mengmeng," she said, "but you can just call me Mengmeng."

"What a lovely name." There was a short silence. She flashed her big eyes at me and waited for me to speak. "So, who do you prefer, your mum or your dad?"

"Uncle," she said pouting, "that's boring. I already told you I'm not a little kid."

"Okay, fine. It wasn't anything really, we just went to the beach."

Mengmeng's eyes lit up and she covered her mouth with both

hands. "Wow, spending the night on the beach. How romantic!"

I tried to explain, "We just went to the beach. Nothing happened."

She burst out laughing. "You've given yourself away now!"

I could have died. I had no idea that kids these days developed so fast.

Our conversation broke off at this point because a journalist came over. All the girls crowded round to try and get in the shot — Old Li's daughter was no exception. The anchor patiently coached the girls what they were to say. Old Li's daughter got a line about the provision of food. There was an old woman among them who was an absolute classic. After the journalist's adjustments to the truth, she suddenly had ten years added on to her age. She looked into the camera and said, "I'm doing fine," but sounding like a survivor in a refugee camp giving the response they usually give in interviews: "I'm still alive!"

Just after midday the sun reached its burning zenith. We had no choice but to get back into our cars for the air-conditioning. When pedestrians walked past we looked at each other through the windows. They all wore sympathetic smiles, making me feel like a caged animal. I couldn't quite figure out whether I had locked them out or locked myself in. After a while I felt like I was suffocating. When I went outside the heat was unbearable. The exhaust fumes were softly gathering and spreading, everywhere mixing with the smog, and rising. I raised my head up fiercely, as if I were looking through a hole in the ozone layer at the sun. The sun seemed on the verge of collapse, like it might crash down onto our heads any moment. In such an eventuality there was only one safe place to be and that was the sea.

Down by the shore I met Old Li's daughter. She'd already

changed into her swimming gear. When she saw me she looked very happy and shouted over, "Uncle!" She asked me to go for a swim with her. Going into the sea by yourself is a very dangerous thing to do. Being Old Li's friend I had a duty to protect her. She swam quite well and her movements were very precise — she had clearly had some training and didn't need protecting at all. We kept on swimming out until eventually we were stopped by the shark net. "Out there is the real sea," Mengmeng said wistfully, "Out there I would turn into a mermaid."

"And me?" I said, "What would I turn into?"

She shook her head. "Who knows? Probably a sea turtle."

To avoid becoming a sea turtle I started swimming back quickly. I could hear Mengmeng's voice rippling behind me. When we were halfway we climbed onto the reef for a rest. Mengmeng shook her hair free and it stuck to her white back. There was another awkward silence. I took the initiative by telling her what I had told Old Li the previous day.

She considered it for a long time, then suddenly batted her eyelashes and beamed, "The traffic jam has been going on for a whole day and night. That Zhu Wen guy must have died of laughter by now."

Just then I looked over her head into the distance. The cars seemed to have become one with the sky.

(Translated by John Mcmillan)

Editor's Recommended Reading
(in Chinese)

Song of Everlasting Sorrow (Changhen Ge) by Wang Anyi

Scratching an Itch (Zhua Yang) by Chen Xiwo

Plain Soup of Greens (Baishui Qingcai) by Pan Xiangli

At the Age of Eighteen (Shiba Sui Gei Wo Yige Guniang) by Feng Tang

How the Duck Flew Up to the Sky (Yazi Shi Zenyang Feishang Tian de) by Xu Zechen

图书在版编目（CIP）数据

化妆：英文 / 李敬泽 主编
—北京：外文出版社，2008 年（21 世纪中国当代文学书库）.
ISBN 978-7-119-05437-7

I. 化⋯ II. 李⋯ III. ①中篇小说－作品集－中国－当代－英文
②短篇小说－作品集－中国－当代－英文 IV. I247.7
中国版本图书馆 CIP 数据核字（2008）第 134637 号

责任编辑　曾惠杰
英文审定　Kris Sri Bhaggiyadatta　May Yee　李振国
装帧设计　视觉共振
印刷监制　冯　浩

化　妆

主　编　李敬泽

出版发行　外文出版社有限责任公司
地　　址　北京市西城区百万庄大街 24 号
邮政编码　100037
网　　址　http://ww.flp.com.cn
电子邮箱　flp@cipg.org.cn
电　　话　008610-68320579（总编室）　　008610-68996177（编辑部）
　　　　　008610-68995852（发行部）　　008610-68996183（投稿电话）
印　　刷　鸿博昊天科技有限公司
经　　销　新华书店 / 外文书店
开　　本　787mm×1092mm　1/16
印　　张　23
版　　次　2014 年 11 月第 1 版第 2 次印刷
书　　号　ISBN 978-7-119-05437-7
定　　价　98 元

版权所有　侵权必究　如有印装问题本社负责调换（电话：68995960）